LOCKED AWAY

A NOVEL

ELLA KHORT

This novel explores intense emotional themes, including trauma and violence, and difficult subject matter exploring themes of survival and recovery.

Corallium Publishing

ISBN: 979-8-9935236-2-0 (Print Paperback), 979-8-9935236-3-7 (Hardcover)

Chapter One

The Present

Still early in the morning, darkness filled the bedroom other than a faint glow of light from behind the Roman shades. Brea's silk nightgown felt damp and clung to her chest and back. Against her thigh, a small foot pushed into her skin. Her eyes adjusted to her surroundings. Looking over her shoulder, she could make out the outlines of two little bodies under the comforter. Alex and Sophie had fallen asleep in bed with her while watching a movie last night. Rolling over, she placed her head on the pillow next to Sophie and felt her little breaths blow on her nose.

Brea closed her eyes, remembering what had woken her—a dream about Hayden. To slow down her heartbeat, she inhaled several slow, deep breaths. Years had passed since the last time she had dreamt of him. Turning onto her side, she reached over to the nightstand to find her phone and knocked it onto the ground. With a groan, she stretched her arm and patted around the floor to find it and, once in her hand, she switched it on. It was three in the morning.

After a dream about high school, she could expect to feel uneasy for the rest of the day, but if she pushed away the memories and busied herself, as always, she would forget again. Brea resisted the urge to look at her phone as scrolling through the news would only further stimulate her, rather than relax her into a drowsy state. Instead, she redirected her focus onto something neutral to meditate on—what she could wear in the morning or what to prepare for dinner. Half an hour passed, and she found herself still awake.

Desperate for a glass of water from the kitchen, she licked her chapped lips but remained in bed to avoid waking the children. She tugged the comforter to pull it over her chest, then paused, seeing Alex's legs twisted in it. Attempting to free the blanket was not worth the risk of waking him up. Frustrated, Brea stared at the ceiling.

When Adam, her husband, traveled out of town for work, she cared little if her children fell asleep in bed with her. In her mind, it was normal for kids to sleep with their parents on occasion, but Adam insisted Alex and Sophie sleep in their own beds, claiming otherwise they would develop poor sleep habits. Tucked in bed with her children, it was the most restful sleep Brea could have.

Twirling Sophie's honey-colored curls between her fingers, she thought of her dream about Hayden. Twenty years had passed since she had last seen him, yet her mind would never allow her to bury him for good. What she found unsettling was not the dream itself, but that in her dream, she had found herself drawn to him rather than fearing him.

Brea closed her eyes, drew in a deep breath and replayed what she could remember of the dream in her mind. She recalled standing in a large white room with two long rows of white metal-frame beds on either side of her. Crisp white sheets made up the beds, and a folded green blanket sat atop the foot of each mattress. Dressed in a white tank top and matching knee-length skirt, Brea held in her right hand a large white suitcase and in the other, her laptop computer.

Puzzled, she scanned the room. She was alone, but beyond the walls, laughter and a crescendo of voices grew in the distance. Turning around, a large glass door appeared. Brea set her belongings on a bed, walked to the door, and stepped into an immense white room filled with dozens of white tables, leather chairs, and sofas. Weaving throughout the room like a chaotic hive of ants were droves of people in white suits. The room hummed with intense energy as people moved about, entrenched in the depths of an important project, shouting and passing papers. Brea, overwhelmed and apprehensive, felt lost amid the chaos.

Among the many moving bodies in the room, a group caught her attention. It took a moment to register, but it was unmistakable—it was Vienna, Jaime, Trevor, Callie and Tara—flawless and polished as they were twenty years ago, but dressed in casual rather than formal white clothing. They languished on the oversized sofas with their legs propped up on the coffee table, and their arms draped over the armrests. Unfazed by the activity encircling them, and unaware of Brea standing before them, they sat with an exclusive air of superiority above all the others. Their presence dominated the surrounding space, and Brea knew from experience that entry into their inner circle was by invitation only.

Then Brea saw him—Hayden—his arresting light-blue eyes watched her as he leaned against the wall with an impassive expression on his face. "Run," she thought to herself, but as Hayden held her gaze, she could neither breathe nor move. Behind him, inky black patches began to bleed through the white walls, and the room grew darker. Colored lights flashed, first in brief pulses, then grew more vivid and rapid and the intensity of the lights forced Brea to avert her eyes from Hayden.

In the distance, she heard a steady beat of music, sensual and familiar, grow louder until an uncomfortable vibration pulsed throughout her body. She crossed her arms over her abdomen and spun around—the room had morphed into a debaucherous nightclub, and she was now submerged in a sea of dancing bodies slithering around her in seductive madness. Beset by a cloud of turbulent activity, she squeezed her eyes shut to block out the overwhelming disorder invading her senses.

On the verge of running, Brea felt an abrupt, inexplicable shift in the ambient energy, and she remained fixed in place—Hayden was behind her—she knew it before she felt his touch. He placed his hands on her shoulders, and the surrounding tumult dimmed and retreated into the background. The weight of his hands and the warmth of his breath on her neck, she found comforting.

Hayden wrapped his arms around her and pulled her against his chest. Brea turned her head, and her lips parted upon feeling his mouth brush against her cheek. It defied logic—her mind told her to run, but she felt an insistent and unexplainable desire to stay pressed against him. The music once again grew louder, and his lips began to flicker rapidly against her skin—he was trying to tell her something but she only heard the thundering music.

"Hayden," she whispered. Upon saying his name, he disappeared, and the frenzy resumed. Desperate to find him, she scanned the crowd, but all she saw were dark shadows and silhouettes of amorphous forms. Bodies collided with her from every direction, fingernails scraped against her skin, and hands grabbed at her hair as she struggled to push through the mass of people. The music grew louder, and she placed her hands over her ears to protect them—she could not find a path of escape through the oppressive crowd until, on the verge of collapsing, it parted. Running until free of the mass of bodies, she stopped upon reaching a large black wall, blocking any further escape.

The air felt thick and it was difficult to breath—Brea was trapped. Anxious and frightened, she turned and saw that the walls and the mob of people were disintegrating as though dissolving in acid. She lowered her eyes and her focus shifted to the floor—tufts of grass sprouted through the black tiles. Brea lowered herself to the ground, ran her fingers through the soft blades of grass and found herself now seated on damp earth in a small clearing, surrounded by a forest of towering trees and moss-covered boulders.

Brea's eyelids and limbs grew heavy with an irresistible urge to lie down and sleep. The fading music gave way to a series of soft chimes, and if she tried to open her eyes, they burned. No longer alone, Hayden sat beside her, tracing her collarbone with his finger. Whispering her name, he leaned down and, with tenderness, kissed her on the lips. Water rose around her, submerging her body and a powerful force pulled her down deeper into the water until she could no longer breathe. Though indecipherable, she heard a voice echoing in the distance, and she woke up.

Brea's psychologist in college, Diane, explained that dreams could be a means of communication from her subconscious mind when stressed. Perhaps there had been a trigger, something in the news or a movie she had seen accounting for her dream, though she could not identify a recent event that had unnerved her. Regardless of the source, her inability to fall back asleep frustrated her. She did not like the idea of taking medication, but from time to time, she wished she had a sleeping pill to take on nights such as this.

Glancing once again at her phone, she sighed, seeing an hour had passed. "Forget it," she whispered and pulled her phone off the charger to scroll the news. Eventually, her eyes would become heavy, and she could try again to fall asleep. When she had dreams such as this, as few as they had become over the years, she knew the distractions of the day would help her bury the dream and, with it, any unsettling memories of her past or Hayden that had resurfaced.

Chapter Two

The Present

Sophie woke up first. Her little hands found Brea's and tugged on her mommy's fingers. When that did not wake Brea, she tapped on her cheeks.

"Can Mommy please sleep more?" Brea mumbled, exhausted, having fallen back asleep after five in the morning.

"No, I'm hungry."

"You're hungry? Let's snuggle, and I promise Mommy will make you pancakes in a little while."

"No, I'm hungry."

"I'll make bacon," Brea added, hoping that did the trick. She paused as Sophie considered the latest offer.

"Okay," she answered.

Brea smiled, pulling her four-year-old closer to her. One minute passed, and a little voice once again said, "Mommy, I'm hungry."

"Okay, I'm getting up. Mommy is only tired from having had a strange dream."

"What kind of dream, Mommy?" Alex said, now also awake. He scooted to the middle of the bed on the other side of Brea.

"Oh, nothing. It was so boring, about going to school when I was little, yuck." Brea smiled and tickled her seven-year-old son under his arm.

"Did someone die?" he asked with concern. It had been a recent theme with Alex, asking more about death. His grandparents were aging, and one of his best friends from school had lost his grandmother three weeks ago.

Brea placed her arm around Alex and squeezed. "Nope, nothing like that. It was about school when I was little," she replied as she kissed the top of his head. Alex had the same honey-colored blonde hair as his sister, lighter than Brea's hair color at that age. Her mouth felt tacky, and her tongue dry. Having a glass of cold water followed by a warm shower motivated her to roll out of bed.

"How about you kiddos watch a show while Mommy takes a shower?" she asked as she squeezed Sophie's toes. Scrunching her toes, she giggled. It was Brea's favorite sound in the world.

They both yelled out an enthusiastic "Yes!" Standing up, she turned on the television, found a cartoon, and tossed Alex the remote.

"No, first a hug, Mommy." Sophie lifted her arms.

Brea beamed and threw open her arms, exclaiming in a loud silly voice, "My most favorite thing ever." Embracing Sophie, she picked her up for a mommy bear hug and nuzzled her face into her daughter's disheveled hair. She inhaled. Sophie's hair smelled of rosewater soap from last night's bubble bath.

"Mm, delicious baby, yummy," she whispered in Sophie's ear. After kissing both her daughter's cheeks multiple times, she placed her down on the bed. Sophie settled next to Alex to watch the show without further protest. As the children were on summer vacation from school, there was no need to rush.

Brea raised the shades to let the light into the room and peeked outside. Seeing the cloud cover, she expected a cool outdoor temperature, setting the stage for a typical day in Ocean Crest Beach. She ambled to her closet and pulled out a blue wrap linen dress and a gold belt to match her sandals. It would be prudent to dress in layers, given that the weather often warmed up by the afternoon. Brea sighed, noting the absence of her cashmere cardigan—she must have left it in the car or at the shop.

After slipping out of her nightgown and wrapping herself in an oversized bath towel, she waited for the water in the shower to warm and examined her face in the mirror. At thirty-seven years old, her skin was still smooth and undamaged, aided by her strict regimen of daily sunscreen and wearing a hat if she spent over fifteen minutes outdoors.

On further inspection, she noticed her roots had grown a bit too long for her liking and she would need to refresh her highlights. Her natural hair color, a shade of caramel-brown, had always inspired many compliments from admirers, though Adam preferred her hair lighter, and she obliged him. Brea made a quick note on her phone to call the salon to book an appointment.

Stepping into the shower, an image of Hayden holding her flashed through her mind. Brea shut her eyes tight and turned up the temperature of the water, hoping the heat would loosen up her muscles and distract her from thinking of Hayden. Squirting a glob of bath wash onto her sponge, she lathered her skin and scrubbed with extra force as though she could wash away the dream. Hurrying to finish, Brea rinsed out her hair and shut off the water.

After dressing, she checked on Alex and Sophie. Engrossed in their program, Brea returned to the bathroom to style her hair and apply her makeup rather than wait for their nanny, Tina, to arrive. Returning to the bathroom, Brea pulled out the tubes of facial cream and makeup from her vanity table drawer to prepare her face for the day.

It never failed to shock her how many products she used compared to her teenage years. Every day she followed a time-consuming ritual with the end goal of having her makeup look "*effortless.*" She chuckled at the absurdity as she began.

Satisfied with her appearance after a quick blow dry, she raced into the bedroom and asked in a chipper voice, "Who is hungry?"

"Me!" her children proclaimed at an ear-shattering volume.

Brea loved every inch of her home. She had poured her love, time, and soul into creating a beautiful home for her children and a sanctuary for herself. Adam had a successful career as a corporate attorney, and after they married eight years ago, he insisted they purchase their dream home despite the exorbitant price.

Adam's parents, generous and eager to dote on their son and new daughter-in-law, contributed a large sum, making the dream home a reality. They purchased the sprawling ranch home in an affluent neighborhood on the cliffs above Ocean Crest Beach, boasting stunning ocean views from the backyard, kitchen, family room, and primary bedroom. Although a luxurious home, the combination of cedar shingles and white shutters lent the home a charming beach house aesthetic.

She had devoted two years to updating the home and perfecting the landscape design of the backyard to her taste. The painstaking work had been worth the effort and patience. The walls, furniture, and kitchen showcased a palette of neutral gray and earth tones with light-colored oak floors and custom stone-colored cabinetry, all in a rustic contemporary style. To add in color, Adam left it to Brea to choose a curated selection of abstract paintings.

As Brea prepared coffee in the kitchen, she recalled the last and only time her parents flew in to visit her the year they completed the renovations and decorating. After a tour of the home, her parents stood in silence in the kitchen, staring out the window with no compliments or congratulations. Instead, her mother complained about the drive up the winding road to their home and the cramped flight.

They sat through an uncomfortable lunch that Brea overextended herself to prepare. Her mother's eyes would travel to the patio doors, and as she rubbed her temples, comment on the excessive bright light entering the room while her father drank beer and contributed little to any conversation. They had not returned to visit since.

Embarrassed, Brea spent the rest of the evening after her parents left apologizing to Adam. He dismissed her apologies, unconcerned with their lack of enthusiasm, believing their behavior resulted from the long flight and fatigue.

Brea smiled and, as always, did not disclose more than necessary regarding her past. On occasion, she would share with Adam that her mother suffered from a vague constellation of mental health issues. He did not press for details, and she did not volunteer more information regarding her childhood. Adam, with an attentive family growing up, could never understand the depth of her complex history with her own.

Sipping a hot cup of coffee, Brea sighed and mixed the batter for the pancakes. Soon, the scent of melted butter filled the kitchen, and her stomach grumbled. Waiting for the batter to bubble in the pan, an idea occurred to her—she could search for pictures of Hayden on her phone. Despite the abundance of social media on the internet for years, this had never occurred to her before. "Why would I do that?" she asked herself.

"Mommy, I'm hungry," Alex cried out. Startled, Brea pressed her hand to her chest. She turned to flip the pancakes, shelving the idea to find a current picture of Hayden.

With the spatula, she flipped the pancakes with careful attention not to let the batter spill over. Sophie would only eat them if they were perfect circles. It was a phase that made mornings stressful for Brea. "Almost ready," she called out as she transferred the pancakes onto a platter. "Shit," she whispered to herself, having forgotten the bacon.

Alex and Sophie shuffled into the kitchen as Brea finished topping off their pancakes with chocolate chips. Seeing breakfast ready, both ran to their usual seats at the wooden kitchen table. Neither of them mentioned the bacon Brea had forgotten.

Pulling out a chair next to Alex, she sat down to finish her coffee and nibbled on a plain pancake. Sophie chatted about her plans for the morning—to paint pictures of apples with Tina, and Alex would read and work on his Star Wars Lego set.

"Well, this is going to be a great day," Brea remarked with a bright smile and ruffled Alex's hair with her free hand. She drained the rest of her coffee and went to the sink to wash the pans and bowls as the kids finished eating.

The traffic during Brea's commute had been light until approaching the arts district of Ocean Crest Beach. This special neighborhood comprised art and furniture galleries, specialty boutiques, and restaurants, attracting tourists from all over the country. The morning delivery trucks and rush of employees arriving at work congested the roads. Brea tapped her fingers on the steering wheel as she inched closer to Olive Street, where she worked part time in a luxury home décor shop named Brine, owned by her best friend Hannah.

Last year, restless from not having worked since marrying, Brea had approached Adam to discuss returning to work after Hannah had offered her a position at Brine. He put up a fight, finding it incomprehensible why she would want to work as they were wealthy and believed it "*beneath her*" to work in retail.

Hannah, charming and well versed in the art of persuasion, shared with Adam that the wealthy ladies in Ocean Crest Beach would covet his wife's spectacular taste and affinity for design, making her a "*local celebrity.*" Then Hannah, appealing to Adam's vanity, laid on the flattery that, drowning in her work, he would be her "*hero*" if he could spare Brea to help her. Adam relented, and they agreed she would work three days a week.

Although Brea enjoyed working at Brine, it had not been the future she had envisioned for herself. Having graduated with a bachelor's degree in English and education, she had planned on teaching and publishing her own novels and poetry. But having grown tired of school, she decided against pursuing her master's degree and instead made an impulsive decision to move to Los Angeles to work as a junior content writer for a marketing firm.

Six years later, she met Adam Tandervon at a party through a colleague in her company. Single and content living in Los Angeles, Brea grew to love her peaceful life. However, as she was nearing her thirties, the desire to have a family had become more pronounced.

The problem had been finding the right man. She found it difficult to trust men and often declined second or third dates if she suspected their intentions did not align with her goals of marriage and children. Adam proved himself different from the usual men she had casually dated. Though attractive with sandy-blonde hair, dark gray eyes, and born into generational wealth, most important to Brea, his personality exuded confidence, charm, practicality, and decisiveness.

Being nearly eight years older than her, he declared himself ready to find a wife, and it had been impossible for her to resist his interest and attention. Despite some initial hesitation, believing herself unworthy of someone as polished as Adam, she gave him her phone number.

To her astonishment, less than a year later, they were engaged. Adam told her she impressed him not only for her beauty, but more for her calm and composed temperament and proclaimed her his perfect future wife. After they married, Brea made a promise to herself that she would continue to embody the qualities that pleased him about her. He offered her a secure life, believing it would shelter her from the anxieties of an unpredictable and complicated world. It would be her version of a perfect life, and it had been, at least for a little while.

Hannah's black Porsche sat in its usual parking spot behind the shop. After turning off the engine, Brea remembered to check the backseat for her cardigan. "Damn," she muttered, seeing it was not there. She grabbed her handbag and yawned. Walking across the parking lot, she sighed, wondering how Hannah, single and out most nights until after midnight, somehow always arrived at the shop before her.

"Good morning," bellowed Hannah from the office at the back of the shop. The wooden floors creaked as Brea made her way to the office.

"Where do you source your energy from? It's astounding," Brea shouted as she stopped by the register and checked under the counter for her cardigan. It was not there. Cursing under her breath, she continued on to the office to join Hannah. Feeling chilly, she regretted not having taken a shawl with her.

Brine sold beach-themed home décor, small pieces of furniture, coffee-table books, and various collectibles. The shop had a minimalist design, with whitewashed wooden paneling, gray paint, chandeliers, dark wood tables and shelving on the walls to showcase the merchandise. The shop attracted wealthy Ocean Crest Beach residents furnishing their beach houses and tourists, drunk on sunshine or cocktails, looking for memorabilia to ship home to remember their vacations by. Brea's favorite customers were tourists, especially coming from countries around the world. She loved to hear stories about their lives and travels.

"Please tell me my cardigan is in here," Brea exclaimed as she burst into the small office, though the size was rather akin to a large broom closet. A small antique refurbished desk, two chairs, and shelving built onto the walls took up most of the space, leaving little room for two people to pass one another without touching. The shelves held labeled boxes bursting with important paperwork, receipts, catalogues, and office supplies. Brea had organized everything in order to maximize the most out of the compact space, much to Hannah's appreciation. Spotting her favorite ivory cashmere cardigan on her chair, Brea let out a sigh of relief.

Hannah looked up and grinned. "You look fabulous today."

"Aww, thank you. I barely slept, but with about fifty dollars' worth of makeup, I'm glad I could convince you I look spry and fresh," Brea replied.

Dropping her head into her hands, Hannah sighed. "Thursday, what a bullshit day. Wait—why couldn't you sleep last night? Were you and Adam up all night having sex?" she followed with a salacious smile.

Brea rolled her eyes. "No. He's out of town, remember? By the way, we're married with two small children. We're lucky if we can eat a meal at the same table. Come on." The truth was, she and Adam had not had sex in over six months.

Since having Sophie four years ago, they had drifted apart. There was an obvious emotional detachment from one another—Brea busied herself with her children and working at the shop while Adam traveled frequently and often worked late nights at the office. Over the recent years, they functioned more like roommates than spouses, though she held on to the tenuous hope of a salvageable marriage. Ashamed, Brea kept her marriage problems to herself.

"Okay, so why are you so tired?" Hannah laughed and pressed on. Brea's dream about Hayden resurfaced. She would not tell Hannah about it, as she knew little about Brea's years in high school. As with Adam, she had never shared her past with Hannah, fearing she would see her as a wounded and weak woman.

Brea lied. "Sophie woke up early this morning, and I couldn't fall back asleep." Plastering a wide smile on her face, she changed the topic. "How about last night? You went out with what's his name, Micha or Michael?"

"You mean Miguel. Oh, he is so sexy. Amazing body, fantastic sex. See, unlike you, I was born to sleep, eat, have fun, and have sex—not to give birth to children and become boring," she teased with a facetious smile.

It was one of the many reasons Brea loved Hannah. She did not have an anxious bone in her body, loved herself, lived her life with abundant confidence, and never apologized for anything unless she had run over a cat or done something egregious.

Brea chuckled as Hannah walked out of the office to open the shop for the day. Hannah had great style and today wore a khaki silk dress, cowboy boots, several long-layered gold necklaces with her long blonde hair pulled into a ponytail. It would be fair to say Hannah had a nontraditional beauty with a narrow face, hazel eyes, and a strong nose. However, her character and charisma created an allure that men found difficult to resist.

"Hey, I'm going to stay back in the office for a bit," Brea called out after Hannah.

The shop rarely received many customers before ten. Brea figured she would have time to check if any online orders had come in overnight and help prepare them for shipment. After working for an hour in the office, she took a brief break to pick up coffee for herself and Hannah from the cafe next door.

She pressed her lips together, seeing the line of five customers ahead of her and leaving little room for her to fit inside. After a minute, the door behind her opened, hitting her shoulder.

"I'm sorry," a male voice apologized behind her.

Brea did not turn, though, glanced to the side, seeing the man in her peripheral vision. "No problem, tight fit in here," she replied. The man squeezed in behind her, and her muscles tensed. She disliked having a man she could not see standing so close to her. Gripping one hand with the other, she rubbed her fingers with her thumb to distract herself.

Eager to return to the store, she glanced at her phone to check the time. To Brea's relief, three people in line ordered together and stepped aside, allowing her to move up several feet.

Despite having more space between herself and the man behind her, she felt an urge to look at him. Pretending she had dropped something on the ground, she stole a glance as she straightened up. Absorbed with his phone, he did not notice her having turned around.

He was a handsome man near Brea's age with short brown hair, dressed in a pair of jeans and a salmon collared shirt. Having allowed her gaze to linger a moment too long, he looked up and met her eyes, giving her a friendly, casual smile before lowering his eyes back to his phone. Brea relaxed and redirected her attention to the chalkboard menu to pass the time.

She returned to the shop with their drinks, surprised to find the store empty. Drinking coffee with Hannah over the next half hour, they enjoyed chatting until a steady stream of customers occupied the store. The shop stayed busy throughout the afternoon and by day's end, she had been quite occupied and had forgotten her unsettling dream of Hayden.

Brea returned home at six o'clock and found Adam in the kitchen pouring himself a glass of white wine. She tossed her purse onto the counter. "Hi. How was your trip home?" she asked, grabbing a glass for herself from the cabinet.

"Fine, happy to be home," he replied, placing the bottle on the counter for Brea. He gave her a clipped smile.

"Where are the kids?" she asked as she poured herself a small glass.

"Playing. Tina made some pasta and salad for the kids. There's enough for us to eat, so you don't have to cook." Adam leaned against the counter, still dressed in his navy suit, with tousled hair. He yawned, appearing exhausted after his flight from Phoenix, where he had been for two days attending meetings for a business merger.

They stood in silence together for several minutes, avoiding eye contact. Adam picked up his phone and started scrolling through his text messages. Brea cleared her throat. "I'm going to check on the kids and start bath time."

Adam mumbled, "Sure," and she left the kitchen to find Alex and Sophie. The children were playing in Alex's room, half-dressed, feral, jumping on the bed and entertaining themselves, making animal noises. Brea could not help laughing as she stood in the doorway. Most of the time she would join in the silliness, finding their laughter and joy contagious, but occasionally a wave of sadness would hit her. A pang of it affected her now.

Her children basked in endless love, affection, and security, but her own childhood, spent alone, had been isolating, cold, and sterile. She had been an only child, and growing up in her home lacked any loving or joyful memories.

These waves of sadness would unexpectedly strike her, sometimes accompanied by an overwhelming anxiety that lingered for hours or days. In their early years of marriage, her low moods broke through her attempts to mask them. Adam, unsympathetic and irritated when these moods of hers struck, coined these episodes as Brea being *"in her zone."*

To avoid his discontent, she would keep up appearances, paste a smile on her face and pretend her emotional pain did not exist. Aside from Adam, Brea felt it important to avoid appearing frail or broken. As a consequence, she did not speak of her past with him or anyone else. Creating a beautiful life for her children was her priority, and to do that, she needed to be the best version of herself, even if that meant ignoring her past and pesky dark feelings that would make it past her defenses.

CHAPTER THREE

THE PAST

B rea held her navy blue backpack on her lap, shifting and tapping her fingers as she sat in the front seat of her mother's car. The street traffic on the way to Black Harbor Public Library had been heavier than expected, and it was five minutes to four o'clock. Brea did not want to be late to the annual Black Harbor Junior Fiction Contest awards ceremony, having won a first prize for her children's book, a charming story about a lonely rabbit who had befriended a honey bee. She did not intend to enter the contest, but her English teacher insisted after reading it and proclaimed it *"extraordinary and heartwarming."*

"This is fine, Mom. I'll jump out here." Although one block from the library, if Brea ran, she could make the ceremony on time. Unbuckling her seat belt, she opened the car door and sprang out onto the sidewalk. It was the middle of March in Black Harbor, and though near spring, the temperatures had taken an unexpected nosedive the past week. Living in a beach city had its charms, but without warning, the cold spells could be biting and unforgiving. A chilly wind blew behind Brea as she reached the doors of the library and she shivered despite wearing a thick wool sweater.

Hurrying through the lobby, Brea stopped at the check-out desk. She asked Mr. Rossie, the librarian, where she needed to go for the awards ceremony.

"The children's library. They're about to start Brea. Congratulations, by the way." He gave Brea a thumbs up. Being a regular at the public library, the staff knew her well.

"Thank you," she whispered with a sheepish smile and hurried away. Reaching the children's library, there were several rows of chairs filled with students and parents. To the left of the podium stood a photographer for the local Black Harbor newspaper. Brea groaned, dreading the newspaper featuring her picture. Seeing her photograph in print, the bullies at school would have more ammunition to tease her.

As a seventh-grade student at Black Harbor Middle School, many of the students did not hold Brea in high esteem. Although an exceptional student and despite the many compliments her parents received, how she was "*exceptionally beautiful*," her peers regarded her as odd. Her long, thick caramel-brown hair, striking amber eyes, and her delicate nose and high cheekbones were not enough to save her from perpetual torture and insults.

The principal reasons Brea was a prime target for daily torture were that she dressed in oversized generic clothing picked out by her unfashionable mother, had a slim figure with no breast development to speak of, and kept to herself. The bullies would taunt Brea in the hallways, hurling insults within earshot of everyone nearby. "*Dork,*" "*No Boobs Brea,*" and "*Boring Brea*" were among the most common slights.

Nevertheless, Brea had a covert plan to turn her life around. During library period, rather than reading, she would often hide behind a book and peek over the top to study Naomi, Black Harbor Middle School's most admired girl in the school, and her friends.

She documented in her journal what she gleaned from over-hearing their conversations—hairstyles, trending nail polish colors, and the boys they wanted to date. In addition, in careful detail, she noted what they wore—short skirts, colorful leggings, ankle boots, brightly colored cropped shirts or tunics, and dresses that were stylish.

After months of careful observation and contemplation, she had compiled a formula of every change she would need to make to fit into Naomi's circle of friends and have the bullies leave her alone. Hair, makeup, confidence, the ability to flirt, a brilliant smile, and, most important, a new wardrobe. The most crucial part of her plan, because it required financing, she had yet to work out.

Her parents were frugal to a fault despite her father's executive position at the family firm, Staxon Financial. Brea's great-grandfather had founded the company eighty years ago, and it had continued on with the tradition of ownership passing down through the generations, with Uncle Pax as the current president.

Brea and her parents lived in Black Harbor, an affluent beach city, in her deceased grandparents' home. Following her stomach cancer diagnosis, Brea's widowed grandmother, having died several months before Brea was born, insisted that her younger son move his family into her home to provide her with care.

The large white brick two-story colonial home with black shutters boasted a lovely exterior, but the interior, frozen in time, resembled a stuffy British country house, complete with forest-green walls, antique furniture, and a 1940s-style kitchen and bathrooms with black-and-white checkerboard flooring, ivory tiling, and drab matching cabinetry.

Uncle Pax, her father's older brother, had been the golden child of the Staxon family, sociable and charming, while Brea's father, Michael Staxon, was a kind man, however introverted and awkward. The two brothers were opposites. Aside from their diametrically opposed personalities, for reasons Brea could not understand, they never socialized together outside of work, including on holidays. It had been since age nine that she last saw Uncle Pax, when her mother made a stop at the firm after collecting Brea from school one afternoon.

Before Brea had been born, Uncle Pax had divorced, and he had fathered only one daughter, whom she had never met. According to Brea's father, the divorce followed a contentious legal battle. Consequently, despite her cousin living in a neighboring city, Tupa Bay with her mother, their paths never crossed.

Unlike her father, Brea's mother was a reserved and cold woman. Her expectations for Brea were that she kept silent, did not bother her with childish emotional outbursts, and obtained excellent grades. Her mother loathed frivolity with no interest in buying anything fashionable or what she deemed to be *"unnecessary."* Twice a year, with no regard for Brea's preferences or protest, her mother purchased and brought home several bags of dreary and ill-fitting clothing for her.

So a metamorphosis would not be possible, though Brea continued to write and dream about it. Lying across her bedroom floor, she would stare at the ceiling and picture herself as Naomi, admired and envied. However, Brea's fate, much to her despair, would be to remain an awkward, unremarkable outsider—unless a miracle happened.

Finding an empty seat at the awards ceremony, Brea tugged at her oversized green wool sweater and pulled up her loose brown corduroy pants. Once seated, she placed her backpack under her seat and focused her attention on the librarian at the podium, who would present the awards.

The ceremony, briefer than expected, ended with Brea receiving her certificate and posing for an awkward photo where the photographer kept insisting that she "*show some teeth*." Thanking the organizers, she checked the clock on the wall, seeing she had thirty minutes until her mother would return to pick her up. Picking up her backpack, Brea went to the fiction stacks to search for a new book to check out.

Passing a table of kids near her age, a mix of boys and girls in private school uniforms she did not recognize, Brea could not help but notice them. They were carrying on with loud laughter and chatter. One girl met Brea's eyes as she passed and squinted, eyeing Brea up and down with a hostile frown. It failed to bother Brea, accustomed to such looks, and at least these kids she would never see again.

Upon reaching her favorite section of the library, Brea sat down on the floor and scanned the titles of the books. Many of them she had read, but a new book on occasion would pop up and grab her attention. Licking her lips, Brea opened the front pocket of her backpack to search for her lip balm. Blindly searching, she snagged the web of skin between her small and ring finger on something sharp—she snapped her hand out of the bag and groaned upon seeing blood pooling between her two fingers.

There were no tissues in her pockets or in her bag, and she let out a sigh. Grabbing her backpack, she lifted herself off the floor and held her hand in the air as she hurried to the restroom. As soon as she reached it, she tried the door with her uninjured hand, but it would not open. Brea exhaled and took two sizable steps backwards, knocking into someone behind her with her backpack.

"Oomph," she heard behind her. Brea whipped around to apologize, stopping in her tracks seeing she had knocked into a boy dressed in the same private school uniform as the rowdy kids.

He had short, dark brown hair and a golden complexion. Brea's mouth opened as she looked into his eyes. They were remarkable, light-blue with thick dark eyelashes. Her cheeks flushed, and she looked away.

"I'm so sorry," she apologized, mortified.

"It's okay, I can take it," the boy said with a smile. Pointing to her hand and seeing blood dripping down her palm, he asked, "Are you all right?"

The door to the bathroom opened, and she turned and hurried inside. Dropping her backpack onto the white-tiled floor, she placed her hand under the sink to wash off the blood. Her wound throbbed.

Brea grabbed a paper towel from the dispenser to wedge between her fingers, then pressed her cut with firm pressure to dull the pain and stop the bleeding. As she gathered her things, she wondered whether the boy would still be outside. Opening the door, she saw him leaning against the wall, waiting for his turn.

"So, are you going to live or should I call an ambulance?" the boy teased.

Brea smiled, meeting his eyes again as she raised up her hand to show him her handiwork with the paper towel. "I think I'll live."

"Umm, can I help you with that? You're bleeding again." The boy pointed to the folded napkin which had slipped between Brea's fingers.

Brea's heart raced in her chest. "Sure." He stepped into the bathroom to grab another paper towel and rolled it up.

He took a moment to think. "Could I have your hair elastic?" She pulled it out and handed it to him, letting her long hair fall over her shoulders. Stepping closer, he took her injured hand and wedged the paper towel between her fingers, then secured it to her hand with the elastic.

Brea studied his face while he worked. His eyes flickered up to meet hers, and he smiled. She held her breath and looked away. Studying her hand, she saw his trick had worked well. The elastic secured each end of the paper towel flush against her palm and the back of her hand. The proximity to him triggered the most thrilling sensation, as though an electric current had shot through her body. As he stood close to her, she inhaled and noticed his fragrance—a subtle, woodsy scent. Perhaps ordinary to others, Brea found it hypnotizing.

"What do you think?" He took a step back and released her hand.

"Good. Thank you," she answered with a shy smile and searched her mind to find something else to say. Neither of them spoke for a moment.

"I think I've seen you here before. Where do you go to school?" Brea noticed he was more self-composed than the boys at her school. His self-confidence and physical appearance made him attractive, though what captivated her was something in his eyes, a depth that made him more interesting and also mysterious.

"I'm in seventh grade at—"

"Hayden, come on, we're leaving." The girl from the table, blonde, pretty and dressed in a navy sweater and matching pleated skirt, had appeared behind them, five feet from where they stood. She eyed Brea up and down—her nose scrunched up and her blue eyes narrowed as she surveyed Brea's attire. Turning on her heels, she pulled Hayden by the back of his navy polo shirt several feet before he turned to face the girl.

Referencing Brea, she overheard the girl begin speak as she hurried away, "Gross, Hayden, talk about lowering your standards, not girlfriend material for someone like you. Let's get out of here—"

Repeating his name to herself, she whispered, "Hayden." She rolled her eyes and exhaled. Although used to insults about her appearance, the humiliation of Hayden witnessing it cut deeper than usual.

Brea sat down on the floor, tucked away deep in the fiction stacks. Before needing to leave through the front entrance, she hoped Hayden and his friends would be gone. In fact, she would avoid the public library for a while in case they returned, fearing further embarrassment even though the idea of seeing Hayden again excited her. Maybe she had imagined it, but something in his smile made her wonder if he liked her.

Twenty minutes later, Brea emerged from the stacks. She peeked around the edge of the shelf nearest the main lobby. Relieved to see their table empty, Brea made her way to the main doors of the library and, upon seeing her mother's car parked twenty feet away, strode down the sidewalk. Reaching the passenger door, Brea squeezed her eyes shut and shook her head. It would be impossible someone like Hayden would ever be interested in her. No one liked "*Boring Brea.*"

Chapter Four

The Present

The week passed with few deviations from Brea's usual routine. The weekend had been hectic, shuttling the children to a birthday party followed by a family trip to the Museum of Natural History, then an outing to the beach on Sunday. Drained on Monday after a day of endless chores, Brea longed for her return to work on Tuesday. Hannah covered Brine on the weekends and closed the shop on Mondays, leaving Brea to cover Tuesdays and Wednesdays, often alone, and with Hannah on Thursdays.

With the shop's success over the previous few years, Hannah planned to hire additional staff, freeing Brea to devote more time to creative projects such as restoring antique furniture. To date, all but one of her pieces had sold within a week of placing them on the floor. She enjoyed tapping into her artistic brain and relished the pride and satisfaction of bringing joy to someone's home with one of her reimagined pieces.

Brea washed her face and brushed her teeth after changing into her nightgown. Adam joined her in the bathroom, though he paid little attention to her as she began her regimen of applying her facial serums and moisturizers. Regardless of the fact Adam showed Brea little physical affection at home or approached her to make love but rarely, Brea continued her efforts to appear youthful and beautiful. When socializing at dinners or events, it pleased him when others complimented Brea on her figure and beauty and, on occasion, he would wrap his arm around her shoulders and drop a kiss on her cheek.

A chasm had grown between them, and Brea placed the blame on her shoulders. Other than the house, his work, or the children, they had little to talk about. Perhaps they never had much in common to begin with, though Brea suspected another reason. Adam knew only the sanitized version of herself she had created to be desirable enough to marry and, as a consequence, little true intimacy dwelled in their relationship.

She questioned whether she even knew her true authentic self anymore, though it mattered little. It would be unfathomable to expose her tainted past to Adam, fearing he would lack understanding and see her as a blemished woman. He came from a wealthy and well-respected family, never had to suffer any traumatic hardships in his life, nor lacked admiration or support from his colleagues and friends. And so, coupled with Adam practicality and confidence, Brea trusted Adam to make all the major decisions in their life in exchange for her beauty and complacency.

On Tuesday morning, Brea ran behind schedule. Her muscles ached, and she had a slight headache from another restless night of sleep. There had been enough time to blow-dry her hair and apply her makeup, though Tina would need to prepare breakfast for the children that morning. Adam had left for the day and would return home late as he needed to attend a dinner with his partners.

Securing her gold hoop earrings, Brea scanned the contents of her closet and settled on a light-blue silk jumpsuit and tan leather sandals. While dressing, she heard Tina calling out to Alex and Sophie, having let herself in through the front door. Slipping into her shoes, she grabbed her purse and hurried to kiss the children goodbye, then bolted out the door.

Driving to the art district, she sipped her coffee and listened to the music on the radio. By the time she had parked and walked into Brine, the caffeine had permeated her brain, and she felt alert. Before reaching the office, she straightened up the book table—it was a quirk, but if she saw the books asymmetrical or misaligned with the tables edge, it would bother her until she could fix it.

At nine, Brea propped the door open with a black rubber stopper. The repetitive chime sounding off every time it opened would irritate her as the day drove on. If she planned to sit in the office, it helped to alert her to a customer's presence but, when alone, she needed to keep her eyes on the floor.

The early morning crawled along with few customers visiting the shop. Brea busied herself jotting down original inspirational messages on the backs of business cards. Although a gimmick, it gave customers a moment of joy, and when they returned, they often requested another card for an uplifting quote courtesy of Brea's imagination. Hearing cheerful chatter, she would glance out the door as people walked past and, later that morning, a steady stream of patrons occupied the shop.

Puffing up her pride, one customer occupied a sizable portion of her time, interested in the set of refurbished end tables Brea had completed two weeks ago. Her lengthy description of the sanding and staining pleased the customer, who then bought the tables. Staying busy for the next couple of hours, she greeted customers, engaged in friendly small talk, and rang up purchases.

At one o'clock, the shop fell empty again. Now hungry, Brea planned to close for half an hour to take a brisk walk and order lunch. She hurried to finish her notes for an item needing shipment to the Midwest later that afternoon. A voice interrupted her thoughts as she placed the papers into an empty folder.

"Hi, Brea."

Looking up from the counter, Brea smiled upon seeing a man standing in the middle of the floor six feet in front of her. He was tall, handsome, and dressed in a fitted black button-down shirt and light-gray slacks.

"Hello," she replied as she tried to place who this man was, knowing her by name.

"I didn't want to startle you, showing up like this. I had wanted to talk to you for a long time, and this was the only way I thought I could."

He was familiar to Brea, his posture and the way he tapped his leg with one finger on his right hand. She stood up from the stool where she had been sitting—before her brain could, her body had recognized him. Her heart beat faster as she looked into his eyes.

"You don't recognize me, I know. It's been a long time."

Brea could not speak. Her lips parted as she sucked in a breath in disbelief. Had her dream been an omen, or could she be having an emotional breakdown from sleep deprivation?

"Hayden," she said as she gripped the edge of the counter with her hands to steady them. "What are you doing here?"

He was no longer the teenage boy she had known, but now a grown man—his frame broader, his face matured, and his dark brown hair shorter. But still, those vivid blue eyes Brea could never forget.

Maintaining eye contact, he walked to close the distance between them. Standing across from her, he lifted his arms to place his hands flat on the counter. Brea took a step back, knocking into the stool behind her. Recognizing his mistake, he pulled his hands back and placed them in his pockets.

"Why are you here?" she repeated.

Hayden inhaled and lowered his eyes to the ground for a moment before looking at Brea again. "I was here three weeks ago with my girlfriend. Mostly you spoke with Avery. I was in shock myself seeing you, and at the time, I was relieved you didn't recognize me. Then a few days went by, then a couple of weeks, and I couldn't stop thinking about you. I needed to come back and try to talk to you."

Brea's eyes darted around the store. The open door made it unlikely they would be alone for long.

"Can we talk, Brea?" he asked.

"You need to leave. No, I can't talk to you." Brea took a step to the side, intending to usher him out.

"Wait. Please," he said, moving his hands up, flexed in a neutral position. He stepped in front of Brea to prevent her from leaving. She froze in place and her eyes fixed on Hayden's hands.

"Could we step out for coffee or something to eat? We won't be alone," he asked, then took two steps back to prove he had no intention of trying to corner her. He swallowed and turned his body to the side to let her know she could pass him or come with him if she chose to. His facial expression and demeanor conveyed a gentle hopefulness Brea might relent and agree to talk with him. As in her dream, a mixture of emotions filled her. Although she wanted to dismiss him, the way he stood before her, humbled, she could not.

Closing her eyes, she sighed, then reopened them to study his face. Brea lowered her head and drew in a deep breath as the memory of Hayden wrapping her hand the day they met flashed through her mind.

"I'll grab my purse," she said, taking several steps backwards.

Hayden nodded. "Thank you," she heard him reply as she turned to walk to the office.

As though walking through a large pool of water, Brea's movements were slow, and her mind remained in a state of disbelief. Reaching the office desk, she reached for her phone and checked the screen. Seeing no missed calls or messages, she placed her phone in her purse and picked up the "Be Right Back" sign to hang on the door.

Hayden, waiting for her patiently, watched her pass him to hang it on the hook. Holding the door open, she gestured with her arm that he needed to leave first. Stepping back two feet, she left plenty of room for him to pass her, then locked the door. Turning to face Hayden, she crossed her arms across her chest.

"I thought we could go down the street to that place on the corner over there," Hayden pointed with his finger. Brea nodded, and they walked toward Lumière, a cafe where one could order pastries or lunch at the counter and sit under a large covered patio.

Her mind turned over what he said as they walked side by side in silence down the street, passing art galleries, shops, and crowded restaurants busy with lunch service. Though overcast in the morning, the clouds had broken apart, leaving behind a beautiful light-blue sky for the afternoon. To Brea, everything now appeared surreal—brighter, the colors more vivid, and every sound louder than usual, as though her brain had woken from a deep sleep.

Brea's eyes narrowed as she recalled what Hayden had told her—that he had seen her several weeks ago. It was astounding to think that her brain had subconsciously recognized him in the store that day and frightening that her mind housed an endless entity of layers she could not understand or control. Her dream had not been a coincidence, but an alert she failed to recognize.

Entering the cafe, Hayden turned to Brea. "What would you like?"

She studied the menu for a minute, having trouble processing the words. "I'll have an iced tea and a fruit cup," she replied, no longer having much of an appetite. Hayden nodded as Brea turned away to find an empty table on the patio. Stopping at the water dispenser, she filled a small plastic cup to the brim and drank it down.

Once seated, Brea's eyes followed Hayden as he stepped up to the counter to order and pay. Taking the table number from the cashier, he scanned the patio for Brea. Meeting her eyes, he paused for a moment, then headed to the table where she sat.

Hayden stuffed the receipt into his pocket and pulled out a chair. The screeching sound of the chair's feet scraping against the concrete startled them both. Sitting down and taking a moment to collect his thoughts, Hayden spoke first.

"This is difficult for me too, B."

"Don't call me B," Brea said with a hard edge to her voice and lowered her eyes to the table. Hayden swallowed. He did not respond and took his time to try again.

"I have been running through what I want to say and how to say it, hoping you wouldn't refuse to see me." He paused again, waiting for Brea's reaction before he continued. Her eyes fixed on Hayden with a blank expression as she waited for him to continue.

"As I said, I was here three weeks ago for business, a potential acquisition my company is considering, and Avery had joined me for a long weekend." He paused again and cleared his throat.

"The hotel concierge recommended we come here for lunch and to see the galleries. It's unbelievable, but by chance we went into your store, and as soon as I saw you talking with a customer, I recognized you. Your hair is lighter, but everything else—your face, the way you talk and move—it's all the same."

Brea met Hayden's eyes. She shook her head, uncertain of where he was going with all of this.

"Anyway, you asked Avery if she needed any help. You said hello to me, but you didn't recognize me."

Hayden paused, waiting to see if Brea would say anything in response. She searched her mind but drew a blank. On any given day, she could have five or twenty conversations with many customers in the store, then soon after, forget.

"I don't remember," she said and ran her fingers through her hair.

"Obviously, I couldn't approach you with Avery next to me. Again, at first, I was relieved you didn't recognize me, but then I started thinking about us and as the weeks passed, I regretted not having said anything to you. So, I came back. I had to see you again." Brea rubbed her eyes, confused about what purpose this discussion would serve—too many years had passed, and it was too late to fix what had happened between them. She did not want to go back to Black Harbor and relive those painful memories.

Hayden, appearing to read her mind, continued, "I'm not looking to throw out a simple apology and expect everything will be all right. I'm not naive that it would take a lot more than that. What I am hoping to propose is what I think would be the best way for you, for us, to find closure and put what happened in the past."

Brea crossed her arms and sat back in her chair. "What makes you think I haven't done that already?"

Hayden lowered his eyes to the table briefly before speaking. "I don't think you have. I followed you on Saturday, and now seeing you, talking to you, I'm certain you haven't."

Brea leaned in across the table, shaking her head, uncertain if she had misheard him. "Wait a minute, repeat what you just said."

"I found out where you lived, and I flew in on Saturday, then drove to your house. Sitting in front of your home, I wasn't sure if I could go through with it. Then I saw you leaving with your family and—I'm embarrassed—but I followed you."

Brea's eyes grew wide. "You did what?"

"Look, I know this sounds crazy, a creepy thing to do—"

Brea's voice rose, and she cut him off, shaking her head with her eyes closed. "Yes, this is all crazy, more than insane Hayden."

"Hold on," he replied. "Please listen to me—it wasn't like that." He took a moment to think. "I wanted to find the right time to talk to you. It was difficult to see you. You're a grown woman now, married, and you have this whole life. The last thing I wanted to do was to make anything worse by coming here."

"Are you kidding me? This is crazy. Normal people would take a chance and call. You followed me with my children and my husband?" Brea rubbed her eyes and forehead. "Hayden, why would you do that?"

"Because I'm hoping you'll give me the chance to explain what happened that night. I want you to know the truth about everything I was going through during that time in my life. You wouldn't give me a chance back then. And after seeing you on Saturday, I knew I had to overcome my hesitation and talk to you. Brea, you are not happy."

"I am," she answered with an edge to her voice. "What are you, a—life coach or a therapist now? By the way, I've seen a psychologist to figure out how much those years at Harvey Slate screwed me up—and you should know—you played a role in that."

"I realize that. Look, as much as you may not like it, I know you. Before you say it, I know twenty years have passed, but that doesn't matter. I bet I still know you like most people don't. The thing is, I'm not only here to apologize or explain—there's something else."

Brea pressed her lips together and raised her eyebrows.

"I could say sorry, give you a quick explanation, and leave. Would that be enough for you?" Hayden asked.

"You already know the answer to that," she replied, averting her eyes. Growing impatient, she tapped her fingers on the table. "Get it out, Hayden. Tell me what you want."

Hayden laced his fingers together and placed them on the table. Before he could speak, the server arrived with their orders, setting down the fruit cup, ice tea and the coffee and muffin Hayden had ordered. "Enjoy," the server smiled at Hayden as she walked away with the order number, taken with his good looks.

"I am proposing we do our pact. Do you remember that night in the car at the beach? Do you remember what we agreed to do?"

Shaking her head, Brea searched her mind for a moment until she remembered. Raising her eyes to meet his, she exhaled. "You can't be serious, Hayden? We were kids, saying a bunch of crazy nonsense."

"Come with me on our trip. You made me promise I wouldn't forget. I didn't, and here I am. All you need to do is show up. I'll cover all the costs. Plus, you can hear my story, and I can explain that night to you and other things you never knew about. I don't want you to fear me. If you hear me out and spend some time with me again, I hope you will know and remember that I am the person you knew before that last night."

Brea blinked her eyes a few times, believing she must have misheard him again.

"Are you crazy? I'm married. I have children. You told me you have a girlfriend. We can't go on a trip together—this is—"

Hayden interrupted. "I know, crazy. It sounds crazy when I say it out loud, but listen to me. You know I see what you won't let anyone else see. Something isn't right, and I think you put yourself back in a cage."

Brea heard his words, but it was as though each one floated in the air and she had to pluck them out, one by one, and put them back together in her mind to process what he was saying. "I think you are—I can't think of anything to say right now other than you have lost your fucking mind."

Hayden inhaled and sat back in his chair, though his resolve remained steady.

"I'm serious, Brea. Do you want to spend the next twenty years like this? I'm not saying everything in your life is wrong, but don't you want to find out what is? You said I played a role in how your life turned out. Well, that night affected my life too. I think we need each other to sort it out. If we go back there together, I think your understanding and, I hope, forgiving me will free us both."

Brea scoffed. "I find it hard to believe you care about me and my life. I think you are trying to manipulate me into fulfilling some kind of midlife crisis fantasy. Actually, I don't know what I'm thinking. This is all unreal."

Hayden sat back, shaking his head. "This isn't about sex—it's about us. It was always different with us, even if you can't admit it right now. I think you'll know it if you dig back down and remember."

"More lying and cheating. Breaking the rules again but tucked away at a secret hotel resort," Brea said in a bitter tone of voice.

"Brea, I don't care about the rules. I don't give a fuck what expert psychologists say or what anyone would say if they found out. Yes, this involves lying, but—Brea, this is you and me. Go back and let yourself remember our story. If we do this, whatever happens, it will stay there. And when we leave, I hope we'll be able to go back to our lives and move forward."

The glass of iced tea Brea had ordered sat untouched. Beads of moisture dripped down the sides, pooling onto the table. She reached over and dipped her finger into the small puddle of water around the base of her glass and drew a long-wet streak down the tabletop.

"Did you ever tell anyone what happened to you or about your past? I mean, other than a therapist?" Hayden asked, looking down at his hands as he played with the edge of a napkin.

Placing her arms on the table, Brea dropped her face in her hands. Hayden waited patiently for her to answer. She shook her head. "No, not really."

"Not even your husband?"

"Adam doesn't know any of it, or anything about you."

Hayden nodded with understanding. Reaching into his back pocket, he pulled out his business card and slid it across the table, leaving it between her elbows.

"I am not expecting an answer today. Think—go back and remember everything leading up to that night—from the beginning. If you decide to do this with me, and if you can figure out a way to do it—I'm with you. You know where we would go. You chose the place already."

Brea opened her eyes and studied the ivory cardstock with bold black print lettering. The card read, Hayden Botero, President and CEO, BoteroX Software Corp.

"I'm staying nearby in a hotel until Saturday morning if you want to meet again. Think about what I said. Go back and remember—all of it. My cell phone number is on the back of the card. Call me when you have an answer. I'm ready whenever you are."

Brea rose from her chair, leaving her drink untouched, though she picked up the fruit cup to take with her. She picked up the card and slipped it into her purse. "Don't hold your breath, Hayden," she replied.

Before turning to leave, she had to ask. "Hayden—are you really prepared to lie to your girlfriend to do this regardless of the consequences if she finds out?"

Without hesitation, he answered, "Yes. For us, I am."

CHAPTER FIVE

THE PAST

In her stifling room on the eve of Labor Day, four-teen-year-old Brea used a dry washcloth to wipe her sweaty forehead. She kicked off her sandals and sat on the wooden floor, switching on her oscillating fan. Cursing under her breath, she resented her parents for refusing to buy her a window air-conditioning unit. Claiming the heat interfered with her sleep and concentration did nothing to sway her father. Steadfast in his declaration, he would proclaim that if humanity had survived without air conditioning for centuries, then, so could the Staxons. Brea rose to walk into the library. In the late afternoons, she found it to be one of the cooler rooms in the house.

An only child, Brea often hid herself in the home library, which in the past had doubled as her grandfather's office. Her father often spent his time in the family room in front of the television and her mother in her bedroom. Neither had any genuine interest in books, therefore leaving the library as her personal sanctuary. Over the summer, Brea spent many lonely days in the library reading novels and writing poems in her journal seated at her grandfather's antique British Colonial desk.

Having studied ballet and modern dance since early childhood, Brea dreamt of becoming a professional dancer until the spring of eighth grade, when her mother pulled her out of her dance academy without warning. To Brea's surprise, on the way home from ballet class, her mother announced the time had arrived for Brea to give up her childish dream of becoming a dancer in order to focus on her grades. Days of crying followed her heartbreak. Dancing had helped her through the first years of middle school before having met Allegra, now her best friend, who had moved to Black Harbor in eighth grade. Stripping off her dreary clothes, she would change into her leotard and transform into a striking alternate version of herself as she danced—beautiful, strong, and confident.

It mattered little to her mother she brought home stellar grades. Her mother remained unmoved. The headmistress of the academy, Miss Amelia, even visited the house to advocate for Brea and shared her sincere opinion that Brea's talent held true promise in pursuing a career as a professional dancer. Brea's mother thanked her, then ushered her out of the house.

After shutting the door, her mother lamented that Miss Amelia had tried to manipulate her by praising Brea's talent *"only because she wanted the tuition money."* Fighting back tears, Brea nodded. If her own mother did not believe she had genuine talent, her dreams were only a childish fantasy, and the discussion closed.

Without dancing, Brea had long and empty summer days to fill. Being a wonderful friend, Allegra invited her over daily, unless when travelling for family vacations. She lived near Black Harbor High School in a newly constructed luxury community. For Brea, although the homes were beautiful, she envied most the central air conditioning and dreamt of living in a home where she would not break a sweat walking to the bathroom down the hall.

Although withheld from Brea, Allegra's parents, the Shays, considered Brea's parents alarmingly hands-off, allowing her to sleep over and visit Allegra's house daily and without question.

On occasion at the grocery store, Mrs. Shay would see Brea's mother, surprised Mrs. Staxon would never remember having met her before. Further, she did not appear to have any interest in the fact that their daughters were best friends. A disturbing coldness lived within Mrs. Staxon, and that made her heart break for Brea.

Mrs. Shay did what she could to help Brea, whether inviting her to eat dinner with them or giving her Allegra's gently used or never worn clothing. The state of Brea's appearance shocked her, as Mrs. Staxon only dressed her daughter in oversized and unflattering clothing. She worried, wondering what that type of detached upbringing would do to a young girl, though Brea harbored a kind heart and exhibited a goodness of spirit.

On Labor Day evening, Brea arrived home with her mother after a day trip visiting her mother's sister, Aunt Emily, an hour's drive west of Black Harbor. Her aunt, a frightful and emaciated woman in her late forties with long auburn hair and small dark eyes, wore only long dark dresses with chunky resin necklaces. She found her aunt's appearance conjured an image of a witch and, to Brea's relief, visits to her home were few.

Aunt Emily had neither friends nor interests other than to complain about her ex-husband and lament how horrible people were in the world. Topics of conversation often revolved around Brea's grades and which university she planned to attend. She would turn to Brea, point a bony finger at her and remind her, "*You can't count on anyone, Brea. Listen to me again. You can only count on yourself in this life. Find an excellent school and make an independent life for yourself so you don't wind up like your mother. Don't let anyone ever see you weak—be smarter than everyone else.*"

Brea's mother would nod her head and hang on every word pouring out of her elder sister's mouth. If she had imbibed excess alcohol, she would wipe away tears as Aunt Emily laid into them about Brea's future.

The one respite was that Aunt Emily lived on a private road with a lake at the end. Once excused from the table, Brea would walk to the lake and, in the summer, collect blueberries from the rows of bushes lining the unpaved road. Humming and pausing to kick small rocks as she walked, she would pop the delicious berries into her mouth one by one.

Aunt Emily owned an old dock on the lake with peeling white paint and rotted wooden corners. Brea would step onto the creaky planks and lie down, daydreaming against the backdrop of the water lapping against the dock as she swayed. Tomorrow would be Brea's first day of high school, and an exciting bevy of prospects lay ahead of her. As she lay on the dock, she closed her eyes, wondering whether she would find a boyfriend, a thrilling possibility she had contemplated these days more often than not.

In the last year of middle school, Brea's wardrobe had improved with Allegra and Mrs. Shays' help. Regrettably, despite a new hairstyle and age-appropriate makeup, she found herself no more admired than before, though the bullying had dissipated as the year had progressed. Allegra, in contrast to Brea, exuded self-confidence and focused on sports, gymnastics, and playing the piano, with no desire for admiration. Her amiable and outgoing nature made her relatable and well-liked by her peers with little effort.

Jonathan, Allegra's older brother, had a similar personality, easygoing and affable. Both siblings had dark brown hair, brown eyes, and adorable cherubic faces. Jonathan, starting his junior year, promised to look out for Allegra and Brea and *"protect"* them from the older boys who enjoyed hitting on freshman girls. Allegra would roll her eyes and punch her brother in the shoulder. Brea would smile, eager to find out if that was true.

That evening, Brea wiggled out of her shorts and T-shirt to change into her pajamas. After a cool bath, she sank into the worn brown leather armchair in the library and switched on the standing lamp with a dusty red lampshade. Anticipating the morning, she lacked any appetite and skipped dinner. To help her relax, she settled down with a cup of tea and a novel she had checked out of the library the day before.

Before opening the book, Brea reflected on the lackluster story she had been told of her parents' marriage. Her mother, Anne, attractive and reserved, was the product of a conservative upper-middle-class upbringing. With the expectation she would secure an educated husband with high earning potential, rather than benefit from higher education, she obeyed her parents and attended college. Halfway through her second year, she met Michael Staxon at a school mixer, and they married the month following his graduation.

Settling into life as a homemaker, five years passed until Anne conceived Brea, and no further children followed. Whether by choice or fate, Brea would never know, as her mother refused to answer her questions about why she had been an only child.

Anne believed her primary responsibilities as a mother included providing basic meals, scolding Brea if she was too *"demanding"* or *"oppositional"* and maintaining a home free of irritating excess noise or disruptions. Brea obliged, having learned at an early age how best to avoid her mother's displeasure and cope with her mercurial moods. The Staxons lived under the same roof, though functioned independently of one another.

It was not until Brea spent more time with the Shays that she recognized the abnormalities within her own family.

Brea moved into her room once her eyes grew heavy, and she had trouble focusing on her book. Lying in her four-poster bed, she listened to the sound of the fan oscillating back and forth. Her eyes moved around her room, settling on her dark wood dresser topped with stacks of her favorite novels. High school represented a thrilling new chapter in her life, and she felt certain that something special lay ahead of her. Love, she hoped above everything else it would be love.

Chapter Six

The Past

To Brea's disappointment, the first few months of high school were rather dull regarding meeting any boys of interest. Her teachers were intimidating, and the immense workload of the honors program often overwhelmed her. Performing poorly in school would never be an option for Brea, and the anxiety of receiving anything other than a perfect report card drove her to stay up late and study throughout the weekends at the expense of her sleep and social life. Her parents' response to her stellar grades had been stoic at best, a pat on the shoulder and handing Brea an envelope with a small amount of spending money. With so little enthusiasm and praise for a superb report card, she never wanted to witness their reaction to an imperfect one.

When she had spare time, Brea visited Allegra's house, took long bike rides, or wrote in her journal and, when weather permitted, read in her detached garage. Years ago, she had converted it into an improvised clubhouse for herself, furnishing it with old patio furniture and discarded bric-a-brac stored in boxes after her grandmother's death.

An unprecedented event, however, interrupted her usual routine for that Saturday evening. Jonathan offered to take Allegra and Brea with him to see a movie with two of his friends,

Anthony and Blake. She knew them, having crossed paths at Allegra's house several times, but had no real opinion of them, other than they were friendly.

Outside the theater, Allegra, Jonathan, and Brea waited only several minutes until Jonathan's friends arrived. It was a cool night, and a subtle smoky scent infused the crisp autumn air. Brea smiled, bundled in her wool coat and scarf, thrilled to be out with an older group of boys, even though they were only Jonathan and his friends.

Brea and Allegra greeted Anthony first, short in stature with light-blonde hair and a hyperactive and humorous personality. Blake, relaxed and easygoing with an athletic build, light-brown hair, and brown eyes, smiled and waved at Brea.

Jonathan bought the tickets, and the group entered the theater with time to spare. Blake offered to buy popcorn and suggested Brea help him carry the snacks. She removed her coat and held it against her chest as she joined Blake in the concession line. Blake turned and complimented her outfit, an ivory cardigan and a new pair of boot-cut jeans. "Thanks," she mumbled, dropping her eyes to the floor, taken aback by his attention.

Since beginning high school, Brea's mother relented on buying clothing for her daughter, and now her father handed Brea a white envelope of money to spend as she liked. She had become an expert at budgeting and tracked when the stores offered the best sales to maximize her resources. In addition, Allegra gave Brea free access to her wardrobe.

Tonight, Allegra had offered to make up Brea's face and had been heavy-handed with the eyeliner and lipstick. While at first self-conscious, the longer Brea studied herself in the mirror, the more she found herself pleased with the transformation. With her hair waved and pulled into a low ponytail with several pieces framing her face, Brea looked older than fourteen and rather sultry. With several couples standing in line ahead of Blake and

Brea, she stared at the popcorn machine as she contemplated an idea for a short story she planned to write for English class.

"How about candy?" Blake asked Brea.

"Sure, whatever you like," she replied.

"I'll pick out two boxes, and we can share. I'll order you a soda too, or anything else you would like," he added with a toothy smile and flushed cheeks. Brea studied his face with a shy smile, suspicious of Blake's offer as a means to impress her.

"Thank you. A soda is fine." She felt flutters in her chest as he turned to order. After he paid, he placed the candy boxes into his coat pockets, then handed her the largest size soda the concession stand sold. Brea's eyes widened, knowing it would be impossible to drink even half of it before the movie ended. "Thanks," she replied, regardless appreciative of Blake's thoughtfulness as they turned to meet Jonathan, Allegra, and Anthony waiting by the far end of the concession counter.

In the theatre, Blake gestured for the others to pass by him so he could sit next to Brea. The truth dawned on her that Jonathan had not offered to take her and Allegra to the movies out of the kindness of his heart, but as a setup for her to spend time with Blake. Despite being an unexpected turn of events, she found it a pleasant one.

Blake removed his coat as Brea took her seat, and the boxes of candy dropped out of his pockets onto the floor. He leaned down to retrieve them with a self-conscious smile. Seeing him now in a different light, she had to admit he was rather attractive. Out of the corner of her eye, she noticed Allegra watching her with a conspiratorial grin on her face. Of course, she had been in on it. This explained the excessive fussing over Brea's makeup. Brea rolled her eyes and mouthed to Allegra, "I'm going to kill you."

Allegra mouthed back, "He's cute."

The theater darkened, and the crowd quieted down to watch the previews. Brea sipped her soda and drew in a deep breath.

Blake looked at her and smiled before turning his attention to the screen. *"Oh boy,"* Brea thought to herself.

During the film, Blake's shoulder would brush against hers when shifting in his seat. At one point, he leaned in close to offer Brea candy. She nodded and he picked out several gummy bears and placed them in his palm. "That's not very hygienic," she teased, with a flat expression. Although initially fooled, he quickly recognized Brea's teasing. He brought his hand to her mouth, pretending he would feed her. Brea chuckled. Careful not to make too much noise, she plucked the candy out of his hand and ate it. By the end of the movie, she had relaxed, though when watching the sex scenes, she did everything possible to avoid looking in Blake's direction until they ended.

Anthony broke off from the group after the movie. The remaining four agreed to walk to the cafe down the street for coffee and dessert. Inside, they spotted a booth with blue velvet upholstered benches on either side of a cherry wood table, large enough for the group.

Brea ordered a hot chocolate instead of coffee, knowing that caffeine would make her too jittery for the night. When the server delivered their orders—cappuccinos for Allegra, Jonathan and Blake and Brea's hot chocolate—they had forgotten the whipped cream.

"Oh no, that's the best part," Brea proclaimed to the table. Blake, a true gentleman, without hesitation stood to fetch a serving of whipped cream for Brea.

Once he was out of earshot, Allegra teased Brea, twirling her hair with one hand and batting her eyes. "Ooh, someone has a crush on you."

"Allegra, shut up," Brea said, her eyes wide with a mixture of embarrassment and irritation. Jonathan smiled and interjected, "He likes you. He's a good guy, so give him a chance."

Blake returned with the whipped cream and, with a proud look on his face, handed the porcelain ramekin to Brea. Dumping the whipped cream into her hot cocoa, Jonathan and Allegra stepped away to call their parents and inform them they would arrive home later than expected. Now alone at the table without the buffer of Allegra and Jonathan nearby, Brea's heart beat faster. He broke the ice to share a tidbit of gossip regarding the movie they had seen.

"So, I heard that the actress playing Maya stole the director away from his pregnant wife. I read that in a celebrity gossip magazine. But don't judge me. I spend a lot of time in my dad's dental office waiting around for him." Brea laughed out loud—not at the gossip, but at Blake's self-deprecating confession. Blake smiled, relieved and proud that he could make Brea laugh.

"By the way, thank you for the whipped cream." Brea scooped a dollop onto her finger to taste it.

"So, where should we go on our second date?" he asked in a casual and presumptive manner.

Brea nearly choked on her whipped cream. "What? Are we on a date?"

"Well, no, but I thought that would be a good way to ask you out on one. An official one," he answered with hopeful eyes, awaiting her reply.

Brea wiped the residual whipped cream off her lips. "Um, yes, that would be great."

Blake beamed, relief washing across his face. "So, can I have your phone number and call you tomorrow?"

"Sure, do you have a pen?" Blake smiled and reached into his jacket pocket, producing a ballpoint pen. Her hand trembled as she took it from him, hoping he failed to notice as she wrote her number on a napkin. Blake took the napkin, folded it over once, and placed it in his jacket pocket along with his pen.

He leaned forward to take a sip of his cappuccino as Allegra and Jonathan returned. They knew what had happened, grinning as they took their seats.

"Okay, so thoughts on the movie?" Allegra asked. "Was there enough sex?"

They all laughed. As they drank their coffees and cocoa, the foursome filled up the following hour, talking over one another about movies, school, and any interesting stories to share regarding their classmates.

Every so often, Brea exchanged a glance with Blake. She wondered if he would try to kiss her at the end of the night or wait until they had their "*official*" first date. Regardless, elation filled Brea. In her mind, now a true high school student, she hoped that soon she would have her first boyfriend.

CHAPTER SEVEN

THE PAST

By the end of May, Brea and Blake had dated for six months. Blake's kindness, and Brea's enthusiasm for having a boyfriend, could not overcome the lack of romantic chemistry she felt for him. When he kissed her, she felt nothing. True, they laughed and had fun together, yet there was none of the electric passion she had hoped for. Over time, she recognized that the glue in their relationship had been her love of spending time with his family, in particular his eight-year-old identical twin sisters. They were adorable and hung on every word Brea uttered.

Discussions at the table with Blake's parents were lively, and they were interested in Brea as a person. She would talk about her love of writing, books she had read, and dreams for the future. Further, they treated her as though her thoughts and opinions mattered when they spoke about politics or current events. Blake's family was the family she wished she had, and that played a role in her motivation to continue on in the relationship, even if it lacked the romance she craved.

Several weeks before summer break, the school aide summoned Brea to the office during her honors geometry class. Annoyed, Brea could not imagine what could be so important as to pull her away from her class. It would make catching up quite difficult if not present to take notes, and final exams were around the corner.

With her hands clasped in front of her, Brea found herself being led to the school psychologist's office. Her mother and guidance counselor sat at a large, round mahogany table inside the office, and Dr. Nelson stood behind her desk. Mounted on the wall behind her were various diplomas and awards.

Brea squeezed her hands together as the group fixed their eyes on her, and Dr. Nelson instructed her to have a seat at the table next to her mother. Her mother, dressed in a white blouse and navy skirt, eyed Brea with a stony expression as she dabbed beads of perspiration forming around her hairline with a tissue.

Dr. Nelson, a middle-aged woman dressed in a light-blue suit with a round face, a generous figure, and kind brown eyes with voluminous curly blonde hair, smiled at Brea and took her seat. Brea had already met her guidance counselor, Ms. Shattenridge, several times, and found her to be gentle-hearted and invested in her student's well-being. Meeting her guidance counselor's eyes for any sign as to the purpose of the meeting, she only gave Brea a slight smile. Dr. Nelson spoke.

"Brea, we're here today to discuss a concern that has come up. Your English teacher found your journal in class yesterday morning and was quite concerned reading through some of your poetry." Dr. Nelson paused and exchanged a glance with Brea's guidance counselor before continuing. Brea wondered why that was a problem and remained silent. She had not re-alized she had left it in class.

"You're not in trouble, Brea. The purpose of our bringing in your mother is to see if there is anything going on, either at home or with your mental health, that we can help with. I spoke with a few of your teachers, and they're concerned about you. It's obvious you have lost weight over the year and you socialize little with the other students in class. I spoke with your mother regarding my recommendation that we schedule you to see a counselor to talk with someone."

Lifting her hands in the air, Brea's mother inhaled. "That's enough. Brea is fine. Is there a problem with her grades?" she asked, leaning forward and placing her hands on the table.

"No, the opposite. Brea has excelled in all her classes. Though we are wondering if the pressure of the honors program may be a bit too stressful for Brea. I can meet with her next year, and perhaps we can consider switching her to a less demanding course load."

"Absolutely not." Brea's mother shouted, spraying several drops of saliva across the table. "The problem isn't Brea. I warned my husband that public schooling was a disastrous idea. If you dare label her as having mental problems, we will hire a lawyer, mark my words. Mr. Staxon will look into enrolling Brea in a private school next year. I won't stand for this. It's insulting and humiliating. Brea will finish out the semester, and she will not return to this school in the fall."

Brea looked down at the floor. She knew better than to plead with her mother.

"Mrs. Staxon, we only want to help, and pulling Brea abruptly out of school, from a familiar environment, could be very traumatic for her."

"We'll have the new school communicate with you for Brea's transcripts." Her mother rose and stalked out of the office, leaving Brea staring at the floor.

Dr. Nelson rose from her chair. "Let me try one more time. I'll be right back." She hurried out of the room to follow Brea's mother, leaving Brea alone with Mrs. Shattenridge.

"Brea honey, is everything all right at home? If you are being hurt, please tell me. I can help you."

Brea's mind raced. Her parents never hit her. She looked into Mrs. Shattenridge's eyes. Dressed in a dark green turtleneck sweater with her brown hair pulled into a bun atop her head, she reminded her of Miss. Amelia—kind, warm-hearted, and attempting to do what she could to help Brea.

"No, Mrs. Shattenridge, they don't hit me. It's only that I write what I feel or think about. I didn't realize my writing was that bad. Can I have my journal back, please?"

Mrs. Shattenridge smiled and handed Brea her journal. "No, not bad, Brea. Your poems are quite moving, though somber. I think for us it was a little shocking to read your words. There was so much sadness."

Pausing for a moment, Brea's counselor chewed her lower lip and sighed. "Look, I'll do whatever I can to help you if your parents switch you to a new school. I won't tell them about this meeting and make sure you have an excellent summary letter and recommendations, not that you need them. Your work speaks for itself. If you ever need me, come and find me."

Brea nodded and stood up. "Thank you. Can I go back to class now?"

"Of course, go ahead, Brea," Mrs. Shattenridge replied.

Walking through the empty halls, Brea rubbed her hands together, dismayed at the unexpected turn of events that would uproot her into a different school. Her mother might change her mind, though Brea doubted it. Once her mother birthed an idea, it sprouted deep roots and there would be no going back.

Opening the door to her math class, her classmates looked neither at her nor seemed concerned about her absence. She picked up her pencil and focused on her teacher, pushing the past twenty minutes out of her mind as she copied down the math problem written on the board.

That afternoon after Brea arrived home, unsurprisingly, her mother refused to speak to her. She had broken a sacred rule—do not cause trouble and create more work for her mother. When her father returned home, she could hear her mother yelling at him in the kitchen. She insisted he call Uncle Pax to find out how to enroll Brea in the same private school as his daughter, Vienna. Her father did not argue, and the discussion ended before it began.

Two days later, her mother knocked on Brea's door amid studying for her French final exam. "You will start school in the fall at Harvey Slate Preparatory. Your cousin Vienna is entering her third year, and Uncle Pax will ask her to help you settle in." Brea stared at her mother, knowing better than to display any emotion or attempt to argue.

Clearing her throat and placing one finger on her lips, her mother continued. "Brea, if you write again in your journal, write only cheerful things from now on. I will not be called in to another meeting because you can't control your emotions. Do you understand me?"

Nodding her head, Brea's mother gave her a terse smile. "We'll pretend as if nothing ever happened. Things will go back to normal. I will stop at your new school tomorrow to order your uniforms."

Brea leaned back on her bed after her mother left the room and whispered, "What is normal about this life?"

The abrupt transfer shocked the Shays and Blake. Brea fabricated a story, though Allegra did not believe it. She claimed her parents believed the public school system had failed to *"challenge"* her, prompting their decision to transfer her to a private school. Blake's face fell upon hearing the news. Devastated, he wrapped his arms around Brea and held her. Brea's instinct had been to pull away, though she resisted to avoid hurting his feelings.

To reassure himself more than anyone else, he said, "Brea, nothing will really change. We'll see each other after school and on the weekends. I can even pick you up on the days when I don't have soccer practice." Brea smiled faintly and gave Blake a small kiss on the cheek.

Allegra sighed, shook her head, then, with an abrupt shift in demeanor, brightened. "Hey, I just realized something, Brea. You won't be 'Boring Brea' there. You can reinvent yourself and be the gorgeous, mysterious transfer. Jonathan went to some Harvey Slate parties, and they're pretty legendary. This could be a good thing."

"Or you could be yourself because you have nothing to prove and you're great the way you are," Jonathan added.

Brea thanked Jonathan for the compliment. Despite her anxiety, the idea intrigued her. She could start over and be whoever she wanted to be. Perhaps transferring to Harvey Slate would be the best thing that could have happened to her.

CHAPTER EIGHT

THE PAST

The summer passed with a quick pace. Brea spent most of the summer at the beach, at Allegra's house, or with Blake. When Blake and Allegra traveled with their families, she spent lazy afternoons at the park reading and writing.

Upon the conclusion of Labor Day weekend, Brea's first day at Harvey Slate Preparatory School arrived. Dressed in her school uniform, a knee-length wool navy skirt and a white-collared shirt, she stood before the administration building at a quarter to eight on Tuesday morning.

Uncle Pax had informed Brea's father he had spoken with Vienna and claimed that his daughter was "*eager*" to reach out and help Brea acclimate to the school. At summer's end, her cousin had yet to call Brea. Per Uncle Pax, Vienna had been travelling in Europe for much of the summer, and Brea assumed the phone call had slipped her cousin's mind. She believed with certainty that on the first day of school, Vienna would seek her out to welcome and introduce her around Harvey Slate.

Brea studied the immense ivy-covered Federal-style building housing the administration offices. Scanning the property from her vantage point, she observed that the other campus buildings were modern beige and white structures with large glass windows.

The Harvey Slate welcome packet stated that each grade level held classes in separate buildings, and three additional buildings housed specialized facilities for art, computer science, and foreign languages. In addition, the campus boasted state-of-the-art amenities, including a dining hall, gymnasium, performing arts center, assembly hall, library, a central outdoor courtyard and sprawling athletic fields.

Brea entered the administration building. The foyer comprised green marble floors and dark wood wainscotting, lending an elegant ambience to the space. On the walls hung an extraordinary number of framed pictures and awards the school had won over the years. Brea spotted the door to the main office on her left.

Entering the office, an elderly secretary, Ms. Irene, dressed in a gray wool dress and a Harvey Slate black blazer, greeted Brea. She directed her to sit in a brown leather armchair until the headmaster could see her.

Five minutes later, Brea met with Ms. Lindsey Joyce, her new guidance counselor, and Headmaster Carter in his office. Following a review of Harvey Slate's history, the school's general logistics, and her schedule, Ms. Irene summoned Brea to meet her assigned student helper for the day.

"Brea, this is Jennifer. She will be your helper today if you have questions. She has permission to leave her courses early, and she will help you find your way around. Think of her as your private tour guide and confidante."

"Thank you, Ms. Irene," Jennifer, a petite redhead with shoulder-length hair, a pale complexion, and dressed in a Harvey Slate navy polo shirt and skirt, replied with a wide smile. Once alone, Jennifer's smile vanished. "Follow me," she said, turning on her heels and motioning to Brea with her hand over her shoulder. Brea, taken aback by the abrupt change in Jennifer's demeanor, turned to follow her with raised eyebrows.

"Brea, the most important thing first—a warning so you don't go off the rails. If you want a spot in the Harvey Slate honors program for junior year, you need to shine. Don't hold your breath because it's only the top ten percent who get an offer and that's about twenty-five students per class. Also, many of the parents red-shirted the boys to give them an academic and athletic edge, adding another layer of competition. Please don't freak out and do something dramatic if you don't make it because Harvey Slate is one of the best high schools in the country. So, unless you intentionally try to ruin your future to piss off your parents, a top college is in the bag."

"Got it," Brea replied.

"Listen as we walk because I don't have time to hop out of class to shuttle you around all day, but if anyone asks you—I did. I'll walk you to first period, but you're on your own for the rest of the day. Write some notes on your schedule. Here's a pen."

Brea's eyes narrowed as she took the pen from Jennifer. "All right."

"Buildings are in this order going clockwise. Write this down."

She did her best to keep up with Jennifer as she pointed to the buildings by grade level and all the structures visible from the central courtyard. Brea drew a haphazard map, doubting she could make sense of it when needing to look at it later. Jennifer widened her stance and listed off a series of characteristics to help Brea distinguish the buildings on the campus hidden from view. Brea shook her head, overwhelmed and unable to write the descriptions fast enough.

"The dining hall has a black bar across the top, and there is an amazing salad bar. The gym has a glass dome. Our performing arts center has scary masks on the plaque by the door. The assembly hall is as big as the gym but has no glass dome, and the library is the big white building next to the freshman building. You following me?" she asked as Brea wrote the last of her notes.

Without waiting for Brea to answer, she changed the subject. "Are you taking the bus home after school?"

"Yes," Brea replied as she shook out her hand, cramping from her burst of frantic writing.

"After school, walk around the gym, past the basketball courts, to the south parking lot. All the buses park there and take off twenty minutes after the last bell. If you miss it, go to the administration building for a taxi voucher or to call whoever you need to call—or find someone to date with a car. Looking at you, that won't be difficult for you to manage." Pausing a moment, Jennifer looked at Brea, raised her eyebrows to see if she understood everything and waited for a confirmation.

Brea nodded. "Yes. I got it."

Jennifer held up a finger one foot from Brea's face. "Final quiz. Where is your history class?"

Brea glanced at her map and pointed to the sophomore building.

"You got it, see fast learner. You'll do great here." Jennifer smiled and ushered Brea to the sophomore building.

"We are in the same gym class in the afternoon. I'll check on you then." Jennifer turned to walk towards the foreign language building.

"Wait," Brea cried out. Jennifer whipped around and widened her eyes with obvious impatience. "Do you know someone named Vienna Cortello?"

Jennifer's lips parted, then narrowed her eyes. "Yes. Why?"

"Well, she's my cousin, and my uncle said she would help me adjust. She never called me, so I figured maybe I could find her. I have never met her, so I don't even know what she looks like."

Jennifer strode back to Brea and grabbed her elbow, pulling her to the side of the sophomore building, then looked around her to ensure they were alone. "You're—Brea Cortello?"

Brea's eyes darted from side to side. "No, we have different last names. I'm Staxon. Cortello is her mother's last name."

"Wow. I see the resemblance now. Interesting. Look, no of-fense to your bloodline, but Vienna is a cold-hearted witch, and her friends aren't any better. Even though she's your relative, be careful. Consider yourself warned again. If you still want to find her, you're on your own." Jennifer turned on her heels and walked in the other direction across the courtyard.

"Thanks—so much," Brea muttered under her breath as she entered the building to find her classroom. What Jennifer had shared about Vienna was worrisome. She inhaled and resigned herself to figuring out the path ahead at Harvey Slate on her own. The last thing she needed was another bully. If her cousin wanted to connect with her, it would be up to her to find Brea.

⁂

The first month of school passed with little conflict or difficul-ties. Brea found she had acclimated to her new surroundings, her schedule, and had found her rhythm. Vienna neither called nor attempted to find Brea at school, and she left it alone.

A week into school, Brea's father asked if Vienna had helped her adjust to Harvey Slate, and she lied, stating that she had giv-en her a tour of the school. Remembering Jennifer's warning, avoiding Uncle Pax scolding Vienna for ignoring Brea super-seded her acclimation to school—she had no desire to land on her cousin's bad side.

As promised, Blake picked Brea up from school on Tuesday and Thursday afternoons. Sometimes they would stop off for coffee or a slice of pizza after school, though often Brea preferred to return home to study. By the end of the first week, she resolved to do everything possible to land in the top ten percent of her class and secure a spot in the honors program for junior year. Blake would grumble, but he understood.

Brea's attempt at reinventing herself had not come to fruition. Most of the girls in her classes were polite, but unenthusiastic about befriending her. She garnered more attention from the boys, as several of them in her history and biology courses had invited her to study in the library with them or to meet out on the weekends. Brea would smile and inform them she had a boyfriend at Black Harbor High School. This piece of information did not hinder them from trying again the following week.

In early October, the weather cooled, and the autumn air was crisp and invigorating. While Brea walked to the parking lot to catch the bus on a Wednesday afternoon, she smiled as she surveyed the campus decorated with fall-themed garlands and pumpkins. Reaching the gymnasium, she passed a boy dressed in black Harvey Slate athletic wear and a baseball hat holding a large duffel bag. He halted in his tracks, and his eyes fixed on Brea as she passed by. Their eyes met, and he smiled at her. Seeing that he was handsome, her cheeks flushed.

Brea averted her eyes and quickened her steps to pass him by. Her heart raced seeing he had smiled at her with interest. Although ashamed of herself, she could not suppress the electric pulses that coursed through her body. She shook her head. "Boring Brea has Boring Blake," she reminded herself. It was not a kind thing to say either about herself or Blake, but it was the truth as she saw it.

Chapter Nine

The Past

The following day, Brea walked to the south parking lot after school to take the bus home. Approaching the gymnasium, she slowed her pace, hoping to see the boy from yesterday. Letdown that she did not see him, she sighed, having taken the time that morning to wave her hair and apply heavier makeup than usual in the event their paths crossed. Though not a complete waste of time, Joshua from biology class appreciated the effort she had put into her appearance, and once again asked if she would meet him out on Saturday. To his disappointment, Brea informed him she had a date with her boyfriend.

On Saturday night, Blake's parents invited Brea to attend a party in honor of their twentieth wedding anniversary. Having been told she would need to dress up for the occasion, she wore a fitted pale-pink sweater with a heart-shaped neckline and a black pencil skirt. Following his parents' anniversary celebration, they would meet Allegra and Jonathan at a Black Harbor High School party. Having attended only one party the previous year, she looked forward to it.

Blake, dressed in a navy suit and tie, stepped out of the car to greet her as she waited for him on her porch. After embracing her, he planted a fleeting kiss on her lips with a level of passion equaling a warm handshake.

"You look beautiful," he complimented, then took her hand to escort her to the car. Brea forced a smile, disheartened once again. Her body failed to respond to his touch or kiss.

Arriving at the elegant steakhouse, Brea surveyed her surroundings. The tall ceilings, geometric Tiffany chandeliers, large black-framed windows, and tables set with crisp ivory tablecloths and yellow rose centerpieces impressed her. Joining Blake's parents in the reserved dining room, they made a fuss to ensure Brea met as many of their friends as possible.

Half an hour later, Brea's face hurt from the endless smiles, introductions, and polite conversation. They were all lovely people, though she found it difficult to enjoy her meal peppered with frequent interruptions to answer questions. Brea left the table to use the restroom once the waiters cleared the dinner plates, and upon returning, found her napkin folded on the table, her water refilled, and a black velvet jewelry box beside her dessert plate.

Brea turned to Blake, seated beside her, with a wide smile on his face. "Blake, you didn't have to buy me a gift."

"Go ahead, open it," he urged.

Brea smiled and flipped open the box. Inside lay a silver necklace with a starburst pendant on a white silk pillow. "Blake, it's beautiful. Thank you," she exclaimed as she lifted the necklace out of the box to place it around her neck. She fastened the clasp, and a wave of guilt washed over her—she did not deserve the gift. After seeing the boy by the gym, she often fantasized about him asking her out. Though filled with culpability, it had not been possible to banish the thought from her mind.

Blake leaned in and kissed her with a light touch on her lips. She stiffened. The guests seated near them broke out in smiles and clapped their hands upon witnessing the sweet scene. No one noticed Brea's sigh of discontent. Blake's kiss felt as though she had kissed her own hand.

The inescapable truth exploded within her—she would never ache for him or feel as though her body lit on fire when he touched her. Despite this realization, Brea resigned herself that staying in a passionless relationship would be better than the alternative of being alone.

Leaving the restaurant, Brea sat in silence, staring out the window as Blake drove them to Doug's house, a student in Blake's class whose parents were away for the weekend. Arriving at the party, Brea studied the spectacular custom Tudor home with a long driveway and a fountain in the courtyard. Despite the chilly temperature outside, there were groups of teenagers scattered in the front yard, smoking cigarettes.

Brea grabbed Blake's hand as they walked to the door, self-conscious about being overdressed in formal clothing and attracting strange glances from their peers. Reaching the front door, she heard a whistle and overheard a boy congratulate Blake that Brea was "*hot*." Blake turned to say thanks, annoyed, but avoided starting any trouble. He ushered her inside.

Despite the size of the spacious living room, the space felt cramped with the massive number of bodies packed inside. The opulent interior of the home resembled a French country estate, featuring parquet wood flooring, antique weathered wood furnishings, yellow wallpaper, and gold ornate framed landscape paintings. Although not to her taste, she found the decor nonetheless elegant.

Brea hesitated to move from her spot. Blake helped her out of her coat, then added it to a pile of outerwear threatening to topple over onto the floor. She placed her hand over her necklace and rubbed the starburst between her fingers. Blake grabbed her other hand, and holding tight, pulled her into the crowd behind him.

"You want a drink?" he asked, raising his voice over the noise and pointing to the kitchen.

"Sure," Brea replied and followed Blake. A dozen half-empty bags of chips and an absurd number of liquor bottles littered the expansive kitchen island. In the kitchen corner, a group of boys she recognized from Black Harbor High School hovered near the keg to fill up their blue plastic cups.

"What do you want? A beer?" Blake offered as he rubbed his thumb against the back of her hand.

"No, thanks. I'll have a cranberry and vodka." Brea did not drink alcohol, but feeling out of place, she would need something to help her relax. The only drink she could think of was what she had seen her mother drink at her Aunt Emily's house. Blake mixed Brea's drink, then handed it to her. Taking a small sip, the taste surprised her. The refreshing drink had a tart flavor with a hint of sweetness, and she could not taste the alcohol.

"Blake!" Brea and Blake turned, hearing a female voice shouting over the music and chatter. A tall blonde in a puffy red and black ski jacket pushed her way through the crowd towards them. Stepping with long strides, she outstretched her arms and, nearing Blake, embraced him. "Blake, I've missed you. I was telling my parents how long it had been since we'd seen each other."

"Yeah, it's been a while. Tell them I said hello and that I'm still sorry I broke your coffee table at your sixteenth birthday party." They laughed as Brea stood between them, staring at the floor.

The girl turned to Brea to introduce herself. "Hi, I'm Kari." Brea smiled. Before she could speak, Blake spoke for her.

"This is Brea, my girlfriend," he said, placing his hands over her shoulders and squeezing them.

"Hi, you guys look so cute all dressed up. I have known Blake since forever, like kindergarten forever. He's such a nice guy," she gushed to Brea.

"He is. It's nice to meet you," Brea replied. She found it interesting that being "*nice*" appeared to be the first thing all people said about Blake.

"I like your jacket. It looks—warm," Brea added, unsure what else to say to Kari.

"It is, yeah," she answered, glossing over the trite compliment. "I came back from a trip with my parents a couple of hours ago, and I didn't bother to change. After four days in Colorado, I had to escape my house and get away from my parents." Kari rolled her eyes as she spoke.

"So, are you a junior or senior? I don't think I remember seeing you before," she asked Brea.

"A sophomore, but I go to Harvey Slate Prep. I don't know many people here," Brea answered with an awkward smile.

Kari grinned mischievously. "Hey, you're better off not knowing most of these people, only the good ones like Blake," she said as she nudged him in the arm. Someone caught her eye, and Kari turned to walk back into the crowd, telling them she would catch up with them later.

"Kari is a sophomore at Boston University—pre-med. Jonathan went on a few dates with her a couple of years ago. Cool girl. I'm hoping we can talk to her more later. Let's find Jonathan and Allegra," Blake suggested, leading Brea through the crowd until finding them.

Over the next hour, they chatted with Blake's classmates and teammates from wrestling. With the alcohol having kicked in, Brea found herself more relaxed and confident as time passed. Joining in conversations felt effortless, and as the night progressed, Brea surprised herself by boldly cracking jokes. After her second drink, she needed to use the restroom. Tapping on Blake's shoulder to help her, he pointed to the hallway where she could find the bathroom.

Turning down the hall, Brea passed several shut and locked doors. Reaching the end, she saw a door cracked open and placed her fingertips on the handle to peek inside. Disappointed, she saw a bedroom at first glance, but then her mouth dropped open seeing a couple on the bed. Shocked, she froze in place, staring at the couple, the girl on top and the boy underneath her with his hands holding her bottom as she rubbed against him. It was a fervid passion she had never experienced with Blake, and although there was a sense of shame in observing this couple, she found herself transfixed in place. Before she could retreat to avoid detection, the boy opened his eyes and saw Brea standing in the doorway.

Stepping back, mortified, Brea tripped over the hall carpet and slammed into the wall behind her. Steadying herself, she straightened up and spun around. A few steps into her retreat, a door opened, and a girl exited the bathroom. Relieved, Brea slipped in to use the restroom and touch up her makeup. Closing the door, the volume of the music and noise dropped a notch, giving her a welcome moment of respite to relieve her full bladder. Now comfortable, she checked her outfit and refreshed her lipstick. Satisfied with her appearance, she opened the door with more force than she had intended and it swung open and hit the wall with a loud bang.

Brea winced and stepped out with her hand covering her mouth, hoping she had not damaged the wall. Turning around, she startled, seeing the boy from the gymnasium leaning on the wall near the bathroom door with his arms crossed over his chest and a blue cup in his hand. A handsome grin spread across his face as their eyes met. He had short, textured brown hair, with an olive-toned complexion and green eyes.

"Hi. You're Brea, right? I saw you the other day by the gym at Harvey Slate," the boy said with an accent.

"Hi, yes—I'm surprised you know my name." Brea smiled, flattered. "What are you doing here? Do you have friends at Black Harbor High?"

"Yes, I know Doug well. And about knowing your name, I may have asked some guys at school to help me out. I was hoping I would have the chance to talk to you one day. I'm Jamie."

Brea opened her mouth to speak. Jamie's bold eye contact made it difficult for her to think clearly. Her heart raced, and she found herself at a loss for words. Averting her eyes, she searched for the confidence she appeared to have lost now in Jaime's presence.

"I saw you holding hands with the guy in the suit. How did he get a girl like you?" he asked, taking a sip of his drink and drawing Brea's attention to his lips.

"Well, he's friends with my best friend's brother..." her voice trailed off, uncertain of how much detail she should share.

Jaime stepped in closer to Brea. "He seems like a nice guy, but—"

He leaned in a few inches from her ear and whispered, "I think you could do better."

Brea's cheeks burned. Lowering her eyes, she studied the fitted, long-sleeved blue shirt he wore, highlighting his athletic build and muscular arms.

"I also think you chose a nice outfit tonight. All the guys out there can't stop checking you out," he added.

Brea chewed on her bottom lip. "Oh, I don't know about that, but thank you," she replied, flattered, yet overwhelmed by his direct flirtation.

Jaime's mouth opened to say something else when they heard someone yell out, "Cops!"

Chaos erupted as over one hundred and fifty teenagers rushed to the back of the house to evade the police. Desperate to avoid an arrest for underage drinking or smoking marijuana, a crowd pushed into the hallway to jump out of the bedroom windows, knocking Jaime and Brea into one another. No one wanted a stain on their impeccable record that could devastate an Ivy League college application.

Jaime grabbed Brea's hand and pulled her with him. "Come on," he yelled over the crowd.

Brea remained fixed in place. "Come on," he yelled again. She let him pull her a few paces, then paused, knowing Blake was searching for her. In the general panic and chaos, she relented as Jaime tugged on her hand again. Jaime led her to the empty bedroom where the couple had been making out, now empty. He pulled her behind him and climbed out an open window.

"Sit on the edge. I'll help you," he instructed Brea. Jaime placed his arms around her waist and lifted her down. His touch sent sparks throughout her body. He grabbed her hand, and they ran across the lawn.

Outside, pandemonium reigned. Partygoers ran and scattered in various directions, shouting to find their friends as others tripped and fell on the lawn in drunken fits of laughter. Jaime held onto Brea's hand, leading her to the back of the property where a gate let them out onto another street. Once clear of the house, they slowed down to catch their breaths and laughed. Other than a few scattered teenagers running down the street, they were alone. Brea shivered.

"My coat," she said between breaths. "I don't have my coat." She had her purse, but without her coat, she would not last long in the cold air of the night. "Blake is going to be so worried about me." Jaime removed the half-zip dark blue sweater tied around his waist and instructed Brea to lift her arms.

"No, you'll freeze," she protested.

"I'll survive. All you're wearing is that sexy pink shirt," he replied with a lascivious grin. "I'll ask Doug for your coat tomorrow and give it to you at school next week. Describe it for me later."

Brea blushed as Jaime stepped close to her. She slipped her arms into the sweater, eager for its warmth. He slid his hands behind her neck to lift her hair trapped under the sweater, then released it, letting it spill over her shoulders. Brushing her jaw with his hand, he zipped it up to the top. Between his touch and the scent of his cologne, masculine and seductive, Brea needed to close her eyes to ground herself. Her lips parted, and her body craved his touch again. Aware of the effect Jaime had on her, it pleased him. He pointed down the wide street lined with tall oak trees and Newport Street lamps.

"Come with me. My friends will wait for me around the corner by the car, and now that the party has broken up, everyone will meet at South Black Harbor Beach. You can find your boyfriend there in a little while."

Brea surveyed the street, conflicted. She wanted to go with Jaime, but worried about Blake's reaction if she left without him. "I'm not sure. I should find Blake. Neither of us has a cell phone."

"You don't have a phone?" Jaime asked, raising his eyebrows.

"Nope, my parents refuse to buy me one. They think it is a waste of money and not appropriate for a young girl."

Jaime whistled. "Well, for sure, he will be there. I'll watch over you until we find him, okay?" He smiled again, and she nodded. Looking into his eyes, Brea found him impossible to refuse. She played with her fingers as she walked beside Jaime down the street, searching for something to say.

Breaking the silence, Brea spoke first. "So, where are you from? I can't place your accent."

"Brazil. I moved here with my parents five years ago, after my family bought a media company."

"Only you and your parents?"

"I have an older brother and sister, but they are married and have their families in Brazil. I travel there for a month every summer to see them. Have you ever been there?"

Brea chuckled. "No, I have never even left the country. So, tell me about your friends, the ones we're meeting. I haven't met many people at school yet."

Jaime described Trevor and Aaron, both juniors like Jaime at Harvey Slate. Aaron was "*solid and loyal*" according to Jaime, and they were teammates on the lacrosse team. Trevor, extroverted and a music fanatic, also having moved to America in middle school from Denmark, knew an incredible amount of information about any major musical band since the sixties. The three of them lived in Tupa Bay. Jaime told Brea that she would meet more of his friends at the beach, and he would introduce her to them later.

"So, Brea, why did you transfer to Harvey Slate?"

"It's a long story. In a nutshell, according to my mother, something about it being better suited to challenge me academically. I'm a bit of a nerd. In fact, tonight has been only the second time I have been to a big high school party and the first time I had a full alcoholic drink," she confessed. Jaime smiled at Brea, finding her innocence endearing. His attention shifted twenty feet ahead, seeing his friends waiting for him beside a black BMW. Raising his hand to greet his friends, Jaime gave them each a high five upon nearing them.

"What's up? You made it!" Aaron and Trevor exclaimed in unison and in high spirits. Aaron, with a stocky, athletic frame, light-blonde hair and brown eyes, dressed in jeans and a zip crew gray sweatshirt, appeared to be self-assured and cocky. Trevor, in contrast, had a darker complexion and jet-black hair, dressed in a blinding white hooded sweatshirt and a matching white baseball cap under a long dark gray wool coat with a pair of expensive headphones around his neck.

"Bro, what happened to you? I thought the cops picked you up," Trevor, speaking with a Scandinavian accent, asked Jaime with a grin as his eyes darted over to Brea.

"Nope, I was helping a beautiful girl. This is Brea. She transferred to our school this year as a sophomore," he replied, then introduced first Trevor, then Aaron to Brea. Brea sensed Jaime's friends were unsurprised by her presence.

"Come on, Brea, hop in. We'll take you with us," Trevor said as he opened the rear door for her. Eager for warmth, she hopped into the car. "To the beach," Trevor exclaimed, turning on the engine and cranking up the music.

Ten minutes later, they arrived at South Black Harbor Beach. A crowd of two-dozen teenagers sprinkled the parking lot, either sitting on the hoods of cars or standing in small groups with drinks in hand. As Brea and Jaime stepped out of the car, they overhead schoolmates shouting on top of one another and sharing their stories of dramatic escape from the police at the party.

Jaime picked up Brea's hand. "Brea, this is most everyone you need to know in my class at Harvey Slate. Let me introduce you to some girls. That's Vienna—"

Brea's mouth gaped open. "Did you say Vienna? That's my cousin."

"Are you joking? She never mentioned her cousin transferring to our school. How is she your cousin?"

Aaron interrupted before Brea could answer. "Welcome to the after-party, Brea. Can I bring you a beer?"

"Sure, thanks," she replied. Although not in the mood to drink any more alcohol, she did not wish to appear prudish.

"Our fathers are brothers, but I've never met her before. I think she was born just after my Uncle Pax and her mom divorced. So, this might be a little strange, meeting her here." Brea cleared her throat and inhaled a deep breath to calm her nerves. Aaron returned with two open bottles of beer, one each for Jaime and Brea. Jaime clinked his bottle with Brea's, and they both took a sip. It was bitter and yeasty. Brea's lips stretched tight across her face, and she frowned.

"I know. Beer isn't the drink of choice for most of the girls around here. In the future, when I see you again, I'll make you a mixed drink," he chuckled and winked. "Come on, I'll introduce you to your cousin. We have been friends since I moved here." As they approached a glossy red Mercedes parked a few spaces from Trevor's car, two girls seated on the hood shifted their attention to Jaime and Brea.

Facing the two girls, with her back turned to Brea and Jaime, stood a girl dressed in a white wool coat, blue jeans, and camel suede high-heeled boots. She had long brown hair, like Brea's, though mixed with blonde highlights. Next to her stood a statuesque girl with shoulder-length dark-auburn hair, dressed in head-to-toe black.

"Hey Vienna, I'd like you to meet someone," Jaime called out. The brunette in the white coat turned to face Jaime. Brea studied her alluring facial features, chocolate-brown eyes, and flawless complexion.

"Vienna, look who I ran into tonight, your cousin Brea," Jamie proclaimed with enthusiasm. Her eyes widened as she fixed her gaze on Brea. Reaching her, Vienna took a step back, and a wide smile formed on her face.

"Oh, Brea, of course. My father had called and shared the—wonderful news you were coming to Harvey Slate. I'm sorry for not reaching out. I've been so busy." Vienna embraced Jaime, kissed him on the cheek, then took a step back and shifted her gaze back to Brea. Brea took a step forward, then back, uncertain if she should attempt to hug Vienna or not. Vienna stood fixed in her place.

"This is Thea. She's a senior at Harvey Slate," Vienna said, introducing the girl with auburn hair on her right. Brea felt a strong negative reaction observing the haughty smirk on Thea's face, as though she had already sized Brea up and decided she was less than.

Though attractive, something malicious lived in Thea's eyes, dark brown and lined with thick black eyeliner. She leaned in to whisper something in Vienna's ear, then with a superior air, greeted Brea with little enthusiasm. "Hi." Brea half-extended her hand to shake Thea's, pulling it back at the last moment, and instead gave her a wave. Thea squinted her eyes at Brea.

"So, Brea, how was your first month at Harvey Slate?" Vienna asked as Thea swiveled around to continue her conversation with the two girls seated on the roof of the red Mercedes.

"I found my way around without a problem. It's such a beautiful school. Oh, and don't worry about not having called. Uncle Pax told my dad you were traveling most of the summer in Europe. That must have been amazing." Brea paused, not wanting to babble and appear insipid.

"It's the same shit—clubs and partying on boats, but it's better than being stuck here all summer. Thea and I were bored after a month, so we went to Japan. You can only hang in St. Tropez for so long until you want to jump off a balcony." Brea nodded with a smile, though unable to relate.

The two girls with whom Thea had been talking with slid off the hood of the car. Both wore expensive black wool peacoats and knit caps. Their shiny blonde hair peeked out from the edges of their hats, framing their faces and showcasing perfect white teeth and flawless makeup. Their appearance, posture, and critical gazes announced their wealth and privilege.

"Hey Jaime," both girls said in unison, taking turns to embrace him.

"Brea, this is Callie and Tara. Many people ask if they are related, but they aren't. They are both juniors at Harvey Slate."

Aaron joined the group as Jamie introduced Callie and Tara and interjected. "Yeah, and they come off like bitches, but they are kind of cool when you know them better, but not much." Although he appeared to be joking, his tone betrayed some truth in what he said.

"Interesting ensemble," Tara commented, dripping with sarcasm as she gave Brea a once over seeing her dressed in Jaime's sweater.

Brea flushed and looked down at the ground, ill-equipped to handle snide comments from these girls. She would have given anything to be accepted by them, to appear witty and confident, but at the moment, her wish to disappear left her speechless.

"Fuck off, Tara," Aaron snapped back. "You wish you looked like her."

Callie and Tara both gave Aaron the finger.

"Ignore them," Jaime said, drinking another sip of his beer. "They can't stand to see a beautiful girl taking any attention away from them." Jaime wrapped his arm around Brea to squeeze her shoulders.

Vienna, ignoring Tara and Callie, studied Brea. "Brea, how are you finding the people at Harvey Slate? Have you made any friends other than Jamie?"

"Well, it's been overwhelming. I want to make friends, but I don't know anyone and, to be honest, everyone is intimidating."

Vienna scrutinized Brea after Thea had confirmed in her ear that Brea was indeed the transfer causing a stir at Harvey Slate. Placing a finger on her lower lip, she considered the unusual fact of meeting a girl as pretty as Brea at Harvey Slate, possessing genuine humility and a sweet disposition. When her father mentioned Brea would transfer to her school, he described her as shy and plain. Shy perhaps, but plain? Anything but.

After all, she had made quite the impression on Jaime, and word had been circulating around school the past week about the new "*hot girl*" who was also "*a sweetheart.*" According to Thea, she overheard a group of sophomore students debating whether the new girl could be "*the better version of Vienna.*" Vienna had hoped to avoid dealing with Brea in the last two years of high school, but upon seeing her and now intrigued, desired to assess her cousin more closely.

"Brea, how about I take you out for lunch tomorrow so we can chat and get to know one another? Then you'll know at least one person on Monday. Of course, other than Jaime," she said, turning to Jaime with a wink. Knowing Brea's acceptance depended on Vienna and Jaime's approval, Tara and Callie raised their eyebrows and left.

Vienna pulled her phone out of her coat pocket. "Tell me your phone number, and I'll call you in the morning."

Brea swallowed. "Umm, Uncle Pax said he already gave my number to you. To the house. I don't have a mobile phone."

Vienna laughed and exchanged a look with Thea, who then turned to walk away. "I might have lost it. Tell it to me." Brea recited her phone number for Vienna, fixing her eyes on Vienna's well-manicured nails as she tapped in the numbers.

"Jaime, we're going to take off. Brea, we'll talk in the morning." Vienna gave Jaime a quick kiss on the cheek, then, to Brea's surprise, embraced her. She stood frozen in place as Vienna wrapped her arms around her.

She watched Vienna, Tara, and Callie climb into the Mercedes as Thea waited for them in the driver's seat. Vienna seemed harmless, Brea thought to herself as she watched them drive off. Even though enthralled to be in Jaime's world, she remembered she needed to find Blake.

"Jaime, I don't see Blake here, and it's late. I need to find a ride home. Do you know what time it is?"

Jaime checked his watch. "Eleven thirty but—"

He paused, appraising Brea's face to see if he could convince her to stay a little longer. "Let's sit in the car so you can warm up, and when Trevor's done talking with the other guys, I'll ask him to drop you off."

Brea hesitated. Although excited by the prospect of sitting once again in a warm car, she worried about what might happen if she sat alone with Jaime in the backseat. Still, she had to admit that although flirtatious, he had been a gentleman since helping her escape the party. Brea agreed and followed Jaime to Trevor's car.

Jaime whistled to Trevor for the keys, who tossed them over. Catching them in one hand, he opened the door for Brea. Slipping into the front seat, Jaime turned on the engine and the heat, then joined her in the back.

"Brea, tell me about your family. What do your parents do?" Brea's cheeks flushed, having missed his question, and lost in her thoughts about how attractive she found him and wondering what she would do if he kissed her. Jaime smiled as though he could read her mind and repeated his question.

Brea focused and cleared her throat. "It's only me. I don't have any brothers or sisters, and my parents—are different. They treat me like a little adult and leave me alone most of the time. So, I suppose that also makes me a little different."

"Well, they must have done something right. I mean, look at you. I wasn't kidding when I said all the guys at the party were watching you, dying to talk to you." Jaime paused and bit his lower lip, drawing Brea's attention to his mouth. She felt a wave of heat rush through her chest. Jaime studied her face and shook his head.

"What? Why are you staring at me like that?" she asked.

"I'm thinking I will not try to steal a girl from another guy, but I think we should be friends." He paused for a moment. "For now." Brea looked away, intrigued yet flustered. Jaime knew he did not need to say anything more. It would only be a matter of time and he would win her.

"I'm going to call you B," he proclaimed. "You like that? You already have a nickname, and we've only been friends for an hour," he joked.

Brea laughed. "Honestly, I do. My name is so strange, I don't know what my parents were thinking. So, I saw you at the gym after school. Are you on a team?"

"Yes, several. Soccer in the fall, basketball in the winter, and lacrosse in the spring."

Brea raised her eyebrows. "Wow, that's impressive."

"You should come to one of my practices. I would like to see you in the stands cheering for me."

"Maybe," Brea replied and looked down at her lap.

Brea forgot about Blake altogether as she spoke with Jaime for another half hour until Trevor joined them in the car, followed by Aaron.

"Anyone hungry?" Trevor asked.

Jaime looked at Brea and grinned. "Yes, Brea is starving. Let's drive to the diner."

Brea did not protest. Won over, she surrendered to enjoying the rest of the night for as long as it would last. As they drove off, she accepted that in the morning she would pay the price for her thoughtlessness to Blake about where and with whom she had disappeared with.

Chapter Ten

The Past

At eight in the morning, Blake called Brea. Having lost her at the party, he had driven around Doug's neighborhood for an hour, trying to find her. Worried and on the verge of driving to her house, he encountered a group of her former classmates in the parking lot of Black Harbor High School. They informed him they had seen her leaving with a boy after the police had broken up the party.

"How could you take off with another guy?" Blake yelled into the phone when Brea answered. "I was worried and drove around in circles looking for you." He paused and waited for Brea to respond. The longer Brea remained silent, Blake grew angrier. "What the hell happened? Aren't you going to explain?"

Brea did not answer, struggling with where to begin and how to explain why she had disappeared with Jaime. She felt drained, having returned home after two in the morning, and her foggy mind struggled to wake up. Blake's pressing for an explanation only irritated her, rather than eliciting an apology.

"Hello? Brea, are you going to say anything?"

"Blake, it was chaos after the police came. I bumped into a boy from school coming out of the bathroom when the police showed up, and he helped me get away. He said most people meet up at South Black Harbor Beach after a party breaks up, so I went with him."

"What? Are you serious? You should have told him to take you home, not party with him for the rest of the night." Brea rubbed her eyes and did not respond.

"This is pretty screwed up, Brea. I don't know what to say. Are you even going to say you're sorry?"

"I'm sorry," Brea replied, yet her tone of voice betrayed her. Her apology lacked sincerity. After spending the night with Jaime and his friends, something irreversible had shifted within her. The euphoria she had experienced with Jaime had felt like a high from an exquisite drug, and continuing on in her banal relationship with Blake would not be possible.

"Did he try anything with you?" Blake asked. Clutching the phone in her hand with a firm grip, she remained silent.

"Do you like him?" Blake's voice subtly cracked.

It was her chance for a clean break. All she had to do was say yes, and she would be free, but she hesitated. Her heart pounded in her chest, and she struggled to find the courage to speak.

"Brea, what are you doing? Do you want to be with me?" Blake asked, despondent.

"I don't know," she answered, her voice barely audible.

"Forget it. I'll make the choice for you—we're breaking up. Don't call me tomorrow or next week to apologize when this guy screws you over." Blake hung up on Brea.

Brea stared at the wall, numb, and hung up the phone. With her fingers trembling, she walked down the stairs to the kitchen for a drink. Filling up a glass with tap water, she brought the tepid liquid to her lips and drained it in several large gulps. Once finished, she placed the glass in the sink and turned around to lean against the counter. Brea's brain failed to process what had happened until several minutes later. Her guilt over hurting Blake notwithstanding, she felt an undeniable sense of relief—she was free.

Thirty minutes later, the phone rang. Brea picked up without hesitation, certain it would be Vienna calling to set up a time for lunch. Allegra spoke without saying hello, breathless and baffled.

"Hey, Blake is here with my brother, and he's a mess. I overheard him saying that you're untrustworthy, heartless, and all sorts of crazy things. What happened last night?"

Brea did not have the energy to explain the complete story, but she knew she could not avoid telling Allegra the truth. Massaging her aching forehead, she ran through the main events of the night. Allegra, captivated by Brea's story, remained silent other than to interject to say "*Wow*" or "*No way.*"

"So, that's it? You guys are breaking up?" Allegra asked after Brea concluded the rehash of the previous night's events.

"I guess. I mean yes. I can't blame him for being angry with me and, to be honest, it's a relief. As nice as Blake is, and he was a wonderful boyfriend, there was something missing. It was like dating my brother," she confessed. "Are you mad at me?"

"What, no way. I mean, I can understand why he was upset, but if you weren't happy, it's all for the best. But—did something happen between you and this guy, Jaime? I promise I won't say a word."

"No, of course not. We only hung out. But he was flirtatious and charming, and he's—so hot. I'm pretty sure he's into me."

"Hey, maybe let the steam blow off of Blake's body first," Allegra teased.

"Oh, shut up. Look, I have to go. I forgot to mention that I met my cousin last night, and she asked me out for lunch today. She seems nice. I think that girl Jennifer was mistaken about her being evil."

Allegra laughed. "Brea, your own cousin doesn't call you for months? Be careful, doesn't sound like she's so nice to me. Call me tomorrow." As soon as they said goodbye and hung up the phone, Brea ran up the stairs to her room with Allegra's words of caution echoing in her mind.

An hour passed, and Vienna called Brea to meet her at a posh lunch cafe on Harbor Boulevard. Brea needed to dress in comfortable clothing, as she would have to ride her bike to meet Vienna. Selecting a pair of jeans and a black fitted sweater she had borrowed from Allegra, Brea hurried to dress herself. Appraising herself in the mirror, she smiled. After the unexpected events of last night, she sensed something life-changing lurked around the corner.

Two hours later, Brea sat across the table from Vienna, stylish and polished, dressed in an ivory turtleneck sweater dress, knee-high boots, and a tasteful assortment of gold rings on her fingers. Compared to Vienna's appearance, Brea felt drab and uninspired and an eerie flashback of her days in seventh grade fluttered through her mind.

They both had ordered lattes and a savory crepe with a side salad. After drinking a dainty sip of water, Vienna began the conversation as Brea picked at her nails under the table.

"Brea, tell me about you? Even though we're related, I know nothing about you. My father never spoke much about your family." Vienna smiled, resting her chin in her hands, appearing interested and holding Brea's gaze intently.

Brea chewed her bottom lip, intimidated by Vienna's presence and commanding poise. Reminding herself Vienna had made the effort to treat her to lunch helped her relax. "Well, I'm interested in becoming a writer. I used to dance, but since starting high school I have been working more on creative writing, stories and poetry. I suppose I'm not a very exciting person, but I want to be one."

"How about your parents? My father says nothing about your dad other than he is quiet and—odd. It seems our fathers are opposites." Brea coughed, uncertain how to respond as she preferred to avoid sharing the dynamics of her family.

"Well, Dad keeps to himself for sure. You know we still live in Grandma Miriam's house. It's all the same. My parents never changed it. If you would like to see the house, that would be great, and Uncle Pax could come too. Mom keeps a bunch of Grandma's old stuff in the attic and in the garage if you want to pick out something to keep."

Vienna raised her eyes to the ceiling and laughed. "I don't see that happening. My father is an asshole. He cheated on my mother and abandoned her when she was pregnant with me. All he does is send us money. I haven't seen him for over a year."

Brea flushed. "Oh, I'm so sorry." Knowing Vienna's strained relationship with Uncle Pax nearly inspired her to confide in Vienna more about her parents, though she held back.

"It's fine. How about Black Harbor High School? Were you popular?"

Brea shook her head. As the truth would be easy to discover it would be pointless to lie to her. "No, not at all. The opposite. I guess everyone thought I was 'odd,' like my dad. I even had a personal band of bullies taunt me until I was in eighth grade."

"People are jerks, Brea—be tough, or they'll walk all over you. It must not have been all that bad in your past high school. Jaime mentioned you have a boyfriend. Tell me about him."

Brea groaned. "Not anymore. He was pretty upset that Jaime helped me last night after the party and that I spent the rest of the night with him. We broke up this morning, but it was for the best. He is a nice guy, but it was like dating a brother or a friend."

Vienna smiled and tipped her head to the side. "Well, you look very innocent and young. I can see how a guy wouldn't find you very—sexy yet."

Brea's lips tightened—she had not thought about it from that angle. Perhaps her own sex appeal had been a problem, but that made little sense, as the issue had been her lack of physical attraction to Blake.

"The good news is you caught Jaime's eye and, everyone considers him to be the best catch at Harvey Slate. Girls at the school would kill to be with him. Do you like him?"

Brea blushed and lowered her head. "He is charming and so good-looking. I'd be lying if I said no, but we just met. Do you have a boyfriend?"

"Yeah, Ben. He's hot, and also a junior, but let's focus on you. I have to admit, I feel a little protective of you, like a little sister. If anyone tries to mess with you, let me know and I'll have your back. No one screws with me. I don't take anyone's shit, and you shouldn't either."

Brea smiled with relief. Having Vienna on her side and looking out for her was welcomed. "Thank you, Vienna."

The food arrived at the table. Brea picked up her fork to eat her salad after letting out a deep breath. Vienna leaned back in her seat and thought to herself, Brea could be a problem. The rumors of her sweet disposition were true. Although Vienna did not mind being feared at school, she refused to be seen as a lesser version of her younger cousin. "Brea?"

Brea nodded and licked her lips as a little dressing dribbled out of the corner of her mouth. "Yeah?"

"A bit of a warning, and I'm serious. Never cross me, all right? You don't want to be on my bad side. I could make your life a living hell at Harvey Slate." Brea's eyes darted from side to side and her smile disappeared. Vienna laughed and waved her hand. "Oh, forget it. You would never do that. Right, Brea?"

Brea shook her head, taken aback by the sudden shift in Vienna's bearing. "No, of course not."

Smiling, Vienna picked up her fork. "So, let me give you the Harvey Slate survival guide. Let's start with the teachers you need on your side."

Brea ate and did her best to absorb Vienna's words. After lunch, Vienna embraced her and said she would see her "*around*." She had hoped to have scheduled a date to see Vienna again, though treading with caution, she did not broach the topic, and intuited it would be best to follow Vienna's lead.

Chapter Eleven

The Past

Brea and Jaime declared themselves a couple two weeks later. Hearing Brea and Blake had broken up, Jaime wasted no time tracking Brea down at school the following Monday and asked her out for coffee that afternoon. That weekend they went out on two dates and the following week spent most afternoons at his house after school. On their first date, when Jaime kissed Brea, she felt what she had always craved—her body flushed from the heat of a passionate kiss.

With Jaime as her boyfriend, Brea's popularity flourished. His charm, gregarious personality, athleticism, and striking good looks made him desired by many girls at Harvey Slate. He had only been single for a short while after his previous girlfriend had moved to France in the summer. The speed of Brea's taking Jaime off the market sent waves through the school.

Vienna's attention to Brea as well enhanced her appeal as she would make a show of embracing her and having a brief chat with Brea when they saw one another at school. Vienna's friends, Thea, Tara, and Callie, would stand flanked on either side of her, remaining reserved with tight-lipped smiles on their faces.

To Brea's surprise, Vienna offered to set up a double date with Jaime, Brea, and her boyfriend, Ben. Brea smiled with enthusiasm and accepted. Having Vienna's attention, albeit brief, and approval was worth its weight in gold. In her mind, *"Boring Brea"* had died. Now she flew close to the sun at Harvey Slate, belonging to an elite group of students, and never would she give it up.

⟡

With no house parties on Saturday night, everyone met at South Black Harbor Beach. Nearing the end of October, Brea dressed to stay warm in her heavy black wool coat and earmuffs. Arriving at the beach with Jaime, Brea surveyed the groups of teenagers clustered around the parked cars and drifting to and from the fire on the shore.

Exiting the car, Jaime grabbed Brea's hand and pulled her behind him, giving high fives to his friends and introducing her to anyone she had yet to meet along the way. Brea struggled to remember most of the Harvey Slate students' names Jaime introduced her to. Regardless, she smiled and attempted to make small talk as they made their rounds.

"Jaime, Beautiful Brea. Good to see you," Trevor greeted them with a jovial smile as he handed Brea a small black gift bag with handles. "Pick out a few. Jaime told me you don't like beer, so I'm going to keep a special stash for you and any of your sexy friends you introduce me to." Brea chuckled and peeked inside the bag containing a dozen airplane-sized bottles of various hard liquors.

Uncertain which one to choose, she looked to Jaime for help. "B, look for vodka. Probably the easiest to go down. And only two. Any more than that and I'll be carrying you into your house."

Brea's eyes widened at the thought. As with Blake, her parents knew nothing of Jaime, and she planned on keeping it that way. The only questions her parents asked her were, "*Are you hungry?*" and "*How was school, Brea?*" On that account, she felt disinclined to share the intimate details of her love life.

"Two max. Understood." Brea searched through the various bottles in the bag. She did not know if they were vodka, so she chose two at random. Unscrewing the first bottle, Brea held it up and drank half of it down. Her face scrunched up in disgust, and her throat burned.

"Oh, that was so gross," she managed to whisper as Trevor laughed.

"Hey, grab her a soda," Jaime told Trevor. "You all right, B?" he asked as he rubbed her back. Trevor ran back with a can of cola for Brea. She drank down several gulps. Reading the label, Jaime snickered. "That's gin, B. No wonder." Finding her naivety adorable, he kissed her on her cheek.

"For your next drink, give me the soda and I'll pour the alcohol into the can for you." Jaime wrapped his arms around her and kissed her again as several juniors from Jaime's class joined them to say hello and meet Brea.

After an hour and ready for another drink, she pulled out her second bottle and handed it to Jaime. "That's rum. I'll get you another soda to mix it with." Trevor joined Brea as Jaime left to grab her a can of soda. Before he could speak, his attention shifted from Brea to someone arriving in the parking lot.

"No way! I can't believe he's out tonight. Hey Brea, come with me. Have you met Vienna's boyfriend? He's in my class too."

Brea shook her head. "No, not yet."

Trevor gestured for her to follow him. "Not surprised. He doesn't come out very often. Come on, I'll introduce you."

Brea yawned and followed Trevor to a black Lexus, slowing to a park about thirty feet from them. Taking off her earmuffs, she fixed her hair and joined Trevor at the car. Reaching the passenger window, Trevor knocked on the glass, and the window rolled down. Nearing Trevor, she overheard him as he spoke to the driver.

"What's up? I didn't think I'd see you out until winter break. Step out and let me introduce you to Vienna's cousin."

The window rolled up before the driver turned off the engine. Brea looped her earmuffs around her arm as a tall boy stepped out of the driver's seat. He gave Aaron a fist bump before turning to face Trevor and Brea, and placed his arms on the roof of the car.

It took a moment, but Brea recognized him—it was Hayden. Brea's lips parted as she inhaled sharply. Locking her eyes on him, she could not believe it. It was the same boy she had met in the library years ago. After that day, she never saw him again, but his face and eyes remained burned in her memory.

"Hayden, this is Brea, Jaime's new girlfriend. She transferred to Harvey Slate last month. Brea, this is Hayden, Vienna's boyfriend. He's in my class and he is the smartest kid in the school, but don't hold it against him. We like him anyway because he's pretty cool." Hayden met Brea's eyes, and she swore she saw a flash of recognition. Standing behind the car, she could not make out his form, but he was now taller, with the same short dark hair and intense blue eyes.

"Hi," she said and held his gaze, hoping he remembered her.

"Hi," he replied without emotion or effort to appear cordial, chewing a piece of gum as he spoke. He had a stoic facial expression, making him difficult to read. Brea broke eye contact, disappointed that he had no idea who she was.

Jaime returned, joining Brea and Trevor at Hayden's car. "Hayden, surprised to see you out without Vienna."

Trevor chimed in. "I was just introducing Hayden to Brea."

Jaime pulled Brea closer to him and put his arm around her shoulder. "She's beautiful, Hayden, isn't she? And she's as smart as you. You two can form a book club together," he teased as he kissed Brea on her cheek.

"Right, well, I'll see you around. Nice to meet you," Hayden replied. He glanced between Jaime and Brea, then walked off to join a group of boys clustered around an expensive sports car.

Jaime turned to face Brea. "He's not exactly the most outgoing guy, but once you know him better, he's cool."

"I thought Vienna's boyfriend's name was Ben?" Brea asked, perplexed.

"Oh yeah, that's a joke between them. No one else calls him that. When they first met, for some reason, she thought his name was Ben. He didn't correct her for weeks, and it became an inside joke between them. She still calls him Ben."

Brea nodded, stunned by this unusual turn of events. She had thought of Hayden over the years since and wondered what would happen if their paths crossed again. His reaction tonight had not been one she considered, and she felt a mixture of embarrassment and hurt.

Jaime stepped in front of Brea. "Hey, is the alcohol hitting you too hard? You're looking a little out of it."

Brea smiled. "Nope, only cold."

Jaime leaned in and kissed her. "Let's go sit by the fire on the beach. If you're up for it, we can go back to my house and watch a movie in a little while. My parents aren't coming home until late."

Brea rubbed her lips together. Up to this point, she and Jaime had only kissed, and although when he kissed her, it sent electric jolts throughout her body, they had not gone further. She looked into his eyes, unsure whether she felt ready for more.

"I promise I'll behave. Unless you don't want me to," he whispered in her ear. "You're the boss and worth the wait, no pressure."

A smile curled on Brea's lips. "Sure." Taking her hand, they walked to the beach to join the party. Curious, she looked over her shoulder to see where Hayden had gone. Unable to find him, she thought to herself that the universe had a strange sense of humor, reminding her that *"Boring Brea"* would haunt her no matter who she dated or how admired she would become at Harvey Slate.

CHAPTER TWELVE

THE PAST

On a cool, windy April afternoon, six months later, Brea sat on the sidelines of the lacrosse field fulfilling her duty as a girlfriend, watching Jaime and the Harvey Slate Lacrosse team practice after school. Jaime's practice trudged along with no end in sight. Brea, wearing Jaime's sweatshirt, zipped it up as high as it would go, then pulled the hood over her head.

Checking her watch a third time, the minutes inched to five o'clock. Rather than eating, she had spent her lunch period in the library to start on her weekend homework, a decision she now regretted. Her stomach growled. As soon as practice finished, Jaime and Brea were meeting his parents for pizza, though she worried she might faint from low blood sugar before then.

That evening, a Harvey Slate Senior planned to host a large house party. His parents owned real estate all over the country and often traveled, leaving his house a frequent site for parties. Jamie planned to drop Brea off at Allegra's house to dress for the evening, and would return to drive them to the party. It had been two weeks since having last seen Allegra. With them attending different schools, and Brea spending much of her free time with Jaime, she worried Allegra could become resentful. Up to that point, Allegra had voiced no complaints.

Scoring a goal, Jaime waved to Brea from the field as he ran past—she cheered and blew him a kiss. Exhausted and stifling a yawn, she checked her watch again. This past month had been challenging. Brea dedicated most weekday evenings to rehearsing for a provocative senior project—a play inspired by Plato's Allegory of the Cave written by a small group of senior students. Brea, cast in a minor role, would perform in only one scene, though it was a solo dance number.

The gods had tasked her character, dancing the symbolic role of "Temptation," to lure the main character, Lucien, from the cave. Once liberated, he would be free to experience the true nature of the world, both good and evil, realities sheltered from him by his life in the cave. Jaime invited his friends to watch the performance the following weekend, despite his reservations about its tedious and philosophical nature. In the spirit of supporting Brea, they had all accepted. Brea had also invited Vienna, pleased she had accepted her invitation, though surprised she insisted on bringing Hayden with her.

Jaime, Brea, Vienna, and Hayden had met out for half a dozen double dates, all of which Brea found more uncomfortable than enjoyable. When she attempted to engage Hayden in a conversation, her efforts were often unsuccessful. Hoping to find a shared interest, she inquired about his classes, genres of films or books he enjoys, ambitions for the future, and countless other topics. To her frustration, Hayden would give a curt, shallow reply with fleeting eye contact, and upon paying the check, or once the movie ended, he stood promptly to usher Vienna out the door.

Brea remained at a loss for Hayden's indifference or, rather, she feared, frank dislike of her. Worse, why his behavior continued to bother her so much she found incomprehensible. She wished she hated him, yet for an inexplicable reason could never abandon the desire of wanting to win him over.

Another oddity had been Vienna's behavior. Brea suspected over time, though uncertain, Vienna gleaned enjoyment, witnessing Hayden's comportment toward her. It filled her with unease, the manner in which Vienna smiled when Hayden tersely answered her questions.

"Ben, you're too moody. Give the girl a break. Even if she isn't interesting, that doesn't mean you can act like an asshole," Vienna would exclaim through laughter, failing to notice how insulting her comments landed on Brea. Hayden would nod and look anywhere other than at Brea. Jamie, unwitting, attentive, and affectionate with Brea, appeared to enjoy their outings together and Vienna's charming and convivial company. Vienna's continued invitations to Jamie and Brea for another double date a few weeks later continuously surprised Brea. Jaime would accept with enthusiasm, and the cycle continued on.

With the enigma of Hayden's behavior, Brea had little time to dwell on it. Between the play and spending time with Jaime or Allegra, Brea had been working late into the night over the weeks to keep up with her schoolwork.

"B, we're done," she heard Jamie shout from the fence. "Let's go."

Brea collected her things and hurried to meet Jaime waiting at the other end of the field. Greeting him with an embrace and a long kiss, she felt her stomach growl again. "Please feed me. I'm going to pass out from hunger," she begged. Patting Brea on her bottom, they turned to walk to the parking lot hand in hand.

Chapter Thirteen

The Past

On the night of the play, Jaime, Trevor, Tory, Aaron, Hayden, and Vienna sat in the center, six rows from the stage. Tory, Trevor's new girlfriend and a sophomore, had a friendly and easy-going personality that Brea enjoyed. From behind the curtain, Brea watched the group talking with one another and observing Hayden, he appeared to be in a better mood than usual, laughing at something Aaron had said.

Brea rolled her eyes, annoyed that Hayden would not give her the chance to be friends. It never failed to astonish her how his persona differed from the day she had met him in the library. She scanned the audience for Allegra and Mr. and Mrs. Shay, though could not find them. Giving up, she closed the curtain. Attempting to rid herself of any pre-performance nerves, she shook her hands and jumped up and down several times. Jaime had seen none of her rehearsals, and she hoped to impress him with the most mature performance to date she would dance.

"Clear the stage except for the cast," the director, Max, announced. The cast gathered on stage in a circle and joined hands. Max praised everyone's dedication and hard work in making the show come together. After a brief exercise to loosen them up, he wished them all good luck and, of course, to *"break a leg."*

Still dressed in her warm-up sweats and slippers, Brea walked offstage to the dressing room to change. She pulled her costume off the rack—a red cropped short-sleeved dance top with matching footless tights over dance briefs. She had styled her hair loose with voluminous waves, cumbersome for a dance performance, though, according to Max, essential for the character to use her hair as a tool of seduction. Who was Brea to argue with the director and his vision?

Thirty minutes into the first act, the curtain closed after the previous scene had ended, and Brea took her mark on center stage. Inhaling through her nose and exhaling through her mouth several times to ready herself, Brea closed her eyes. With her back to the audience, she outstretched her arms on either side of her, and tilted her head back as the curtain opened. The music began, and the lights cued, casting an orange-red glow over the stage. The main character, Lucien, stood in front of the cave prop near the wings on Brea's left.

Her movements—slow and deliberate—carried her across the stage in a series of turns and arabesques. Temptation danced toward Lucien, reaching out for him and falling into his arms. She tried to pull him with her, her hands on his shoulders, but he resisted.

Using her body to create angular shapes followed by a combination of bold jumps, she tried but failed to capture his attention, then transitioned to a series of sensual floor work. Reaching Lucien, she tempted him to take her hand, yet he resisted and pushed her away. With a rapid series of chain turns, she crossed the length of the stage.

This push and pull continued as Temptation danced a series of seductive variations. Failing to lure Lucien, she intensified her efforts with another series of floor work. Reaching Lucien, this time he lifted her, walked Temptation across the stage, then placed her down. He tried to escape, but she gripped his hand, and he dragged her across the stage to the cave. As she stood, Lucien embraced her from behind and their torsos rolled together in a slow circle before he released her and stepped back.

In the ending series of chain turns and jumps, Lucien's last attempt at resisting her failed. Overcome with desire, he fell to his knees, then dropped onto all fours. Temptation rolled over his back, with her legs extended in the air as her hair spilled over his shoulders. Standing over him, Lucien collapsed onto the floor.

Moving back into her original starting pose, Temptation extended her arms out once again, this time facing the audience in triumph as the music ended.

Applause erupted from the audience. Brea, out of breath and radiant, strained her eyes to look into the crowd, seeing Jaime, Trevor, Tory, and Aaron clapping with broad smiles, whistling and cheering. Brea's face fell when her eyes settled on Hayden.

Neither clapping nor smiling, he sat still with an intense expression on his face, staring at Brea on the stage. Stunned and off her mark, Brea stood in place in the curtain's path as it hurtled towards her to close. At the last moment, she took a step back to avoid being hit.

After the final bows, Brea rushed backstage to change, then met Jaime and the others in the lobby. Running into Jaime's open arms, he embraced her and lifted her several inches off the floor to spin her around in a circle. "You were amazing, so sexy. But I'm going to beat that guy's ass on stage for putting his hands on you like that," Jaime teased and planted a kiss on her lips.

Allegra and her parents appeared. Mrs. Shay offered Brea a beautiful bouquet of hot pink roses. After sharing how professional and polished Brea had been on stage, they took turns giving Brea a quick embrace. Brea thanked them for coming, appreciative of their support as her own parents had missed the show.

Before Brea had left for the theatre, her mother complained of a sudden "*horrendous*" migraine. Declaring the stage lights and the clapping would make the headache worse, she refused to attend the performance. Further, she insisted Brea's father remain home with her in the event her condition worsened. Brea, although bothered, had expected her mother would conjure an excuse to avoid attending the play.

Aaron, Trevor, and Tory then congratulated Brea, embracing her and praising her performance. She thanked them all, her cheeks flushed with embarrassment from the abundant attention.

Tory announced as she embraced Brea, in front of Allegra's parents no less, "I am so turned on. Show me some of those moves."

Trevor's eyes grew wide and mouthed, "Thank you," to Brea. She laughed, flattered, and proud she had impressed them all.

"Let's go to Nigel's. He's having people over tonight," Jaime said, standing behind Brea with his arms wrapped around her shoulders and chest. Brea had never met Nigel, though she remembered Jaime having mentioned him being a freshman in college and used to play on the Harvey Slate soccer team with him.

"Where are Vienna and Hayden?" Brea asked, scanning the lobby.

"They'll meet us at Nigel's," Trevor replied as he turned to usher the group to the exit. "Vienna was being a pain in the ass. Something about going back home to pick up something she forgot. She dragged Hayden out of the theatre in a bad mood."

Brea's smile shifted to a frown, unable to shake the image in her mind of Hayden's strange expression from the audience. She would overcome her ambivalence and ask him for his thoughts on her performance. Jaime called out Brea's name to wake her out of her trance. She grabbed her bags and followed him through the main doors of the performing arts center.

Nigel lived in a modern three-story luxury home on South Black Harbor Beach. Brea's eyes widened as they entered the front door, and she let out a small gasp. The foyer featured a twenty-foot ceiling with skylights and polished marble flooring. As they made their way to the back of the house, Brea scanned the rooms, taken with the various large-scale sculptures and contemporary furniture. Most striking were the abstract paintings displayed on the walls throughout the home.

Past the dining room, they entered a vast living room attached to a gourmet modern kitchen and floor to ceiling windows overlooking the beach.

"This place is like a museum. Won't his parents flip out if they find out he's having this party?" Brea whispered to Jaime.

"Nah, it's not that many people, and as long as nothing breaks and we stay away from the art, it's fine," he answered.

Brea studied the thirty-odd teenagers milling around the kitchen and lounging on the expensive furniture throughout the house. Brea raised her eyebrows. Jaime was a tad overconfident, believing everyone could control themselves after having several drinks.

Nigel, with outstretched arms and an expansive manner, greeted them. "Jamie! What's up, my man?" he bellowed as he made his way across the living room floor from the kitchen, drink in hand. Jaime informed Brea in the car that Nigel, a freshman at Harvard, had returned home for the weekend as a favor to his parents to house-sit. He then described Nigel as the most notorious ladies' man to have attended Harvey Slate.

Studying him, Brea took notice that he had an attractive face, athletic frame and polished style of dress. He carried himself with confidence, and she understood how his charm and charisma could win over a fair number of girls. However, she perceived something superficial and disingenuous about him that turned her off.

"Brea," Nigel greeted, eyeing her with a libidinous appraisal. "I've heard about you, and everything they say is true," he boldly proclaimed to Jaime. Wearing an olive-green body-hugging dress and platform sandals, Brea regretted her outfit choice, making her a target for untoward comments. Still, Jamie often reminded Brea he preferred her to dress in a feminine style, with makeup and her hair styled when they went out, and Brea desired to please him.

She produced a tight smile, seeing through his charms thanks to Jaime's candid description of his tricks to flirt with and seduce girls. Nigel picked up on her reserve. "Ooh, she has a feisty side, this one. You can tell by her eyes," he teased, laughing a little too generously at his own joke.

"Brea, make yourself comfortable in the living room with the girls. We'll make you a drink. Jaime, follow me so we can figure out the baseball game tickets for next month." Jaime squeezed, then let go of Brea's hand as he walked off with Nigel, leaving her alone.

Turning to face the living room, Brea spotted Tara and Callie seated on the sofa. At larger parties or at the beach, she could easily avoid them. At smaller gatherings, she endured their painful discussions about music videos or nasty gossip regarding girls they considered inferior and worthy of vicious criticism.

"Oh shit," Brea muttered under her breath as Tara caught her eye. Tara looked through Brea as though she had seen a piece of garbage she needed to step over. Her gaze drifted to Vienna, engaged in a conversation with other Harvey Slate juniors. Brea's heart dropped into her stomach. Seeing Vienna meant Hayden would be somewhere in the house. She wished it did not matter to her what he thought about her performance—but it did. And if he had hated it, childish as it would be, she declared to herself, she would hate him.

Seeing a space on the sofa across from Tara, Callie, and Vienna, Brea drew in a breath and ambled to the sofa, greeting everyone with a smile and a wave as she sat down. Brea looked over her shoulder to see if Jamie had mixed her drink, though observed him still engrossed in conversation with Nigel. On the verge of turning her head, she paused, seeing Hayden standing at the far end of the kitchen counter, looking in her direction. Brea averted her eyes. Although wanting to speak with him, she needed more time to prepare herself before approaching him.

"Brea, you were amazing in the play tonight." Brea turned to smile at Sonia, a junior at Harvey Slate, who often starred in the musicals by virtue of her spectacular singing voice. Anjali, a junior as well, and Sonia's best friend, had become a favorite of Brea's as well, sharing her love of reading, and she had a fabulous sense of humor.

"Thank you. It's an amazing number, and it took a lot of work to prepare my body for the role. I couldn't believe Max chose me to perform it," she replied. Brea's eyes darted among the girls as she answered. Perhaps mistaken, she picked up on a whisper of hostility behind Vienna's narrowed eyes.

"Do you want to dance in the future as a professional?" Anjali asked.

"I used to, but now I'm interested in writing. Fiction and poetry, that sort of thing."

Vienna sighed, then changed the topic. "I saw this French movie last week. It was a sexy thriller you all have to see." The girls shifted their attention to Vienna as she described the plot and her opinion of the film.

Amid Vienna's critique, Brea felt a tap on her shoulder. Looking up, she blinked twice upon seeing Hayden standing beside her holding two drinks. Meeting his eyes, she opened her mouth, though no words escaped her lips.

"Jaime asked me to give you this. He'll be here in a minute," Hayden said, dressed in an ordinary white V-neck T-shirt and jeans, yet she found the attire on him striking. Brea took the cup from his hand, and her breath hitched as his fingers brushed against hers.

"Thanks," she replied. Hayden's mouth opened, but he said nothing. Hesitating a moment, he turned from Brea to join Vienna on the sofa. He propped himself on the armrest, positioning himself across from Brea. Crossing his arms across his chest, he held his drink in one hand and made fleeting eye contact with Brea.

"Hayden, what did you think about Brea's performance?" Sonia asked. All side conversations halted to hear his response. Brea's heart beat faster. Taken by surprise, he coughed, as he had been in the middle of taking a sip of his drink. Stalling, he cleared his throat before he spoke.

"It was—good," he responded elliptically. Again, he met Brea's eyes, then looked down at his arms.

"What a detailed critique, Hayden," Callie jested as she laughed.

Vienna rolled her eyes. "Hayden was bored, and he didn't even clap," she announced callously to the group. "Sorry, Brea, you didn't impress him," she added and fixed her eyes on Brea with an icy glare. Sonia and Anjali's mouths dropped open, stunned by Vienna's cruel comment. Tara and Callie looked at one another with raised brows, the insensitivity shocking even to them, though no one dared to challenge Vienna's brutal assertion.

Hayden shook his head with no attempt to disguise his contempt for Vienna's disparagement, hurting and humiliating Brea. "Shut up, Vienna. You're such a bitch," he shot back, albeit in a cool tone of voice. Mouths gaped open and everyone froze, astounded by Hayden's harsh shutdown.

Jaime and Nigel, chatting as they walked, halted in place upon reaching the group, seeing the stunned expressions on everyone's faces, not having witnessed the event, only the aftermath.

"What did we miss?" Jaime asked, looking side to side with a perplexed frown on his face.

The shock of Hayden's atypical behavior stunned everyone into silence, and no one responded to Jaime. Vienna shook her head and opened her mouth to let out a sharp exhale. Eyes seething with fury, she glared at Brea.

"Fuck you, Hayden. Nigel, call me a taxi—I'm waiting outside," she commanded, knocking into Hayden with her oversized handbag as she stood and stormed past him. All surrounding conversations paused as everyone at the party tuned into the drama unfolding in the room.

Nigel took a few steps backwards to call the taxi. Slapping Jaime's shoulder, he said, "Tell me everything when I get back."

Stopping beside Brea before exiting the room, Vienna leaned down to whisper into her ear, "Wipe that virtuous look off your face. They buy it, I don't." Brea looked into Vienna's eyes, bursting with disdain.

"Vienna—" Brea attempted to speak, but Vienna straightened and strode out of the room.

"Hey, what happened?" Jaime asked again, eyes wide.

Tara and Callie, lacking true loyalty to Vienna, snickered having witnessed Hayden's outburst. Sonia and Anjali's mouths continued to hang open in astonishment.

Brea focused on a large-scale painting on the wall behind the sofa where Vienna had sat. The large canvas represented either a violent black hole or a windstorm, with red, yellow, and black aggressive brush strokes. Seeing Hayden crouch down before her broke her meditation.

"Brea, what she said wasn't true. You were—stunning on that stage, I mean it." Looking into Hayden's eyes, she saw the same gentleness she had seen once before, the day they had first met at the library. She saw something else in his eyes—a subtle sadness.

"I'm going to talk to her," Hayden told Jaime as he rose, turned, and left the room.

Jaime, still lost, searched for someone to explain what had happened.

"Vienna insulted Brea's performance, implying she sucked, then Hayden told her to shut up and called her a bitch," Anjali obliged to fill Jaime in.

"That's messed up. Brea, all Vienna does is shop for clothes and throw up her dinner. She doesn't know shit about culture," Nigel remarked, having returned and overheard Anjali's rehash. He shook his head as he sat in Vienna's vacated spot on the sofa.

"B, she's jealous. Don't let her get to you," Jaime said, rubbing Brea's shoulders to comfort her.

Brea pressed her cheek against Jaime's hand, exhausted and eager to return home. Hayden left and did not return to the party, leaving Brea perturbed. The way Hayden had looked into her eyes, something within her had sparked. She wanted more from him, though remained at a loss what she desired. And if Hayden had found her performance "stunning," it did not explain his intense stare from the audience—and she wanted an explanation.

Chapter Fourteen

The Past

B rea returned home from Nigel's at two in the morning. Early in her first year of high school, Brea's father announced she would have a curfew of midnight, though never followed through on enforcing it. Without fail, her parents retired at ten o'clock and slept through the night, allowing Brea to return home when she chose. On the rare occasions Brea returned home after dawn, if her mother or father were awake, she would tell them she had fallen asleep at Allegra's house, and they would nod without question.

Sleeping until late morning, Brea woke up famished and trudged down the stairs to make herself breakfast. She needed to hurry, as Allegra's mother would soon pick her up for a shopping trip. Brea's sixteenth birthday on Friday prompted the mall excursion, and the only gift she had requested from her father had been money to spend. Entering the kitchen, she saw her mother seated at the table with a cup of coffee and a crossword puzzle book. Her father had left to run his usual weekend errands and would not return until the late afternoon.

"Hi Mom," Brea said, catching sight of the unwashed dishes from the previous night's dinner piled in the sink. Eyeing the plates, soiled with crusted streaks of food and crumbs, Brea turned her head in disgust, and her stomach turned. She would wash them herself later, otherwise, they would sit in the sink for days.

"Brea, there isn't any milk left for cereal. I'll do some shopping tomorrow when you are at school." Brea's mother kept her head down as she spoke and continued to stare at the crossword puzzle page. In the margins Brea saw notes, yet the puzzle itself sat empty.

"Sure. I'll make toast, then I need to take a shower and dress for shopping with Allegra and her mom." Brea stood by the sink for several minutes in silence, wondering if her mother would ask about the performance.

Over the school year, Brea's mother had paid less attention to her appearance and, to a large extent, had grown reclusive. Often, she complained of severe fatigue and asked Brea to shop for groceries as she waited in the car. The shopping list her mother handed her never varied, remaining unchanged with the same two dozen items. Having done this task for her mother many times over the previous months, she no longer needed a list to reference in the supermarket.

Brea studied her mother, her face free of any makeup and her shoulder-length brown hair tangled and unwashed. Her lack of grooming and dress, wearing a ragged blue floral nightgown, made her mother appear older than her age. Lately, something in her mother's eyes had changed as well, an emptiness she found more tragic than her appearance. Although Brea often joked her family lived in their home as ghosts, her own mother now resembled what she imagined being a living apparition.

"Mom, my performance. All of my friends thought I danced the part well. The number was beautiful."

Her mother looked up at her with a blank expression on her face. After a brief pause, she produced a tight-lipped smile.

"Wonderful. Maybe we can watch the recording someday," she replied, sipping her coffee.

"No, forget it. It was only a performance for a senior project. Not that important, Mom." Brea rubbed her forehead. Her temples ached as she grabbed the bread, removed two pieces, and placed them in the toaster. From the refrigerator, she took the butter dish, sighing as she closed the door, seeing it empty other than a bag of apples, carrots and leftovers.

"Mom, do you like our house? Living here?"

Irritated by another interruption, her mother looked up once again at Brea. "What? Why are you asking me that? It's only a house with things. Things don't matter."

"So, what does matter?" she pressed.

"Brea, I don't know what you're asking me here. I would like some quiet, all right?" Breaking away from Brea's eyes, her mother scratched her scalp in several places in rapid succession, then slammed her hand down on the wooden kitchen table. After a pause, she picked up her pencil and refocused her attention on the crossword puzzle.

The toaster popped. Brea snatched the slices of bread, frustrated and lacking the courage to explain to her mother what her aim had been—a connection with her mother similar to the one Allegra had with her own mother.

Brea shook her head, disillusioned that any sort of meaningful relationship with her mother would one day materialize. She needed to reconcile that affection or intimate conversations would never occur within these walls, only the sounds of a television program or creaking steps when someone stepped on the old wood floors. Brea scraped off the crumbs embedded in the stick of butter before slicing several pieces for her toast. Sandwiching the two pieces of bread together, she retreated up the stairs to shower and dress.

Later that afternoon, Brea, Allegra and Mrs. Shay sat in the mall food court. In honor of her birthday, Mrs. Shay insisted Brea choose where she would like to eat. With no deliberation, she chose her favorite kiosk that served enormous portions of noodles and egg rolls. Embracing a self-indulgent afternoon at the mall, the three of them ate until they were too full and laughed as Allegra's mother shared ridiculous stories about her neighbors having bought chickens for their backyard.

After their meal, Mrs. Shay asked the girls if she could accompany them to a boutique to buy Brea a birthday present. Brea attempted to decline with grace, though Mrs. Shay insisted, and they set off into the mall. Allegra pulled Brea into an expensive clothing store she never shopped in considering her meager clothing allowance.

Black velvet sofas with gold trim flanked the length of a black stone table in the center of the boutique, and the designer garments hung on gold-painted wooden hangers. The saleswomen, dressed in elegant attire, lavished attention on Brea and Allegra as they browsed. Brea overheard the sales associates and Mrs. Shay commiserate about what they would give to have the figure of a teenage girl again.

Following their clothes selection, a sales associate ushered the girls to the fitting rooms. One by one, Brea tried on different styles of jeans, slip dresses, blouses, and skirts until reaching her favorite outfit—a black-and-white striped skirt with a black spaghetti string camisole made from a stretchy jersey material, soft and luxurious to the touch.

A sales associate brought Brea a pair of black-and-white sandals to try on to complete the look. Stepping out of the dressing room to look in the mirror, Mrs. Shay smiled.

"Oh, honey, you look great. If you love it, that's your gift."

Allegra agreed. "Brea, it's gorgeous—wear it on Friday for your birthday to the party."

"Great idea. Oh, I love it. Thank you, Mrs. Shay." Brea accepted the gift with joy and turned to embrace Allegra's mother.

"You deserve it, honey, never forget that," Mrs. Shay whispered in her ear as she held her.

A sobering thought appeared in Brea's mind. She had no memory of her own mother having embraced her—ever. When Brea flipped through her family photo album, any baby or childhood pictures of Brea featured her alone or standing erect next to one of her parents. Squeezing her eyes shut, she steadied herself not to ruin the experience of this wonderful afternoon, and refused to allow any tears to fall.

Friday night, Brea waited on her porch for Jamie, dressed in the outfit Allegra's mother had gifted her. To celebrate Brea's birthday, Jaime made dinner reservations and afterward, they would pick up Allegra and drive as a group to another party at Doug's.

At six o'clock, Jaime's silver Audi pulled up in front of Brea's house. Seeing her on the porch in her new outfit, Jaime, dressed in a pair of jeans and a fitted dark blue button-down shirt, jumped out of the car to meet her at the bottom steps of the porch. "B, you look beautiful," he exclaimed, pulling her in for a kiss.

"Thank you. This outfit is brand new, even the shoes, so I would like to avoid anything that could cause stains tonight." Jaime took Brea's hand in his, led her to the car, and opened the door for her. On her seat sat a large rectangular white box tied with a blue satin ribbon.

"You can't open it until after dinner," Jaime instructed.

"Of course," Brea agreed without protest. Settling into her seat, she placed the gift on her lap and held it for the duration of the drive. A short while later, Jaime pulled up to the valet stand of an elegant beachfront restaurant in South Black Harbor with a modern white precast concrete exterior. Once inside, the hostess ushered them through the restaurant to a table beside a large window overlooking the beach. Brea surveyed the elegant interior showcasing oak floors, tables covered in beige linens with matching upholstered chairs and bronze sculpted pendant lights hanging from the ceiling.

"Jaime, this place is beautiful," Brea declared in awe as a member of the waitstaff pulled out her chair and she sat down. Jaime smiled and ordered two sodas for the two of them. After reviewing the menus, Jaime caught Brea up on the latest news he had heard from Aaron regarding Vienna. After the fight last weekend with Hayden, she planned to take off several days from school the following week for a trip to a hotel spa, courtesy of her mother for "*recuperation.*"

"That girl is high maintenance, so spoiled," Jaime remarked after thanking the server for bringing them their sodas. With a smile, he added, "Nothing like you. Not only are you beautiful, you're a sweetheart." Brea smiled and nodded, concealing her enthusiasm, knowing Vienna would be absent from school for several days.

Since Nigel's party, if Vienna passed by Brea on campus, she would give her a cool smile and half-hearted greeting. The tension between them had been thick and impossible to ignore. Brea remained at a loss as to why Vienna had turned on her at the party and perplexed regarding the comment about her being "*virtuous.*"

Jaime chattered throughout the meal about his upcoming lacrosse game and summer plans to travel to Brazil. As Brea picked at her seafood capellini, she let him prattle on, her mind wandering. With a polite smile, she nodded at various points of the conversation to appear attentive, though she found it difficult to stay focused. At one point, she attempted to share the plot of a book she had read the previous week that had inspired her to write a poem. Uninterested, Jaime changed the subject. Brea forwent dessert to hasten Jaime paying the bill as she was eager to pick up Allegra. Although the party would be like all the rest, drinking and gossiping, tonight she would have her best friend at her side.

Being in Jaime's circle of friends had proved to be a tiring and monotonous routine, demanding constant socializing and the upkeep of a flawless physical image and composed behavior. Having Allegra with her helped her remember the times when her life was simpler. Still, she dared not complain. This version of Brea was at least admired, respected, and desired. She never wanted to contemplate the possibility of "*Boring Brea*" returning.

"Show me the birthday present from Jaime," Allegra commanded as she climbed into the back seat of Jaime's car. Brea lifted a top-handle gold leather handbag and dangled it in the air for Allegra to admire. Brea had already transferred the contents of her old purse into her new one to flaunt at the party. Allegra took it from Brea's hand to inspect it closer. "Oh, it's amazing.

Nice job Jaime. Brea loves gold—good boy! You pay attention." Allegra patted Jaime on his shoulder. "Brea, you need to show Jaime later how much you like the gift, if you know what I mean."

"You know what, Allegra, you are right. It was very expensive, and think about all the time and effort it took to pick it out, wrap it—"

Jaime turned his head to Brea with a wink and a grin.

"Stop it, you two. And I know, Jaime, that you didn't wrap it. The box and ribbon are from the store," Brea shot back with a side-eye and playful smile. All of them laughed, and Jaime turned up the music for the rest of the drive.

Staring out the window, Brea thought more about whether she was ready to have sex with Jaime, having meditated on the topic over the previous several weeks. Although he never pressured her or brought up the subject, she figured it would be only a matter of time until he inquired when she would consider losing her virginity. While she enjoyed intimacy with Jamie, found his kisses arousing and allowed him to touch her body wherever he desired, she could not decide.

She knew in theory the importance of waiting for the right person, though did not understand how one knew the right person had presented themselves. Her mother, unhelpful, had never sat Brea down to talk about dating. The only education regarding romance and sex she had gleaned was from novels or overhearing stories from girls at parties who were having sex.

Brea, lost in thought, turned to Jaime when she noticed Jaime pulling into Trevor's driveway. "Why are we at Trevor's? Are we picking him up?"

"Nope, he's going to drive tonight so I can drink." Brea looked at Allegra with wide eyes. When Jaime drank too much, which was rare as he wanted to stay in top shape for sports, he could either become excessively high-spirited or quarrelsome. Brea sighed, knowing the futility of protesting.

Exiting the car, they went to the door and rang the bell. A breeze blew through the cool night air, and when stretching her neck back, Brea saw a cloudless sky filled with immeasurable stars and marveled at its beauty. "Jaime, look up."

Jaime narrowed his eyes with a perplexed expression on his face. "Why?"

"The stars—they're beautiful," Brea replied. Jaime chuckled, missing the point, and knocked on the door again. Trevor opened the door with his typical boisterous energy as he greeted everyone. Behind him stood a group of people—Aaron, Callie, Tara, Tory, Hayden and two of Jaime's lacrosse teammates, Dominic, and William.

"Whoa, who's driving? We have way too many people," Jaime exclaimed as the crowd exited Trevor's house. An uproar of arguing over who drove the last time, who wanted to drink, and who would sit shotgun erupted. Brea rolled her eyes, finding the pettiness of the discussion irritating.

Tory jabbed Brea's arm and begged her and Allegra to ride in Trevor's car, so that Tara and Callie would have to sit in the other one. When Brea asked if that would bother him, Jaime winked and nodded for her to go with Trevor, despite his lacrosse friends' insisting he come with them. After further discussion, Dominic volunteered to drive, and they decided Jaime, Tara, Callie, and William would ride with him, and Trevor would drive the others.

As the groups split, Aaron called shotgun in Trevor's car. Hayden groaned, but did not argue.

Tory linked arms with Brea and whispered. "You missed some more Vienna-Hayden drama. They had a nasty fight in the backyard, and she took off, ditching Hayden here."

"Why were they fighting?" Brea asked.

"Who knows, but there was a lot of cursing and yelling from Vienna."

Brea glanced at Hayden. He met her eyes for a moment before looking away. Reaching the car, Tory and Allegra climbed into the backseat first, followed by Brea. Hayden tried to squeeze in next to her, but it was too tight.

"Brea, you're tiny. Sit on Hayden's lap. The drive is short," Trevor suggested.

Brea hesitated. "I won't have a seatbelt," she replied.

Trevor and Aaron laughed. "Hayden, hold on to her because if something happens to her, Jaime will kick our asses," Aaron said.

Brea sighed, lifted herself up for Hayden to sit down, then lowered herself to sit across his lap at an angle. Trevor turned on the music and backed out of the driveway. Hayden slipped his arms around Brea's waist and gripped his left arm with his right hand in the event Trevor had to stop short. They hit a bump on the ridge where the driveway met the pavement. Instinctively, Hayden pulled Brea tighter against him.

His mouth brushed against her shoulder as she fell back from the momentum. "Sorry," she said and readjusted herself on his lap. She heard Hayden exhale, though he remained silent.

"Am I hurting you?" she whispered, turning her head towards Hayden.

"Yes," he answered, meeting Brea's eyes. Her eyes widened. Hayden chuckled, failing in his attempt to feign seriousness. Brea smiled, this being the first time Hayden had teased her. Another bump in the road resulted in his jaw brushing against the back of her shoulder. Her eyes fluttered shut as a wave of heat coursed through her body—and she wished it would happen again.

Ashamed of herself, Brea opened her eyes and turned her head. "Allegra, how is Jonathan doing?" she asked to distract herself from her inappropriate thoughts. Having interrupted a conversation between Allegra and Tory, she paused and thought for a moment.

"Good, ready to graduate. He can't wait to go to Europe with Blake in the summer. It's all he can talk about, and it's driving me crazy," she lamented. The group fell into a conversation about their favorite places to travel in Europe. Brea, having nothing to contribute, remained silent and focused on every movement Hayden made when he shifted underneath her. She found the feel of his breath on her skin decidedly erotic.

As everyone continued to talk over one another, Brea turned her head over her shoulder to look at Hayden. "I heard about Vienna, that you are still fighting. I'm sorry about last week, if I had something to do with it."

"Don't worry about it. We've been having problems for a while," he answered and met Brea's eyes, their faces close to one another. The car bucked as Trevor fumbled his first attempt to parallel park and had hit the accelerator with too much force. Brea's face nearly hit Hayden's. Again, he tightened his arms around her waist. Brea felt her heart race upon feeling the strength of his arms around her.

Once parked, everyone exited the car, and Brea lifted herself to let Hayden slide out first. He held the door open for her to step out. Jaime jogged over to Brea and wrapped his arms around her to kiss her on the mouth. Hayden slammed the door shut and turned to walk towards the house.

"What's with him?" Jaime asked.

"He had a fight with Vienna at Trevor's, and she left him there."

Jaime whistled. "Come on, B, let's go inside."

Brea recognized some students from Black Harbor High School among the various clusters of people standing in small groups, either smoking cigarettes or weed, and holding large plastic cups in their hands.

"I love what you're wearing, Brea." She turned to find the person speaking to her. Seeing Sasha, a sophomore at Harvey Slate in her ceramics class, standing with a group of girls, she smiled. She had short dark hair styled in a pixie cut and multiple piercings in her ears and nose. Brea took Allegra's hand to introduce her to Sasha as Jaime joined a group of his lacrosse teammates.

"Hey Brea. We heard there was some drama between your cousin and Hayden at a party last weekend. What happened?" Amy, a Harvey Slate sophomore, asked.

Another classmate of Brea's interjected. "Can I just say something? On what planet is Vienna your cousin? She is scary, and you are the sweetest person."

Brea opened her mouth to speak, then closed it as Allegra interrupted the conversation to ask Sasha about her piercings and steered the topic off of Vienna. Brea nudged Allegra in the arm with appreciation, and a slight smile formed on her best friend's face.

Amy lit a cigarette and offered one to the group. Although she hesitated, Brea desired to try one. Amy flicked on her lighter and moved closer to Brea. Jamie appeared beside Brea and ripped it out of her mouth, throwing the cigarette across the lawn. Pulling her with him into the house by her arm, he said, "No way, B. I don't want you smelling like an ashtray. Let's go inside." Brea looked back at Allegra, who rolled her eyes, having witnessed Jaime's brazen disregard for Brea's autonomy.

"Jaime," Brea exclaimed in disbelief as he pulled her into the house. "That was so rude." At the bar, Jaime mixed a rum and cola for Brea. Judging by the taste, he had poured a substantial amount of rum into the drink. Brea drank it without comment.

"Jaime, come here," Aaron called from across the room. He excused himself, telling Brea he would return soon. Sipping her drink, Brea strolled around the room with no particular desire to talk with anyone until spotting Jonathan and Blake. Smiling at her, Jonathan gestured to Brea to come and join them. Brea hesitated. She had not seen Blake since they had broken up. Of all places, the universe brought them together in the same spot where they had last seen one another. Approaching them, she gripped the handles of her handbag tighter.

"Hi Jonathan. Blake, it's good to see you. I should have known I would see you here tonight," Brea remarked with an awkward smile. Blake smiled and nodded his head as Jonathan embraced her.

"Is Allegra here with you?" Jonathan asked and scanned the room.

"Yeah, she's outside." Jonathan excused himself to find her.

"How have you been?" Blake asked. Appearing to be at ease with no ill will towards Brea, she relaxed.

"Good, busy. Harvey Slate is kicking my butt, but I'm keeping up. I submitted some of my writing to win a scholarship for a youth writers' program held every summer. I'm hoping I'll hear in the next month if I won, but I'm not getting my hopes up."

"That's great. I'm sure you'll win a spot," Blake replied.

"Allegra told me you're going to college in Boston. That's exciting news. Congratulations."

"Thank you. I can't graduate fast enough." Blake averted his eyes for a moment, appearing to hedge about whether to ask her something. "So, are you still dating that guy? Allegra told me he wound up asking you out."

"Yes, Jaime, he's around here somewhere. How about you? Are you with anyone?"

Blake smiled, then sipped his drink. "Yeah, do you remember Kari? The girl in the ski jacket you met a while ago. The one who had known me since kindergarten? We've been dating for a few months."

"Wow," Brea exclaimed. "She seemed nice. And Jonathan doesn't mind? You mentioned he used to date her."

Blake blew out a breath and pursed his lips. "Nah, it was a while ago for them, you know, no big deal." After a brief pause, Blake smiled. "By the way, I'm sorry about how things ended with us. I think I was a little harsh, but I was angry and hurt."

Brea shook her head. "No, I get it. You were right to be angry. That night, the moment swept me away and the way I behaved—I'm sorry, Blake, I mean it."

"Apology accepted. It's in the past. Well, you look beautiful tonight, and I wish you good luck with that writer's program. I'll see you around." Blake placed his hand on Brea's shoulder to let her know they were square. Brea stepped in closer, and they shared a warm embrace. He gave her a brief kiss on her forehead before he left.

"Bye," she said, watching Blake disappear into the crowd. Turning in a random direction, Brea stumbled upon a group of Harvey Slate Seniors she recognized and joined them amid a conversation on the topic of finding college apartments. Brea attempted to appear interested, but after twenty minutes, beads of sweat formed on her forehead as the crowd grew larger and the stuffy air became insufferable

She scanned the room for Jaime, hoping to lure him to step outside for fresh air, when she locked eyes with Hayden. Watching her from across the room, he sat on a sofa with his chin in his hand. A group of boys seated around him had set up a card game and, although he appeared to be a part of the game, he fixed his attention on her.

Feeling pain on her toe from a newly formed blister, she longed to sit in the empty spot beside him. But she knew sitting near him would not be a good idea, having learned tonight that proximity to Hayden aroused within her another complicated feeling—desire.

In an abrupt motion, she turned, and navigating through the crowd, headed into the kitchen. Thirsty, Brea found bottles of rum and vodka on the kitchen counter. She searched for something to mix the alcohol with. Opening the oversized stainless-steel refrigerator, Brea was thrilled to find ice-cold cans of soda. Grabbing and opening one, she drank a quarter of it before adding in a short pour of rum. Pulling out a stool, she breathed a sigh of relief as she sat, taking the pressure off her feet.

Enjoying the solitude and rest, Brea played with the scattered cocktail napkins on the counter, folding them into various shapes to entertain herself. Half an hour passed before Jaime entered the kitchen and found her.

"You doing all right? You look a little tired—or maybe even drunk," he asked, amused.

"I'm fine," Brea said, finding it difficult to articulate her words more from fatigue rather than having consumed too much alcohol.

Jaime picked up her soda can and tossed it into the garbage can. He grabbed a bottle of warm water from the counter and handed it to Brea. "Hey drink this. I'm cutting you off."

Brea yawned and took a few sips of water. "Thanks. Jaime, I'm tired and ready to go home soon."

"Home? No way, it's your birthday, and everyone is going to meet up at the old campgrounds for a fire. Some guys from the lacrosse team who graduated last year are home for the weekend, and I don't see them often." Jaime looked away from Brea, his irritation obvious. She loathed the idea of hiking the trails to reach the abandoned campsite in her sandals, but she lacked the nerve to refuse Jaime.

"All right. Let me finish this water and stop in the bathroom," she conceded. Jaime grinned and wrapped his arms around Brea, pleased she had caved.

"Some guys want to do a couple of shots first. Meet me by the fireplace in five minutes," Jaime said and walked out of the kitchen, leaving Brea to finish her bottle of water. Once empty, she tossed it into an overfilled garbage can and set off to the bathroom. If she was fortunate, she hoped to find some bandages in the bathroom to cushion her blister.

Allegra declined to go to the campsite, deep in discussion with sophomores from the Black Harbor High School cheerleading squad, and hoping to glean helpful advice for tryouts the following month. She did not conceal her irritation that Jaime had maneuvered Brea into leaving the party and told her she would catch a ride home with Jonathan. Disappointed and apologetic, Brea embraced Allegra and told her she would call her in the morning before finding her way back to Jaime.

Jamie, Trevor, Tory, and Brea stepped out into the night. While Brea had sat in the kitchen, Hayden had left the party, having caught a ride to pick up his own car. He told Trevor that he would meet them at the campgrounds. In Brea's mind, she figured he left to avoid another crowded car ride and the possibility Brea would need to sit close to him.

CHAPTER FIFTEEN

THE PAST

Arriving at the trails in Raven Woods Park, the group waited for Trevor as he rooted through his trunk to find a flashlight. "I found two, let's go," he announced, and the group set off. Brea cursed under her breath stepping onto the dirt path, but kept in mind her good luck of having found two bandages from Doug's bathroom to lessen the pain of the blister on her foot. She yawned and stumbled along the trail. A chill ran through her body, and she wished she had brought her cardigan to shield her from the cool night air. Though she longed to go home and burrow under her comforter, she held back her complaints and continued on.

While chatting with Trevor and Tory, Jaime pulled Brea along behind him with one hand and held a bottle of beer in the other. Brea observed a hint of slurring in Jaime's speech. Remaining silent and focused, she stepped with caution and scanned the ground to avoid tripping on a rock or a root.

At the end of the ten-minute walk, the group reached their destination, the ruins of an old campsite. Having shut down decades ago, the only remnants were half-rotted platforms from torn down cabins and scattered large rocks near a clearing for bonfires. Now it served as a rest spot during the day for hikers and, unbeknownst to the police, a secret spot where teenagers gathered for late-night after-parties. A sizable fire blazed in the clearing near the rocks, with scattered groups of Harvey Slate students distributed amid the grounds, appearing quite intoxicated, howling in laughter, and tripping over one another.

Hayden, dressed in a black puffed vest over his white long-sleeved T-shirt, sat on a flat rock in front of the fire holding a bottle of water. His eyes locked on Jaime and Brea as they neared him. Jaime let go of Brea's hand to give Hayden a fist bump.

"Hey," Jaime said.

Hayden stood up and offered his seat to Brea. Grateful for the opportunity to rest, she thanked Hayden, sat down, and sighed. Several of Jaime's old teammates called him over.

"I'll be back in a bit," Jaime said and leaned down to give Brea a kiss on the top of her head. She watched him walk away to join a group of graduates, leaving Hayden and Brea alone in front of the fire.

"You look cold. Do you want this?" Hayden asked Brea, pulling at the edges of his vest.

"No, I'm fine. Thanks," Brea said, sitting close enough to the fire to stay warm. She planned to remain where she sat until either Jaime's enthusiasm for partying waned or he became so drunk Trevor would have to drag him out. Attempting to ignore the awkward silence between her and Hayden, she looked down and, with her feet, played with the small rocks scattered on the ground. Brea groaned seeing her brand-new sandals caked with dirt.

Hayden cleared his throat. "Brea, I forgot to wish you a happy birthday earlier. Did you have a good time at the party?"

"Thank you. No, I didn't. And now, being here, I'm honestly just—bored and tired." Exhausted and grouchy, she had nothing left in her to feign cheerfulness about being stuck in the woods, dressed in a wildly inappropriate outfit. But the blame lay on her own shoulders for pushing aside her needs and having allowed herself to be persuaded.

Hayden crouched down in front of Brea. "Me neither," he replied, looking into her eyes with a smile forming on his lips. Brea and Hayden chuckled in solidarity. As they held one another's gaze, something shifted, and the energy between them felt as though they were old friends. Hayden drew in a deep breath, sat on the ground beside Brea and turned to face the fire.

"These weekends and these parties have become endless versions of the same night—drinking, hearing stories about things that happened when someone was drunk last weekend, spreading rumors, hooking up. It's never been my scene. I need a compelling reason to come out nowadays," he confessed.

"What was your reason tonight?" Brea asked, curious.

The corners of Hayden's mouth turned up slightly as he looked into the fire. He vaguely answered. "I had one tonight."

On the verge of pressing him for a more detailed answer, Brea caught sight of Jaime crossing the clearing towards them. He headed to Brea, sleeves rolled up, and with a furious expression on his face. Reaching her, he halted his steps and snapped, "Follow me."

Alarmed, Brea rose to follow Jaime into the woods. Hayden, concerned, stood up as well. As she stepped forward, she lost her footing, stepped on a large twig and rolled her ankle. She would have fallen to the ground if Hayden had not caught her by the arm and held her up.

Hayden attempted to intervene. "Is everything all right? Do you want me to come—"

"No, it's fine," Brea replied, interrupting him. Hayden released his grip on Brea's arm. Jaime, with his hands clenched into fists, paused and waited for Brea to follow him into the woods.

"B, what happened at the party?" Jaime barked upon reaching a distance far enough from the campsite where no one could see nor hear them. Brea trembled, cold once again, no longer having the warmth of the fire. Speechless, she searched her mind for what she could have done at the party to make Jaime this angry.

"What? What are you talking about?" Brea cried out, unable to identify the reason for his outrage.

"B, I'm pissed. The guys said they saw you all over your ex-boyfriend."

Brea's heart raced. "No—that isn't true. We talked for a little while. He has a girlfriend. I gave him a hug only to say good-bye—that's it. I promise."

"I need to know that I can trust you, and I don't want you touching other guys or them touching you. It's humiliating my friends think my girlfriend is flirting and putting her hands on another guy. What if I did that with Tara or Callie in front of you?"

"It wouldn't bother me because I trust you," Brea exclaimed. "Jaime, this isn't a big deal. I didn't think that would upset you."

Jaime looked down at the ground and shook his head. "This is bullshit. You can't even see why this is a problem. Find a ride home, B, or leave with another guy. I don't care." Jaime turned and strode back to the campsite.

Brea stood fixed in place, feeling as though her body had switched off. Her mind raced, unclear whether they were only fighting or if Jaime had broken up with her. Closing her eyes, she pictured the humiliation on Monday, facing Harvey Slate if he had. Opening her eyes in a panic, she knew she needed to find Jaime, apologize, and then beg for his forgiveness until he took her back. The haze lifted, and she regained motor control of her body. Taking several steps forward, Brea crossed her arms over her chest to stop her body from trembling.

"Shit." Brea winced as she stepped on a root and the strap of her sandal put more pressure on her blister. She took her time, taking slow steps back to the campsite, and stopping every few steps to wipe her tears with the back of her hand. Her purse sat on the rock where she had left it. Scanning the after-party, she cursed again. Jaime had left, and she did not see Trevor or Tory. No one appeared to have witnessed what had happened except for Hayden. As soon as he saw her emerge from the woods, he went to her.

"B, are you okay?"

Brea continued on her path to the rock to pick up her handbag. "You've never called me B before," she said through trembling lips.

"I guess it's rubbing off on me," he responded, taking off his vest and placing it on Brea's shoulders, seeing her pallid and shivering.

"He's pissed at me because I saw Blake, my old boyfriend. We were talking at the party, and I hugged him when he said goodbye. I'm such an idiot," she said in a shaky voice, not bothering to wipe the fresh tears sliding down her cheeks.

Hayden gripped her shoulders. Bending his knees to position his face in Brea's line of vision for her attention, he did his best to comfort her.

"Hey—it's not your fault. He's been drinking, and it's his pride." Brea would not raise her eyes to look at Hayden.

"He left without you, though. Dick move," he muttered under his breath. "Come with me. I'll drive you home."

Brea wiped her eyes and nodded. "Sure, thanks."

"I'm this way. Follow me." Hayden stepped forward and pointed a small pocket flashlight in the direction they needed to walk through the south side of the park. Her foot hurt, yet knowing every step she took brought her closer to home suffused her with enough motivation to place one foot in front of the other. Brea and Hayden walked side by side in silence for several minutes, listening to the birds and branches rustling in the light wind.

Hayden looked at her a few times before speaking, wrestling with what to say to help her feel better. "Do you want to hear a story?"

"Yes, please," Brea blurted out, willing to listen to anything to help pass the time or help her forget about the fight with Jaime. "Is it a true story?"

"You'll have to listen and decide for yourself," he replied with a spirited smile.

Brea nodded, intrigued. "Okay, tell me."

"When I was in first grade, there was a yearbook cover contest. The one where they have all the kids draw something and they choose the best one for the yearbook cover."

"Sure. I remember those," Brea replied.

"Well, our teachers made a big deal about it. They told us we were all extraordinary artists and that it would be a great honor to win. I had this thing about trying to impress my dad because not much impresses him. So, I thought about it for days, obsessed with finding the perfect idea. I went home and looked through all the magazines and picture books we had in the house until I remembered the perfect one I needed. I had seen it once before, but my mother had seen me looking at it and ripped it out of my hands, telling me it was an 'art' magazine."

Brea laughed, knowing where Hayden's story headed.

"Well, I found it again in my parents' bedroom. I looked through it until I found the perfect picture. I drew it and submitted it in a big yellow envelope. The next day at school, I was called to the principal's office. My mom was there with a school counselor. The principal sat me down, pulled out the envelope and asked me, 'Son, how do you explain this?' Then he took out my picture." Hayden paused and laughed for a moment. "I had copied a picture of a naked lady, boobs and everything, with two star-shaped stickers for the nipples."

Brea stopped walking and burst out laughing. She could picture the entire story in her mind—a little boy version of Hayden, perplexed, and at a loss for words with little understanding of what he had done wrong. Hayden joined in, laughing along with her.

"So, I'm guessing your Hustler-inspired naked lady picture did not win, and you failed to impress your dad."

"Nope. And my mom made sure my dad never found out. He doesn't have a sense of humor. But—I asked my principal if he thought I was a great artist."

They laughed again and continued on the trail, soon reaching the edge of the woods. Brea gasped in relief at seeing Hayden's car parked. He unlocked and opened the door for her to jump inside. Once Hayden started the car, he cranked up the heat for Brea.

"Do you care if I take off my shoes? My feet are killing me," Brea asked.

"Not at all. I can't believe you came here dressed in that outfit. Why didn't you go home to change first?"

"I don't know, live and learn, I guess," Brea muttered as she unfastened the straps of her sandals.

Looking over his shoulder, Hayden checked the road before pulling out of his space. As he drove, Brea studied his profile. She remembered that as a boy, he had struck her as handsome, though now she recalled there had been something more profound about him that drew her to him.

Hayden sensed Brea's eyes on him and his eyes met hers for a moment before looking back onto the road. "What?" he asked, smiling, wondering why she studied him with such intensity.

Brea's cheeks flushed, and she looked away. "Um, nothing. I was only thinking about how I would describe you if I were writing about you. How would I try to describe what you looked like to a reader."

"Oh. Not sure how to respond to that," he replied with an amused grin.

"Sorry, I know that sounds strange. I'm not trying to creep you out. It's something I'm more interested in this year. Creating characters to write a book or a short story rather than focusing so much on poetry. So, it's something I do when I see someone interesting."

"I'm flattered you think I'm—interesting," he said with an attractive grin, triggering Brea's heart to beat faster.

"So, what are you into, Hayden? I mean, this is the first time we've had more than a three-second conversation over the past six months so you need to think of some things to tell me about yourself," she teased, picking up her legs onto the seat and angling her body towards him.

"True. Well, I'm interested in math and computers. The plan is to study software engineering and start up a company in the future—become filthy rich, date a Playboy model, you know," he answered with a cheeky smile.

"So, then you'll have a muse for all of your future artwork, too. You could be the next Tom Wesselmann," Brea remarked, playing along. Hayden turned to Brea with a wide smile, laughing and impressed with her wit. She listened as he shared with her more about his classes, impressed to discover not only had he earned a spot in the honors program every year, but held the rank of first in his class. She seized the opportunity to ask for advice on how to secure a spot for next year, which he shared in detail.

"Do you take a lot of dance lessons? Your performance blew me away," Hayden said after exhausting what advice he had to share regarding the honors program.

"Oh, that's a sad story. I wish, but not anymore. My parents have a short list of what they will pay for and what they expect of me—go to a top university and be independent. My mom's sister has brainwashed her, so the only things that matter to my mother are grades and not depending on a man. And dance wasn't on that list, no matter how much I loved it. I cried in secret for days when my mom pulled me out of the dance academy. But even if I had cried in front of her, it wouldn't have mattered. She is a cold woman."

Hayden nodded and listened without interruption as she continued. It surprised her she felt comfortable sharing with Hayden the details of her dysfunctional family, and she appreciated he did not spin what she said into a pointless pep talk as an attempt to make her feel better. Reaching Brea's house, Hayden placed the car in park and turned to face her.

He spoke, though hesitated before beginning. "You know, Jaime will sleep it off, and tomorrow it will be all right. Vienna is that way too, reactive, especially if she drinks."

Brea nodded and looked out the window, hoping that would be true, though she felt unsettled. Jaime adored her, was proud of her, and protective of her—but deep inside, a tiny voice told her something in their relationship was flawed. Being with Hayden tonight had turned up the volume of that voice, making it more difficult to ignore.

"You know, I'm glad we talked tonight. I thought you didn't like me, Hayden. It's been difficult to read you," Brea said as she unbuckled her seat belt.

Hayden shook his head, turning to look out the windshield, then back at Brea before answering. "Right. I can see why you would have thought that. No, it's nothing like that."

He paused for a moment. "The thing is, it's complicated with Vienna. She is threatened by you, and it has made it difficult for me—"

Brea's eyes widened as she interrupted him. "Hayden, that's crazy. How could someone like her be threatened by me? I have done nothing to her. If anything, I have been extra careful around her ever since she warned me not to cross her."

Hayden's eyes narrowed. "Wait, what? Explain that to me. She warned you not to 'cross her?'

Brea's stomach dropped, knowing she had said something she should not have. "Hayden, I need to stop talking because I don't want to be the reason you both have more problems."

Hayden looked down and shook his head in disbelief. "Don't worry about it. I won't mention anything to her about that. Look, you did nothing to her, but it's complicated, and I can't get into why that is tonight."

Brea frowned and rested her head on the headrest. "So, what can you explain, then?"

Hayden continued. "I'm not like Vienna or the others. This whole scene. I've been along for the ride since I've been with her. I'm someone who prefers to keep to myself—more on the shy side. It can come across like I'm a jerk, I suppose, if you don't know me."

Brea nodded. "If I'm being honest, maybe once or twice, I thought to myself you were a jerk."

Hayden chuckled. "I can't blame you for that."

"But to me, mostly you appear to be reserved, smart, and maybe mysterious. I'm not seeing the shy part, though."

"Don't forget to mention handsome," he joked, rubbing his jaw and chin. Brea laughed, appreciating this playful side of Hayden.

Looking out the windshield, Hayden sighed. "All of this preoccupation with image and who's the most popular—I hate it."

Brea lowered her eyes to her lap, ashamed of her personal obsession with popularity since she had been a little girl. "Well, I have to be honest again. Before Harvey Slate, all I dreamed about was being popular. I was an odd kid and bullied in middle school. I thought if I could be someone like Vienna, my life would be perfect. Ugh, it's too embarrassing to talk about."

"You could never be Vienna. You two are so different," Hayden exclaimed with an intent expression on his face. Brea suspected Hayden meant that in a good way, though uncertain.

Hayden inhaled. "Maybe what you went through in middle school, although awful, helped make you who you are today. I don't think you have a cruel bone in your body."

Brea closed her eyes and sighed. "I don't even know who I am today."

Hayden clicked his tongue and inhaled. "I know what you mean. I think you'll figure it out, though." She smiled—coming from Hayden, she believed him. Hayden opened and then closed his mouth, appearing to struggle with what he wanted to say next.

"B, to answer your question from before. I do like you—the problem is—I'm not sure how to be around you." Looking away, Hayden covered his chin and mouth with his hand as though to prevent himself from saying anything more.

She needed to ask him the question she had been wondering ever since seeing him at the beach. "Hayden, do you remember the first time we met?"

Hayden continued to stare out the windshield. "Yeah, at the beach when you were with Trevor and Jaime."

Brea looked away, disappointed he did not remember the library after all. She shook her head and told herself it did not matter. The important thing to focus on was what their relationship would be from now on. But what exactly? His answer, saying he did not know "how" to be around Brea, puzzled her.

She cleared her throat. "Well, Hayden. Thinking about 'how' you can be around me, let's aim for friendly or we can skip right over to being friends?"

Hayden turned to look at Brea without answering, his expression indecipherable. Brea licked her lips, embarrassed for her misguided assumption that they had reached a turning point in their relationship and he wanted her friendship. "Okay—well, forget it for tonight. I'm going in. I'll see you next week at school." She looked straight ahead and opened the door.

"Thanks for the ride," she called out over her shoulder as she hurried out of the car.

Reaching the top step of her porch, she turned around, seeing Hayden with his eyes lowered and his hands on the steering wheel. "Forget it," she muttered under her breath. Brea entered her home and shut the door, leaving Hayden behind.

Chapter Sixteen

The Past

Something pressed Brea's legs and arms against her body, and her neck ached. Extending her arms, her fingers touched a hard, clear, smooth surface. Panels of thick glass surrounded her. Finding herself trapped in a glass cube covered with her handprints, she cried out in terror. The air was thick, damp, and Brea could not breathe. Dressed in a white bra and shorts, beads of sweat dripped off her skin. Underneath her, she saw a concrete floor beneath the glass, cracked and stained with oil splotches. The glass cube sat in a large empty room with red brick walls covered with patches of peeling white paint.

In desperation, she screamed, but the glass cube trapped her voice inside. Her mother, dressed in a black lace ball gown, with long white flowing hair down her back, passed her by carrying an empty silver tray. Brea pounded on the glass with her fists, screaming for her mother's attention. She glanced at Brea with a vacant expression, then continued on, ignoring Brea's pleas for help.

Startled awake by her phone ringing, Brea opened her eyes and placed her hand on her chest. It took her a moment to realize she had woken from a nightmare. Rolling onto the floor, Brea crawled to her cordless phone and answered.

Brea heard Jaime's voice, sincere and apologetic on the other end. "B, I'm sorry. I overreacted last night, and what I did was terrible, leaving you at the campsite. I know I can trust you, and I don't know what I was thinking. Can I pick you up so we can talk?"

Brea sighed with relief. Jaime did not have to beg or plead his case to convince her to forgive him. "Of course. I'm sorry too, because I should never have hugged Blake. It meant nothing to me other than saying goodbye to him. I promise I'll never do that again. I understand why that would upset you."

"We're good, B. Let's forget about it. I'll pick you up at ten and we'll go to the beach for a walk, all right?"

"Yes, I'll see you soon, bye." Brea hung up and clutched the phone to her chest, relieved the fight meant nothing and they were still together. Glimpsing herself in the mirror, drenched in sweat with her hair damp and stringy, she drew in several deep breaths to slow her heart rate.

"Right. Tea, a shower, and everything is back to normal." Brea winced. The memory of Hayden's arms wrapped around her waist in Trevor's car flashed through her mind. Shaking her head and squeezing her eyes shut, she willed herself to push away any thoughts of Hayden. She needed to focus on Jaime, only him.

❦

Six weeks passed, and in early June, Brea prepared for final exams. After their fight, she spent as much free time as she could with Jaime—studying after school at his house, appearing at every party, and attending all of Jamie's Regional High School All-Stars Lacrosse Team games.

Her busy schedule left her with less time to sleep, and the stress had triggered an uptick in her nightmares. Still, ensuring Jaime remained happy and reassured of Brea's devotion took priority above all else. She only needed to hang on another week and then, once reaching the other side of exams, she could catch up on her rest.

To Brea's surprise, since the night he had driven her home, Hayden had made more of an effort to be "*friendly*" with Brea. Rather than avoiding her, he would stop in the courtyard at school or, when seeing her out on the weekends, say hello and chat.

However, although unsurprising, her relationship with Vienna had deteriorated. Vienna no longer scheduled double dates with Jaime and, though clever enough to conceal overt hostility towards Brea, her condescending and passive-aggressive comments made for awkward nights at parties or at the beach when their paths crossed. Having turned on her, Brea resigned herself to believing a Staxon family curse made any close family attachments impossible.

The weekend after final exams, Jaime played in the Regional Lacrosse All-Stars final game on Saturday afternoon. Having been a fast-paced, high-scoring game, Jaime's team led by one goal. The offensive team had the ball. With only fifteen seconds left in the fourth quarter, the crowd cheered wildly as Jaime used a legal body check and, though the player attempted to stay on his path to score, he dropped the ball. Jaime scooped it off the ground, took off across the field, and that was time. Jaime's team won the game.

Brea and Tory jumped out of their seats, hugging and screaming with the rest of the crowd from their seats. As Jaime ran down the field, he kissed two fingers and held them up to

Brea. She beamed with pride, pointed to the jersey she wore with his name on it, and blew him a kiss. Everyone in the stands who had traveled from Harvey Slate chanted Jaime's name and took turns giving Brea enthusiastic high fives.

Trevor pointed to Brea, laughing and shouting, "That's your man! Give him some love."

After the game, the group looked forward to celebrating the night at a Harvey Slate party. Brea waited for Jaime by the main gate, running to jump into his arms upon seeing him.

"That was for you," he whispered in her ear.

Jaime dropped Brea off at home after the game and would return to pick her up in two hours. After a shower and taking her time to style her hair and apply her makeup, she slipped into a fitted ivory dress with a large midnight-blue flower stretching around her hip and torso.

Studying her reflection, she smiled and ran her fingers through her hair. Tonight, having kept the news to herself all week, she would tell Jaime she wanted to have sex with him after the party. In preparation, Brea lied to her parents that she would sleep over at Allegra's house and spend the night with Jaime as his parents were out of town until Monday.

Brea held her overnight bag in her hand and descended the stairs. She had packed the essentials—pajamas, a change of clothes, toiletries, and a box of condoms. Before leaving to wait on the porch for Jaime, she stopped in the living room to say goodnight to her parents. Her father sat in his armchair reading a magazine and drinking a beer. He looked up at Brea with surprise. "Well, you're all dressed up," he remarked.

"Allegra's parents are taking us out to celebrate. She made the cheerleading squad." Though Allegra had won a spot on the squad, Brea found it easier to lie rather than to tell her father she planned to attend a high school party.

"Great. Have fun," he said, returning to his reading.

"Where's Mom?" Brea asked, surprised she had not seen her since returning home.

"She said something about needing to buy books, probably still at the bookstore."

Brea sighed. Periodically, her mother would develop an obsessive fixation on various projects and activities—knitting, New Age medicine, or learning a foreign language were a few of many examples. After following Brea around the house for hours, her mother would sit on the edge of Brea's bed and prattle on about her latest interests. Without warning, one day the fixation would disappear. It could be days or a couple of weeks, and she would be back to her usual self, dressed in a housedress, neglecting to groom herself, and roaming the house with a mug of tea in one hand and her notebook in the other.

"I'm going to wait outside for my ride. Allegra's brother offered to pick me up. Remember, I'm sleeping at Allegra's tonight, so I'll see you tomorrow morning."

"Good night," her father said, his eyes fixed on the magazine in his hands.

Staring at her father, Brea had a rebellious thought. What if she confessed her plans for the evening? She wondered what his reaction would be. *Hey Dad—I'm going to a raging high school party. I'm going to drink alcohol and lose my virginity to my boyfriend. You've never met him, but don't worry, I stopped at the drugstore yesterday and I bought a box of condoms.*

Blinking several times, she believed his response would be the same, "*Good night.*"

She picked up her bag and left to wait on the porch. The warmth of the evening enveloped her skin, and the scent of damp earth and freshly cut grass perfumed the air. Brea, brimming with confidence, adjusted her dress, eager for the night ahead. The lights of Jaime's Audi appeared, and Brea stood on the top step of the porch as he slowed and parked. When Jaime jumped out of the car, she smiled, finding him handsome dressed in a gray fitted T-shirt, dark jeans, and sneakers. He jogged over to Brea, his eyes bright, and with a wide smile. Wrapping his arms around her, he pulled her in for a kiss.

"You look gorgeous," he whispered in her ear.

"Thank you," she replied as she buried her face in his neck and inhaled the scent of his aftershave. Taking her duffel bag from her hand, he escorted Brea to the passenger seat to open the door for her. Once in the driver's seat, Jaime placed his arms on the steering wheel. Brea's eyes scanned over his body. The sight of his muscular arms, half-covered by the sleeves of his T-shirt, prompted a flush of desire. She fought the impulse to tell him to skip the party and take her back to his house, but she held back. This was Jaime's night to celebrate his game, and she wanted to keep her secret a little longer.

Jaime had arranged for Trevor and Tory to meet them at Vittorio's for dinner before the party. Once inside, Brea scanned the restaurant. Dozens of black-and-white framed pictures of Italian cities, baseball players, and vintage foreign-film posters covered the white walls. Couples, families, and groups of students occupied every worn black wooden table.

Seeing Jaime, half the restaurant cheered, and some stood to greet and congratulate him on the game. Ten minutes passed before they could step in line to order, and as soon as they did, the owner of the pizzeria shouted out, "Big winner here," attracting more attention to Jaime. Giving Jaime a high five, he offered pizza to him and Brea, free of charge. Brea, loath to stain her light-colored dress with pizza sauce, accepted one slice of white pizza and a soda water to partake in the celebration.

Trevor and Tory joined them several minutes after a table opened. Tory, with shoulder-length dark brown hair and a dia-mond-shaped face, was athletic, even-tempered, and witty. She followed a simple formula for her style of dress—jeans, a top, and a pair of heels that accentuated her tall and lean figure. Brea smiled as she sat down next to her and they chatted. Over the months, they had become good friends, and Brea always looked forward to spending time with her.

Once their orders arrived, Brea shared the news she had won the scholarship spot in the youth summer writing program, and they congratulated her with zeal. Her program coincided with Jaime's five weeks in Brazil, ensuring they would not lose any remaining time together before the school year started. With Jaime being gone for so long, it would leave Brea on her own for a sizeable chunk of the summer, though, at least now she had her program to look forward to.

Arriving at the party, they approached the house. The bass of the music thumped and vibrated well outside the walls of the home. Brea could picture the scene inside—half the girls were dancing in the middle of the living room, fueled by mixed drinks, and a group of boys with beers in hand surrounded them, staring, with gaped mouths as they targeted who they would hit on later.

Opening the door for Brea, Jaime ushered her in amid the cheers and congratulations from schoolmates who viewed Jaime as king tonight. Beaming and returning endless high fives, Jaime kept one arm around Brea, and if any of the boys eyed her too long, he would pull her in close and kiss her on the cheek or her shoulder. Her dress revealed a subtle amount of cleavage, and her bare, lean legs attracted an abundance of attention. Jaime relished that the other boys desired Brea, knowing she belonged to him.

Aaron hurried over to greet them, then looked Brea up and down. He took a step back, shaking his head as he shouted to Jaime above the music, "We'll keep an eye on her tonight and keep the losers off her."

Jaime nodded, going in for another high five. Brea rolled her eyes, finding the attention unnecessary, as there were twenty other girls in the room in similar outfits. She found the remark offensive that they believed she could not divert the attention of a sloppy, drunken boy on her own and yet, she allowed the comment to roll off her shoulders. Jaime guided Brea through the party to the bar.

"What would you like?" he asked, surveying the various liquor bottles and holding them up to examine how much remained in each one.

"Surprise me."

Jaime mixed Brea's drink as she scanned the room. Her eyes landed on Hayden, dressed in a burgundy T-shirt, jeans, and a white baseball cap, standing beside the fireplace in the living room and speaking with an unfamiliar girl. Brea studied the petite brunette wearing tight black shorts and a pink cropped peasant blouse. A chin-length bob accentuated her perky face and bow-shaped lips.

Perceiving eyes on him, Hayden turned his head. After a slight double-take, he locked onto Brea's eyes. His facial expression, difficult to interpret, puzzled Brea. She smiled and waved to him. He inhaled, looked up at the ceiling, and gave her a half-hearted wave. Brea averted her gaze to the floor with a twinge of embarrassment, believing she must have appeared pathetic, waving to him like a child eager for attention. Jaime wrapped his arm around Brea's shoulders and handed her a drink.

"Who are you looking at?" he asked, trying to follow her line of vision.

"Oh, Hayden is with a girl I don't recognize," she replied, searching her mind for something else to add in the event Jaime found it suspicious she was eyeing Hayden. "I love her top. I'm wondering where she bought it."

"Is that all you girls think about—shopping? Let's go talk to them, and you can ask her." Brea swatted Jaime on the shoulder in jest. By the time they reached Hayden, the girl had walked away.

"Hayden, how are you?" Jaime asked as he gave Hayden a high five.

"Good. Hey, congrats on the game," Hayden said, his eyes darting between Jaime and Brea.

Vienna joined the group. "Hey baby," she purred, slipping her arm around Hayden's waist and then kissing him on the cheek. Hayden did not react and stared ahead.

Observing Brea for a moment, she eyed her up and down. "Nice dress, Brea, very sexy. I'm sure Jaime won't be able to keep his hands off of you tonight." Placing her hand on Hayden's chest, Vienna squeezed in closer to him. "Right Ben? Can't you picture it? Give your girlfriend a hot kiss, Jaime, let's make her blush."

Jaime wrapped his arms around Brea from behind, then kissed her on the cheek. Hayden remained nonreactive other than to look into Brea's eyes for a moment before dropping them to the floor.

Vienna sighed. "Ben is in a mood tonight. His mother has been sick for—what? Has it been a couple of months now? All kinds of doctor's appointments. But I'll work my magic to turn his mood around tonight when we're alone, and he'll forget about it."

Brea narrowed her eyes at Vienna, finding her behavior and insensitivity appalling. Although Hayden appeared to be his stoic self, Brea could sense something bothered him. Concerned, she leaned her head to the side.

"I'm sorry your mom has been sick. Do the doctors have any idea why?"

"Thanks. No, not yet," he answered in a cool tone of voice, raising his eyes to hers.

He lifted his cup to his mouth. Brea noticed a cut across his knuckles, and the surrounding skin appeared raw and red from a recent injury. Hayden saw her eyes lock onto his right hand and he lowered it to his side to hide it from her view. Brea opened her mouth to ask him what had happened to his hand, but did not have enough time to question him.

"I'll be back," Hayden said, then with an abrupt motion, brushed Vienna's hands off of him and turned into the crowd. Brea continued to watch Hayden as he walked away. With his aloof demeanor and behavior mirroring their past interactions, she felt dismissed.

Vienna smiled and shrugged her shoulders. "Jaime, come with me. I want to talk to you about something. Brea can spare you for a bit, right?" she said with a saccharine tone.

"Of course. I'm going to look for Tory," Brea replied and pasted on a reciprocal plastic smile. Jaime squeezed her shoulder, and Brea turned to walk into the kitchen. A mess of scattered empty cups, garbage, crumbs, and empty snack bags covered the counter. Surveying the kitchen, she discovered several cans of unopened soda in a crinkled brown paper grocery bag and took one to drink. After clearing some space, she pulled herself up to sit on the counter and enjoyed the solitude for several minutes until Anjali and Sonia joined her. The three of them chatted about their summer plans and any Harvey Slate gossip worth discussing until one hour later, Jaime found Brea.

"Hey, I lost you for a while. Come back in," Jamie said as Anjali and Sonia ventured back into the party.

"I'm ready to go," Brea replied.

Jaime glanced around the room, his facial expression shifting from enthusiasm to annoyance. He did not want to argue about it, but he wanted to stay. "Come on. This is my night, and I've barely had any time to spend with you since I've been busy talking to so many people."

Brea smiled, hooked her leg around Jaime's thighs to draw him in close to her and kissed him. Before she spoke, she grazed his ear with her lips and then whispered, "How about twenty more minutes? Then you can take me back to your house, take off my dress, and you can do anything you want with me tonight. I'm ready." Jamie trailed his hands up Brea's back, and the sudden tension in his muscles betrayed his growing desire. He pulled back his head several inches until cheek to cheek with Brea.

"You sure?" he whispered hoarsely.

"I am," she answered, pulling back her head to meet his eyes.

"Right, let's get out of here."

"I said twenty minutes," she replied through laughter.

"Nope, we're out. Let's go." Jaime lifted her off the counter, and they eagerly escaped the party.

Chapter Seventeen

The Past

On the last day of school, Brea learned she had secured a spot in the honors program for junior year. Waiting in the courtyard by the fountain after school, Brea hoped to find Hayden and share the news with him. Her eyes grew wide, seeing Vienna approaching her, changed out of her uniform and dressed in a blue-striped sundress. Tearing the aviator-style sunglasses off her face, she strode over to Brea and halted, leaving only one foot of space between them.

"Brea. I wish I could say it's nice to see you, but I won't. I'll assume you heard the news, but don't get your hopes up—you can't have them both." With a snide grin, Vienna stalked off towards the administration parking lot. Brea, perplexed, shook her head and inhaled. At the moment, she failed to understand Vienna's cryptic warning and did not care to think further about it.

Two hours later, as everyone gathered at the beach to celebrate the start of summer break, Tara and Callie broke the news that Hayden and Vienna had broken up the previous night with no hope for reconciliation. According to Vienna, she ended the relationship because she could no longer tolerate Hayden's *"moodiness"* and claimed he *"bored her."*

Hayden appeared neither that afternoon nor at any of the beach or house parties over the following two weeks. Brea wondered when she would see him again, and although she knew thinking of him could only lead to trouble, the possibility of him disappearing for the rest of the summer bothered her. In contrast, to Brea's relief, Vienna and her mother had departed on a two-month trip to Europe and Asia, freeing her from stressful encounters with her cousin throughout the summer.

Brea and Jaime spent most days at the beach, swimming in Jaime's pool, and having sex when his parents were away from home. On the first night she and Jaime had sex, it was a tender moment, and Jaime had been gentle, having warned her about the initial discomfort she would feel. But sex had not been as she expected. It felt good, and she enjoyed the intimacy, but she did not know if she should feel more. Her inexperience and bashfulness prevented her from asking Jaime, and she resigned herself to feeling pleasure in his desire for her and apparent sexual satisfaction.

In several days, Jamie would leave for Brazil, and Tory, Allegra, Sonia, and Anjali would scatter over the weeks to travel with their families on summer vacations. Brea would fill her empty days on her own, though she did not mind. She looked forward to having an abundance of time alone to read, ride her bike to the park, and work on her writing. Having a vacation from the endless rounds of parties coupled with the time-consuming effort of dressing up and maintaining the affable version of herself she portrayed could not begin soon enough.

Until then, she had one last event to make it through. This weekend Tory's parents were taking a short trip, and she had asked Brea, Anjali, and Sonia over to help her host a small party at her house with the usual circle of Harvey Slate friends and a select group of college students home for summer break.

After a grueling shopping trip to the grocery store, debating what to serve, the girls gathered in Tory's kitchen, preparing platters of fruit, hot appetizers, sandwiches, chips, and cookies. Jaime and Trevor had offered to set up the bar in the living room while the girls changed and fixed their hair and makeup in Tory's room.

Warm colors, antique art, pottery, and rustic yet refined furniture decorated Tory's large Tuscan-style home and, in contrast, hot pink walls and black furniture decorated her bedroom. Enjoying themselves, they listened to music and leisurely chatted until they heard Jaime yell up the stairs that guests were arriving.

With one more glance in the mirror and satisfied with her appearance, dressed in a red skirt and matching tank top, she touched up her red lipstick. Although not her typical style of dress, Jaime had mentioned how much he loved the color red on a woman, and Brea desired to please him. The girls teased her that for the rest of the night, they would call her "Sexy B."

Once downstairs, Brea entered the kitchen to check on the platters of food one final time. Jaime came from behind, wrapped his arms around her waist, and slipped a jewelry box into her hand.

"What is this?" she asked, surprised by the spontaneous gift.

"A gift for my gorgeous girlfriend. Open it."

Brea flipped open the top of the box and gasped at the 18K gold bow pendant necklace encrusted with pavé diamonds. "Jaime, it's gorgeous—thank you." She attempted to kiss him, but Jaime pulled back.

"Whoa, red lipstick. Kiss me after you wipe it off." Brea's lips stretched tight, thinking to herself, it was only lipstick, not cyanide. Pushing her annoyance aside, with a gentle touch, she lifted the necklace from its box and wrapped it around her neck for Jaime to fasten the clasp.

Taking Brea's hand, Jaime led her to the foyer. Stepping before the mounted gold console mirror, she studied her reflection—it was a stunning piece of jewelry. Jaime squeezed her hand, kissed her on the cheek, and then turned to rejoin the party. Holding her gaze on the mirror, Brea touched the pendant with her fingers. Although a beautiful necklace, she could not help but think it screamed ostentatious and did not match her personal style.

"You look very—red." Brea turned her head, seeing Hayden leaning against the wall that divided the foyer from the living room, dressed in a white V-neck T-shirt, gray-blue shorts, and tennis shoes.

"I'm not sure if that's a compliment," Brea replied with a furrowed brow as she looked back into the mirror.

"It's not your usual look."

Brea shook her head and exhaled, rotating to look at Hayden. "It's only an outfit and some lipstick. I don't understand why everyone is making such a big deal about it."

"I'm not trying to insult you. It's only that—you look like you're trying to be someone else."

"Hayden, leave me alone," Brea replied. He paused and looked over his shoulder briefly before meeting her eyes again.

"I can't," he replied with intention.

Brea's eyes narrowed, convinced Hayden was purposely playing with her head—the fleeting looks, acting like a knight in shining armor after the campsite, charming one day, then distant with her on another. A wave of anger washed over her.

Before she could open her mouth to respond, Callie's voice yelled out from the living room. "Hayden, come in here. I have to ask you a smart-person question."

Brea glared at Hayden, and she wanted answers. "Hayden, what—"

"Now! Hurry, or I'll drag you in here," Callie shouted louder.

Hayden released an exasperated sigh before turning to walk into the living room. Brea paused a minute to compose herself and, needing a drink, strode through the living room to the bar. Her heart beat at a frantic pace as she poured rum into a glass, followed by half a can of cola.

Looking over her shoulder, Hayden met her eyes as he spoke with Callie and Tara. Brea pressed her lips together and looked away. Draining half her drink, she added more cola and decided that, as of tonight—she hated Hayden. He was toying with her, and she did not know why.

Brea stormed out of the room into the kitchen, pulled out a garbage bag, and cleaned the counter of empty cups and bottles on the food table. This was Tory's home, but she felt restless, irritated, and needed something to occupy her as she attempted to calm herself. Once the alcohol perfused her brain, her agitation tempered.

Manufacturing a smile, Brea rejoined the party, having moved outside onto the patio. Hearing dance music, rather than sitting with Sonia and Tory at the outdoor dining table, she changed course and joined in with a group of girls dancing on the far end of the patio.

Laughing and dancing provocatively, she caught Hayden watching her, leaning back in his seat with his hand covering his mouth and chin. She continued, her purpose to taunt him, though she had no clear end goal in mind other than her wish for him to feel as conflicted, confused, and frustrated as she did in his presence.

After several songs, Brea grew bored with dancing, then made her rounds through the party to greet and chat with everyone except for Hayden. If he sat with a group she joined, she refused to look at him. If he tried to speak to her, she would excuse herself and leave in an abrupt and cutting manner.

By eleven-thirty, only a handful of boys remained in the living room, including Hayden. Drained of energy, Brea closed her eyes and let the boys' conversation fade into the background as she lay on a chaise lounge. Not long after, Jaimie placed his hand on Brea's head and scratched her scalp. Turning to look at him, she yawned.

"No, come on, come out with me and the guys to the beach," Jaime pleaded as he sat down beside Brea and massaged her calves.

"No way, I need sleep. Please, can you drop me off and have a boy's late night?" Brea asked, hoping he would not put up a fight. Jaime nodded, observing her genuine exhaustion. Taking her hand, he helped her to stand. While Jaime stopped in the restroom, Brea shuffled into the kitchen to say good night to Tory. After rejoining Jaime in the living room, they said their goodbyes to the remaining group, and Brea noticed Hayden had left, having slipped out unnoticed.

Chapter Eighteen

The Past

Jaime dropped Brea off at midnight. Waving from the doorway, she signaled for him to leave before stepping inside. She slipped off her shoes, climbed the stairs, and once in her room, switched on her light. Letting out a puff of air, she undressed, wiped off her red lipstick with a tissue, then unfastened her new necklace. She packed it away in the box and placed it on her dresser.

While seated on the edge of her bed, she pulled a clean white tank top over her head and, though she tried not to, thought about Hayden. The effect he had on her was maddening. Despite his perplexing and inconsistent behavior, Brea found herself drawn to him and, although ashamed of herself, it excited her when she had caught him watching her throughout the evening.

Brea dropped her head into her hands and mumbled to herself, "Go to sleep," knowing that if she stayed awake, attempting to sort out her convoluted feelings for Hayden, she would drive herself insane. Further, she hoped to wake up early and ride her bike to the park and write. Without a solid night of sleep, she would wind up spending the early part of the day watching television.

About to lie down on her bed, she froze upon hearing a strange noise—she did not know what to make of it, though it sounded as though something had hit her window. Motionless, she sat on her bed until hearing the same sound ten seconds later. Hurrying to the window, she moved the curtain aside and peered out. Hayden stood on her front lawn and, seeing Brea at the window, waved for her to come down.

Brea threw up her hands to communicate her irritation and bewilderment. Hayden waved again for her to come down. With a forceful exhale, she held up a finger for him to wait, then closed the curtains.

"Are you kidding me?" she whispered as she searched her floor for a pair of pajama bottoms or shorts. In the corner of her room, she found her pink sleep shorts and slipped them on. Turning off her light, Brea crept down the hall and stairs after making sure no sounds came from her parents' bedroom. Once through the foyer, she opened the front door to step out. Seeing Hayden at the bottom of her porch, she turned to close the door, then crossed her arms as she pivoted around to face him.

"Hayden. What are you doing here? And how did you even know that was my room? It could have been my parents' room."

"Last time I dropped you off, I saw your bedroom light switch on a few minutes after you went in."

Brea sat on the top step of the porch, clasped her hands together, and dropped them onto her lap. "What do you want, Hayden? Wait—before you answer, tell me if you're going to be nice or act like a jerk, because I can't keep up anymore and from now on, I'd like a warning."

Hayden sat on the bottom step and looked up at Brea, his eyes awash with vulnerability.

"I remembered you."

Brea held her breath for a moment before she spoke. "What do you mean?"

"I lied to you. In the car that night. I remembered meeting you in the library years ago." Hayden paused and took a deep breath. Brea continued to look into Hayden's eyes, her heart now beating fast in her chest.

"I remember everything from that day—your hand, how shy you were, the way you looked at me, your giant sweater." Hayden smiled as Brea let out a small laugh.

"I can't explain it, but when I saw you in the library, even before we spoke, something pulled me to you—it was like we were supposed to meet. After that day, I went back and tried to find you at the library, but I never saw you again. I thought if I ever found you in the future, then the universe meant for us to be together. And that night at the beach, as soon as I saw you, I knew it was you, but I was in shock. And all I could think about was how the universe screwed me over, finding you again, but you were with Jaime."

Brea closed her eyes as Hayden's words washed over her. Her thoughts raced, impairing her ability to think straight.

"I thought I could do it—pretend as though we had never met and ignore everything I felt for you. It was so complicated with Vienna and you being with Jaime. The last thing I wanted to do was tell you how I felt and put you in an impossible situation. But after tonight—now I have to tell you. When I see you, it's torture, and I can't help but think everything is wrong. It should have been us, you and me, from the beginning."

Brea shook her head. She did not want to hurt Jaime, though her heart ached as she listened to Hayden. "*It should have been us,*" echoing in her mind.

Hayden continued. "I am not asking you to say or do anything. I'll leave, but I don't want you to be angry with me or think I don't care about you. I have done everything I could to keep my distance from you, not because I don't like you—but because I do—so much."

Brea's lips parted, though she could not find the words to express what she felt. Her throat tightened as she attempted and failed to suppress her tears. Holding his gaze, all of her anger, confusion, and frustration vanished. Hayden stood, then knelt before Brea. He placed his hands on her face and, with his thumbs, wiped the tears that fell on her cheeks. They searched their minds for what to say next, knowing, despite what they felt, they could not be together—fate had brought them back together too late, and it was heartbreaking.

Looking into one another's eyes, the only thing Brea could say was "Hayden." They way she said his name served as confirmation that she shared everything he felt. The beautiful truth had unchained them, and the proximity to one another was too irresistible to push away. They leaned close to one another and, with a gentle touch of their lips, kissed—and it felt right, soft, and tender. Their kiss became more passionate and everything tangible in the world felt as though it ceased to exist.

Breaking apart to look at one another, they laughed in recognition of their mutual relief knowing the truth of their feelings—then kissed again. Needing to be closer, they stood up from the steps to embrace and eliminate any space left between them. Desire alone could not explain it—but something else more powerful, like coming home after the world had beaten you up and done its worst only to find peace in the place you most belonged.

"Hayden, we should move off the porch, but you can't come inside," Brea whispered.

"Should we go for a drive?"

"No. Let me think a minute." Brea had an idea. "Let's go into my garage." Brea held out her hand for Hayden to lead him into her backyard. Careful not to make excess noise, Brea opened the wooden gate. They walked down the path to the garage in silence and slipped in through the side door.

"So, this is a sort of sanctuary for me where I hide out sometimes. It isn't very stylish, but I like it in here." Brea lifted her arms to present the space to Hayden. Reaching up to a shelf, she found her reading flashlight and turned it on.

Hayden smiled and chuckled. "I like it, B. Did you do all the—uh—decorating in here?" he asked, pointing to the various posters, tacked up blankets and old scarves Brea hung to conceal the stacked boxes. On the floor, Brea had laid out an old woven rug to keep her feet clean when she took off her shoes.

Brea straightened out the cotton blanket she kept over the loveseat. "Please don't call me B. That's a Jaime thing. Coming from you, it's strange. How would you like it if I called you Ben?"

"Point taken. I'll try. Slips out sometimes," he said, sitting down on the loveseat. "Which book is your favorite?" Hayden gestured to the stack of books on the carpet.

"All of them. They're like my babies. I can't pick only one," Brea replied and sat beside him.

Hayden froze as though something had startled him.

Brea looked at him with wide eyes. "What is it? Is someone coming?"

"No, I realized there could be mice in here or worse, rats," he announced with alarm.

"Of course. This is a garage. This is like their haven." Attempting to suppress a smile, she then asked, "Are you scared of mice, Hayden?"

"Oh yeah, terrified," he admitted.

"Do you want to leave?"

"No, not yet. But if you see me bolt outside and cry, you'll know why." They both laughed.

Once their laughter slowed, Brea looked into Hayden's eyes and sighed. The tension and confusion between them had vanished, and now the only thing left between them was their need for one another. He pulled Brea in and kissed her again as she shifted onto Hayden's lap, straddling him. Brea slipped her hands under Hayden's shirt. Her fingers explored his skin, beginning on his back, circling around to his chest, then up to his shoulders. The touch of his skin—warm, smooth and taut over his muscular arms and back—felt magnificent on Brea's fingertips.

Pulling back from their kiss, Hayden met Brea's eyes. "Vienna can't find out about us. I don't want to explain the entire story tonight, but she can't. She'll come after you, and I don't want you to get hurt."

Brea nodded. "I know. We have to pretend tonight never happened."

"Yeah," he mumbled, his eyes falling somber. "I don't want this to be a secret, but I don't know what else to do right now."

"Even though I feel the same as you, Hayden, I can't hurt Jaime—I just can't do that to him. He would hate me. Everyone would."

Hayden nodded with understanding.

"And we can't have sex," Brea added.

"I know," he said as he played with a tendril of hair that had fallen over her shoulder.

"What are we doing? What is this?" Brea muttered, not expecting an answer.

"I don't know. But the idea of leaving and not touching you—"

"I don't want you to leave or stop touching me. I know that makes me a horrible person—a cheater and a liar," Brea professed, lowering her head.

"Don't say that," Hayden said, pulling back to look into her eyes. "You're none of those things. Look, I'm the one who put you in this situation. This is my fault." Brea wrapped her arms around Hayden and dropped her head on his shoulder.

"Brea, I know what I'm about to say makes little sense, and what we're doing is wrong, but somehow with us, it's as if the rules don't apply. I can't explain it, but I feel it. Maybe one day things can be different."

They sat in silence, listening to the rustling of a branch tapping against the garage window. After a minute, Hayden kissed Brea's shoulder. She followed by kissing the crook of his neck. That simple kiss sent Hayden over the edge. Pulling apart, Hayden moved his hands to cradle Brea's face and kissed her once again. She ran her fingers through his hair as he dropped his head and kissed the tops of her breasts peeking out from her tank top. Brea moaned, throwing her head back.

"Hayden, I don't know if I'll be able to pretend tonight didn't happen."

"Me neither, but I don't want to think about tomorrow," he whispered and kissed Brea again with an ardor that fueled their desire for one another. Brea removed Hayden's shirt and then her tank top. His scent and the touch of his bare chest against hers unleashed a rush of heat through her body. She kissed his shoulder, neck, and then took his earlobe into her mouth as she pressed her fingers into his back. Hayden let out a groan and moved his hands to her bottom to pull her closer to him. Feeling him firm beneath his shorts and between her legs, Brea began to move her hips. The pressure of his erection between her legs sent pulses of pleasure throughout her body with an intensity she had never felt before.

Hayden's hands on her bottom tensed, and he pressed her deeper into him. Possessed, she rocked her hips faster, her lips parted, and she wrapped her arms tighter around his neck. The passion and pleasure intensified until Brea and Hayden both cried out, and a wave of euphoria overcame her mind and body. Brea tipped her forehead against Hayden's. Their chests and faces were damp with perspiration, and their breaths were rapid.

They looked into one another's eyes and smiled before kissing again.

"Hayden, what was that? It felt incredible," Brea whispered.

Looking into Brea's eyes, a tender smile spread across his face. "You never had an orgasm before?"

"Oh," Brea whispered and smiled. "No. Can we do that again?"

Hayden chuckled and pulled Brea in close to him. "I'll need a few minutes."

"Hayden," Brea said, watching the floor just beyond the edge of the loveseat.

"Yes?"

"Don't freak out, but I think I just saw a mouse run under the loveseat."

Hayden squeezed Brea tighter against him and groaned. "I really hope you're joking."

Brea smiled and kissed his neck, deciding it would be better not to tell him the truth—they had not been alone that night in the garage. They both laughed, and any thoughts about tomorrow, Jaime, Vienna, or the future were suspended and left to float away in the night air. Neither of them wanted this moment to end, so they stayed for as long as they could in the darkness, the only place where they could hide together.

Chapter Nineteen

The Past

Three weeks passed, and Brea and Hayden kept to their word. They did not speak of the night they had shared and kept their distance from one another. With Jaime being away for the past three weeks in Brazil, Brea had only attended one Harvey Slate party with Tory and Anjali the previous weekend. Although she and Hayden tracked one another throughout the party, occasionally making eye contact and sharing a knowing smile, they stayed apart.

What Brea found difficult to endure were the long nights in her stifling room bursting with hot, thick summer air, making it difficult to fall and stay asleep. Dressed in her tank top and underwear, she would wipe the sweat from her forehead and chest as she lay in bed. Often, she fantasized about Hayden lying beside her, tracing her collarbone with his fingertips and kissing her neck. When desire overwhelmed her, she would creep down the stairs into the kitchen and open the freezer door to temper the ache of her arousal.

In the mornings, Brea rode her bike to Nuthatch Park to write. Often, when she thought of Hayden, she would roll onto her back and look up into the trees. Placing her fingers on her lips, she remembered the taste of his mouth, cinnamon, and fought the urge to touch the most intimate places on her body. A cruel universe cursed her with the heartbreaking memory of Hayden's touch, a memory she would recall and never experience again. That afternoon, Brea shook out her hands and legs to force Hayden out of her mind. "Ugh, stop," Brea ordered herself. She needed to focus on her work and resign herself to the fact that there could be no hope for them—they had only one night together, never to be repeated.

When at home, to cope with her guilt, she would amble to the library and write Jaime an email. Half the time it worked to refocus on Jaime and push any thoughts of Hayden into the back of her mind. As the weeks had passed, finding what she should write to Jaime had become a struggle as he did not appear to appreciate her long-winded descriptions of the park or opinions on the books she had read. Her questions always circled back to any recent adventures he had to share with his siblings, nephews, and nieces, the dishes his grandmother had cooked, and then she followed up with comments from his prior email.

Relishing the warmth of the sun on her face, Brea inhaled, then set to work on her short story titled "On the Street," about a runaway seventeen-year-old girl leaving a troubled home to live in New York City. Her dreams of liberation dashed, the protagonist finds herself homeless and struggling to survive on the streets. The tone of the story, moody and dark, made it an interesting read, yet she now struggled on the ending, having decided on a tragic one.

Brea wished she had someone to share her writing with, but Allegra was in Barbados, and she did not feel comfortable sharing her work with Jaime, worrying he would struggle to separate her authorship from her as a person. He appreciated her for her beauty and jovial company, and she worried that if he saw the darker side of her, he would find it disturbing.

As the hours passed, and the end of the afternoon neared, Brea packed her belongings to ride her bike home. Evenings over the past week had been difficult to endure as her mother's mood state had shifted into one of her energetic spells. Last night Brea's mother followed her from room to room, perseverating on building a candle-making business. For two hours she regurgitated information from a library book regarding infusing scent into wax and the importance of aesthetically pleasing packaging—Brea's ears bled from listening to the endless cycle of recapitulated text.

On Friday, late in the afternoon, the phone rang amid her mother's loquacious ramble on the benefits of essential oils. Brea eagerly picked up the phone as her mother left to use the bathroom.

"Hi B," Tory said with enthusiasm, having returned from a week in Florida visiting family.

"Tory, hi. How was your trip?"

"Boring. I need to get out of the house and away from my parents. I just hung up the phone with Trevor, and Hayden's having a small party at his house tomorrow night. Trevor will pick us up. Please come! I can't imagine being stuck with Tara and Callie all night by myself."

Brea hesitated. She had to admit she burned with curiosity to see Hayden's home, and they had proved they could keep their distance from one another at the previous party.

"Sure, what time are you picking me up?"

"Six. We can stop off for dinner before we go to his house."

Brea looked forward to a party for the first time in a while, considering the unpalatable alternative, staying home with her parents and spending another evening listening to her mother carry on about candles. Hanging up the phone, she rubbed her shoulders and devised a plan of escape before her mother returned from the bathroom. Sneaking out of the house, Brea crept into the garage with her journal and a glass of iced tea.

Once seated on the loveseat, an image of Hayden holding her against his bare chest infiltrated her mind.

"Think about your gorgeous boyfriend," Brea whispered to herself. She rolled the icy glass of iced tea across her forehead to divert her attention from the sensuous image in her mind, then picked up her pen, settling on exorcising her impure thoughts into a poem. Brea chewed on her pen until she thought of a title, "Stolen Night."

The following evening, Trevor and Tory arrived at Brea's, honking the horn to let her know they were outside. On her way out, Brea said goodbye to her father, seated in an armchair and reading the newspaper in the living room. He looked up for a moment, wished her goodnight without inquiring where she would head to for the evening or when she would return home, and returned to his reading.

Brea, pensive throughout dinner at Vittorio's and the car ride to Hayden's, fixed her gaze out the window and fanned herself with her hand. She wore a blue ombre strapless summer dress to stay cool, though with the hot weather, the fabric already clung to her skin from her sweat. Wearing her hair loose had been a mistake. Brea searched her purse, hoping to find an elastic to tie up her hair, finding the damp pieces stuck to her back irritating on her skin.

Hayden lived in East Black Harbor on a large piece of property in a sprawling gray brick French-style ranch home with custom large-grid windows. This gathering, invitation only, would include only Harvey Slate students, meaning that rather than two hundred teenagers, there would be around fifty.

Having entered the backyard through the side gate, Brea and Tory made their way through the crowd, exchanging brief greetings and promises to catch up later. Spotting Anjali seated at a table with a group of girls, they joined her. Once seated, she offered to pour Brea and Tory a drink from an open bottle of dry, sparkling wine from a cooler on the table.

Although Brea preferred something sweeter, she welcomed the cold and refreshing drink, hoping to temper her nerves as she anticipated seeing Hayden. The girls chatted about their vacations and filled one another in on any gossip some may have missed while traveling. The light conversation allowed Brea's mind to wander. When needed, she could rely on occasionally nodding or sharing a generic comment to feign her attention.

Brea scanned the patio, having yet to see Hayden. Clustered across the patio and lawn, pockets of schoolmates chatted or played drinking games. At the far end of the large patio, Trevor and Aaron sat at a table playing poker with a group of boys from the lacrosse team. Brea, curious to see the house, excused herself, telling Tory she needed to use the bathroom, then slipped into the kitchen through the patio doors.

She gasped at seeing the stunning interior of Hayden's home. In the custom kitchen, she beheld white and glass-paned kitchen cabinets above sleek black marble counters, built-in high-end stainless-steel appliances, and tasteful decorative bowls filled with lemons. The pristine white marble floors, polished to a high sheen, rendered the illusion of walking on milky glass.

Running her fingers along the counters, she fantasized about what it would be like to eat dinner with his parents. Brea imagined herself dressed in a pale-pink cocktail dress and high heels, clicking on the marble floor as Hayden pulled out an ivory upholstered chair for her at the elegant black walnut dining table. After dinner, she would praise his mother for the wonderful meal she had cooked, then offer to help serve dessert as Hayden slipped his arm around Brea's shoulders.

Obnoxious laughter from the patio halted Brea's fantasy, catapulting her back to reality.

From the kitchen, she stepped into a large, luxurious living room, featuring oversized ivory sofas and a grand fireplace with built-in custom cabinets. Attractive black, ivory, and beige pillows decorated the sofas and, on the shelves and coffee table, sat an assortment of photographs, books, and sculptures. Long ivory curtains lent the room a dramatic air, emphasizing the high ceilings.

A subtle fragrance of lavender and vanilla perfumed the home. Eyeing the sofas, Brea sighed, wishing she could settle onto one of them, barefoot and with her journal in her lap. She pictured Hayden seated across from her with a book in his hand.

Continuing through the room, she peeked into a less formal family room on her right. On her left, she saw a spacious foyer, guest bathroom, and a hallway. To her right, past the family room, was another hallway. She knew she should pretend to use the guest bathroom, then return to the party, but her curiosity had a hold over her, and she continued to explore. Turning right, she walked down the long hallway.

Taking her time, she passed several closed doors and continued down the hall. Reaching the end, she heard music coming from behind a door on her left. She tipped her head closer, listened, and heard no voices coming from inside the room.

She told herself to turn around and return outside, but something inside her felt certain this was Hayden's bedroom, and she felt compelled to look inside. Placing her fingers on the handle, she pushed it down—the door was unlocked.

Opening the door several inches, she looked inside and saw the signs of a teenage boy's room—khaki-colored walls, espresso wood bedroom furniture, a desk, and framed posters of various music bands and sports teams hanging on the walls. Brea checked over her shoulder. Seeing no one, she entered the room and closed the door behind her. Drawn ivory-colored curtains, similar to those in the living room, hung on wrought iron curtain rods. A stack of hardcover books sat on the desk. With a smile, she picked one up and turned it over to read the back cover.

"Brea?"

She swung around and dropped the book on the desk. Hayden stood in the doorway of his bathroom dressed only in a pair of light-gray shorts with his hair wet from having come out of the shower.

"Oh, I'm so sorry," Brea blurted out, her face flushed from her brazen disregard for propriety. "I was curious to see your house, and I heard music coming from inside. I don't know what I was thinking." Turning to leave the room, Brea hurried to the door. Reaching for the handle, she froze as Hayden spoke.

"Lock it," he said.

Brea held her breath. Moving her hand, she pushed the button to lock the door and turned to face Hayden. Their eyes met and, without hesitation, flew to one another. Hayden dropped the towel in his hand to the floor and picked Brea up as she jumped into his arms.

With an urgency and fervor as though starved for one another, she wrapped her legs around his waist and they kissed. No substitute existed for this exhilarating feeling. Hayden tasted like cinnamon, and the warmth of his skin against hers felt intoxicating.

He pulled his head back. "We can't stay in here too long—someone will notice we're gone. I came in to take a shower and change after Aaron knocked into me with a full beer."

"Okay, really quick," she replied, leaning in to kiss him again.

Hayden laughed, his eyes bright, amused she did not hide her desire for him. She wanted him to hold her and touch her, no matter the cost or consequences. They kissed again, and her arms wrapped around his shoulders. Knowing they had little time, she wanted to touch as much of him as she could. Brea did not care—she dug herself in deeper as she lost herself in the warmth and insistence of his tongue in her mouth. Although reckless, her desire for Hayden felt beyond her control, and at the moment, she justified they belonged to one another and, as Hayden had said, perhaps the rules did not apply to them.

Hayden carried Brea to his dresser and sat her down. With his hands free, he ran his fingers down her thighs and, reaching the hem of the skirt of her dress, pulled the fabric up to her hips. Kissing her neck, he moved one hand between her legs. He traced around the edges of her panties with his fingers and then slipped them underneath the fabric to find the perfect spot to tease and apply pressure. Brea let out a loud moan. With his other hand, Hayden covered her mouth and laughed. "Shh," he whispered.

But Hayden did not stop touching her, wanting to bring her to a climax. She nearly cried out again when he used his fingers to push deep inside her. Hayden kissed Brea, muffling the sounds escaping from her lips as he continued to use his fingers in a delicious rhythm. It did not take long before he brought her to orgasm, and he pressed his lips deeper into hers to remind her not to make any noise. Brea dropped her head on his shoulder, her breath slowing.

"Oh no, Hayden, I'm in trouble," Brea whispered.

Hayden wrapped his arms around her and kissed the top of her head. Hayden exhaled and chuckled. "I should have turned up the music," he teased. Brea laughed.

"I don't want you to leave, but you should go outside. Someone is going to notice you've been gone for a while and come looking for you," Hayden said in a subdued voice.

They pulled apart from one another, locking eyes. They knew being caught would have grave consequences, regardless of how right it felt to be in one another's arms.

"Hayden. This is impossible. We both know this can't go anywhere, and with Jaime, I'm so confused," Brea said in a somber tone as she rested her head on Hayden's shoulder. Her heart filled with melancholy and guilt—for betraying Jaime and believing herself to be a horrible person—it mattered little that her feelings for Hayden were genuine and true.

Reading her mind, Hayden pulled back to look into her eyes. "Don't feel bad. Don't do that to yourself. It's not only you. It's me, too. It's just that somehow things got all screwed up. We'll figure it out. It will be all right." Hayden kissed her again with tenderness, then placed his hands on her waist to help her off the dresser. Taking Brea's hand, they walked over to the curtains. Hayden separated them, revealing a set of glass-panel French doors, and opened the doors wide enough to poke his head out.

"No one is there. You can go through these doors to the patio from here. Go right and make another right," he instructed.

Hayden cupped her face with his hands and gave her another gentle kiss on her lips. He then checked outside once more. Satisfied, he stepped aside as he motioned with his hand for her to go. Brea stepped out the doors, but Hayden grabbed her hand before she could walk away.

"If anyone asks where you were, say you went to my parents' room to use their bathroom because you were sick. Tell them you were lost, and you left through the front door. Their room is down the other hallway."

He dropped her hand as Brea nodded. She hurried along the side of the house, looking around her to make sure no one had seen her. As she turned right to step onto the back patio, she bumped into Tara and Aaron amid a conversation.

"Where were you?" Tara asked.

"Oh, I got lost. Someone was in the guest bathroom, so I had to find another one. I felt dizzy from the heat," she answered with a cool demeanor.

"Sure. Hope you're better now," Tara replied with an unconvincing air of concern while boorishly cracking the gum in her mouth. Aaron appeared to study Brea intently through narrowed eyes, though she convinced herself she was only being paranoid. Tara stepped aside to let her pass without further questions. Brea rejoined her friends at the table, sat down, then poured herself a refill of sparkling wine. No one appeared to have noticed her disappearance. Several boys joined the girls at the table to propose a card game, and the girls accepted.

Brea glimpsed Hayden exiting his kitchen through the patio doors. Their eyes met. He gave Brea a slight smile and a subtle nod, then joined Trevor at the poker table. Hayden glanced at Brea after he sat down. An ache set in her chest, knowing it would not be possible to make it out of this situation without someone getting hurt. Brea sank into her seat, knowing that regardless, the future held inevitable heartbreak for her.

What Hayden and Brea failed to see, observing these subtle interactions between them, was Aaron, leaning against the wall with a scowl on his face.

CHAPTER TWENTY

THE PAST

Two nights later, Trevor and Tory picked up Brea for a party on the grounds of a Harvey Slate graduate's parents' country club. A gathering made possible after having paid off the security and maintenance staff to look the other way. As Trevor pulled up in front of Brea's house, she hurried to the car only to slow her steps upon seeing Hayden seated in the back seat. Remembering Hayden's mouth on hers in his bedroom, Brea bit her lip to stop herself from smiling. She opened the door and sat down, greeted Tory and Trevor, then mumbled hello to Hayden under her breath. Their eyes met for a moment, smiling at one another before Hayden looked out the window.

Tory was in high spirits and wanted to make the most of the night, as she would leave for Spain in two days. "I'm getting drunk tonight," she cried out. Trevor cheered and Brea chuckled. Although a lively energy bubbled in the car as they drove, Brea and Hayden struggled with how to appear natural with one another. Failing to accomplish this task, they avoided speaking to one another.

Five minutes later, Trevor pulled up in front of Anjali's house. Anjali, waiting on the sidewalk, jogged over to the car and opened the passenger door where Brea sat.

"Scooch in, Brea," she said. Brea glanced at Hayden. He held his gaze straight ahead and with his hand, covered his mouth. Pressing her lips together, she shifted to the middle, smoothed down the skirt of her dress, and plopped her purse on her lap. While fastening the seatbelt, her leg pressed into Hayden's—to deflect from her desire to touch his leg, she clasped her hands together.

Shortly after they drove off, she felt Hayden shift in his seat. His arm pressed into hers and she closed her eyes. Every muscle in her body, now tense, ached for him to press in closer as they continued to drive, and Brea found it difficult to focus on the conversation in the car.

Trevor pulled into the supermarket parking lot and parked in an isolated space at the far end of the lot. "We're going to see if we can get a case of beer," he shouted over the music before turning off the engine. Trevor and Tory sprang out of the car, leaving Anjali, Hayden, and Brea in the backseat as they unbuckled their seatbelts to wait, uncertain how long it would take Trevor to convince someone to buy the beer for him.

"Do either of you want anything? I'm going to run in for gum and a drink," Anjali asked. Hayden shook his head.

"Yes, a bottle of water, please," Brea requested. She reached into her bag to take out a few dollars for Anjali.

"Don't worry about it, my treat," she called out as she closed the door, leaving Hayden and Brea alone in the back seat.

Brea turned her head and spoke. "Hayden—"

Before she could finish, Hayden kissed her.

The touch of his lips against hers—though ambrosian—did not succeed in overriding the half-hearted pocket of resistance her mind mustered to protest the brazen exhibition of impulsive passion. Hayden placed his hand on her leg and traced her thigh with his fingers. Brea groaned and then mumbled through his kiss. "Hayden, we can't. This is stupid. We're going to get caught."

"I don't care. I'll take an ass-beating. This is worth it," he replied, his voice low as he brushed her lips with his.

Brea closed her eyes and surrendered to her own desire for Hayden. "Okay, nice knowing you."

Hayden kissed her again, deeper, and Brea guided his hand under her dress to travel up her inner thigh. Upon reaching the desired destination, his fingers pressed in between her legs. Brea gasped and slipped her hand under the band of his shorts. Pleased to find him firm and responsive to her touch, she squeezed with gentle pressure, and he moaned.

Driven by frantic, urgent passion, they explored one another's bodies. "Hayden, this is crazy."

"Right, I'll stop. You're right, this is wrong," he said, his voice hoarse, though he did not stop touching her.

"No, don't stop. Wrong is good right now. It feels so good, Hayden," Brea whispered, out of her mind. Her body was on fire, and she did not want him to stop.

Hearing laughter in the distance, they pulled their hands back to themselves and froze. The fear of being caught roused them out of their reckless abandonment of logic and reason.

"Hayden, now we have to stop," she exclaimed, then wiped her mouth.

Hayden sighed and leaned back in his seat. Tilting his head back, he stared at the roof of the car. "If I could go back, I would have said something sooner. Things could have been different, Brea."

Brea shifted to straighten her dress and smooth down her hair. "Hayden, we have to stop torturing ourselves—"

Before she could finish, Tory and Anjali's laughter interrupted her. The car doors opened, and they climbed into their seats.

Having found a college student to buy alcohol, Trevor followed a minute later, holding a case of beer. "Let's go," he bellowed after storing it in the trunk, and they drove off to the country club. Brea and Hayden sat close to one another for the remaining car ride, enduring the torture of their arms and legs pressed together. Brea could only focus on the memory of his hands on her body.

For the remainder of the night, they kept their physical distance, but when they saw one another and their eyes met, they exchanged an elusive smile. A swift heart lurch, followed by an ache of despondency, would emerge when her eyes grazed over Hayden's lips or hands. It was clear—forgetting would not be possible if she allowed herself to be alone with Hayden and it would only be a matter of time until someone caught them.

At the end of the week, she would leave for her writer's program, and developing a strategy to refocus her energy on Jamie had become paramount—if she did not distance herself from Hayden, she would wind up alone, a target for Vienna, and despised by all at Harvey Slate.

Chapter Twenty-One

The Past

The following Friday, Brea arrived at the youth writers' program, held that summer at a beachfront resort in Port Hammonsville, a two-hour drive north of Black Harbor. Scanning the hotel ground floor, Brea's father located the program check-in table, leaving her to explore the lobby as he greeted the program director seated next to a crate of folders.

The hotel, though not what many would define as luxurious, was a well-maintained property with a charming boutique feel and modern design. Brea studied several large-scale canvas paintings depicting the ocean at varying times of the day, from sunrise to sunset. Struck by their beauty, she felt a wave of serenity wash over her, believing it to be a good omen for the week to come.

Seeing a map of the hotel mounted on the wall, she moved closer to study it. Apart from the hotel rooms, the resort offered an outdoor swimming pool, a restaurant, a fitness center, a media library, and several conference rooms.

Brea met her father at the check-in table to introduce herself to the program director, Sherilyn, and to thank her for the scholarship. Sherilyn greeted her, then finished briefing her father on the various amenities, rules, and logistics parents needed to know if an emergency occurred. Brea's father listened, attentive with hands clasped before him, and shook his head when asked if he had questions for her.

Sherilyn handed Brea a hotel map, room key, and a program for the week's activities, then Brea and her father stepped out of the lobby to retrieve her luggage from the car. Placing her bags on the ground, her father patted Brea's shoulder, mumbled goodbye, and settled in his seat.

She watched her father drive away. Once his car was out of sight, she stretched her neck to the sky, finding the heat from the scorching sun invigorating. Knowing she had left Black Harbor behind for an entire week filled her with a sense of relief. Unfolding the paper map she held in her hand, Brea studied it to find her room. Picking up her backpack and duffel bag, she returned to the lobby.

The configuration of the resort—a basic rectangle—held the pool, courtyard, and seating lounges at its center. Three wings housed hotel rooms, and the fourth wing contained the remaining amenities. A path on the other side of the pool gate led the guests to a small private beach.

Brea, pleased at having discovered her room had an ocean view, hastened her steps, eager to settle in and unpack. She found her room at the end of a long white hallway on the second floor. Fortunately, her bags were light as she required very little clothing for the week—several pairs of shorts, T-shirts, pajamas, one sweatshirt, running shoes, and two bathing suits. She had gladly left her makeup, hair dryer, and other high-maintenance grooming items behind at home. The next week would be only for Brea to write, attend courses, practice meditation, and swim.

Reaching her room, she opened the door and saw two sets of wooden bunk beds made up with crisp white sheets and folded cerulean blankets at the base. Prints of various types of seashells hung on the baby blue walls and a hot pink suitcase, a backpack, and a large tan duffel bag sat on the top bunk bed on her left. Brea preferred to sleep on the bottom, terrified of rolling out of the bed as she slept, and for that reason claimed the bottom bunk bed. Other than several scuffs and scratches on the dark wood floors, the furniture appeared new and the room well maintained. Opposite the bunk beds, there were two wooden dressers, a desk, and a floor lamp.

Brea sat down in the chair at the desk to rest. She swiveled around to face the window and gazed at the ocean for a moment of welcomed peace. When ready, she opened the top two drawers of the dresser nearest her bed to unpack and arrange her clothes. On the verge of bringing her toiletries into the bathroom, Brea heard voices approaching the door in the outside hallway.

After struggling for a moment with the key card, a petite blonde with curly hair and a freckled complexion, dressed in an army green T-shirt and denim shorts, opened the door. "Hi, I'm Amanda," she said, greeting Brea with a lively smile as she entered the room.

Behind Amanda entered a tall girl with light-brown hair pleated in two braids, dressed in overalls over a bathing suit. Waving and introducing herself to Brea as "Mia," she stumbled into the room carrying a black suitcase and a backpack.

"Nice to meet you. I'm Brea."

"So, we found out from Sherilyn that our fourth roommate had to pull out of the program last minute, so it will only be us three in this room," Amanda informed Brea.

"Did either of you know her? Hopefully she's all right," Brea replied.

"No, but I doubt it was anything tragic. But hey, now we have extra storage space," Mia joked as she motioned with her hands to the empty bunk bed. The girls laughed and then exchanged where they were from, year in school, and general small talk.

Mia and Amanda were friends, having flown in from Florida to attend the program.

"Do you have a boyfriend?" Mia asked with a smile.

"Yes, his name is Jaime. I have my photo album with me for our meet and greet later, if you want to see."

"Yes," they cried out in unison and shuffled over to Brea's bed, sitting down on either side of her. Now that the universal icebreaker of discussing boys had begun, the residual awkwardness in the room vanished, and the girls were fast friends.

"I had a boyfriend, Matt, but we broke up last month because—well, he thinks he might be gay," Mia shared.

"Oh, I'm so sorry," Brea replied with raised eyebrows, unsure of what else to say.

"Mia, he's gay. I tried to tell you last year, but you wouldn't listen," Amanda said, shaking her head. Brea smiled and refocused on her photo album. She flipped through several more pages until reaching the section with pictures of her and Jaime at various parties and gatherings over the recent months. Brea settled on showing them a picture of her with Jaime after a lacrosse game.

"Shut up!" Mia said. "Brea, your boyfriend is freaking hot," she exclaimed.

Amanda grabbed the album out of Brea's hands for a closer look. "Oh yeah, totally," Amanda agreed. She flipped through the pages to survey the other photos.

Amanda's eyes widened as she pointed to Hayden in a group picture. "Holy shit—who is this? He's sexy."

"That's Hayden, one of my—friends," she replied, attempting to answer nonchalantly. She had inflected the word "friends" and hoped that Mia and Amanda had failed to notice.

"Brea, can we move to Black Harbor and go to your school? These boys are hot," Mia cried out again in disbelief. Laughing, Brea took the photo album from Amanda and tucked it into her bag.

Brea did not plan on discussing anything about the mess she was in with Jaime and Hayden. She changed the topic, hoping the conversation and the questions ended there. "Is anyone thirsty? I could use a soda or something."

"Sure, let's find the vending machines," Mia replied.

Amanda and Mia quickly unpacked their bags before they headed out to explore the hotel. Later that evening, there would be an orientation in the conference room to meet the advisors and other program participants, leaving the girls several hours of free time.

Evidently boy-crazy, Mia was especially eager to scope out the boys. Brea smiled to herself and rubbed her temples as the girls strolled and Mia listed her requirements for a boyfriend. Brea refused to consider talking to another boy unless it centered on writing. For the next week, she would pretend the opposite sex did not exist.

At seven o'clock, forty-eight participants found themselves seated in a large conference room divided among tables of groups of six with a group mentor. Sherilyn led the orientation with an overview of the courses, breakout sessions, special projects, and various activities available to all the participants over the week.

"Kids, if you are interested in any activities when you are not in breakouts, workshops, or mentorship, please check out our activities schedule in the program folder you received at check-in. We have morning yoga, guided meditations, pool activities, movie nights, and so much more," Sherilyn boasted into the microphone. Next, she reviewed some of the general goals of this program. In summation, the most important ones being to show respect for your fellow writers, critique with purpose, take part with enthusiasm, and begin your personal journey to free yourself from whatever holds you back from your unique creative voice.

Brea's group comprised an equal number of boys and girls. Her mentor's name was Audrey, a thin, raven-haired college junior from Columbia University, dressed in a stretchy black bodysuit underneath a pale-blue Japanese floral kimono robe. Everything about her radiated hip. She had a small tattoo of a turtle on her wrist and wore her thick, lush hair piled on top of her head with a pencil sticking out. Audrey was the type of woman who could have been a muse for a Picasso or Matisse painting if she had been born earlier in the twentieth century, with her straight, narrow nose, dark eyebrows, and full, rosy lips.

"Hello fellow young writers," Audrey addressed the group.

"My name is Audrey. I'm an English major at Columbia, and for the past two summers I have volunteered as an advisor and mentor for this annual youth writer's program. The written word serves to further humanity as we record history and learn from our mistakes, attempt to capture what it means to be human, inspire ingenuity, foster imagination, and feed the souls of others. The lifeblood of authorship lies within you all, the next generation of writers with your novel and authentic voices."

A boy seated beside Brea whispered under his breath, "What is this, the Super Bowl?" Brea smiled—Audrey's introduction had moved her. For a twenty-one-year-old college student, she appeared far older than her years—wise, intelligent, confident, and articulate. Going around in a circle, Audrey asked everyone to introduce themselves. Her group included students from all over the country and interested in various genres of writing—fiction, screenwriting, playwriting, and journalism.

"Our first task tonight, and perhaps the most important one, is to come up with a group name. This is a big deal, so let's take our time here," Audrey announced with a sly smile. An animated discussion and raucous laughter followed as they threw out one ridiculous group name after another.

"Balzac's Balls."

"Hard Dickens."

"Hymen-g-way."

Every few minutes, the group exploded in obnoxious laughter, becoming so disruptive that Sherilyn had to scold them to quiet down. "Wow, you guys are going to be a fun group. You'll all be writing porn one day to be sure," Audrey exclaimed as she wiped away tears from her eyes after having had a good laugh.

Once the group settled down, they brainstormed a serious list of names. The group agreed on "Predilection for Fiction." Audrey gave the group a thumbs up with enthusiasm and moved onto the next order of business, to select at random their final group project, named "The Final Draft." Audrey explained the rules. Together, the team would write a collective project—a short play, movie scene, collection of poems, or a short story—then recite or perform it before the entire program on the final night.

Brea had the honor of choosing the genre out of the box for the group. Shutting her eyes, she inserted her hand into the box and plucked out a small folded piece of paper. Clearing her throat, Brea read out the assignment. "Write an anthology of poetry or an epic poem based on the following theme—family, love and pain." Several members of the group groaned, having hoped for a short play or a creative short story. Audrey refocused them with a pep talk, reminding them that sometimes the shortest prose could be the most powerful.

After some debate, the group settled on each participant writing an individual poem rather than a group epic poem. They postponed further discussion until their first group breakout in the morning. Audrey shared how impressed she had been with her group's enthusiasm, then released everyone for the night.

Brea joined Mia and Amanda, waiting for her at the entrance. Amanda's group had selected a short screenplay, to the envy of Mia, as they both planned on becoming screenwriters. Mia's group would write a short story, and already she had several romance-themed ideas to share in her morning breakout group.

In the days that followed, Brea woke for beach meditation at seven in the morning. Sitting on a yoga mat facing the ocean, Brea would surrender herself to guided meditations. The warmth and light of the rising morning sun on her face felt as gentle as a soft kiss. She allowed her mind to empty itself of fear, desires, judgements, and inhibitions. Her thoughts would jump from one to another, and Brea sent them away like ripples from a dropped pebble into a body of water until her mind emptied. Never had she known such a contented peace.

Brea had no trouble burying her guilt and thoughts of Jaime and Hayden after a few days in the program. Her mind was centered and stimulated with like-minded people. Life there was simple—dress comfortably, eat, and let your mind wander or focus on creating something deep and meaningful for yourself and others.

As Brea had suspected, Audrey turned out to be one of the most extraordinary people Brea had met—grounded, observant, unique, and thoughtful. She was herself through and through. After several mentorship sessions with Audrey, Brea wondered if she had sold a bit of her soul to be Jaime's girlfriend. Her life at Harvey Slate had been the metamorphosis Brea had always desired, though contingent on being with Jaime and concealing the dynamics of her family, her pain, and insecurities. If anyone knew her true self, would they continue to respect her or ridicule her?

Beyond daily meditation, she found the food to be the most exceptional part of the program. Her favorite being the hot breakfast buffet. Never had Brea been privy to such an expansive offering of all you can eat meals. While there were some variations on the daily menu, Brea would walk into the conference room welcomed with hot platters of French toast, pancakes, eggs, bacon, sausages and assortments of bagels, pastries, fresh fruit, yogurts, and juices. Lunches and dinners rotated among pasta bars, Asian dishes, hot sandwiches, pizza, roasted chicken, steaks, and pork chops served with roasted or mashed potatoes, steamed vegetables glazed in sauces, and a large salad bar.

Amanda and Mia would stare at Brea's plate, piled high with food, in disbelief. "*Where do you pack it away?*" and "*Don't your parents feed you at home?*" they would ask with wide eyes, eyeing Brea's slim figure. Brea, embarrassed, would smile and continue eating. After she ate, the fullness wrapped around her like a warm hug.

On Wednesday afternoon, Brea joined Audrey in the media library for her mentorship session. Entering the room, Brea spotted Audrey seated in an oversized black leather armchair with her bare feet propped up on a matching ottoman. Wearing red overalls over a black halter top and her hair covered under a silk scarf, Brea made a note to herself to copy her outfit. On

Audrey's lap sat a thick black-and-white notebook with pink and yellow square notes peeking out from the edges, clips, and sheets of notes jammed in between the pages. Looking up and smiling at Brea, Audrey gestured for her to take a seat in the armchair across from her.

"Hi Brea. I hope you are doing well. I bet you went to morning meditation," Audrey started off.

"Yes, it's been incredible. I'm going to make sure I keep it up when I'm back home in a few days."

"Good. Let's start off with your poem for The Final Draft."

Brea cleared her throat as she pulled out her copy written on a lined notebook page. Her fingers trembled, hoping to impress Audrey.

Audrey closed her eyes as she listened to Brea recite the poem, concentrating on her words and tipping her head from one shoulder to the other. When Brea finished, Audrey opened her eyes and paused before speaking.

"How's it going so far, Brea?"

Brea blinked several times in confusion, uncertain what Audrey meant by her question. "Do you mean with this poem—what I think about it?"

"No, the program. How's it going for you overall?" Audrey clarified. Brea nodded as her eyes darted around the room, attempting to come up with something intelligent rather than banal to comment on.

"Great. I just came from that character development workshop, and I think the tips for creating a strong backstory were helpful."

"Right," Audrey replied, disappointed with Brea's answer. Removing her legs from the ottoman, she pushed it away, then planted her feet onto the floor and looked into Brea's eyes. Brea shifted in her seat and folded up her draft—she placed the paper on her lap with two fingers as though she held a soiled rag.

"Brea. What has struck you the most being here—something about you, how you are feeling?" Audrey asked, looking deep into Brea's eyes.

Brea released a tense chuckle. "This will sound stupid, but it's the truth—the food."

"If it's your truth, so be it. Tell me why?"

"Because I've never eaten so much in my life," Brea answered with a shrug, looking down at her lap.

"Close your eyes. Tell me more."

Brea complied, closed her eyes and took a moment to clear her mind before she spoke.

"When I walk into the dining room for every meal, I know that when I leave, I won't feel empty. And it never disappoints me. The food welcomes me with kindness, and it says, you can have whatever and everything you want—and I'll fill you up. There is—abundance and warmth. Someone stacks and layers the rolls and pastries on wooden trays in circles, not just to feed me, but to send a message that I was worth the extra time to make it look beautiful. Even the butter is whipped and piped into little bowls just for me—not sitting half-melted in an old butter dish caked with burnt bread crumbs. This isn't food for survival. It's like a home. It's love. And I feel—so special."

Brea wiped her eyes, then opened them. Her cheeks felt hot, and she wanted to run out of the room.

"Brea, that was your voice. You, woven in with your words, your pain. That draft in your lap—the technique is excellent. Your teachers in school would praise it and perhaps read it out loud to the class, but it was missing you. Don't impress me with technique. Dig deep and pull it out of you. I think you should start over. And by the way—never be afraid to write about food. Shit, look what that did for Hemingway."

Brea laughed and composed herself after a deep breath. "What if what I have to say is too sad? I don't want to be the sad writer who walks into a river with stones in her pockets."

Audrey smiled at the reference to Virginia Woolf, then turned her head to gaze out the window for a moment. "Brea, let me tell you something. The saddest thing is when you try to be what or who you aren't. Look, what this program is about—I mean the workshops are great, but this experience is to remove yourself from your daily life and focus on your internal world. You need to tap into what is deep inside of you to help you tell your stories to the world—even if they are somber." Audrey sat back in her chair and tapped her notebook with her fingers.

Brea meditated on Audrey's words. What she said to Brea echoed her own voice, deep inside of her, that she tried to ignore—she was not living as her true self. Every day she presented herself on campus at Harvey Slate, to Jaime, or attended a house party, she morphed into a character version of herself she thought she needed to be. If she was agreeable, accommodating, charming, and untroubled, then she would never be *"Boring Brea"* again. But at what cost?

Interrupting her thoughts, Audrey continued. "Brea, let me share something difficult to write I've been working on. I'd like for you to share your impressions when I'm finished reading it to you." Brea slipped off her sneakers and grabbed her pen and notebook, ready to focus on Audrey's words, having learned more from her in fifteen minutes than in years of school.

Chapter Twenty-Two

The Present

Amber streaks of light peeked under my door
Tip toe down the hall, one foot another led
Mama in the kitchen, scratches on the floor
She said it is time, my apron, time to bake the bread
Unhappy child, my mama hurt me so
Not from her hand, her silence was the dough
Years ago, a choice was made; there is little here to save
And you will never fit here, girl, unless you're well behaved
I am so hungry, Mama, if only you could shake
Seeds of tenderness, I too could grow like bread
She looked away and deeply sighed
No tears, my mamas mad
So, I learned to smile instead.

Brea read the poem she had written twenty-one years ago for
The Final Draft several times before returning it to the scrap-
book where it lived, protected by a thin plastic sheet.

Did she understand the depth of what she had written at that
age? As she read it now, it broke her heart. Having her own

children, the effort to be present and consistent was challenging, no doubt, but she showed up every day, no matter the mistakes she made or how exhausted she felt. Her children's moods sometimes confused and frightened her, but she committed to loving and supporting them, even when she felt lost.

In contrast, her mother had only accepted compliance, silence, and had been incapable of affection or tolerating any of Brea's emotional needs. Neither could her father. He coped with life and the uncertainty of raising a child by withdrawing behind the television and drinking beer.

On the floor of her bedroom, Brea sat with her legs crossed and a wool blanket over her shoulders. Seeing Hayden had triggered a flood of memories impossible to halt. Lost in her mind, it had been difficult to focus on the drive home, and walking in the door, Brea mumbled to Tina that she felt unwell and needed to rest. Tina fussed over Brea, seeing the state she was in—aloof and disheveled. She offered to stay late to prepare Sophie and Alex's dinner, give them baths, and then put them to sleep. Brea had gratefully accepted, walked into her bedroom, and locked the door.

Her eyes fixed on a picture of her holding Alex the day after he had been born. Fat, angry tears trickled down her cheeks, and she did not bother to wipe them. With the air trapped in her chest, she sobbed at the realization she had betrayed herself as a young girl. Instead of recognizing and dealing with her pain, she had locked the wounded girl inside a box and buried her deep down, believing that if she ignored her and created a perfect life, she would achieve happiness. Brea had made this mistake twice in her life and, now that Hayden had unlocked the door, she could no longer ignore the young girl's pleas to be heard.

An idea came to her, the one thing she could think of in the moment to see her way through—write. Picking herself up off the floor, Brea walked to her desk, opened the drawer, and took out a pen and a pad of paper. The last time she had written anything meaningful had been in college. She had stopped writing to stuff down her sadness along with the darkest pieces of her past she had wanted to hide from.

So many years had passed, and she wondered if she could liberate that part of herself. It lay dormant, buried deep within her mind, in a dark, dusty room with a dirty window blocking the light. Brea closed her eyes. She imagined this empty room with white walls and a wood floor where black typed words floated in the air like dust particles. A white streak of light appeared through a small clean patch on the dirty window, illuminating a spot on the dusty floor.

Brea walked to the window and, with the edge of her sleeve, wiped away a large circle of grime. Leaning over, she looked through the clearing. Straining her eyes, she saw the ocean—it was Black Harbor. She needed to keep going back.

Picking up the pen, Brea shook it and tested it. A small scribble of black ink appeared on the page—and then the words flowed like her memories.

Chapter Twenty-Three

The Past

On Saturday, Brea and her father arrived home late in the afternoon. Her week had been a welcome break from Black Harbor, and she returned with a new level of confidence in her writing. Audrey and her peers had proclaimed the poem she had written for The Final Draft as "*bitterly beautiful*," "*raw,*" and "*honest.*" Brea did not write it with perfect technique, but it was her truth.

Placing her bags on the floor of her bedroom, Brea fixed her eyes on her phone and contemplated whether to call Jaime. He had arrived home the day before, but she hesitated if she felt ready to contact him. It had been a gift to be without the weight of Jaime, Hayden, and Harvey Slate tied around her neck throughout the week.

Brea wiped her forehead and stepped out of her shorts, mourning the loss of the air conditioning at the hotel. Lowering herself to the floor, she switched on her fan, and stared at the delicate floral-patterned wallpaper. A realization dawned on her—the key difference between Hayden and Jaime.

She cared for Jaime, and he adored Brea, though unlike with Hayden, their relationship lacked a deeper emotional connection. With Hayden she could say what she thought, bring him into her dusty garage where she hid from the world and give him a tour without shame. Her tears did not bother him—he wiped them away with his fingers without judgement. Jaime, in contrast, harbored a more externally focused nature, and wanted Brea to stay with him in a place of exuberance and enthusiasm—she only felt comfortable being what she thought he wanted her to be.

Shaking her head, Brea did not know what to do with this realization. It did not change the fact that she had betrayed Jaime and that being with Hayden would not be possible without dire upheaval and certain retaliation. She unpacked her bags, settling on having one more night to herself, and would call Jaime in the morning.

Descending the steps to the ground floor, she walked into the kitchen to put on the kettle for a cup of tea. As she lit the stove, she heard her mother's footsteps on the creaky wooden floor in the dining room. Brea braced herself, unknowing what kind of mood her mother would be in.

Dressed in her nightgown and clutching a book on watercolor painting against her chest, she greeted Brea upon entering the kitchen. "How was the drive? You arrived home later than I thought you would," her mother asked as she pulled out a chair at the table and sat down.

"The drive was fine. We had a late start after the farewell lunch. I took my time saying goodbye to the advisors and the friends I made."

"Are you hungry? There is some chicken and spaghetti in the refrigerator?"

"No thanks, maybe later. I'll have some tea for now." Brea eyed her mother. She appeared to be in a neutral mood and calm. "Mom, do you want to hear about the program? It was amazing."

Her mother inhaled and stared at the wall in front of her with a vacant expression. "All right," she replied, her lips curving into a small smile.

Brea's eyes brightened as she pulled out the chair opposite her mother. "I don't know where to start. Well, the best part was working with my mentor, Audrey. She is the type of writer I want to be—comfortable with who she is, confident, brilliant, and she thinks I have a lot of potential. There were group meditations on the beach every morning that—"

She paused, seeing her mother's eyes blank with no apparent comprehension of Brea's words. "Mom?"

Her mother blinked as though waking from a trance. "Sounds wonderful. I'm glad you're home." Picking up her book, her mother stood to leave the kitchen. "I'm going to sleep. I'll see you in the morning."

Brea nodded and closed her eyes, frustrated with her naive hope that her mother would be interested in her life. The kettle whistled, and Brea fixed her tea, meanwhile scolding herself for her feelings of disappointment and resentment. When would she learn her mother would not change?

The familiar cold emptiness of her home swept over her as she climbed the stairs to return to her bedroom, reminding her that without Jaime and her circle of friends at Harvey Slate, she would be alone. Brea regretted not calling him. She wished he had picked her up, taken her out, and told her how beautiful she was as he held her in his arms.

Though she believed she did not deserve Jaime's love after betraying him, she was now resolved to do everything necessary to keep him. The alternative, being alone, would be too painful to consider.

The following morning at eight-thirty, Brea called Allegra to tell her she had returned home, knowing she would be awake earlier than Jaime. Excited they had the chance to see one another after almost a month apart, Allegra invited Brea to come over for lunch. Brea accepted, then read for an hour in bed until she figured Jaime would be awake. Jaime picked up the phone after five rings, half-asleep, and perked up hearing Brea's voice.

"B, I missed you. Can I pick you up in an hour and we'll go to the beach?"

Brea hesitated before answering—she knew she had made a mistake. Jaime would find it insulting that not only had she called Allegra first but would also have lunch with her before seeing him.

"Sorry, I promised Allegra I would have lunch with her. Could you pick me up at her place around one o'clock, or can we meet up tonight?"

Jaime scoffed. "B, I've been gone for five weeks and you called Allegra first?"

"I'm sorry. I missed you so much, and I can't wait to see you, but she's always up early, and I didn't want to wake you up. Should I call Allegra back and let her know I'll see her tomorrow instead?" Brea regretted backtracking. She should be able to stand up for herself and explain to him that her friendship with Allegra is as important to her as her relationship with Jaime.

"No, see her. I'll pick you up at her house at one. My parents are gone for the day, so we can come back here and figure out what we're going to do tonight."

"I'm sorry, Jaime. I'll see you soon, bye."

"Bye." Jaime hung up, his tone of voice unsettling. Brea hung up the phone, worried she had made a mammoth error and that this would cause another fight with Jaime.

Sitting on the sofa at noon in Allegra's living room, Brea shared several of her poems while Allegra's mother fixed lunch. Figuring her poem from The Final Draft was too sad and personal, she had left it at home. Instead, she chose contemplative poems about meditation, friendship, and reflections on nature.

Brea apologized several times throughout lunch that she could only stay until one. Allegra's frown communicated her displeasure that Jaime had hijacked Brea from her once again. Allegra hesitated to express her irritation, worried it might strain their friendship, but she found it tiresome that he dominated Brea's free time.

At one o'clock, Brea stood outside Allegra's house waiting for Jaime, chewing her right thumbnail and shifting from side to side. Dressed in a simple pink cotton sundress, flip-flops, and with her hair in a bun, she worried Jaime might find her lack of effort to dress up for him as another insult. Her room had been hot throughout the night, affecting her ability to sleep well, and she had lacked the energy to put much effort into her appearance that morning.

Wiping the sweat off her forehead, she dried her hand on her dress as Jaime pulled up in front of Allegra's house and honked the horn. He did not step out to greet her, confirming his anger. Brea hastened her pace to the car and opened the door to climb inside. He turned to Brea with a tight smile.

"Hi," she said, forcing a bright smile on her face despite her unease, and leaned over to kiss him. He did not push Brea away, but his lips remained tight and stiff as she kissed him.

"Hi. How was Allegra?" he asked with a detached air.

Fastening her seatbelt, she replied. "Good. We had lunch and made plans for tomorrow morning to grab coffee. She was a little upset I couldn't spend a lot of time with her today."

Jaime shook his head and pressed his lips together. He hit the gas pedal with a heavy foot, and the car sped up rapidly. "Jaime," Brea cried out, startled. He eased up on the gas yet did not respond to Brea's cry of surprise. As they drove in silence, a knot appeared in Brea's stomach and her mind raced—she needed to apologize and beg for his forgiveness. It would be the only way to prevent a fight. If she could be humble, compliant, and demure, Jaime would forgive her.

Arriving at Jaime's expansive Mediterranean-style home, Brea followed Jaime in silence up the walkway to the side entrance. He unlocked the door and held it open for her with one arm. Brea passed through the vast kitchen and struggled to find the right words to earn Jaime's forgiveness as her eyes darted around the room from the exposed wooden ceiling beams to the walnut cabinets. Reaching the living room, she abruptly swiveled around to face him.

"Look, I'm sorry. I know you're mad at me. I missed you so much, and I'm so sorry I messed up. Please come here," Brea pleaded and held out her hand. Jaime lowered his eyes to the floor, contemplating whether he was ready to accept her apology.

"Please, Jaime. I'm sorry," Brea whispered near tears. Jaime exhaled and went to Brea. His facial expression softened as he wrapped his arms around her.

"Don't cry, B, I missed you too." Jaime squeezed Brea tight against his chest and she let out a sigh of relief.

"Let's go upstairs. I've been dreaming about you naked in my bed," he whispered into her ear. Brea smiled and kissed him. Jaime, reassured, removed the purse from her arm and tossed it onto a sofa. He took Brea's hand and led her up the stairs to his bedroom.

After sex, Jaime appeared to have forgotten the entire incident. As they lay in bed, he told Brea about his last days in Brazil spent with his older brother on a boating trip. Brea listened as she lay on Jaime's bare chest. Although not unpleasant, being intimate with Jaime had been more difficult than she had expected. His touch and taste were so different from Hayden's, and she felt waves of guilt wash over her during the act.

To connect with Jaime as they lay in bed, Brea attempted to share with him her experience writing her poem for The Final Draft. She gave up, noticing his interest waning, and never made it to her pivotal mentorship session with Audrey. Wondering if she should offer to share some of her writing with him, she held back. If he had been interested, he would have asked, and the fact he did not was hurtful.

Brea spent most of the week with Jaime at the beach and socializing with various Harvey Slate friends. Allegra, despite her growing annoyance, remained silent. Still, she did not hesitate to call Brea on Thursday morning with exciting news—to invite Brea to a black-tie hospital fundraising event at an estate in South Black Harbor on Saturday. Upon learning Jonathan could not attend the event, the Shays' close friends, who were hosting, invited Allegra to bring a guest.

"Brea, I don't care if Jaime proposes to you and wants to have your wedding on Saturday. You are coming with me, or we need an intervention about Jaime," Allegra insisted.

"Of course," Brea exclaimed. Allegra shared with Brea the details of the event—a cocktail reception, a live auction, a catered dinner, and a live band. "Wow, it sounds like it will be a Great Gatsby party," Brea commented.

"I love you so much I'm going to let that one slide even though it was so nerdy," Allegra replied through laughter.

"Ha ha. I have to go. Jaime is picking me up soon, so I have to take a shower."

Allegra sighed. "Sure, make sure Jaime takes you off your leash when you have to use the bathroom."

Brea's mouth dropped open. "Allegra, what's your problem?"

After clearing her throat, Allegra chuckled to diffuse the tension. "Nothing. Forget it. I'll see you on Saturday. Come to my house at two. We'll hang out and get ready together."

Brea agreed before she hung up the phone, then lay down on her floor, ill at ease with Allegra's remark about the leash. Perhaps Jaime absorbed much of her free time, though she reasoned Allegra did not understand the sacrifices needed to keep a boyfriend happy. Leaving her room to walk to the bathroom, Brea pushed Allegra's comment out of her mind. Jaime would arrive in an hour to pick her up to watch a movie at his house, then in the evening they planned to meet Tory and Trevor at a Tupa Bay coffee shop.

Since arriving home, she had little time to write and wished she could have a free day to ride her bike to the park and write in her journal. To her relief, however, she had fallen back into her familiar routine with Jaime and had not seen Hayden since her return to Black Harbor. His absence made it easier to pretend he was in the past, though escaping all thoughts of Hayden had not been entirely possible—she still thought of him when she lay awake in her bed at night.

The memory of Hayden's eyes looking into hers would invade her mind, and her heart would race. To steady it, she would press her hand to her chest, draw in a deep breath, and then whisper Jaime's name several times. With enough practice and patience, she hoped she could coach her brain to bury any thoughts of Hayden. Thus far, her attempts had been unsuccessful.

Chapter Twenty-Four

The Past

Saturday evening, Brea and the Shays arrived at a luxurious beach estate home for the charity gala. Several valet parking staff circled the car to open the doors for the ladies, and Brea stepped out of the car dressed in a champagne metallic column gown she had borrowed from Allegra. She wore her long hair waved in a twisted ponytail and a pair of understated gold teardrop earrings.

An abundance of lanterns and overhead lights cast an empyrean glow across the property, captivating Brea. Magnificent floral arrangements of white hydrangeas, peonies, and roses decorated the walkway.

"This is incredible," Brea whispered to Allegra, seeing servers in ivory dinner jackets holding polished silver trays with champagne filled crystal flutes at the top of the walkway. An usher escorted Brea and the Shays along a path around the house where the event was to take place. The weather had cooperated with the event coordinator, and the evening air was temperate and permeated with a faint scent of sea salt.

Reaching the vast backyard, they stepped onto an expansive stone patio spanning the length of the home. Two bars, each surrounded by a small crowd of guests awaiting their turn to order cocktails, sat at either end of the patio. Steps from the patio led down to an immense lawn with a colossal white party tent housing the band, dance floor, and dinner tables. A tent for the cocktail buffet sat opposite it. Similar to the front of the house, the lighting design included strung-up lights overhead and lanterns around the property. A white deck and steps led down to the beach at the property's end.

Mr. and Mrs. Shay soon split off from Allegra and Brea to mingle, leaving the girls to explore the party on their own. Allegra wore a strapless azure cocktail dress with a full tulle skirt, making the girls quite the pair as they descended the patio steps.

A server stopped before Allegra and Brea, holding a tray of champagne glasses. Hoping the server would not ask their age, they held their breaths and reached for a flute. The girls smiled at him as he nodded his head and continued on.

Brea grabbed Allegra's hand and pointed to the cocktail buffet in awe. From the tent ceiling, sky lanterns floated above two thirty-foot tables covered in ivory satin linens and draped with chiffon bunting. Atop the tables were numerous silver trays of sushi, charcuterie platters, and seafood towers piled high with crab, prawns, oysters, and lobster tails.

"Allegra, I have to be rich one day," Brea proclaimed under her breath. No further seduction was necessary—this life was better. Allegra grinned and laughed off Brea's comment as a joke, though she meant it, and a longing filled her. She believed it impossible that sadness could exist if one possessed all this opulence and beauty.

Scanning the crowd, Brea noted they were the youngest guests at the party until seeing a group of teenagers seated in a lounge area on the periphery of the property. A tall boy with wavy blonde hair dressed in a black tuxedo waved to Allegra and Brea.

"Allegra, do you know who that is?" Brea asked. Looking over her shoulder, Allegra turned her head in the direction Brea pointed to.

"That's Jacob," she replied, the corners of her mouth forming a slight smile.

"He's cute. Who is he?"

Flipping her hair over her shoulders, she turned back to Jacob and held up a finger to let him know she would be a minute. "He's the son of my dad's friend from college. He goes to Westgate Prep and will be a junior. We've sort of hung out over the years, but the last time I saw him was around two years ago. He's so much taller now."

"And cuter?" Brea teased. "Go talk to him."

Allegra sighed. "Sure, let's go."

"Not me—you! I'll keep myself busy and come join you soon." Allegra raised an eyebrow and turned to join Jacob and his friends.

Remembering the buffet, Brea swiveled around and strolled to the tent. Picking up a cocktail plate, she piled on prawns, fresh berries, and onion tart canapes. She enjoyed the savory tarts between bites of shrimp and popped the juicy berries into her mouth until her plate was empty. If she had not been in such an elegant society, she would have licked the salty brine off her plate—the food tasted that delicious.

Finishing the last of her champagne, Brea searched the crowd for another server with a champagne tray. Unable to find one, she felt bold enough to try her luck at the bar. Brea went to the patio, then hesitated, disheartened, to see sizeable crowds in front of each bar.

Her feet were already beginning to ache in her heels, and waiting in a long line would be torture. Changing her strategy, she spotted an empty high-top cocktail table. The hemline of Brea's dress was low enough that she could slip off her shoes and tuck them under the tablecloth without it being obvious she was barefoot. She bent down, bumping into someone passing by.

"Oh, excuse me, I'm so sorry," Brea apologized to a handsome gentleman appearing to be in his mid-twenties with dark-blonde hair and brown eyes. Taken aback by the sight of Brea, a beautiful young woman he had never met, he smiled in surprise.

"That's all right." Turning to the man at his side, he excused himself from their conversation and joined Brea at the table.

"Can I help you find something you dropped?" he offered as he set a tumbler of scotch on the table.

"No, thank you. My plan was to take my shoes off and give my feet a break," she confessed.

"Ah, got it. If you want to go for it again, I won't tell anyone. As long as you tell me your name and let me talk with you for a bit," he replied with a flirtatious grin. Dressed in a tuxedo and a black tie, rather than a bow tie, he appeared more casual, and his friendly demeanor was decidedly less stuffy compared to the older men at the party.

"Sure." Brea bent down to slip off her heels and kicked them under the tablecloth. "My name is Brea. I'm a friend of the Shays. I'm here freeloading." Brea smiled as the gentleman's eyes widened at her confession. There would be no point in attempting to appear as though she were a wealthy socialite who belonged at the party.

"Nice to meet you, Brea. I'm Marco. Can I offer you a drink? Anything you want, since you are—uh, freeloading off my parents, as you say," he replied, amused.

Brea's eyebrows raised. "Oh, sure, thank you. By the way, your home is beyond beautiful."

"Thanks, but it belongs to my parents, not me. So how old are you, Brea?"

"Sixteen."

"Oh wow, I would have guessed at least twenty or twenty-one. Now I legally can't hit on you," he declared after he let out a whistle.

Brea laughed. It was obvious he was not a creep, only straightforward and direct.

"Well, I also have a boyfriend, so I guess that's two strikes."

"Of course you do. If I had met you when I was in high school, I would have done anything to have you be my girlfriend." Brea rolled her eyes in jest and waved off his conjecture.

"So, Brea, what would you like to drink?" he offered.

"I'll have a glass of Champagne, thank you."

Holding up his hand, Marco caught the attention of a passing waiter. "A bottle of champagne for the table." The waiter nodded and hurried off.

"I can't drink an entire bottle of champagne by myself." She did not intend to offend him, but rather wished to avoid drinking too much and vomiting in front of Marco.

"I'll join you, and don't worry, I'm not trying to get you drunk. I have to say, I'm stunned. You don't look or carry yourself like a sixteen-year-old girl. You must be quite a young woman of the world."

Brea lowered her eyes, readying herself to disappoint him with her answer. "No, I'm not interesting at all. I've lived in Black Harbor with my parents my whole life. I haven't even been to Europe. Maybe it's all the reading and writing I spend most of my free time on."

"You're pretty tough on yourself, aren't you?" he asked, pausing as the waiter returned with a tall champagne bucket filled with ice, a bottle of champagne, and glasses. He presented the bottle to Marco for approval, then he popped the cork. After filling their glasses, he placed the bottle in the ice-bucket and with a nod, turned on his heels and disappeared into the crowd.

"So, tell me about your boyfriend, Brea." Marco held up his glass to Brea to salute her. She reciprocated his gesture and took a small sip, savoring the crisp, dry flavor of the champagne.

"His name is Jaime. He's handsome, outgoing, and he is—I don't know. We're kind of different. Sorry, I don't know if I want to talk about him. Things have become complicated with us." Brea shook her head and looked off into the distance at the tents on the lawn.

Marco took another sip. "I remember being your age and having my first girlfriend. I didn't know what I wanted. It was all hormones and attraction. You'll learn, make mistakes but—stay away from the bad ones," he advised, tipping his glass towards her.

"Are you a bad one?" Brea asked with a humorous tone of voice.

"Oh yeah, the worst," he teased.

"Why is that?" she asked, playing along.

Marco laughed. "No, seriously, I'm not at all. The truth is, I'm one of the boring types, but I still made my fair share of mistakes, chose the wrong girls, and broke a few hearts myself. That's what you do in high school."

Brea sighed. "I know all about making mistakes. It seems like I can't stop myself from making them lately," she admitted.

A brief smile crossed Marco's lips. "Finding yourself in a pile of shit happens. How you find your way out of it and what you do after is where you learn. What about your mother? Have you talked to her about it? I mean, what do your parents think about Jaime?" he inquired, reaching for the champagne bottle to top off their glasses.

"My parents don't know about Jaime, or if they do, they don't care. My parents are odd and not involved in my life. We live in the same house like ghosts. It's embarrassing, and I don't like to talk about it." Brea paused and looked away.

"So, you have to figure out how to dig your way out of all the piles of shit yourself?" he asked. Brea nodded to confirm the sad truth.

"That must be hard. See, my parents were the opposite. They were involved in everything I did. If my mom could have brushed my teeth for me until I was eighteen, I think she would have. By the time I was in my last year of high school, I couldn't leave fast enough. I only applied to schools that were at least a thousand miles away from home, and after I received my acceptance letter to Stanford—I left as soon as I could after graduation. It was the best day of my life, even though I know my parents only wanted the best for me. I can't imagine what it would have been like to live with cold indifference. That sounds lonely."

"Lonely—that summarizes it nicely." Brea averted her eyes from Marco and pressed her lips together, hoping to change the subject. Marco received Brea's subtle message that this was not a topic she wished to further discuss.

"You mentioned writing before? I can see that. I am picking up on a creative deep vibe from you as though you have something important to say about this world. And you are—drop dead gorgeous." Brea scoffed and turned her head, uncomfortable with the compliment.

"No, no, not like that. Go with me here. I'm inspired to act brotherly, so listen to me, if my advice is worth anything. There are going to be a lot of guys out there who will want something from you. Be careful. They may not care about treating you well and might try to make you feel special to get something from you. Boring guys like me aren't so bad when you're my age."

A slight frown formed on Brea's face. Marco appeared to be sincere, but the last thing she wanted to hear was a condescending warning she needed to *"be careful."*

"What about you, Marco? What do you do for a living?"

"I am starting my last year of medical school at Stanford in the fall. The plan is to match into a hematology-oncology residency program. Maybe even work towards a PhD, but I'll see how it goes."

"Wow, that is incredible and not boring at all!"

"I don't always remember that, so yes, thank you. Look, I've enjoyed talking with you, but I promised my parents I would walk around and meet some people. I wish you luck, Brea, and if our paths cross again in the future, I will look forward to it." Taking her hand in his, he kissed it and with a grin turned to walk away. She had to give it to him—the man had charm for a *"boring guy."*

Brea scanned the party. She spotted Allegra and Jacob seated beside one another on a striped patio loveseat in the lounge area, engrossed in conversation. Brea, once again hungry and bordering on intoxicated, slipped into her heels and left the bottle of champagne behind. She walked down the patio steps and then across the lawn, to rejoin Allegra.

"Well, hello," Brea said with a grin on her face as she approached her friend. Jacob stood to greet Brea as Allegra introduced them. His interest in Allegra was obvious, seeing the manner in which he smiled and fixed his eyes on her. When the chimes rang, calling the guests to dinner, Jacob asked Allegra if he could find her afterwards for a dance.

"Sure, of course," she replied and her cheeks flushed. Jacob excused himself and left to find his parents.

"You seemed to have a lot of fun with Jacob," Brea commented, giving Allegra a gentle nudge with her elbow as they turned to walk side by side to the dinner tent.

"He's hilarious. We talked, and maybe I'm crushing on him now," Allegra confessed with a coquettish smile. They entered the tent and took their seats across from Allegra's parents.

After dinner, they spent the rest of the night dancing and talking with Jacob. At one point, Brea glimpsed Marco on the edge of the dance floor and waved to him. He raised his glass with a nod and pointed to her bare feet with a thumbs up. Brea laughed and thought to herself, if a boring guy like Marco could offer her a life like this one, it would be a good one.

⋇

At eleven-thirty, the Shays slowed to a stop in front of Brea's home. Jaime, seated on the porch steps, sat up straighter seeing the car pull up.

"Everything all right, honey? You want us to stay?" Mrs. Shay asked with furrowed eyebrows.

Brea opened the door and replied, "No, it's fine. Jaime probably came by to talk to me about plans for tomorrow or something. Good night. And thank you again for inviting me to join you tonight. It was amazing." Brea smiled to reassure Mrs. Shay before exiting the car.

The Shays drove off as Brea stepped onto the sidewalk and stood fixed in place, observing the manner in which Jaime glared at her with a hard expression.

"Jaime, what are you doing here?"

Jaime rose from the steps in silence. As Jaime walked slowly to Brea, she felt her heart race. Before reaching her, he turned his head and took a deep breath.

"Is it true? I really hope it isn't true, B. Did you have sex with Hayden?"

Brea resisted the urge to close her eyes. Her throat tightened and the muscles in her neck and shoulders tensed. "No, Jaime."

He took a step closer, staring into her eyes to decipher whether she was telling the truth.

"Aaron pulled me aside tonight at the beach. He told me that you and Hayden went missing from his party while I was in Brazil. He noticed your messed-up hair and makeup when you came from the side of the house onto the patio. Then he saw Hayden come out of the house a minute later, and that made him suspicious."

Brea averted her eyes from Jaime's. Her selfishness prevented her from telling Jaime the truth. She did not want to hurt him, but more than that, she was terrified of losing him and being alone. "No, we didn't have sex. It was so hot that night that I needed to cool off in the bathroom. Then I got lost trying to find my way back to the patio." Brea's voice shook, and her fingers trembled.

Jaime's head dropped, and he rubbed his eyes before looking at her again. "B, I don't believe you. I want to—but you won't look me in the eye. Being honest with me and being able to trust you—those are the most important things." Brea met Jaime's eyes again. The mixture of pain and distrust behind them was unmistakable. She looked away and fixed her eyes on the ground, unable to speak.

Jaime gave her ample time to respond, but she could not conjure a convincing reason for him to believe her. He shook his head and exhaled. "This is the second time I've had to question you about another guy. Brea, I can't do this again. As much as it kills me, I'm done." He tilted his head back to look into the sky and closed his eyes.

Brea's voice caught in her throat. Squeezing her eyes shut, she briefly covered her face with her hands. "No, Jaime, please," she begged and took several steps towards him. Jaime held up his hand to stop her.

"Out of respect, I will not repeat any rumors, and I asked Aaron not to say anything to anyone else." Brea sucked in a deep breath, frozen where she stood. Jaime turned away, then quickened his pace to his car. Pausing a moment, he placed his hands on the roof. His distress was obvious despite his resolve. In an abrupt motion, he ripped open the door, climbed inside, and drove off without looking back at Brea.

It was over, and the weight of her guilt for having betrayed Jaime and lying like a coward pulled her down into an infinite depth of self-loathing—she would suffer the consequences she deserved. No amount of pleading would save her, and there would be no reconciliation this time.

Brea forced herself to move one foot in front of the other to her porch. To her surprise, she did not cry as she climbed the steps to unlock the door. The keys were in her hand, though she had no memory of taking them out of her purse. After stepping inside, she shut the door and stumbled into the living room where she sat on the couch and stared into the darkness. Eventually she fell asleep, and when she woke at dawn, still in her dress, she sat up and remembered what had happened. Jaime ending their relationship had not been a dream—she was alone again, and there was no one to blame other than herself.

Chapter Twenty-Five

The Present

Brea sat on the stool at the Brine sales counter with her eyes fixed on the door. When someone entered, she held her breath, convinced it would be Hayden. It was near impossible to focus, and she often fumbled over her words as she greeted customers or answered questions.

At noon, the store emptied of customers, and Brea's head ached. Leaning against the counter, she massaged her forehead, increasing the depth and pressure over time to rub away the tension. Her mind felt empty, and her body numb. Brea stared at the counter, unaware of the minutes passing as she continued to rub her temples in vain. As though a bell chimed, she snapped back into the present with a desperate urgency to leave the store. Bolting to the door before another customer could enter, she locked it and placed the "Closed" sign on the hook.

An irrational thought appeared in her mind. What if she were having a breakdown? Perhaps yesterday's encounter with Hayden was a prolonged hallucination? "Stop it, Brea, you are fine. You're not losing it," she told herself.

Reaching the office door, another frightening thought halted her steps—is that not what her mother had believed—that she did not have mental health problems? Years ago with her thera-pist, Brea had pieced together that her mother had a mental ill-ness, which she had no insight into or acceptance of. Racing to the mirror, Brea braced herself in the event she saw her mother's reflection staring back at her.

With a tremulous exhale, she lifted her eyes and Brea saw her own reflection. She dropped her face in her hands and inhaled several slow, controlled breaths. It was real. Hayden had been there, and her mind had unleashed a storm of memories she had buried for decades. Naturally, she felt overwhelmed by the flood of emotions. After all, that was why she had locked it all away—to avoid feeling anything, and now her bill had come due.

Grabbing her purse, she shut down the computer and switched off the lights. She needed alcohol. Brea drove fast and recklessly, searching for a place where she could have a drink. One mile up the coast highway, she spotted Oceanus, a beach-front restaurant where she and Hannah had celebrated Brine's one-year anniversary.

Entering the restaurant, Brea informed the hostess she would only need a seat at the bar. She lowered the sunglasses sitting on her head to cover her eyes as the large windows, white walls, and light oak flooring made the brightness intolerable. Pulling out the first empty chair she came upon, she sat down and scanned the cocktail menu. Brea nodded to the young female bartender dressed in a white tuxedo shirt and a black vest to attract her attention. With a warm smile, she walked over to greet Brea.

"I'll have a mojito and a glass of water." Brea rummaged through her purse to find a pain reliever. She sighed with relief at finding her travel-sized bottle of ibuprofen. Taking out two pills, she placed them on the bar and waited for the bartender to serve her drinks.

"Would you like to open a tab?" the bartender asked with a polite smile when she returned and set down Brea's drinks. Brea dropped the pills on her tongue and swallowed them down with a large gulp of water. She nodded, reached into her wallet, and handed her a credit card.

"Could you make me a Grey Goose over ice when I'm done with this?" Brea dismissed the bartender's reaction, noticing her eyebrows knit together and blink twice before she nodded and turned to walk to the register. The bartender likely believed her to be an alcoholic, surly and desperate to chase away a hangover or withdrawals, though she cared little.

Brea caught sight of herself in the mirror behind the bar—she looked terrible. Lifting her sunglasses, she studied her reflection, seeing her hair limp, unwashed, and her complexion pale, having only applied minimal makeup that morning. Placing her sunglasses once again over her eyes, she picked up her drink, grateful at least she had worn a clean gray sundress and had applied deodorant before leaving the house that morning.

Drinking half her mojito in one shot, she sat back in her chair and massaged her neck. In ten minutes, she would no longer care about her appearance once the alcohol made its way into her bloodstream. She swirled her drink in her glass and chuckled—if alcohol was a poor coping mechanism, so be it for today. Right now, it was a life vest she needed to cling to so she would not drown. "Fuck the experts," Brea muttered to herself, repeating a variation of what Hayden had said the day before.

Brea scanned the restaurant, glimpsing the cheerful couples and business colleagues enjoying the ambience and elegant dishes placed before them. They sat content and calm, and Brea's distress and loneliness felt that much more palpable.

Shifting her focus to the windows, she watched people strolling on the beach as they enjoyed the mild weather and sunshine. Her gaze moved beyond them, and settled on the ocean. It hypnotized her as she watched the waves crashing onto the shore, then pulling back into the ocean in illimitable repetition.

The bartender, seeing Brea near finished with her first drink, placed the vodka rocks in front of her. Drinking down the last of the mojito, she pushed the glass away from her to the opposite edge of the bar, and then picked up her second drink.

Brea contemplated the mysterious nature of the mind as she watched a young couple laughing on the other end of the bar. It baffled her how so many years had passed since Harvey Slate, yet her mind, so powerful, could summon the emotions, sounds, and sensations she had experienced over twenty years ago—they were as clear and true as if she had been reliving the past.

A truth she could not deny struck her. Brea could stay busy, work, take care of her children and pretend her past was irrelevant, yet it lived in her, stored in her bones, and most unsettling were the memories of Hayden and how much he had meant to her. Brea shook her head and shut her eyes. "Impossible, it's crazy," she whispered to herself. She could never do what Hayden asked. "Impossible," she repeated and sipped her drink.

Stopping herself at two drinks, Brea paid and left the restaurant, then walked along the beach to clear her head before driving home. Compared to earlier, her nerves had steadied, but her sadness clung to her like a wet sheet, refusing to relinquish the hold it had over her.

Hayden told her she needed to go back and remember all of it, as if she had a choice now. She could not shut the door of her mind even if she tried. Although wanting to blame Hayden for triggering her distress, she could no longer deny he spoke the truth—her pain, she had enshrouded under a character version of herself created for Adam, as she had done with Jaime.

Years ago, Hayden saw behind the mask she wore at Harvey Slate—he knew her true self. And remembering Hayden's tenderness only amplified her confusion because she now recognized that beneath the memory of their last night together, she had buried their entire relationship. He claimed she was missing pieces of the story, but she questioned if what he had to tell her would truly change anything in the present.

As she seated herself on the sand, Brea ceased to resist and allowed her mind to continue walking backwards in time. Could she find something in her memories that would make her consider going on this journey of understanding and forgiveness with Hayden, and, if she did, could it help her? If she did nothing, Brea feared her desolation, like the waves of the ocean, would crash into her conscious mind, only to recede into a cycle of endless perpetuity.

Chapter
Twenty-Six

The Past

In October, two months after Jaime ended their relationship, Brea found their paths rarely crossed at Harvey Slate, though not entirely by coincidence. Brea stopped attending parties and, to avoid him at school, she cleverly steered clear of idling in the courtyard and cafeteria, and took an alternative route to the bus parking lot. Neither of them disclosed the reason for their breakup, and while there were rumors that Brea was a prude or Jamie had lost interest, they soon faded after the first month of school.

Several days after the breakup, Hayden called Brea to check on her as news of their split had circulated. He informed her that though Jaime had not confronted him about Brea, Aaron did. Hayden lied, denying anything happened between them. Although painful, she told Hayden she needed some time alone, and that when ready to talk to him, she would let him know. Hayden respected her wishes, and neither called nor attempted to speak to her at school.

When Brea missed Hayden, she would remind herself that caution dictated they keep their distance from one another. The hopeless reality, more than ever, remained that a genuine and open romantic relationship between them was impossible—it would only confirm Aaron's story as truth to Jaime, and Vienna would orchestrate a brutal campaign of retaliation against her. When Vienna saw Brea at school, she would either ignore her or flash an arrogant smile, pleased that Brea no longer had Jaime and had withdrawn into the social outskirts of Harvey Slate.

During the afternoons or on the weekends, Brea often kept to herself, going for long walks, studying, writing at the park, or riding her bike to the public library, though she was fortunate to still have her girlfriends. Tory and Anjali had called her after the breakup, reassuring her that although she and Jaime had broken up, they were her friends and would remain so. Trevor and Aaron, for obvious reasons, remained loyal to Jaime, so while as a group they would not socialize together, the girls would invite Brea out for shopping or for girls-only nights out. And she still had Allegra, though she was dating Jacob and often occupied with cheerleading practice or games.

The weather had shifted to the cool autumn climate typical of Black Harbor, and in the midmorning, a rainstorm arrived without warning. Though the janitors worked with swift determination to dry the slick floors, puddles of grimy grey water from umbrellas and soggy shoes collected in the halls of the Harvey Slate buildings.

Having worn brand new ballet flats with smooth, polished soles that day to school, Brea fretted she would slip, and as a result, took extra caution to take her steps at a slow pace. Having left her sweater at home that morning, the air, cold and heavy, gave Brea a chill dressed in her navy skirt and a white blouse. Crossing her arms across her chest, she made an effort to warm herself as she drifted through the hallway.

Brea worried she would be late for pre-calculus, her least favorite class that year, having ambled down the halls with sluggish footsteps and lingered at her locker in search of her graphing calculator. She had the misfortune of being stuck with the most unpleasant teacher Brea had known, Mr. Wortherman.

He delighted in torturing and witnessing the sight of his students squirming in their chairs as he taught at a relentless pace. The energy in the classroom, fraught with tension, piled on additional layers of anxiety as the students wrote frantic notes and devoted every ounce of mental energy to keep up with the lesson. The halls were nearly empty and Brea groaned, needing to use the restroom and ensuring she would be late.

She hastened her steps to the stairwell, nearly slipping as she reached the bottom of the staircase, though she managed to grab onto the rail in time to steady herself. Looking up, she froze in place seeing Hayden, dressed in a gray Harvey Slate sweater over a white dress shirt and navy slacks, at the top of the staircase. He raised his eyebrows with a slight smile, showing he had been waiting for her to appear. Brea could not suppress the wistful smile spreading on her lips at the sight of him.

Neither spoke as she climbed the steps, taking her time, one by one. Reaching the top, Hayden whispered, "Follow me." Brea looked up and down the length of the hallway, ensuring they were unwitnessed entering the empty classroom he led her to.

"Hi. How are you?" Hayden asked.

"Late—and I have to use the bathroom," Brea replied as she rubbed her forehead, regretting having shared the bit about needing to use the bathroom.

"This won't take long." Hayden smiled, perceiving Brea's embarrassment.

"How did you know where to find me?"

"I'm resourceful. I have my ways." Brea cocked her head to the side with wide eyes. Hayden chuckled. "I asked Ms. Irene for your schedule this morning—she loves me. I told her I needed to find you because I found your American history paper, and it was critical that I hand deliver it to you."

Brea let out a light laugh. "So, what did you want to talk about? I need to get to class."

Hayden rubbed his mouth. "I know you said you needed space, but I wanted to talk to you and see how you've been doing. You're kind of like a ghost now. But I suppose that's what you wanted, I mean, with everything that's happened." Hayden rambled in an uncharacteristic manner.

Hearing the chimes signal the start of class, Brea shut her eyes and clicked her tongue against the roof of her mouth. "Well, I'm late for pre-calculus with Mr. Wortherman. I have to go and face my humiliation." As she turned to take a step towards the door, Hayden moved in front of her to prevent her from leaving.

"Wait. Could we talk after school or this weekend?" he asked with a hopeful expression on his face.

"Hayden, I don't know. That could be a bad idea," she replied, avoiding eye contact.

"I know, but I don't feel great about the way things turned out, and I don't want to leave things like this between us. We can drive somewhere else, out of Black Harbor, and no one will see us. What if I pick you up on Saturday morning? At eleven?"

Brea raised her eyes to meet his. She could not deny to herself she missed him and, although complicated, figured perhaps finding closure would be in both their interests.

"All right," she conceded.

Hayden let out a breath and nodded his head. "Great. I'll pick you up at eleven on Saturday and wait out front for you."

"I'll see you on Saturday," Brea confirmed, raising one corner of her mouth in a half-smile. Although unwise, wrong, and reckless, she wished he would embrace her. She had coped with her loneliness for the past couple of months, but now, in proximity to him, she longed for the warmth of his arms around her.

They looked at one another for a moment, lingering, the pair of them appearing to struggle with finding the courage to voice something unsaid. Hayden dropped his eyes, then stepped aside, allowing Brea to leave first. Walking past him, she kept her eyes ahead and hurried out the door.

Chapter Twenty-Seven

The Past

Brea called Allegra for an emergency meeting at the Shays' house later that afternoon. Allegra sat on her bed eating a bowl of cereal, and her eyes followed Brea as she paced back and forth in front of her. In the past, Brea had told Allegra the story of meeting Hayden in the library, though, fearing her judgement, had withheld her complicated feelings for him over the previous year and her infidelity. After running into Hayden at school today, for an inexplicable reason, she determined the day had arrived to tell Allegra the entire truth. Brea hesitated about where and how to begin.

"Brea, stop, you're going to give me a headache. What is it? Tell me already."

Concluding her pointless exercise of traversing the length of Allegra's room from one side to the other, she halted in front of her best friend, turned to face her, and drew in a deep breath.

"First, agree to something. Don't interrupt me. Let me finish the entire story and say nothing until I'm done. Do you agree?"

Allegra squinted her eyes at Brea. "Sure. Agreed."

Shoveling another spoonful of cereal into her mouth, she motioned with her hand for Brea to begin. She told her the story in full, omitting the sexually graphic details yet giving Allegra the general idea.

Allegra waited patiently for Brea to finish, nodding her head, and honoring the agreement to refrain from any verbal interruptions. Upon Brea's conclusion, Allegra sat in silence, gazing at the ceiling with her mouth hanging open in amazement. Brea threw up her hands to show Allegra she could now speak, cry out, or admonish her.

"You know, this isn't that surprising. The few times I saw you with Hayden, I sensed he had a thing for you. That and from your double date nightmare stories, there was something kind of odd happening there. He pretended not to like you because he liked you—it makes total sense," she announced, as though the explanation for his behavior had been obvious all along.

"Are you kidding me? Wait—do you think Jaime knew?" Brea blurted out with wide eyes, then changed the topic, her mind agitated and jumping from one thought to another. "Allegra, why didn't you ever say anything to me before?"

"I don't know. I thought you were in love with Jaime, and it didn't matter. You were so focused on keeping Jaime happy—all the time." Allegra did not conceal the disdain she harbored when she said, *"all the time."*

Brea sat on the floor with her legs crossed. "Anyway, it's all a mess. Vienna hates me, because she knew how he felt about me. Ugh, and she had warned me from the beginning not to cross her." Slapping her hand against her forehead, Brea continued on. "Being with Hayden—it's impossible. Jaime would know we lied, and everyone at Harvey Slate would despise me. I can't go backwards and suffer through the next two years like I did in seventh grade—the looks and the name calling."

Allegra's face softened, empathizing with Brea's fears. "Look. We make mistakes. We're teenagers. Talk with Hayden and move on—but don't make out with him—that will derail you."

Brea dropped her head into her hands and nodded in agreement, unable to dispute Allegra's sage advice.

Allegra continued, "Look at the positives. You still have friends at school, and you have me, even though it feels like we live in separate countries sometimes." Walking over to Brea, Allegra sat beside her on the floor and placed her arm around her shoulders. "Brea, you can't hide from Jaime and Vienna forever, you know. Eventually, you are going to put on a nice outfit, go to a party, and stop sitting at home reading Jane Austen novels. If I know you, and I do, there aren't any parts left to underline in *Persuasion*."

Brea produced a half-smile. "You know me—too well."

Allegra squeezed Brea's shoulders. "Brea, what do you really want from Hayden? Be honest with me. I mean, do you have intense feelings for him like you would die without him?"

Brea closed her eyes. "Of course, I have feelings for him. I feel comfortable with him, and I can say what I'm really thinking. He liked the seventh-grade dumpy version of me, which I don't understand at all, but he did. And when he touches me or we kiss—I can't describe what it feels like without embarrassing you. Still, it doesn't matter what I feel. We don't have a choice, so I have to move on. It's better anyway that I focus on myself for a while—be without a guy."

Allegra smiled and attempted to lighten the mood. "Cool. So, no need to shave your legs. It will free up your schedule to study more."

Brea laughed. She was relieved Allegra knew the truth. Although not absolved of her sins, her friend's lack of judgment and support lessened the guilt and belief she was an irredeemably horrible person. Brea would meet with Hayden and find the closure she needed to move on to the next part of her story.

Chapter Twenty-Eight

The Past

Despite having fallen asleep after one in the morning, Brea woke up early. Pushing aside the stack of books on her nightstand, she checked the time on her alarm clock. It was seven-thirty and, being wide awake, it would be pointless to stay in bed and try to fall asleep again.

Brea shivered in the chilled morning air, a consequence of her father's frugality in keeping the thermostat low to save money during fall and winter. After rolling out of bed, Brea snagged her navy sweatshirt off the floor before leaving her bedroom to walk downstairs and fix herself a cup of tea.

Finding herself alone on the ground floor, she took care to avoid making excess noise as she filled the blue enameled teakettle and set it upon the stove to boil the water. Rather than waiting in the kitchen, she meandered into the family room and sat on the olive-green damask sofa. Brea shivered again. A subtle, earthy scent undulated in the room, and the air felt weighted and damp.

Staring out the window into the backyard, she saw that the sky was overcast, though the rains had stopped. Her gaze fixed on the branches of a tree—lifting, dropping, and bobbing in the blowing wind. She wondered where Hayden would take her later that morning when her father interrupted her thoughts, entering the family room with the newspaper in his hand.

"Brea, there was a note for you sitting on the porch," he said, handing her a white envelope.

"Thanks," she replied, taking the envelope and turning it over. She saw her name handwritten on the front. Waiting until her father left the room, she slipped her finger under the flap held closed by a piece of clear tape. Inside she found a note: "*Sorry, can't make it today. I'll find you and explain later, Hayden.*"

Brea crumpled up the note and sighed. That Hayden had gone through the trouble of writing a note rather than calling was odd. Hearing the teakettle whistle, she stood and shook her head. There would be no point in mulling over whether Hayden had changed his mind or whether something of true importance happened to warrant cancelling their outing.

She fixed herself a quick breakfast, then trudged up the stairs to read in bed until settling on a plan for what to do with her free day. Two hours later, Brea picked up the phone to call Allegra.

Allegra, certain it was Brea, answered after two rings. "Are you panicking because Hayden is picking you up soon?"

"No, that's not why I'm calling. He cancelled anyway, and before you say anything, I don't know why. He wrote a note and left it on my door. Something came up, I guess," Brea replied, hoping to stave off any further discussion about Hayden.

"Annoying. So, are you pissed?"

"No, it's fine. He said he'll explain later. Anyway. I was hoping we could do something today. Maybe a movie? I need a break from being a hermit."

"Wow, get ditched more often. It's Brea reverse psychology," Allegra teased.

"Ha ha," Brea replied.

"I wish I could, but I'm going out with Jacob and his parents to see a play this afternoon and then dinner. How about tomorrow? We can go to the mall. Call Tory and see if she wants to meet us."

"Sure. I'll call you tomorrow morning." Brea hung up the phone. She paced around her room several times, contemplating how to spend her day, and settled on venturing outside the house. Rather than visiting the library, she would ride her bike to Harbor Coffee House and work on her poem for the Harvey Slate Gazette's writing contest. If selected, her piece would print in an exclusive edition in December devoted to creative writing, and the deadline to submit approached.

The crisp autumn air and the sight of the colorful leaves on the trees created a tranquil atmosphere for Brea's bike ride. Invigorated upon reaching the cafe, she hopped off her bike and entered the cafe with a bright smile. Dozens of vintage framed photographs and posters, interspersed with large overstuffed bookshelves holding books and board games, adorned the crimson walls. Seeing an abundance of open seating in the cafe, she stepped in line at the counter.

Brea ordered a cappuccino and a double-chocolate muffin. Spotting a vacant brown leather sofa with a long coffee table, she claimed it and unpacked her journal, notebook, and pencils as she waited for the barista to call her name for her order.

An hour passed, and Brea went to the counter to order another coffee. She returned to her seat and noticed a boy now seated across from her dressed in a fitted light-blue plaid shirt and jeans with short, textured platinum-blonde hair, and darker facial stubble. He was reading a book. Brea glimpsed the cover, but she could not see the title clearly. Picking up her notebook and pencil, she focused her attention on her poem. After letting out an audible exhale, she shook her head, stuck on an awkward line in her poem and uncertain how to correct it.

"What are you writing?" a voice asked, grabbing Brea's attention.

Her eyes darted upwards, seeing the boy seated across from her, studying her as he leaned back with one foot propped on the coffee table. With the book dangling from his hand, he lifted his arm and draped it over the top of the sofa. Brea felt her cheeks warm. His facial features and silver-gray eyes captured her attention and there was something in his demeanor—a confident edge—that made her stumble over her words.

Brea lowered her eyes, finding the intensity of his gaze rather intimidating. "Oh, I'm working on a piece of writing for a school newspaper contest."

"Interesting. What's it about?" His voice had a smooth, melodic rhythm that drew Brea in.

"It's a poem, a sonnet about winter. My school runs a special edition in December for creative writing. I figured writing something about the cold weather might improve my chances of being selected."

"So, you must go to Harvey Slate," he announced with a wide smile, as though he had solved a great mystery.

Brea raised her eyebrows, surprised he had surmised her school from her reply. "Yes, do you go to Harvey Slate? I've never seen you there before."

"Yes, well, I used to and graduated over a year ago. I'm Cylis. What's your name?"

"Brea. So, how did you know I go to Harvey Slate?"

"The December creative writing edition. I'm a writer too. I had a few pieces published in that edition when I was in school," he replied.

A broad smile formed on Brea's face. "Really? I'll have to look them up in our archives. Where are you going to school now?"

"I'm taking a break this year. I've been traveling over the past few months, and I won't return to school until next fall. Could I read what you wrote?"

Brea inhaled and pressed her lips together. "I don't know. Do you really want to read it? It's an early draft, and I'm stuck on a line. The wording and the rhythm aren't quite working."

"Come on, maybe I can help you out." Leaning forward, he ran his hand through his hair, then placed his elbow on his knee and cradled his chin in his hand. The way he moved—deliberate and sensual—struck her. His eyes fixed on Brea's, and she could not help but feel flattered Cylis had taken an interest in her. She tipped her head to the side, as though hypnotized by his gaze.

"All right, here." Brea handed him her notebook, unable to avert her eyes from his.

Taking it from her with his free hand, he held it up and focused on the page. Brea studied his face and eyes, moving from side to side as he read through the poem. When finished, he lowered the notebook down and locked eyes with Brea.

"This is good. I see what line you're talking about."

He rose from his seat and maneuvered around the coffee table to join Brea on the sofa. She pushed aside her journal and papers to clear a spot for him. As he sat down, the scent of his cologne—a spicy, resinous scent—diverted her attention. Taking Brea's pencil out of her hand, he erased the line she had indeed been stuck on. After a minute, he wrote a line, then reread her poem.

"Here, read this and tell me what you think."

Taking her notebook from his hand, Brea read through her poem. It was brilliant. He had rearranged several words and replaced "white" with "opaline." The adjustments were transformative.

"This is amazing. I was stuck on this for days. You read it once and fixed it in sixty seconds." Brea turned to face him with a look of astonishment.

"Sometimes you have to take a step back and give yourself a bit of distance. If you're too close to it, you can get lost in your head." He sat back and angled himself to face Brea.

"Thank you. I mean it. I had a mentor in this writing program last summer, Audrey. She was so cool, and she could see something and correct it just like you. Everything she touched was genius." Brea smiled as she reread the line Cylis had written.

"Well, I'd like to meet you here again. I can bring what I'm working on, and you can give me your opinion."

Brea's mouth opened, stunned yet intrigued. "Are you sure? I'm only in high school. I don't know how valuable my opinion would be."

Cylis grinned. "Based on what I've read so far, I'm impressed. Do you have anyone else you trust your writing with?"

Brea shook her head. "Not really, my teachers."

A winsome smile appeared on his face, and he clasped his hands together. "Now you can have me. Let's meet back here on Monday at four o'clock and bring me some more of your work."

Brea nodded, and her heart beat faster. "Yes. Monday at four. I'll be here," she confirmed as she pulled her hair into a ponytail and twisted it over one shoulder.

Cylis pointed to his book on the sofa. "Do you mind if I hang out with you while I read? I won't interrupt you, promise."

"Not at all, but I want to hear about what you're reading later. I'm always looking for a good book," she replied. Brea looked into his eyes again. There was something magnetic about his persona that drew her to him and his being a writer led Brea to believe that fate must have brought them together. Cylis tapped his chin as though he needed to contemplate carefully entering such an agreement, and she chuckled.

"Will do," he said, tapping her on the knee before he stood. Brea's eyes followed him as he returned to his seat on the sofa opposite her. He had a seductive charisma unlike anyone she had met before that rendered her unsettled, yet exhilarated.

Picking up her notebook, she focused on her page. She felt Cylis's eyes watching her and met his gaze with a timid smile. With a slight upturn in one corner of his mouth, he returned his attention to his book.

CHAPTER
TWENTY-NINE

THE PAST

On Monday, Brea arrived at school with twelve copied poems from her journal in a folder. She hurried to the library during her lunch period to reread her poems for any necessary last-minute adjustments. Arriving home from school, she would have little time, enough only to change before biking to town for her meeting with Cylis.

Seeing her usual table free, she claimed it. After placing her folder, backpack, coat, and water bottle on the table, she ventured into the fiction section. If Cylis brought a book, she hoped to read alongside him once they finished critiquing one another's writing. Meandering through the stacks, Brea smiled and replayed in her mind every detail of her chance encounter with Cylis. True, Brea had planned to stay single, but if someone found a chest of gold, would they leave it behind or take it and bask in their good fortune?

Brea took her time leafing through several books until picking up an Oscar Wilde novel she had yet to read and settled on checking it out. Approaching her table, she slowed to a halt, seeing Hayden seated in her chair. He did not appear to notice Brea as she walked towards him. Her eyes widened seeing him reading a page from her writing folder, and she quickened her steps to rip the poem from his hands. Nearing the table, she paused—his mouth curved into a smile as he read and it was clear he appreciated what she had written. Reaching the table, Brea placed her hands on the surface and leaned down.

"Did you find something interesting?" she asked, keeping the volume of her voice low. Hayden's eyes flickered up to meet Brea's. Leaning her head to the side, she glared at Hayden to communicate her irritation.

"Do you go through everyone's stuff without permission or only mine?" she continued.

Hayden leaned back in his chair with a devilish grin, confirming that, yes, he was completely comfortable welcoming himself into her personal space. "Is this about us?" he asked, placing the paper on the table and sliding it over to her.

Brea rubbed her forehead before glancing at the paper, though she did not need to—it was obvious he had read the poem inspired by their first night together. Looking down, she saw the title, "Stolen Night."

"It's good. I mean it," he said, his blue eyes fixed on Brea's. Her face softened. She sighed and pulled out the chair opposite Hayden to sit down.

"Thank you," she replied, attempting to conceal her embarrassment. Obviously, Hayden had been there with her in the throes of passion. Still, it had been a personal and emotional account of what had happened between them that night.

"What are you doing in here? Did you come here to find me?" To avoid alerting anyone else to his presence at the table, she whispered, even though the isolated table sat tucked away in the back corner of the library. And, although unlikely that anyone of consequence would be in the library during her lunch period, she did not want to tempt fate.

"Yes, to tell you why I couldn't see you on Saturday." Brea put up her hand to stop him—it did not matter.

"It's fine, Hayden. No explanation is necessary." Rather than falling into a discussion about their past indiscretions, she preferred having the time to reread her poems.

"Well, I'm still going to tell you," Hayden continued, ignoring Brea as she scoffed at his insistence.

He began again. "My mom is still sick, getting worse over the past couple of months. No one could figure out why until Friday. She met with the neurologist, and he diagnosed her with early-onset Parkinson's disease. She's devastated, and I had to stay home with her all weekend," he said as he rubbed the back of his neck and stared at the table.

"Hayden. I'm so sorry, I—I don't know what to say. What does that mean? I don't know what that is." Brea's heart ached for him seeing the anguish he attempted to conceal behind his eyes. If she could have, she would have wrapped her arms around him, yet she worried about being seen. "Are you all right?"

Hayden raised his eyes to meet hers. "Me? I don't know, not really, but I'll have to be. It's a neurological disease that progresses and affects how you move. She could live with it for a long time, but the doctors are worried because it seems to have already progressed rapidly. She's often in pain and has muscle spasms. They're starting all kinds of medications to see if they can slow it down and help her feel more comfortable, but they have side effects, and it's hard to say how she'll do on them."

Brea exhaled and pressed her hands together. "Hayden, what can I do?"

"Well, I wanted you to know I didn't change my mind or blow you off. Can we go somewhere after school today to talk?" he asked, then tapped his fingers on the table, awaiting her reply.

Brea hesitated, wanting to choose her words with care. She did not want to lie to Hayden, but telling him the truth about Cylis would be awkward. Opting for vague, she answered. "I have something I need to do after school today, so I can't. And this week I'll be busy with the poem I'm writing for The Gazette special edition. How about we try for Saturday again?"

Hayden eyed her with suspicion. He could tell Brea was trying to conceal something from him. Averting his eyes, he pressed his lips together. "Sure. I'll pick you up on Saturday at eleven. We can take a drive and go out for lunch." Brea turned her head to make sure nobody was close by, then nodded.

"Brea, one more thing, could you—"

"What?" Brea asked after Hayden paused.

"Could you read me the last four lines of your poem? I want to hear you read it to me." Looking down at the table with a slight smile on his face, he drummed his fingers on the table, waiting for her answer.

Brea observed him with a wary facial expression, uncertain of his intentions in making this request. "Fine, if you promise to leave when I'm done," she replied, and Hayden conceded with a nod.

Picking up the paper, Brea cleared her throat and read aloud.

"Softly in stealth, innocence washed away
A starved heart bled purple, now red
The ache of desire in darkness fulfilled
His touch, rampant and untamed, left nothing unsaid."

Brea lifted her eyes to meet Hayden's. He had watched her as she read.

"Did you ever write a poem about another guy? About Jaime?"

"It's not a contest, Hayden. I write about a lot of things."

"But did you?" he asked again, insistent.

"No," she answered truthfully after thinking for a moment, surprised with the realization that she had never written a poem about either Jaime or Blake. She shook her head and sighed. "Look, I will see you on Saturday. Now leave—let me finish what I'm doing," she said, shooing him away with a good-natured gesture of her hand.

"Yes, ma'am," he obliged with a grin as he stood, then strolled away, turning back once to look at Brea before disappearing around the corner of a bookshelf. Brea laughed. Perhaps after everything that had happened between them, they could be friends. Maybe not—time would tell.

Chapter Thirty

The Past

Entering Harbor Coffee House that afternoon, Brea scanned the room for Cylis. Her heart fluttered at seeing him seated at a four-top table with a hardcover book and a notebook stacked in the center. Brea approached him, eager and curious to see what he had brought for her to read. Cylis met Brea's eyes with a wide smile as he leaned back and crossed his arms in front of his chest. She sat in the chair opposite him and clasped her hands under the table, hoping to steady her skittish fingers.

Brea observed they had dressed in a similar color palette and style. She wore a black fitted Henley long-sleeved shirt with a pair of dark blue jeans, and Cylis, a black sweater, light-gray jeans, and a black cafe racer leather jacket, hung on the back of his chair. Brea took it as a sign that they were indeed like-minded and ideal for one another.

"How was Slate today?" he asked as Brea unpacked her book, journal, and folder.

"Good. I'm in the honors program, and it's kicking my butt, but I'm managing."

"Wow, I'm impressed. That was not something I would have been able to handle at Harvey Slate. I'll order you a drink. What would you like?"

"A large coffee with cream. Thanks."

Cylis rose from his chair to walk to the register. Brea, transfixed by his movements, placed the tip of her thumb between her front teeth while watching him walk. She held her breath, studying the gestures he made with his hands as he leaned over the counter to order, musing his bearing was like that of a seductive rock star.

Seeing him return with their coffees, Brea cleared her throat, inhaled, then picked up her folder. "So, I have twelve poems here in different styles and themes. These are some of my most meaningful pieces, and I would like your honest critique. What did you bring for me?"

Cylis held up his notebook. "I have a short story I'm working on. It's about an actor who finds himself engulfed in the dark side of the entertainment industry. It's bleak, but I'm interested to hear what you think about it."

Brea chuckled. "I'm not afraid of dark or sad writing. It's a long story, but that's the reason I wound up at Harvey Slate."

"Oh, a bad girl. Your school expelled you for your writing? I knew there was something interesting about you the moment I saw you."

Brea laughed. "I didn't get kicked out. I'm not that edgy or naughty. My mom pulled me out and transferred me to Harvey Slate because she was angry with the school for making too big of a deal out of the writing. Anyway, let's read. I have to be home by seven tonight. I have a French and a pre-calculus quiz this week."

"School is a waste of time. It gives you a false sense of security—people believe they are intelligent because they have a degree. The only reason I'm going back in the fall is because my parents are forcing me."

Brea's eyes widened. "I see you have strong opinions on the subject. You mentioned you're taking off this year. Where were you last year?"

"Yale. The short version is I had some trouble with my classes, and it pissed off my parents. I'll tell you the full story another time. Come on, turn it over." Cylis held out his hand for her folder.

"So, what do your parents do? Based on what you said, it sounds like they feel school is important—I'm guessing they won't let you move to Paris to become a writer."

Cylis chuckled. "No, definitely not. They own a film production company. Same old story—only child, they expect a lot from me, work all the time, and I'm alone a lot, blah blah blah."

Brea's ears perked up. "Alone, that sounds like my house. Except my parents are always there, but they ignore me. I don't have any brothers or sisters either. I have a cousin, Vienna, but I only met her when I started at Harvey Slate last year."

Cylis sat up straight. "Wait a second, Vienna, as in Vienna Cortello? She's your cousin?"

Brea nodded to affirm that it was true, and Cylis whistled.

"She's something else—a gorgeous girl, but cold. A lot of guys wanted to nail her, and most of the girls wanted to be her or were terrified of her. I think there's a novel there now that I think about it."

Brea shook her head. "Right, well, I can speak from experience—that sounds about right. I'm on her shit list, even though I'm her cousin."

"What did you do to her?" Cylis asked, intrigued.

Brea produced an awkward laugh to buy time, then changed the subject. "It was nothing interesting. So, you mentioned traveling. Where were you?"

"I was backpacking through South America for three months. It was amazing. I met interesting people, improved my Spanish, wrote, and ate amazing food. It's a different world over there with real culture—not the superficial way of life the people around here surrender themselves to. Anyway, now, it's all about writing until I go back to school in the fall. So, enough talking, let's read."

Brea rubbed her finger across her chin in awe of how intelligent and provocative she found Cylis—qualities that remarkably enhanced his sex appeal.

They settled into their seats to read for the following hour. When finished, Brea exhaled, impressed by Cylis' meaty short story with an enthralling storyline and a multi-faceted and richly developed main character. Despite her minor notes, she declared it a solid piece of writing.

Cylis picked out "Stolen Night" as one of her best pieces. When he finished reading the last line aloud, Brea regretted having kept the poem in her folder. Hearing another boy read her most private thoughts and feelings about Hayden felt peculiar—bordering on a betrayal of the intimacy she shared with Hayden. They read and chatted for another hour, and when it was time for Brea to leave, Cylis asked if he could call her during the week.

"Do you like foreign films? There's an independent theater in Tupa Bay showing a Spanish film at one o'clock on Saturday. Would you come with me?"

Brea, forgetting her plans with Hayden, did not hesitate to accept. "Yes, definitely."

Cylis handed her a pen. "Write your number in my notebook." Leaning down over the table, Brea's hair spilled over her shoulder. Cylis reached out his hand to push it back for her, and she turned her head to meet his eyes. He grinned, and her cheeks flushed.

"There you go." Brea straightened up. Cylis rose from his chair and leaned in to kiss her cheek. His lips lingered a moment longer than she would have considered a platonic kiss to be. She froze in place, hoping he might kiss her on the lips.

"Bye," Cylis said in a low voice.

"Goodbye," Brea whispered, then turned to leave, wanting more but thrilled with the anticipation of seeing him on Saturday. Walking away from the table, she placed her hand on her chest and, upon feeling her heart racing, dropped it to her side as she exited the cafe. Cylis's eyes followed her until she disappeared from sight.

Chapter Thirty-One

The Past

A sigh of frustration escaped Allegra's lips upon hearing the tapping sound of Brea's pencil hitting the page of her notebook. The following afternoon after her meeting with Cylis, the girls sat at the Shay's kitchen table with their homework as Mrs. Shay prepared them a snack and cold drinks. Distracted by thoughts of Cylis, Brea struggled to concentrate and peppered Allegra with frequent interruptions to talk about him.

"What do you think I should wear when I see Cylis again?" Brea asked as Allegra endeavored a third time to focus on her chemistry homework.

"Brea, you're driving me crazy. I don't know, a hot pink halter top. I'm sure he's in love with you and will marry you after you graduate high school, too." Allegra smirked at Brea and attempted to return to her homework once again, now having lost where she had left off.

Mrs. Shay, listening, chimed in. "Allegra, don't be rude. Brea, if I could share a little wisdom—maybe give it some more time and learn a bit more about him before you jump in too fast. It's difficult to know a person in the beginning when you're swept up with having met someone new and exciting." Brea sighed and rested her head on her fist. The advice made sense, but Cylis was seductive, clever, and, him being a writer, made it easy to relate to him—there would be no reason to wait if he desired her.

"He's different from the other boys—brilliant and interesting. Plus, we have writing in common. When I have something to say or contribute, he values my opinions, and he has these incredible, almost silver eyes that make me want to—"

Brea stopped herself before finishing her sentence and looked down at the table with wide eyes. Mrs. Shay, not being a stranger to teenage hormones, chuckled.

"Gross—not in front of the parent," Allegra said after she groaned and threw her pen onto her notebook with force.

"Hey, I understand. I'm not that old. Although he is an older boy, Brea. You should consider that you are both in very different places at your ages. It may not seem like it, but there's a world of difference, even with only three or four years when you're sixteen." Allegra's mother smiled and waited for Brea to acknowledge she heard her. Satisfied when Brea nodded, she exhaled.

"I'll leave you girls to finish up your homework. Here are some carrot sticks and a fruit salad," she said and placed the platter in front of the girls. "Fresh iced-tea is in the refrigerator in the glass pitcher." After wiping up the counter, Allegra's mother left the kitchen.

Brea looked at Allegra, watching her with raised eyebrows and her lips stretched tight in disapproval.

"Allegra, what?" Brea blurted out.

"Nothing, it's just you said you wanted to be alone. Now, you're jumping all over another guy and—"

"And what?" Brea asked, her face crumpling.

Allegra paused and shrugged her shoulders. "Nothing, let's do our homework so we can have time to watch a movie after.

By the way—don't forget you have the Hayden situation this weekend to deal with too," Allegra cautioned.

"Well, I'm going to cancel with Hayden and tell him something came up since Cylis asked me to see the movie at one o'clock. There won't be enough time for me to see Hayden. Anyway, it's better for us to leave things in the past and move on. Let's get serious. I can focus now, I promise."

Allegra shook her head. "I hope you know what you're doing, Brea," she said and grabbed a handful of carrot sticks with a resigned exhale. She knew Brea better than anyone and worried she was on the verge of throwing herself into another relationship when what she needed was to be alone.

Brea, high on Cylis, ignored Allegra's disapproving looks. She lowered her eyes to her math textbook and bit her lower lip not to interrupt Allegra again.

Chapter Thirty-Two

The Past

A snowstorm swept through Black Harbor, leaving a foot of snow on the ground in mid-December. The wintry landscape, coupled with strung-up frosted ivory lights, white pine wreaths, and balsam fir garlands, saturated the city center with holiday charm. Many of the Black Harbor neighborhoods vied to be voted the best decorated, and without fail, Brea would always smile seeing each home decorated more lovely than the previous one. As expected, Brea's home stuck out on her street every year as the one dark house with no holiday cheerfulness. The sole decorations the Staxons owned were a six-foot artificial Christmas tree and stockings.

Regardless of the lack of festive decor, Brea, in her younger years, eagerly awaited Christmas. It had been customary for her father to buy a box of Belgian chocolate truffles and peppermint candy canes the week before Christmas, and they would decorate the tree with a holiday film playing on the television.

This year Brea unpacked the tree ornaments and, with half-hearted effort, decorated the tree. The tradition of candy canes and chocolates had died out years ago and today, she decorated alone while her father sat in front of the television and Brea's mother, having been in one of her angry spells over the recent weeks, isolated herself in her bedroom.

Her mother only ventured out of her room either to rummage through old boxes in the attic or to storm throughout the house, declaring she lived in a miserable city and that Brea's father had ruined her life. These episodes were impossible to predict, with no identifiable trigger or pattern. They could occur several times a year, or a year could pass in between, and the duration was incalculable.

At night, she heard the sounds of her mother moving throughout the attic—sliding boxes, dropping objects, and shrill cursing. When Brea was a child, her mother's erratic behavior would frighten her. At sixteen, now accustomed to it, rather than being fearful, she had adopted methods to cope.

Having finished decorating the tree, Brea snuck into the kitchen and swiped a beer from the refrigerator. She tucked it into the waistband of her sweatpants and hurried upstairs to her room. Seated on the floor, she opened the can with care to avoid spilling the foam onto her rug. Though Brea disliked the taste of beer, she aimed not to enjoy it, but to ease her tension.

Brea had consumed half the can when she heard her mother's heavy footsteps upstairs, followed by the unsettling sound of the old floorboards creaking. She boxed her ears with her hands—the sound unnerved her. Picking up the beer, she drank down the last half, then threw the empty can across the room into her garbage bin.

Stomp. Creek. "Fuck," her mother shouted from the attic, followed by a crash as another heavy object fell onto the floor. Brea turned on the music in her room to drown out the sounds coming from above. With her winter sonnet on the cover, Brea eyed the December edition of The Harvey Slate Gazette on on the floor beside her bed, and thought about Hayden. She had cancelled on Hayden twice to meet on the weekend and, soon after, he gave up trying to reschedule with her. Despite Brea's avoidance of seeing him outside of school, they would greet one another and exchange brief small talk if they passed one another in the halls or in the courtyard, depending on whom else was present.

Now that she had Cylis in her life, Brea devoted her energy to pursuing him. He was enigmatic, and he never failed to make her feel special, praising her precocious talent and level of maturity compared to her peers. There was a single problem—she found the tedious pace at which their relationship progressed mystifying.

They met at the coffee shop several times a week to write and to critique one another's work. On the weekends, they went to the movies or to Tupa Bay Tavern, a dive bar where they could drink and play pool with no need of identification. However, to Brea's frustration, they were stuck in a gray zone, somewhere between friends and dating. Although Cylis showed her affection, held her hand and placed his arm around her when they sat next to one another to read, he only kissed her on the cheeks or forehead.

Being too timid to confront Cylis to clarify his specific intentions regarding their relationship, she lived in a state of tortured silence. However, she had recently learned some interesting information from Anjali and suspected it could be the reason he desired to take things slow with her.

Anjali, having remembered Cylis from high school, informed Brea that he had dated another Harvey Slate graduate in his class named Eva for two years. Allegedly, they had an intense relationship, and she had broken his heart after they graduated—leaving him for an artist, a painter ten years her senior, and following him to New York City as his muse and model.

On Friday night, while playing pool at Tupa Bay Tavern, Brea worked up the courage to ask Cylis about Eva.

"Hey Cy, I heard from one of my friends at school you used to have a girlfriend, Eva. What was she like?" Brea twisted the gold bracelet on her wrist, waiting for Cylis to answer her question, and curious to find out as much as she could about her.

Cylis straightened up and paused his efforts to hit the green ball into the corner pocket. "I still hang out with Eva when she's in town, so I wouldn't say 'was.' She's an artist, impulsive, inspired, unique. We have a connection that will never die. But—she needed to be free. She isn't conventional, and she didn't want to be with only one person."

Brea studied Cylis as he meandered around the pool table. Every movement he made fascinated her—the way he shifted his weight onto one leg or lifted the pool stick onto his shoulders. Brea bit her thumb, desperate for him to walk over and kiss her.

"So, do you still want to be with her, or is it all in the past now?" Brea chewed her thumbnail, hoping for the answer she wanted to hear.

Cylis's eyes livened as he neared Brea. "If it weren't, would that make you jealous?" Stepping in front of Brea, he pushed a tendril of hair that had fallen on her cheek behind her ear.

"I don't know," she mumbled as she dropped her eyes to the floor. Cylis kissed Brea on the forehead before returning to the pool table to take his shot. Closing her eyes, Brea wanted more.

"Cy, there's a Harvey Slate Party next Saturday. Do you want to go?" He made his shot and knocked the ball into the pocket. Picking up a shot of whisky, he drank it down.

"Sure, I haven't been to one of those parties in a while. I'll tell you what, I'll call Eva. She's coming back into town. I'll invite her to come too."

Brea swallowed. The news was unexpected and unwanted. "Oh. Sure—if you want to. How about I meet you there? Anjali will drive me and the girls." Being stuck in a car with Eva would be torture. Brea preferred to meet her at the party and impress her with a confident entrance.

"Sure. Get up. It's your shot, Brea. If you want to win, play the game," Cylis taunted. Brea smiled, reading deeper into what he had said. He was right. If she wanted him, she would need to show him she was as good as Eva—if not better. Saturday was an opportunity, and Brea accepted the challenge.

CHAPTER THIRTY-THREE

THE PAST

Anjali, Tory, and Brea drove to the party at a Harvey Slate senior's home whose parents were out of town for the weekend. Tapping her fingers on her legs, Brea shifted in her seat. Tory had prepped Brea that Jamie would be at the party tonight with Trevor and Aaron, though it bothered her little. Rather, her restlessness stemmed from her preoccupation with meeting Eva.

It had taken longer than usual for Brea to decide on her attire that evening. Cylis often saw her dressed in jeans and a long-sleeved T-shirt. Tonight, she needed to appear sexy and confident, yet casual to avoid appearing desperate and over-dressed. After careful consideration, Brea chose a pair of ivory stretch slim-fit pants, an off the shoulder sky-blue sweater, and camel ballet flats. She had curled her hair in soft waves and left it loose down her back.

Upon entering the house, the girls tossed their coats onto a growing pile of outerwear in the formal living room. Down-stairs, the party was underway, and the girls followed the signs with arrows directing them to the rear of the home. Reaching the family room, a spiral staircase led them down to an immense entertainment room with window walls, a custom black-lacquered contemporary bar, and indigo-blue upholstered seating sets spread throughout the vast space. Pop Art-style paintings, no doubt original artwork, depicting bar scenes and liquor bottles, hung on the walls.

A deck overlooking the beach, filled with teenagers smoking cigarettes and marijuana, spanned the length of the room on the other side of the windows. Brea scanned the crowd inside. Her heart stopped spotting Cylis from behind, dressed in a light-gray fitted sweater and jeans, standing beside a girl with long pale-blonde hair—it had to be Eva. They were engaged in a conversation with several people Brea did not recognize, likely other graduates. Tory and Anjali broke away to join Sonia on the other end of the room, leaving Brea alone.

Approaching Cylis, Brea caught sight of Hayden on the balcony through the window wall. His eyes locked onto Brea, and his mouth opened, as though he wanted to say something to her. She looked away, plastered a large, inauthentic smile on her face, and braced herself to meet Eva.

"Hi Cy," Brea said, touching his arm. He greeted Brea with a warm smile, placed his arm around her and squeezed her shoulders. Eva, dressed in a black wide-leg jumpsuit and clunky boots, turned to look at Brea. She had large chocolate-brown eyes and a fair complexion. Barefaced other than a layer of berry-colored lipstick, Brea found her face uniquely attractive.

Cylis introduced Brea. "Eva, this is Brea. My young protégé." He let go of Brea's shoulder and slipped his arm around Eva's waist. Brea did a slight double take at hearing herself described as a protégé—she did not appreciate being infantilized.

"Hi Brea. I've heard about you. You're a poet, is that right?" Eva smiled thinly, articulating her words in a slow, breathy voice. Despite her seemingly kind disposition, Brea found her demeanor bizarre, as though she were high on a psychedelic drug.

Her eyes met Brea's, but gave the impression she looked beyond her.

"Yes, but I also write short stories and I'm hoping to write a novel one day. You're a model in New York. That sounds amazing—I would love to see a piece you posed for."

"I stopped modeling this past summer to paint and sculpt after discovering I'm more than a naked form. Looking at you, Brea, I think I could do something transcendent with you. I see you nude, lying in a field of grass, holding a large sewing needle laced with pink thread. What do you think, Cylis, would Brea pose for me?"

Cylis grinned and kissed Eva on the cheek. "I don't think she's ready for you, Eva. Few people could handle your sexual energy other than myself."

Eva and Cylis smiled at one another with a knowing glance. Cylis moved his hand to her bottom and rubbed it as Eva rested her head on his shoulder. "It was nice to meet you, Brea. Think about it—if you would like to pose for me." Eva returned to the conversation with her friends.

Brea's face fell. Observing how Cylis looked at Eva, it was clear their bond and affection for one another had remained strong, and it felt as though a dagger bore into her heart. She cleared her throat. "Cy, I'm going to get some air." Placing his hand on her shoulder, he gave it a gentle squeeze, then let go.

"Come back soon," he replied and shifted his attention to the group.

Brea fought the impulse to search for an empty room in the house where she could cower and cry, but her stubborn resolve would not allow her to give up on Cylis. After all, she lived in Black Harbor and had shown her loyalty to him, unlike Eva, who had broken his heart and only visited on occasion. She had not imagined his feelings for her—all she needed was more time.

Withdrawing from the group, she made her way to the bar, grabbed an empty plastic cup and filled it with a generous pour of vodka. She drank it down, then refilled her cup with a rum and cola. After inhaling a deep breath, she swiveled around and spotted Nigel at the other end of the room watching her. Brea had not seen him since the night of her performance.

Catching her eye, he sauntered over with a wide grin and shining eyes. "Well, hello, if it isn't the beautiful Brea. If I'm not mistaken, you and Jaime broke up. Sad news for Jaime, but fantastic news for me."

Brea smiled. "Hi Nigel. Yes, that's true. How have you been?" Nigel wore a stylish mulberry-purple hued sweater, designer jeans, spotless white tennis shoes, and his hair styled with a generous amount of gel.

Eyeing Brea's bare shoulder, he bit his lower lip. "I'm great, but now that I'm seeing you, marvelous. You should know better than to wear something that shows just the right amount of skin—it drives a man crazy."

Brea held her breath to prevent herself from rolling her eyes. Under no circumstances would she go home with Nigel tonight, and yet, she childishly hoped that Cylis would see her with him and, in a jealous rage, storm over to pull her away from him. As a result, she deferred her impulse to excuse herself and smiled. With little shame, she engaged in flirtatious banter with Nigel until another graduate, she vaguely remembered having met in the past, interrupted them a short while after.

"Nigel, Brea—want to join me to smoke a joint on the balcony?" he asked.

Brea shrugged her shoulders. "Sure. I've never smoked, but why not?" Nigel took Brea's hand and led her through the crowd to the balcony. Once through the door, they wove into the group, and she found herself face to face with Jaime and Vienna. Brea and Jaime locked eyes only for a moment before he gave Brea a tight-lipped smile and then excused himself to reenter the house.

With a wicked sneer splashed across her face, Vienna witnessed the interaction with delight. Beside her sat Tara and Callie, perched on the railing, gawking with cool smiles and raised eyebrows, eager to see what dramatics they might witness over the ensuing moments. Brea felt the familiar wave of guilt and regret wash over her as she watched Jamie shut the door behind him. Although she wished he could be friendly with her, she had to accept that it would be unrealistic to expect Jaime would embrace her and make small talk.

Standing further down the balcony, Brea spotted Hayden with a group of seniors she did not know very well. His eyes fixed on her with concern in seeing her proximity to Vienna. Nigel slipped an arm around Brea from behind and pulled her closer to him. He inhaled a drag of the joint, then blew out a cloud of smoke that wrapped around Brea's head, and she winced, finding the scent rank and earthy.

"Take a small hit, Brea," Nigel said, handing the joint to her. She took it and held it between two fingers, fixing her eyes on Vienna as she inhaled a puff. As the smoke filled her lungs, an awful burning sensation filled her chest. She coughed violently, and tears filled her eyes. Vienna burst into laughter, enjoying watching Brea suffer.

"Stop trying to be cool, Brea. You don't know how to smoke," she exclaimed with the venomous intention of embarrassing her in front of as many people as possible. Nigel slapped Brea on her back several times. Once she stopped coughing, he placed his hands on her shoulders and, with his fingers, traced several circles on her bare shoulder.

"She's good. It's always hard on you the first time you smoke, doesn't matter," he reassured Brea, then bent down to kiss the crook of her neck. Brea stiffened.

Vienna rolled her eyes and smirked. "So, Brea, I hear you're hanging out with Cylis a lot. If you didn't know, let me do you a favor—he's been with Eva for years."

Brea coughed again and excused herself. "I'm going to the bathroom. I'll be back in a minute." Nigel squeezed her shoulders, letting go as she spun around to return inside. Part of her wanted to plant a kiss on Nigel's mouth, only to shock Vienna, but she decided against it, not being in the mood to play games for her sake.

Vienna called out after her. "I have to say it, Brea. Everyone knows you're throwing yourself at Cylis, and it's kind of sad. It doesn't matter how much coffee you drink with him—he doesn't want you. I'm only trying to help you out so you don't fucking embarrass yourself in front of the entire school."

Brea rotated at her waist and flipped Vienna the middle finger before turning once again to return inside. The surrounding crowd went crazy, shouting and laughing, and Tara and Callie, wide-eyed, cackled with malevolent delight. "Whatever, she deserves it," Vienna proclaimed in a haughty tone of voice. She returned her attention to a group of sophomore girls who had been hanging on her every word before Brea had appeared.

Brea held back her tears—she refused to let anyone see her cry as she manuevered and pushed through the crowd. She climbed the spiral staircase and strode through the house. Bursting out of the front door onto the paved walkway, she surveyed the area to ensure she was alone, then gasped, sucking in deep breaths of bitter cold air as she let the hot tears fall down her frozen cheeks. She could fake her strength in front of others, though not to herself—and now, most concerning, she had openly declared war against Vienna.

Vienna, always an opportunist to torture someone, would seize any available chance to hurt Brea. But, Vienna's cruel nature aside, after seeing Cylis with Eva tonight, Brea could not deny Vienna's claims that Brea's feelings were possibly one-sided.

Cylis, having seen Brea upset as she hurried through the room, had followed her outside. He pulled her into his arms to comfort her. "Hey," he whispered several times. "What's wrong, Brea?"

Brea shook her head. She could not tell Cylis what happened with Vienna on the deck, but she needed to know if he wanted to be with her as much as she wanted him. Instead, she rose onto the balls of her feet to kiss Cylis on the mouth, and for a moment he let her, then pulled away with a slight smile of condescension.

"Brea, what are you doing? You want to kiss me?" he asked, brushing the hair out of her face with his hands.

"I don't know what I'm doing. I'm so confused, and I don't understand you and Eva," she answered. Inside, she knew what she wanted—for him to love her—but to say those words out loud felt too honest and pathetic.

Cylis pulled her into an embrace. Brea inhaled his scent, a fragrance of leather and pepper, and pressed into his chest. "It's all right, you're a special girl to me," he repeated twice as though he held a wounded bird in his hands. Tears welled up in her eyes again, and she did not stop them from falling. Cylis rubbed her neck and held her against him as she cried.

The door opened abruptly, and they stepped back from one another. It was Hayden. Seeing Brea crying, his posture stiffened and his jaw clenched. He stepped towards Brea.

"Hey, do you mind if I take over here?" Hayden said with an authoritative stance.

Cylis turned and stepped in front of Brea at an angle. "I don't know. Are you the reason why she's like this?" Cylis straightened his posture and glared at Hayden.

Hayden took a step forward and crossed his arms in front of his chest. "No, are you?" he challenged. Upon seeing Brea wearing only a sweater, Hayden removed his black wool coat and stepped around Cylis to set it upon Brea's shoulders. Cylis and Hayden then turned to face one another. Cylis took another step closer to Hayden, boasting a pompous air of superiority as though it was obvious he outmatched Hayden and needed little excuse to engage in a fight. Brea observed Hayden's body tense and his right hand clench into a fist at his side.

Brea feared the situation was on the verge of escalating. "It's okay, Cylis, I'm good. It's not about him. I need to talk to Hayden for a while," she said, placing her hand on Hayden's arm to diffuse the tension.

Hayden grinned at Cylis in victory, then arrogantly gestured towards the door to show Cylis that was his cue to get lost. As Cylis stepped away to return inside, Hayden called out after him, "Oh, and tell Eva I said hi—it looks like she missed you in there." Cylis scowled at Hayden through narrowed eyes, though, as he stepped into the foyer, before closing the door behind him, his expression shifted and a half-smirk danced across his face.

"Brea, look at me." Hayden moved into Brea's line of vision for her to focus on him. "What are you doing? Smoking pot? Hanging out with Nigel and this guy? What's wrong with you?" Hayden asked with an edge in his voice.

"Nothing, having a good time. What about you? What was that with Cylis? A bit much, don't you think?" Brea asked, raising her voice.

"No, it wasn't. Fuck that. He's playing with you. Him and Eva were together for two years, and when she comes back to town, they're all over each other. Everyone knows you're chasing after him, and he's using you to fill the gaps. I can't believe you are falling for his bullshit," he spouted off and threw his arms up in frustration. Brea sucked in a deep breath, and tears once again filled her eyes—it hurt to breathe.

Hayden moved closer to her, softened his stance and wrapped his arms around her. "I'm sorry. That was harsh." He held her as she cried. Pulling back after a minute, he bent down to look into her eyes. "Let's go. We're getting out of here. Grab your coat and we'll go somewhere to talk, drink a coffee or something."

Brea drew in a deep breath to steady her voice. "Coffee? Do you think that's a good idea right now?" she asked.

"Well, we can order decaf if you're worried," he answered, attempting to deadpan, but cracked a smile at his lame joke.

Brea laughed through her tears. "You know what I mean, Hayden," she said, gesturing towards the house.

"Yeah, I know. Jaime or Vienna won't see us. Meet me at my car. I'm parked across the street. I'll warm it up." Brea nodded, then handed Hayden back his coat. She slipped inside to let Tory know she was leaving.

Chapter Thirty-Four

The Past

Brea met Hayden at his car. Before opening the door, she glanced over her shoulder to ensure no one would witness their leaving the party together. She felt immense relief sinking into the passenger seat, finding the interior warm and Hayden's presence comforting. Brea clicked her seatbelt, and after letting out a breath, laid her head against the seat to look out the window as they drove off.

"We'll drive to Seaport Harbor. There's a twenty-four-hour diner near the beach, and we won't run into anyone we know that far out." Brea continued to stare out of the window as the world passed by. Her body felt heavy, and crying had congested her nasal passages. Drawing in a deep breath through her mouth, she hoped that by the time they arrived at the diner she would be able to breathe though her nose.

Hayden grinned. "I saw what happened with Vienna. Nice move, by the way, giving her the finger—aggressive and effective."

"I'm going to pay for that, but she was being a little cunt baby," Brea muttered.

Hayden's eyes narrowed at Brea's insult, and he laughed. "I don't know what that means, and it sounds creepy. If you made that up, please don't say that again—ever," he teased.

Brea grinned. "Maybe. I can't promise I won't because it's a conversation starter." The mood lightened as they laughed together. Hayden raised the volume of the music and continued to drive.

They arrived at the diner at a quarter past ten. Other than a few scattered cars, the parking lot was empty, and inside there were several customers seated at the counter eating hamburgers or drinking coffee. A server passed them by and told them to sit wherever they liked. Brea followed Hayden to a booth, and they sat down.

The ambiance inside was what one would expect of a twenty-four-hour diner built in the nineteen sixties, brightly lit with beige-and-white checkered floors and a long row of orange vinyl booths set opposite a long counter with stools. Classic rock music played in the background at a low volume, making conversation possible.

Brea ordered a chamomile tea and a slice of coffeecake, and Hayden, a coffee and an order of French fries. The server collected their menus and hurried off for their drinks.

"So, what are we going to talk about?" Brea asked, toying with her napkin and folding it into a triangle. Hayden fidgeted with the butter knife on the paper napkin in front of him, turning it over with his fingers several times until he dropped it and fixed his eyes on Brea.

"Look, what happened between us—I meant what I told you, that it should have been us together from the beginning. I also felt a lot of guilt about the whole situation. I still do. It doesn't feel good that I put you in such a difficult position, and I'm sorry about that."

"I know Hayden. We don't need to apologize to each other—anyone else, but not to each other," Brea said, sinking into her seat.

"I miss talking to you. I hate it when I see you at school and you walk by, pretending half the time like you don't know me, as though nothing happened between us. It shouldn't be this way."

Brea shook her head, uncertain where he was going with this conversation. "What are you saying, Hayden? You want us to come clean now?"

Hayden released a loud exhale as he looked out the window. "I don't know. I don't have all the answers. There would be consequences."

Brea ran her fingers through her hair and stretched her neck. "Hayden, you saw me tonight. I am confused about Cylis and I don't understand my relationship with him. It's a mess. I'm a mess. Not to mention everything that happened with us—I couldn't handle it if everyone found out I cheated on Jaime. It would be another pile of shit I'm not strong enough to find my way out of right now."

The server returned with their orders, though neither of them was hungry at the moment. They stared at their plates without moving. Shaking his head, Hayden added cream to his coffee, then threw his spoon down, hitting the plate and making a loud noise. The other patrons turned to look at Brea and Hayden.

"I'm serious about Cylis, Brea. Stop with him. I don't know what he's doing with you, but I don't like the way you look. You look sad, and you've lost weight. I saw you hitting the bar pretty hard tonight and now moving onto weed. Don't you see he's dragging you down and he will not give you what you deserve?" Hayden blurted out, his tone of voice laden with exasperation.

Brea ate a forkful of her coffee cake and shook her head. It was too sweet, and her stomach turned. She threw down her fork on the plate, and another loud clink reverberated in the diner. "Shit, Hayden, you're one to talk. It isn't like you were getting down on one knee begging to be my boyfriend," she exploded with little regard for the attention she drew towards them.

"Is that what you want?" he asked, placing his hands flat on the table and looking into Brea's eyes. She held his gaze, searching to decipher what he wanted. Frustrated, she looked away.

"Look, Hayden. Cylis is perfect for me. We have writing in common, and I know he likes me. True, I don't understand why we aren't in a full relationship, but I'm sure there is a good reason. I just need to be patient, and he'll come around—I'll have to see what happens."

Hayden shook his head. "I think he's going to string you along because he does like you, but he isn't over Eva, and he doesn't want you to be with anyone else. But what really worries me—seeing him tonight, and now that I'm paying attention—I think there's something off about him."

"Stop Hayden. You clearly have a biased opinion. Also, he's an artist, so of course he might seem a bit 'off' to you. Look, I'll sit him down and have a serious conversation with him to find out where he stands with Eva and if he wants to be with me, all right?"

Hayden scoffed and stuffed a French fry into his mouth. "Hope it's worth it. Maybe you can be the next Sylvia Plath. Just don't stick your head into an oven if it doesn't work out with him," he retorted.

"Hayden. It is going to be fine. Honestly, after tonight—I get it. I'm going to talk with him and clear everything up. I promise."

"Brea, you should walk away and not look back." Hayden stared into Brea's eyes with a resolute expression to convey he meant every word he said.

She dropped her head onto her arms, folded in front of her on the table, and groaned. "Please let's drop it. I don't want to think about it anymore tonight." After a moment, she rolled her head to the side and studied Hayden as he ate. "So—what? Are we going to be secret friends now?"

Hayden smiled and reached over the table to pull her plate towards himself. With his spoon, he scraped the whipped cream off the cake, shook it onto the side of the plate, and helped himself to a large bite.

"I guess, we'll just—see what happens," he said, mocking Brea and her naivety. Brea scoffed as she straightened up to add cream to her tea.

"Hayden, how's your mom? I'm sorry I never asked you about her again. That was a shitty thing I did."

Hayden's expression altered, and a slight frown formed on his face. Brea watched his hands clench briefly into fists, then he stretched his fingers out and tapped them on the table. "Not good. She's not eating very much, and—it's tense at home. But her symptoms are stable for now. The worst of it is my dad. He's angry all the time. I mean, he always has been, but—" Hayden drew in a deep breath. "You know what, let's talk about something else, anything else," he said, bringing his hand up to rub his forehead and eyes.

She tilted her head. "Sure, but if you want to talk about it with me, you can." Hayden nodded but did not respond. Changing the subject, Brea shared with him her thoughts about trying her hand at writing a play. Hayden, visibly relieved to talk about something else, threw out ridiculous themes Brea could write about. His prize idea was for her to write a Harvey Slate murder mystery with her pre-calculus teacher revealed as the killer.

They ordered another round of drinks and filled the time—sharing funny stories, reviewing the colleges Hayden had applied to, and discussing the most recent books they had read. The events of the night at the party had faded away by the time they paid the check. Hayden checked his watch. It was half past midnight. Although reluctant to leave as they were enjoying one another's company, they agreed it would be best to go, as they had a lengthy drive back to Black Harbor.

Before departing, they stopped to use the restroom. Seeing her reflection in the mirror, Brea fixed her hair, then touched up her eye makeup. Satisfied with her appearance, she hurried to leave, knowing Hayden was waiting for her. Brea paused outside the ladies' room upon seeing him leaning against the door frame at the entrance. Observing him, handsome in his black sweater with his coat in one hand and the other in his pocket, she felt an ache of desire to embrace him. Hayden straightened his posture and smiled, seeing Brea.

"Ready?" he asked, and Brea nodded. Neither of them moved for a moment, pausing to look into one another's eyes. Stepping outside, other than the staff cars parked by the side entrance, they saw only Hayden's car in the lot. They raised their eyes to the night sky, black and sprinkled with infinite stars. "It's amazing, isn't it?" Hayden commented. Brea nodded in agreement and sighed. A cloud of vapor formed from her breath in the frigid night air, and Hayden saw Brea shiver. Taking her hand, he hurried her to the car and, once inside, he turned on the engine and cranked up the heat.

He removed a pack of gum from his pocket and offered Brea a piece. She checked the flavor—of course, cinnamon. With raised eyebrows, she took one, unwrapped it, and placed it in her mouth.

Turning her head to study Hayden's profile, she watched his jaw moving up and down as he mindlessly chewed. The bright lights from the diner highlighted the angles of his face, and her eyes fixed on his mouth. She felt her heart beat faster. Hayden did not need to drug her, but offering her a simple piece of that cinnamon gum had flipped a libidinous switch deep inside her.

Now conscious of Brea observing him, his head turned to look at her. Her cheeks flushed. She smiled and looked away to fasten her seatbelt, but Hayden's arm reached across to stop her.

He took her hand and pulled her closer to him. Their eyes locked, and Brea tilted up her chin and parted her lips. He knew that was the signal for him to kiss her, and he did. Brea's body remembered him, and she moaned. Hayden responded and kissed her deeper.

The gum in their mouths moved around until it stuck together in one piece in Brea's mouth. They pulled back a few inches and laughed at the absurdity. Hayden placed his hand under her mouth, and Brea spit the gum into his hand. Along with the gum came a trail of saliva. He groaned and opened the door to throw it on the ground. After shaking his hand, he wiped it on his jeans.

Both of them laughing, Hayden placed his hands behind Brea's head and pulled her in to kiss her again. His fingers fumbled to unbutton her coat, and as she slid her arms out one by one, Hayden pushed it off her shoulders. Once free, she climbed onto his lap to straddle him as best she could in the tight space. Hayden pushed the seat button to move it back as far as it would go to create more room.

Hayden slid his hands down her back until reaching her bottom. With his hands under her thighs, he pulled her closer to him, and a rapid flush of heat spread throughout her lower body. She moaned as Hayden's lips trailed down her neck. Brea rocked her hips back and forth, feeling him firm beneath her, and with each movement, a deep, growing pleasure bloomed within her.

Their bodies moved together in synchronicity, and though the moment of passion was fervent and erotic, it also felt familiar and safe. Being with Hayden, kissing him once again, was like coming home. They both knew this could only be another stolen night, but their need for one another suppressed any hesitation or rational thought. Brea moved her hips faster against Hayden, bringing them close to climax. Kissing her with earnest passion, their mouths parted, and his tongue's touch brought her over the edge into a state of incomparable euphoria. As their breaths slowed, Hayden held Brea against him. Pulling back to look at one another, he kissed her again with a light touch of his lips.

"What do we do now, Hayden?" Brea whispered.

"I don't know. I didn't know if you would kiss me, but I'm glad you did," he replied.

"It was the gum. I'm kind of addicted to it. Or at least, when you chew it around me, I am," Brea murmured with a kindling smile.

Hayden grinned mischievously and pulled her in closer to him, holding her tight in his arms as Brea rested her head on his shoulder. "Now I know your weakness."

Brea closed her eyes and inhaled, finding his scent comforting. "Hayden, what is this—I mean, what are we? And why is it that when I'm with you, I can't control myself?"

Hayden sighed. "It's the same for me. Brea, look—"

"Hayden, let's not spoil it," Brea whispered and shook her head. It would be better if Hayden did not answer. If she continued to fool around with Hayden, it would ruin her chance with Cylis, someone who could offer her an authentic relationship—she did not want to give up on him yet.

"It's late. Let me take you home," Hayden replied, then pushed the loose strands of hair that had fallen on her cheeks behind her ears. Sliding back into her seat, Brea clipped in her seatbelt as Hayden shifted the gear to drive back to Black Harbor.

❧❦❧

The drive had lulled Brea to sleep. Hayden woke her by rubbing the back of her head with a light touch. Opening her eyes for a moment and then closing them, she mumbled, "No, I don't want to go in," dreading the icy cold walk to her front door and the icy cold house she would have to sleep in. Hayden sat back and closed his eyes to wait until Brea felt ready to go inside. Unaware of how long they had stayed in the car together, Brea eventually stirred and opened her eyes. She looked at Hayden, resting with his eyes closed. "Goodnight, Hayden," she whispered.

Hayden smiled. "Goodnight." He turned his head towards her and opened his eyes. Brea put on her coat and exited the warm car to step into the bitter cold air. She hurried up the walkway to her porch and turned around after reaching the top of the steps. Hayden watched to ensure she made it inside the house before driving off. She fumbled with her keys, opened the door, and disappeared into the darkness.

Chapter Thirty-Five

The Present

Brea rolled over, struggling to fall asleep. She fixed her eyes on Adam's bare back. He had joined her in bed several minutes before, having stayed up late to work in his office after dinner. Remembering the night with Hayden in the diner, she wiped away the tears in her eyes.

Unable to sleep the previous night, she had called Hannah earlier that morning, telling her she felt ill and needed to stay home. Hating to lie to Hannah, she reasoned it had not been a complete fabrication, as her mental state in truth balanced like a wobbly rock set upon the tip of a pencil. Her withdrawal and isolation for the past two days necessitated spending the day with Alex and Sophie. She missed the two most precious, incredible people in her life and, further, she needed a break from her fiery memories.

Before lunch, Brea had sent Tina home early so she could take her children to the park for a picnic. Afterward, they drove to the public library to play in the kids center and pick out new books. Trailing behind Sophie and Alex in the children's section, she had a temporary pause from the potent feelings that had flooded her body over the previous two days.

Brea pulled out a beloved picture book she would read as a child and opened it. Recalling how the smell of the paper soothed her, she lifted it to her nose and inhaled. A faint smile stretched over her lips—the scent acted like a salve, palliating the emotional wounds that had reopened since seeing Hayden at Brine.

Now in bed, she watched Adam's back expand and contract from his slowing breaths. She desired tenderness and comfort, what she felt with Hayden all those years ago when she felt alone and lost. Lying next to Adam, she felt an urge to reconnect with him, and there was no alternative but to initiate it, no matter how awkward it felt.

"Adam," she whispered.

He grumbled, "Yeah?"

Brea lifted her arm and extended it towards his shoulder. Upon feeling the touch of her fingers on his skin, she hoped he would roll over, look into her eyes, and hold her. Finding and saying the words out loud—that she needed his affection—was too difficult. She hesitated, pulled her hand back and shifted her body closer to him.

"Brea, what are you doing? I can't sleep with you pressed against me like that," Adam mumbled.

"It's been a rough couple of days," she whispered.

"Get some sleep then," he replied, rolling onto his stomach.

Brea inhaled a deep breath. "I think we should talk, Adam—about us." Brea pressed her hand to her mouth, surprised she had said the words out loud.

"I think we should sleep, Brea," he muttered.

Brea rolled onto her back and stared at the ceiling. Her heart sank. The memory of Hayden wiping her tears away on her porch filled her chest with an unbearable ache.

Was she ever held by Adam the way Hayden had held her? Or had Adam filled her with the feeling that as long as they were in one another's arms, it mattered little if the world fractured and disintegrated around them? She felt desperate for it now, when she needed it most. Adam lay a foot away from her in physical distance, yet an endless desert of detachment separated them.

Brea sat up and turned to look over her shoulder at her husband. He made no movements nor indication that he noticed. She left the bedroom. Walking down the hall and into the foyer, she grabbed her purse off the double-pedestal console table and carried it with her into the kitchen. From the refrigerator water dispenser, she filled a glass to the top, placed it on the white marble counter, and sat down on a stool.

She surveyed her pristine custom stone-colored kitchen cabinets and stainless-steel appliances. Licking the corner of her mouth, she thought to herself, if someone snapped a photograph of her kitchen, it could print in a home décor magazine. But if they opened up the pantry, they would find a disorderly mess of snack bags, old boxes of crackers, expired jars of various pasta sauces, and grocery bags bursting out of a drawer she never recycled. Her eyes flickered up to the ceiling, meditating on the fitting metaphor for her life.

Opening her purse, she pulled out Hayden's card and stared at the print. He told her to call him if she wanted to see him again, something that day she never believed she would consider—but now she did. After tapping the card on the table several times, she shoved it back into her purse and dropped her head into her hands.

Although occupied with Alex and Sophie earlier, her journey through her past had slowed, for reasons unrelated to the activities of the day. Brea had reached the point of needing to dive into the last six months of her junior year. It would be the most difficult time to remember—she feared it, yet more than ever, felt the weight of necessity to go back there.

She needed a solid night of sleep, but the idea of returning to her bedroom lacked appeal, and as she surveyed her surroundings, she felt her entire home confining. The urge to move fresh air through her lungs motivated her to grab the folded blanket on the couch and venture into the backyard.

Careful to close the doors behind her with a light touch, she stepped onto the lawn in her bare feet. The grass felt slightly damp, but soft. She spread out the blanket, lay down and stretched her arms and legs while looking up into the sky.

Finding the air lighter and sweeter outside, a phantom heaviness lifted off her chest, and the breaths came easier as she rubbed the blades of grass between her fingers. In the night's quiet her eyes grew heavy, and before falling asleep, she thought how outlandish it would be if she woke up covered in snow.

Chapter Thirty-Six

The Past

Harvey Slate went on a winter holiday break for two weeks, and snowstorms passed through Black Harbor, burying the unfortunate residents who had not traveled for the holidays under a thick blanket of snow. Brea's friends, including Cylis and Hayden, had departed on family vacations, leaving Brea housebound and alone for the duration of the break.

On Sunday afternoon, the day before Harvey Slate would resume classes, Cylis called Brea to invite her to visit an art museum with him the following Saturday. Although Brea had considered Hayden's warnings about Cylis, she ultimately dismissed his concerns. On the phone, Cylis, apologetic about Eva, reassured her they were no longer together and that he was looking forward to him and Brea *"becoming closer."* He then mentioned Hayden, asking if there was something between them.

"I hope not. I don't think I could share you, Brea," he said, his tone of voice dejected. Brea, moved by his sentiments, reassured him she and Hayden were not dating, then accepted his invitation.

After her conversation with Cylis, Brea found her mother seated at the dining room table cluttered with a tabletop easel, a canvas pad, oil paints, brushes, and art books. During Brea's break from school, her mother, no longer agitated and irritable, would sit for hours, if not all day, at the table painting. Brea would check on her and, if she had not eaten, brought her a cup of tea and a sandwich or a plate of leftovers from the previous night's dinner.

With extra time on her hands, Brea had taken it upon herself to clean the home, estimating the last thorough cleaning had been over five years ago. After finding a plastic bag filled with old hand towels and a mop in the broom closet, she filled a bucket with hot water, vinegar, and dish soap and then worked her way throughout the home one room at a time, wiping away thick layers of dust on the shelves, counters, and tables. It took her two passes in every room with a broom to clean up the dust and debris, then she washed the hardwood floors and baseboards.

The physical exercise benefited her, lulling her into a meditative state. With her body occupied as she washed and polished, she would develop her storylines, or write ideas for new poems on a yellow legal pad she kept on the kitchen counter.

When passing her mother seated at the table, she would grab Brea's hand and ask her opinion on her painting. The majority were still life or landscapes, copied from an art book, and often well done. After praising her mother's work, a proud smile would appear on her mother's face. She would let go of Brea's hand and resume her painting.

With a rag in hand and dressed daily in an old sweatsuit with a bandana tied around her head, Brea cleaned the house from top to bottom. Her mother did not appear to notice, nor did she thank Brea.

When Brea had finished cleaning for the day, she would sit at the dining room table with her mother after preparing a pot of tea, then read or write in her journal. Often, they sat in silence and, on occasion, her mother would share with Brea interesting facts about famous artists or a new technique she had discovered to apply to an unfinished painting.

To Brea's surprise, her anger and resentment over the break had softened into pity and a maternal desire to care for her mother as she listened to recited sections from the art history texts. Still, knowing her mother, she knew her mood would inevitably shift, and it would be impossible to predict in which direction—these weeks of tranquility were sure not to last.

The following day, the second semester at Harvey Slate began, and Brea returned to school, eager to hear Tory and Anjali's stories of their travels. It was not until the middle of the week that Brea ran into Hayden in the courtyard, rushing to her American History class. Both of their faces were rosy from the bitter icy winds and it was too cold to stay outside and talk. He asked if she would meet him in the library after school, and Brea accepted.

Once classes had ended for the day, Brea found her usual table in the library. Seated, she hung her coat on the back of her chair and pulled out her math textbook to begin her homework. Shortly after, Hayden joined her. Having laid his coat on the empty chair beside him, he settled in at the table and they caught up on their winter breaks.

"I'm jealous you stayed home and could sleep in and read. I'm exhausted. It was more like a working family tour than a vacation," Hayden lamented.

"Right, well, I functioned as a housekeeper while everyone else was off touring the world—but I won't complain. Watching the snowfall during the storms was soothing, like meditating. Also, I did a ton of work on my writing, so I think I'm set for the second semester of English."

Hayden smiled and lowered his eyes, hesitating a moment before he spoke. "I bought you something in Sicily. I saw it in an antique shop and thought of you."

Brea's eyes brightened, moved. "Hayden, you didn't have to do that." Pulling a small red cardboard gift box out of his backpack, Hayden slid it across the table to Brea. She opened it, and a tender smile spread across her face. "Hayden, it's beautiful. I've never seen anything like it," she exclaimed as she ran her fingers over the blue enamel brooch in the shape of a butterfly.

"It's a long-tailed blue butterfly. The woman in the shop told me a local jeweler made it in the nineteen-twenties." Brea took the brooch out of its box and pinned it to her sweater.

Seeing it on Brea, a wide smile stretched across Hayden's face. "So, can we do something on Saturday? I was thinking more about the secret-friends thing, and if that's what it has to be for now, let's do it."

Brea's mouth opened and then closed. She would not lie to Hayden about Cylis. "I can't. Cylis is picking me up and taking me to the art museum for the day."

Hayden's face fell, and he looked away from Brea. "Really Brea? Do you think that's a good idea?" he asked, the tone of his voice laced with exasperation.

Brea inhaled sharply. "Hayden, I'm a big girl, but I can reassure you we spoke, and he's ready for us to take the next step. It was interesting. He was concerned that there was something going on between us—"

Hayden cut Brea off. "There is something between us, Brea."

Her heart sank in her chest. "You know what I mean, Hayden. I could have an actual relationship with Cylis and be happy now."

Shaking his head, he raised his voice. "Brea, he is going to hurt you. That smirk on his face at the party when we were outside—I don't understand how you can't see it." Brea rolled her eyes, insulted that Hayden considered her a naive child, incapable of caring for herself.

"Hayden, I can't trust your opinion of Cylis, for obvious reasons."

"Did he say, 'Brea, will you be my girlfriend' or did he say a bunch of bullshit about how special you are and you heard what you wanted to hear?" Hayden's expression of anger fueled Brea's irritation.

"Hayden, lower your voice," she exclaimed in a stern tone. "No, he didn't use those exact words, but essentially—yes. At least I'm pretty sure—stop confusing me."

"Brea, I can't sit by and watch you do this to yourself. If you wake up—and I hope you do—then we'll talk." Hayden stood up, grabbed his coat and bag, and strode out of the library.

Brea dropped her head into her hands and fought against the tears forming in her eyes. She loathed the idea of Hayden being angry with her. It hurt—but he was wrong. He had to be, and she would prove it to him.

Chapter Thirty-Seven

The Past

Located in a beach city east of Tupa Bay, Cylis drove Brea to the art museum on Saturday late morning, a repurposed private estate historically owned by a wealthy nineteenth-century real estate magnate. The art collection resided in the main residence, a large gray stone mansion with white shutters and an entrance overlay of ivory marble and matching grand columns.

"Are you hungry?" Cylis pointed to a sign by the stairwell leading to the museum cafe.

"A little. I could have something small." Brea followed Cylis down the stairs, wishing she could shake her foul mood. Upon joining him in the car, Cylis's kiss, landing on her cheek for only a moment before he turned his head, lacked any of the passion or affection she had hoped for.

Ruminating on her fight with Hayden as they drove, she could not push his warning out of her mind. She now doubted her belief that things were going to be different with Cylis and that Hayden had been right. Her pride did not want to accept that possibility.

"Cy, this place is gorgeous," Brea proclaimed, surveying the museum cafe—brightly lit and elegant, with marble cafe tables, gold resin royal chairs and candle chandeliers hanging from the ceiling.

"Not as beautiful as you. I missed seeing you for the past few weeks." One corner of his mouth turned up. Brea flushed. Cylis' admission confirmed that his intentions were genuine and Hayden was mistaken.

"I'm buying, so order whatever you'd like." With one hand, he tilted up Brea's chin and planted a fleeting kiss on her mouth. A radiant smile stretched across her lips as Cylis led her to the dessert display—a large counter with an expansive assortment of gourmet French pastries behind a glass window. Her eyes scanned the marvelous selection of patisserie.

She chose a small, round chocolate mousse cake. Cylis took Brea's hand in his as they walked to the counter to order. He ordered a coffee and salad for himself, then for Brea, her dessert, and a glass of lemonade. Finding an empty table, they sat down and discussed the various halls they would prioritize visiting that day.

"Brea, after the museum, let's go back to my house. I finished a short story, and I would like your opinion." The server arrived with their orders.

Brea thanked the server. "Of course, happy to. And I haven't seen your house yet—I can discover the secrets you hide there," she teased. As she ate the first bite, she closed her eyes. The flavor of the chocolate mousse sitting atop a layer of cake, covered with a glossy dark chocolate ganache and fresh berries, melded into the perfect balance of bitterness and sweetness. Cylis smiled and sipped his coffee, though left his salad untouched. He sat back in his chair and fixed his eyes on Brea as she ate her dessert.

"Wow, try this, Cylis."

"No, I'm enjoying watching you eat it," he replied.

"You are missing out," Brea taunted as she ate another large forkful. "So, I think I might impress you today. I spent the winter break with my mother while she painted and I read several of her art books. If you're lucky, I might share some fascinating art history with you."

"I think we should enhance the experience of this day," Cylis announced with a mysterious grin. Brea furrowed her eyebrows.

"Do you trust me?" Cylis sat up straight and pulled his chair in closer to the table.

Brea's mouth opened, but she hesitated. "Yes," she answered after a pause.

"Do you want to be close to me?" Cylis placed his chin in his hand and covered his mouth.

Brea nodded, intrigued. "I do."

"Here." Cylis dove his hand into his pants pocket and pulled out a small plastic bag. Inside were two pink pills, both stamped with a smiling face.

Brea's eyes widened and she leaned forward to examine the pills. "I don't know, Cy, what are those?"

"Have you heard of ecstasy?" Cylis studied Brea's face to gauge her reaction.

"Yes, but I've done nothing like that before. Could it hurt me?"

"Brea, I wouldn't give you something that would hurt you. It will make us feel like we're the closest two people could be together. I've done this with Eva before—many times. Don't you want to feel that way with me?" Brea's heart raced as she stared at the pills on the table. Although she wanted Cylis to see her as adventurous as Eva, the idea of taking a drug frightened her.

Cylis extended one hand and brushed Brea's cheek with his finger. "Let's walk around the museum, and we'll drop it once we get back to my house."

Brea pursed her lips and lowered her eyes to her hands. "Let me think about it, Cy."

Cylis's eyes flickered to the side and a faint hint of irritation in his facial expression betrayed him. He drew in a deep breath and slid the bag closer to him before returning it to his pocket.

"Come on, let's walk around," he said as he stood, averting his eyes from her. Conflicted, she rose. Brea did not want Cylis to believe her to be closed-minded and immature, or worse—that he would pull away as they prepared to take the next step in their relationship.

She followed Cylis in silence up the stairs into the main hall of the museum and into the featured exhibition—a Matisse and Picasso side-by-side exhibition. As she contemplated Cylis' proposal, Brea struggled to relax and enjoy the artwork. He spoke little with her, and when she took his hand, he would soon let go and move on to another painting without her. This continued as they walked through the Impressionist, American art, and Dutch painting halls.

Reaching the Post-Impressionist wing, Brea's favorite period of art, they studied the collection of Gauguin, Cezanne, Seurat, and Van Gogh paintings. Fascinated, Brea examined the vividly painted canvases. Some possessed a contradictory moodiness despite their bright colors—she struggled to find the vocabulary to describe what she felt until she came upon a painting that gave her pause. Scrutinizing *In the Waves*, 1899, by Gauguin, a painting of a nude woman with auburn hair positioned with her back to the viewer, a profound wave of sadness overcame her.

The figure appeared to rise out of the ocean like a siren in a sea of dark emerald-green tumultuous waves. Brea averted her gaze to break the hypnotic effect the painting held over her. Cylis moved closer to her and took her hand. Her eyes returned to the painting. She allowed the tears to roll down her cheeks and wiped them away with her free hand.

"What do you see, Brea?" Cylis asked.

"It's beautiful," she replied, her voice wavering. "Her neck, the way she's stretching it—I can't tell if she's extending it like that to seduce someone or if she's trying to catch her breath—calling out for help, but no one can hear her."

Cylis squeezed her hand. "I hear you, Brea," he whispered into her ear. Dropping Brea's hand, he placed his arm around her shoulders and pulled her against his chest.

Brea looked into his eyes. "Let's go back to your house and take the pills." In that moment, she believed Cylis to be the only person who understood her, and she wanted to be as close to him as they could be, as he had been with Eva.

Chapter Thirty-Eight

The Past

One hour later, Brea and Cylis arrived at his home. He lived in a secluded wooded area on the northern border of Tupa Bay in a dark gray contemporary home with large windows spanning the length of the second story. Brea stepped out of the car, impressed with the peace and tranquility of the property.

"My parents are gone for the week. We have the entire house to ourselves." Cylis took Brea's hand and led her inside through the garage. The interior as well reflected a modern design with light wood flooring, ivory walls, and a sleek, minimalist style of gray and black furniture, shelving, and large-scale framed abstract photographs on the walls. The kitchen featured unusual dark gray cabinetry extending from floor to ceiling. If not for the sink in the center island, Brea would have mistaken the kitchen for an elaborate storage unit.

As expensive and well-decorated as the home was, it was not welcoming. The aesthetic, being too modern for Brea's taste, resembled a nightclub rather than an inviting home. Cylis removed his coat, then helped Brea out of hers, draping them both on a kitchen counter stool. Feeling warm, Brea removed her wool sweater, leaving her dressed in a black tank top and gray jeans.

Handing Brea a glass of mineral water, Cylis removed the small plastic bag from his pocket, then took care to empty its contents onto the marble counter. With a finger, he pushed one pill to Brea. She stared at it for a moment, then glanced at Cylis beside her. A slight smile formed on his face when she met his eyes. She picked it up, placed it on her tongue, and with a large sip of water swallowed it before she could change her mind.

"Good girl," Cylis grinned. Taking the glass of water out of Brea's hand, he popped the other pill into his mouth. "Sit down in the living room and get comfortable. I'll grab the manuscript." Cylis leaned down to kiss Brea on her cheek, then left the room. Over his shoulder, he called out to remind her it would take about thirty minutes for the drug to take effect.

Brea opened her mouth wide to draw in a deep breath, hoping to calm the flutters in her stomach. Seeing the large glass windows in the living room, she strolled over to gaze outside. She studied the dense landscape of evergreen trees surrounding the property, musing there was an eerie beauty to the woods. Brea imagined how frightening it would be if lost in them at night, uncertain of what could be hiding in the depths of the forest.

Turning around, her eyes landed on a modular black leather sofa in the center of the living room where she could sit and continue to enjoy the view as she waited for Cylis to return. Although stylish, she had trouble finding a comfortable position as it felt rigid and dense beneath her. She lay down across the length of the sofa, and her eyes drifted to the ceiling, wondering if this drug would do what Cylis claimed—make them feel closer and more connected.

Staring at the ceiling, Brea hummed and lost track of the time until she checked her watch. Cylis had been gone for almost twenty minutes. Brea slipped off her shoes and socks. It may have been the effect of the drug, but the room felt warmer. She wiped the beads of sweat forming on her forehead, then dried her hand on jeans, wondering if perhaps the heating had malfunctioned.

"Cy, it's so hot in here. Can you check your thermostat?" Brea called out, but she heard no response.

Brea sat up and fanned herself with her hand, leaving an imprint of sweat behind her on the sofa. Cylis returned to the living room with his manuscript in hand. He had changed into a white tank top and a pair of gray sweatpants. This was the first time Brea had seen the upper half of his body fairly uncovered—he was lean but muscular, with a large tattoo on his left shoulder blade.

"What does that symbol mean—your tattoo, with all the flames?" Brea asked.

"Hephaestus. Greek god of fire."

"That's intense, but so cool," Brea said, giving him a thumbs up in approval. Cylis smiled and handed her the typed manuscript.

"Should I read or do you want to tell me about it first?" Brea thumbed through the manuscript, estimating there were thirty pages.

"No, start reading and I'll make us a drink." Brea settled in, lifted her legs onto the sofa, and read. Beads of moisture continued to accumulate on her forehead and above her upper lip—she wished she had a towel to dab her face.

Returning to join Brea, Cylis handed her a cold drink. Hot and thirsty, she drank half of it down. It was bitter, a mix of vodka and a blend of citrus juices. Placing the glass on the coffee table, she continued reading. Cylis sat on the sofa several feet from Brea, watching her as she read.

The plot of the story centered on an older man with thanatophobia, an intense fear of mortality. To cope with his phobia, he seduced sixteen-year-old girls with a predilection for brunettes.

As the story progressed, she felt an increasing sense of disquiet. It was clear Cylis had used Brea as inspiration for the female main character—flawed and wounded. The story took a darker turn. Disturbed, she read a violent and explicit sexual scene.

Halfway through the manuscript, Brea felt waves of something coursing through her body as though she were lifting off the sofa, akin to riding an ocean wave. Placing the manuscript on her lap, she turned to Cylis.

"Cy, I'm feeling something. It's like I'm on a roller coaster, and I can feel my heart beating so fast. It's uncomfortable."

"Don't be scared of it. Let go. It's kicking in," he replied with an impassive expression.

Brea blinked her eyes several times. The waves felt somewhat pleasant, though a knot of anxiety had likewise settled in her chest. "Cy, do you feel it?" she asked, closing her eyes.

"I do. Brea, what do you think of my story?"

"I think you put me in it, and it's strange. It's dark, and I can't finish it right now." A wave of nausea and unease rolled through Brea.

"But the last half is the best part. I'll read it to you." Cylis shifted closer to Brea, took the manuscript, and with his free hand, rubbed her neck.

Brea laid her head on the top of the sofa. She felt an odd mixture of apprehension and heaviness in her body, coupled with intense physical waves of heat. "No, let's finish it later Cy, I feel strange."

Cylis chuckled. "Fine." He tossed the manuscript onto the table, and the papers scattered onto the floor like leaves caught in a gust of wind.

"Stand up. Come here." Cylis rose from the sofa and held out his hand to Brea. She fixed her eyes on his hand and traced the veins in his arm to his biceps. "Do you want to be closer to me now?" he asked. Brea shifted her gaze to his face, and his silver-gray eyes bore into her with intensity.

"Yes," she answered, looking into his eyes. If he held her, perhaps the frightening sensations coursing throughout her body would abate.

"Follow me to my room. I have an idea." He continued to stand over Brea, holding out his hand with a self-possessed expression.

"What is it?" Brea asked as her eyes fixed once again on his arm.

"I want to watch you dance."

Brea looked at Cylis, his eyes rooted to her with a piercing gaze. She felt her cheeks burning, then wiped her forehead. "Cy, I can't. I'm too hot."

"Take off your jeans. Watching you dance with your legs covered would ruin it."

"I don't know, Cy, I'm not comfortable." Brea placed her hand on her chest—her heart beat faster than she knew it could.

Cylis leaned down, gripped Brea's waist, then lifted her off the sofa. His strength surprised her. Lowering his face in front of hers, Cylis smiled. "You said you trusted me, Brea. Is that true?"

Brea swallowed, ashamed to admit how uncomfortable she felt. Dancing on stage in her leotard and tights had never bothered her, but what Cylis asked of her—to dance for him dressed only in her tank top and underwear—felt too raw and sexual. She had hoped for more romantic intimacy with him.

"Yes, I trust you. It's only that you've never really kissed me and you're asking me to take off my pants." Cylis moistened his lips and, with an assertive grip, placed his hands behind her head and kissed her. The invasion of his tongue into her mouth, both startling and aggressive, caused her to stumble.

"There. Let me help you." Cylis unbuttoned her jeans and lowered them off her legs. Brea rubbed her hands together. She did not stop him despite feeling conflicted and self-conscious. Eyeing her with a faint smile, he threw her jeans onto the sofa, then ran his fingers up her outer thighs. "Brea, your skin feels amazing."

More exposed than she felt comfortable with, Brea crossed her arms in front of her chest and pressed her trembling hands against her body, hoping to still them. Cylis placed his hand on her lower back and led her down the hallway to his bedroom.

After entering his room, he walked her to the center, stopping several feet in front of his bed, made up with a black comforter and two large white pillows. Cylis took several steps back from Brea, placed his hands behind his head and stretched his neck to look at the ceiling before speaking.

"Brea, let's think of this as a game. You want to play, right?"

Brea did not respond as she surveyed his room, finding the black painted walls and ceiling disorienting. On the walls hung several large black-and-white photographs of ominous-looking landscapes.

"Brea?" Cylis repeated as he turned on his stereo with the remote. Standing before her, he widened his stance, and she nodded while wiping the sweat off her forehead and chest. Although she wanted to leave, and her hands would not stop trembling, she felt embarrassed to refuse Cylis.

"I want to watch your body move. Start dancing."

"I don't understand, Cy, watching me dance isn't a game." Cylis circled around Brea, then from behind wrapped his arms around her, and kissed her earlobe.

"You wanted us to be closer. And if you want that, do what I'm asking for. That's part of the game to get what you want," he whispered into her ear. Brea wiped her forehead once more and relented. She would dance for him to one song, and then it would be over.

"Okay, but then let's go outside. It's too hot in your house." Cylis did not reply. He removed his shirt and tossed it onto the floor as he crossed the room. With the remote, he changed the song and cranked up the volume of the music. Lying across the bed on his side, he gestured for Brea to begin.

Brea hooked her hands behind her neck and moved to the music while Cylis watched, dragging his fingers across his lips. After a minute, Brea paused and clutched her hands against her abdomen. "Cy, I don't want to do this anymore. I don't like this." She found the song unduly sexual and dark, and the volume was so loud, the beat of the bass reverberated in her chest.

"Brea. You want to be close to me, and I want to watch your body move to the music," Cylis called out. Brea studied his expression and found the grin on his face unsettling. She shut her eyes and danced again. Closing her eyes somehow lessened her discomfort, though her hands felt numb and continued to tremble. Most unsettling, she could not inhale a deep enough breath to satisfy her, as if the air had thickened.

When the song ended, her body jolted upon feeling Cylis's hands touch her bottom. Standing before Brea, he slid his hands up her back, reached her collarbone, and moved aside the damp pieces of hair stuck to her chest. He dropped his head and kissed her neck. Brea felt an aversion to the touch of his lips on her skin, and she took a step back. With force, Cylis grabbed her arms and drew her nearer to him. He lowered the straps of her tank top and bra, exhaled, and used his fingers to trace the curves of her breasts.

Brea pushed away his hands. "No, Cy. Turn off the music. It's too loud, and I don't feel good. Please stop touching me." She attempted to pull up her straps when Cylis placed his hands on her shoulders and gripped them firmly. He was strong, and it hurt when his fingers pressed deep into her skin. "Cy, please," she pleaded. Her body trembled as tears formed in her eyes, spilling over her cheeks and forming thick lines down her face. Shutting her eyes, she dropped her head.

"Open your eyes, Brea," Cylis commanded over the music. Brea startled and obeyed, but fixed her eyes on the floor.

"Look at me," he directed with a forbidding tone of voice. Cylis pinched her chin and with a firm grip, tilted her head up as she raised her eyes. Seeing the menacing smile on his face, she attempted to turn her head, but he would not allow it.

"Brea, you said you wanted to play. Game's not over yet—got it?"

Brea sucked in a sharp breath, and her stomach sank. They were alone in his house, in the woods, and there was no one to help her—he had her trapped, and she would not be able to fight him off.

Cylis released his grip on her chin only when she nodded. Frightened and immobile, she lowered her eyes as Cylis lifted her off the floor. As he carried her to the bed, Brea's only thought was that she wished the ceiling would split open so she could see the trees above her—but all that surrounded her was black paint and darkness.

✦

That night, in silence, Cylis drove Brea home, and she neither spoke nor looked at him as they slowed to a stop in front of her house. She stared blankly ahead, and it felt like someone else controlled her body when she stepped out of the car and onto the pavement.

Reaching her front door, she was unaware of the time, though the house was dark and her parents were sure to be asleep. Brea entered her home, feeling as if she had fought in a battle—her body heavy and her mind numb. The moment she stepped into the foyer, she became nauseated and hastened her steps to the bathroom. She made it in time to vomit in the toilet and then lay down on the cold black-and-white tiles.

Unaware of how many minutes or hours had elapsed since having lain on the bathroom floor, eventually Brea became thirsty. She lifted herself and walked into the kitchen. Opening the refrigerator, she pulled out a carton of milk, drank and nearly emptied it, and left it on the kitchen table. Her surroundings, dull and surreal, felt like a dream, or rather, as though she was amid a lucid dream after waking from a nightmare.

Brea did not remember walking up the stairs or entering her bedroom, but at some point, found herself seated on the edge of her bed, still dressed. Leaving her bedroom light on, she lay down, hoping Hayden would drive by, see it on, and throw a stone at her window.

Chapter Thirty-Nine

The Past

The winter resisted letting go of its hold over Black Harbor until early April. Tired of the interminable gray skies and sporadic snowstorms, the stubborn cold weather gave way to spring. The Harvey Slate Junior class had progressively shut down nearly all social activities over the previous several months to study for the SAT. By March, weekend parties had mutated into group study sessions at coffee shops, the Harvey Slate library, and the kitchen tables of generous parents willing to provide endless snacks and coffee for overachieving teenagers.

Brea studied at home or at the public library, preferring to work in isolation rather than with her friends as she had little patience for interruptions from Tory or Allegra, who took regular breaks to buy coffee or to take a walk. Her need to score high on the SAT had crossed the line into obsession—the harder she studied, the easier it had been to push away memories of Cylis. And as the months passed, the shame and revulsion she felt diminished, made easier since Cylis never attempted to call or find Brea again—vanishing as though he had never existed. Her efforts to forget him proved so effective, she sometimes wondered if that day at his house had been only a nightmare.

After that day at the museum, Brea told her parents she had caught the flu and stayed in bed for four days. On the second day, buried under her covers, she decided two things—what had happened was her fault and she would tell no one what Cylis had done to her. Without question, Allegra, Tory, and Anjali believed Brea's lie that she had given up on waiting for Cylis and had ended their friendship.

When Brea returned to school, Hayden found her in the library to apologize for his behavior and their argument. She accepted his apology and then revealed that she and Cylis were no longer speaking after discovering he was not interested in a committed relationship. Hayden suspected Brea held back something from him, but he did not press her further, relieved Cylis was out of her life.

Hayden would meet Brea at the Black Harbor Public Library and call to check on her over the months. Although she tried to conceal it, Hayden observed that something within her had shifted—a subtle melancholy and a resigned indifference to the world around her. He half believed her claim that the SAT added a layer of stress on top of her usual studies, and did not press the topic of seeing her other than when they met at the library. Brea told Hayden she would re-emerge in the spring with the rest of the junior class, and he hoped that would be true.

Following the SAT, the junior class's social scene reawakened, and a Harvey Slate party coincided with Brea's seventeenth birthday on Saturday. Two weeks earlier, Jasmine, a graduating senior, learned that her first-choice college had accepted her. As her parents were out of town, she planned a celebratory party. No one cared about Jasmine's acceptance, but they cared deeply about the chance for a dissolute party after a brutal winter and endless, intense studying. Tory, Anjali, and Allegra insisted Brea come to the party despite her hesitation.

Arriving at Jasmine's house, Brea looked out the window of Anjali's car at the large Cape Cod-style home with black shutters and a steep roof with dormer windows. A large white sign with a black arrow tacked on an oak tree ferried everyone towards the side of the house. There, an open white wooden gate welcomed everyone to the party in the backyard.

Tory, Anjali, Allegra, and Brea entered the gate to find one hundred teenagers scattered throughout the yard, exuberant and engaged in conversations, dancing, and playing drinking games. It was a cool night, yet warm enough to stay outside for the duration of the party. Ivory frosted lights decorated the beams of the large covered patio, and in the yard's corner sat a stone outdoor fireplace with beige patio furniture beneath a wooden pergola.

The girls walked in a row of four to the small white canopy tent on the lawn, where a folding table and several coolers housed the bar. Brea fixed herself a rum cocktail with pineapple juice and scanned the crowd. Grateful to dress in something other than her Harvey Slate uniform or a sweatsuit, tonight Brea wore a mauve jersey cotton dress, ballet flats, and had washed and styled her hair with loose waves. Drinks in hand, the girls strolled through the yard to greet and chat with their classmates. Soon after, Tory and Anjali broke away upon seeing Trevor arrive at the party.

Brea groaned, knowing that not far behind would be Jaime, and sure enough, a minute later he entered with Aaron and a group of three girls. Jamie held the hand of a petite blonde trailing behind him—she knew Jaime would move on, even so, it was difficult to witness his new relationship paraded in front of her.

Jocular and appearing to be his usual gregarious self, Jaime greeted other Harvey Slate classmates with enthusiasm and a broad smile. Watching him, Brea felt a hollowness in her chest. It felt like a lifetime ago she had been Jaime's girlfriend, naive in her belief that the world was a kinder place than it is. Now she felt damaged, having seen the true nature of the world sprinkled with dark and violent landmines.

Jaime's date, conventionally attractive and dressed in a tight red skirt paired with a hot pink fitted shirt, wore a vacant expression on her face. Suppressing a smile, she wondered if her facial expression betrayed a lack of intelligence or drug use. Her two friends were taller and plainer, both blonde as well, dressed in jeans and shiny polyester tops. The two of them were engaged in an animated conversation, gesturing with their hands as they walked.

Brea drank the entirety of her cocktail in several gulps. Allegra nudged her on the arm.

"Hey, you want to slow down there? We have all night." Brea shrugged her shoulders.

"You know, me and Tory were on the verge of having an intervention with you until you agreed to come out tonight. I can't lie. We've been worried about you."

Brea nodded. "I know, sorry. With school and the SAT, I've been obsessed with studying. But it's behind me. I just need some time to relax and catch up on sleep," Brea replied in an effort to reassure Allegra.

Allegra pursed her lips together as she studied Brea, uncertain if she believed her. She then added, "By the way, Jacob is going to meet us here soon. I saw him three times in the last month between the SAT and spring break." Brea rubbed her forehead, embarrassed she had been self-centered and neglected to ask Allegra about her relationship with Jacob. Reflecting further, she now knew she had been a terrible friend since transferring to Harvey Slate, focusing only on herself and taking her friendship with Allegra for granted.

"Hey Allegra, I'm sorry I've been gone for so long. I haven't been a best friend to you for a long time," Brea said, sincere in her apology and fighting back tears.

Allegra took a step closer to Brea and sighed. "Hey, I know that you're in a different school and all kinds of shit happened over the year. And to be honest, I haven't been one hundred percent supportive either. You know I wanted to punch Jaime and Cylis more than once, but, look, we're going to be fine. What's going on with you?" she asked, enveloping Brea's shoulder with her arm.

Brea wiped her eyes. "I don't know. Maybe it's because I'm seventeen today, but I feel like I'm seventy. I've made so many mistakes, and I don't know how to fix things."

Allegra inclined her head to the side with a smile and then embraced Brea. "Why don't we plan a sleepover and eat a stack of grilled cheese sandwiches next Saturday? We can talk all night, and it will be like old times."

"That would be—just what I need." Brea managed a half-smile, though she felt numb, lacking faith anything could piece her back together. Tory waved to Brea and Allegra, motioning for them to join her and Trevor near the fire.

"Go ahead. I'm going to eat something, and then I'll meet you over there," Brea said. Allegra left, and Brea made her way to the snack table on the patio. She filled a plastic cup with cubes of white cheddar cheese and black grapes. As she ate, she surveyed the party for anything of interest to focus on when the world around her slowed to a screeching halt.

A boy with short platinum-blonde hair dressed in a white tank top and jeans drew her gaze, and her chest seized as if she had been shot. The boy turned around. She gasped in relief at seeing she had been mistaken and it was not Cylis. Rubbing her eyes, she extended her neck to look up, making it easier to open her airway and usher a large breath of air into her lungs. Her hands shook as she hurried to the bar for another drink.

Reaching the table, Brea poured a shot of vodka into a cup and drank it down. Desperate to fix another cocktail, she searched for the rum, picking up the bottles one by one to read the labels, then slamming them down in frustration, and almost knocking one over. Finding the rum, she poured it into her plastic cup one-third of the way full, then topped it off with a half-can of cola. It was strong, but Brea needed it to calm herself down. The alcohol would shuttle to her brain, and the panic would temper shortly. All she needed to do was breathe and wait.

Brea sipped her drink and as she turned to leave, she caught Hayden's eye, standing on the periphery of the patio with a group of his classmates. Witnessing her distraught and bingeing on alcohol, he mouthed to her, "What the fuck?" Ignoring Hayden, she strode across the lawn to meet Allegra, Tory, Anjali, Trevor and several boys from the football team.

Engaged in cheerful conversations before the fire, no one appeared to notice Brea seat herself beside Allegra. Though she attempted to pick up the thread of the general discussion, the sinuous red flames of the fire—angry and violent—continuously drew her gaze and focus away from the group. It was odd. She knew it was fire and it would burn her without apology, yet she felt hypnotized, and the urge to touch the flames overtook her. The ease with which the fire lured her, she found disturbing, though she could not blame it. After all, she thought to herself, that was its nature—alluring and destructive—like the demon within Cylis.

As time passed, the party spiraled into chaos. In one corner of the lawn, a loud argument broke out between two seniors from the football team, fighting over a girl, and while some groups of teenagers were drinking shots and screeching out toasts, others were screaming insults or shouting over one another to tell a funny story. At the party's center, a mass of girls danced, grinding with one another to the loud music as boys catcalled and egged on the dancing girls to make out with one another.

In making a wise decision, Brea poured out her remaining drink and stood to find a bottle of water and another serving of food. An overwhelming desperation to separate herself from everyone took hold of her mind. Coming to the party tonight had been a mistake, and she wished she had stayed home to read in her garage.

Searching through the bags of snacks, Brea grabbed a handful of pretzels and then washed it down with an ice-cold bottle of water. Her eyes fixed on Jaime and his date, standing twenty feet from her on the patio. The girl held a beer in one hand and a red leather top-handle purse in the other, similar in style to the gold bag Jaime gifted Brea on her birthday last year. Studying her, Brea continued to ponder why she had a persistent, vacant look on her face when she felt two hands clap onto her shoulders from behind.

"Her name is Bianca. She's gorgeous, right? Moved here from New Jersey last month. Jaime adores her. I think she's the right girl for him," Vienna purred into Brea's ear.

"Yeah, she seems—awesome," Brea replied with a smirk as she brushed Vienna's hands off her shoulders, then turned to face her.

With a malevolent smile pasted on her smug face, Vienna attempted to taunt Brea. "So, are you still hung up on Cylis? It's kind of sad that you were hanging on to his dick while he walked in the opposite direction." Brea looked up into the sky and exhaled as Vienna continued.

"It was pathetic, B. Everyone was and still is laughing at you behind your back." With a cruel chuckle, Vienna removed a small leaf that had fallen onto Brea's shoulder.

"Vienna, I'm certain that one day you're going to discover the sad truth that you're pathetic," Brea replied with an icy glare and walked away—her fear of Vienna no longer had a hold on her. Brea had the misfortune in her young life to have met true evil face to face, and it had become clear Vienna only personified a tragic caricature of someone who wanted to be the villain. In truth, the worst Vienna could do to her would be to spread rumors and gossip like a petulant child.

It did not bother Brea if her peers believed she was pathetic and had chased after Cylis. What tortured her was the shame she carried with her, believing that what had happened to her had been her own fault. Despite Hayden's warning, she had persisted in her efforts to pursue Cylis and, as a result, she had walked into his trap.

Vienna's over-inflated ego did not register Brea's comment. Only she felt irritated that her pokes at Brea had failed to wound her cousin. Vienna sauntered off into the crowd, reassuring herself there were more interesting people to insult and intimidate that evening.

Done for the night, Brea walked across the lawn. Spotting Anjali, she lied, telling her she felt unwell and had found a ride home. It would be a long walk, but she cared little. The night air and exercise would help her relax and clear her mind. Jasmine lived near Black Harbor High School, and Brea estimated she would reach her house in forty minutes. Taking her time, Brea strolled down the street. Her feet would ache by the time she arrived home, but her early escape from the party would be worth the price.

The air was crisp and light. Brea drew deep breaths as she walked, imagining that with each inhale, she could cleanse her body and wash away her sins and regrets. If only it were that simple, still, at the moment it was the only strategy she had to soothe herself. She halted her steps as she passed a cluster of honeysuckle bushes. Perhaps it was a good omen, she thought to herself.

Honeysuckles only bloomed in late spring and summer, and they were one of her joyful memories as a young child. She remembered at four or five, holding a large branch on an Easter Sunday. Pulling off the flowers one by one, she would crush the blossoms between her fingers, lift them under her nose and inhale, feeling tranquil and contented. Brea leaned in to inhale the sweet, characteristic fragrance, hoping at that moment to recapture the same feeling from her childhood.

Although a pleasant scent, it failed to lift her mood. Continuing on, she found comfort in the echo of her hard-soled shoes hitting against the concrete. As she reached the corner to turn, she heard a car engine speeding up, growing louder from behind. Brea's steps slowed to a stop—turning around was unnecessary because she knew it was Hayden.

Was this not the pattern? Brea falls apart, and Hayden turns up to put her back together. The car came to a stop in the middle of the road, and the engine idled. Perhaps he, too, recognized the absurdity of their odd relationship and thought twice about whether he should stay or leave her alone to spiral downwards.

"B," Hayden called out to her. Brea did not move. "Get in, Brea." She turned, seeing Hayden watching her through the windshield. To avoid being seen, Hayden motioned for her to hurry, and after drawing in a deep breath, she went to him.

Chapter Forty

The Past

Brea opened the door, sank into the familiar seat, and buckled her seatbelt. Neither of them spoke. Turning to look at Hayden, she sighed. "Hi," Brea muttered, pushing the loose strands of hair stuck to her face behind her ears.

"Why did you leave?" Hayden asked, his expression stolid.

"I don't know. Why didn't you say hello or bother to talk to me while we were there?" she shot back.

"You know the answer to that. You were hitting the bar pretty hard over there. Are you trying to hurt yourself on purpose now?" Brea shook her head and looked out the window without answering.

"Are you mad at me?" he asked, incredulous.

Sucking in a breath, Brea shook her head. "No. I'm sorry. It isn't you. I thought I wanted to go home, but I'm feeling edgy. Maybe we could go somewhere for a little while so I can clear my head?" Giving Hayden a half-smile, Brea now felt a sense of gratitude he had found her.

"You hungry?" he asked.

"Not really."

Hayden thought for a moment. "Well, I know where we can go then," he said, shifting the gear, then stepping on the gas.

They drove in silence for several miles until they pulled up in front of Hayden's house.

He put the car in park and left the engine on. "I'll be right back," he said, jumping out of the car and jogging up the driveway to the garage. Brea rested her head on the window, gazing out at the streetlights as she listened to the hum of the engine. Hayden reappeared several minutes later, holding a folded plaid wool blanket. Once inside, he tossed the blanket onto the back seat and pulled away from the curb.

"I'm going to take you to this private beach I found one night. We're not supposed to go there, but I haven't been caught yet. We'll need to make one stop on our way."

"Is that where you take all your secret friends? Actually, don't answer that yet. I've been wondering, Hayden—do you have any friends?" Brea teased.

Hayden grinned and replied, "Nope. And you're the first person I'm taking there."

Brea smiled. "As I suspected." She checked her face and hair in the sun visor mirror, hoping she did not look disheveled, although with Hayden, it mattered little. He often saw her looking like a mess. Other than a few spots in the corner of her eyes where her eye makeup had smudged, she looked put together, though her lips felt dry. Digging into her purse, she found her lip balm and applied a thick layer.

Hayden pulled into the supermarket shopping complex and parked in front of the store. As he opened the car door, he turned to Brea. "You need anything?"

"Yes, a bottle of water, or whatever they have that's cold to drink." He stepped out and closed the door. Brea's eyes followed him enter the supermarket through the "Exit Only" door, propped open to let out the remaining customers. Brea checked the time—it was ten minutes to eleven, and the supermarket was about to close. Thirsty, she was glad they made it in time.

Restless in the car, Brea stepped outside to wait in the fresh air. There were several empty cars parked in the lot. She strolled around Hayden's car in circles until pausing to lean against the hood. Stretching her neck, she looked up into the vast night sky with patches of stars peeking out from between the clouds. Brea rubbed her neck to work out the muscle tension.

Hayden exited the store with two bottles of water in hand and slowed his pace upon seeing Brea leaning on the hood of the car. "What did you need to buy? Don't tell me it was porn," she said with a disapproving smirk as he joined her on the hood.

"No," he answered with narrowed eyes. "Should I go back in?" he joked.

Brea clicked her tongue, then smiled, amused as usual with their proclivity for good-natured banter. Flashing a mischievous grin, Hayden dug his hand into his pocket, produced a pack of cinnamon gum and held it up to show Brea. Brea's smile faded as she looked into Hayden's eyes. Hayden, disturbed by her change in facial expression, scrambled to apologize. "B, I was just messing around—"

Brea kissed him—without permission or apology and rolled over his leg to stand before him. Hayden dropped the bottles of water and gum to wrap his arms around her. His hands slid down her back to pull her in tighter as she lifted her arms to run her fingers through his hair. His scent—cypress and musk—intensified her desire for him.

They paid no attention to the time as they kissed, lost in one another until they heard the engine of a car speeding by on the road, and they pulled apart. Although alone in the parking lot, it would not be a good idea for them to act recklessly. Hayden tipped his forehead against the bridge of Brea's nose.

"Come on, let's go," he whispered. After picking up the water bottles and gum, they reentered the car and drove to where Hayden planned to take Brea.

Twenty minutes later, Hayden turned onto a private road lined with luxury beach homes in South Tupa Bay. Most were unoccupied in the off season until early summer. Hayden mentioned a security guard patrolled the area, but he often saw him sleeping in his car. As they turned into the neighborhood, Hayden pointed out the security guard, and they both laughed when they saw him asleep in the driver's seat.

Hayden drove into a driveway that curved around the final house on the street. If the security guard woke and drove down the road for a routine check, he would not see them. A magnificent view of the beach welcomed them from where they parked—a full moon had risen, illuminating the sand and the white foam of the waves crashing on the break against the shore.

"How did you find this place?" Brea asked.

Hayden removed his seat belt and turned to Brea. Hypnotized by the beauty of the ocean, she stared at the waves. Hayden reached over to unbuckle her seatbelt, then gave Brea a quick kiss on the lips. Turning towards him, she slipped off her shoes and lifted her legs to lay them across Hayden's lap before leaning back against the door.

"Last year, my dad was in one of his angry moods and lost it with my mom. I could hear everything from my room, and it became really intense. I had to make sure she was all right, and then—"

As she listened, Brea's expression shifted, and Hayden saw a sadness burgeoning in her eyes. He paused. "I don't want to go into all the details, but after I knew she was safe, I had to leave for a while. So, I left and drove around for hours until I found this place." He turned his head to look out at the ocean.

Brea meditated on his words before responding. In her home, it was the opposite—ice cold. She could not imagine what it would be like to live with someone who had a volatile temper. "It isn't fair," she said, staring at the water. "We don't get to pick our parents. But I guess none of it is fair, right?" she added, not expecting a reply. Hayden continued to gaze out of the windshield and rubbed his thumbs against his fingers.

"You know what's strange? It's my birthday today. Like last year at the campsite when you drove me home. Why does it seem like the universe brings us together for you to rescue me?" she asked abstractly, again not expecting an answer.

Hayden turned to face Brea. "I'm sorry. I forgot to tell you happy birthday." He checked his watch. "So, we have another twenty-five minutes to celebrate. Should I swipe some champagne from my house, or we could buy a package of cupcakes at the gas station?"

Brea chuckled. "No. I'm done with drowning myself in alcohol tonight. It feels good just to sit here."

Hayden thought for a moment. "How about a birthday present? Everything is closed, but if you tell me what you would like, I'll get it for you tomorrow."

Brea smiled. "What about a coupon or an IOU?"

Hayden nodded. "Anything in particular you had in mind?"

"How about this? If I need you again one day in the future, even if it's fifty years from now, you'll come and help me."

Hayden smiled. "What kind of trouble? Do I need to learn combat or train with weapons?" he teased.

"Maybe. Seriously, promise me that if you see I'm stuck in a pile of shit, come pick me up, take me to Mexico for a week, and help me sort it out."

Hayden put out his hand. "Agreed. How about since we missed my birthday this year, you do the same for me? Then it's more like a pact."

Brea laughed and shook Hayden's hand. "Deal." Hayden laid his head back. Their eyes remained fixed on the water and they sat in the silence until Brea asked him about his plans for graduation. Many colleges had accepted him, and graduation was approaching, but she did not know which one he had chosen.

"MIT," he replied, staring straight ahead with a blank expression and a neutral tone of voice.

"Hayden—congratulations," Brea exclaimed, straightening up for a moment with a broad smile. "You don't seem very excited."

Hayden groaned. "I am, but it's complicated. I'm worried about my mom and leaving her alone with my dad. I'm not sure if I want to go." Brea pressed her lips together. She understood his conflict, though felt compelled to bolster his enthusiasm and encourage him not to deprive himself of this extraordinary opportunity.

"I understand why you would be worried, but—you have to go, Hayden. You have worked so hard, and I can't imagine your mom would let you give up the chance to go there. It could change your life. I think it would break her heart if you gave that up to stay home with her." As she spoke, a pang of sadness hit Brea, realizing that soon Hayden would be gone. Even though the intimate nights they had spent together had been few, somehow knowing he was in Black Harbor, she felt less alone.

Hayden nodded. "Let's change the subject. What have you been writing lately?"

Brea gave Hayden a sheepish smile. "Song lyrics. I thought that if I wrote an interesting song, maybe someone could perform it at the senior showcase next spring.

"Really? Sing one for me."

"What? No way. I only wrote the lyrics—I'm not a singer."

"Come on, I don't care how you sound. I want to hear it," he pressed.

Brea attempted to shift the topic of conversation twice, but Hayden was relentless. After going back and forth for several minutes, they compromised. She would recite the lyrics to one of her songs, and he accepted.

"Is the song about your parents?" Hayden asked when she had finished.

"Yes." Brea smiled, impressed he had made that connection. The song was how she imagined her parents fell in love before everything broke apart into the life she now knew. "I have to believe at some point they loved each other. Or at least maybe they had some level of excitement about getting married and having children. You would never know it now. My house—it's a lonely place to be." Brea paused and stared into the distance. "My dad is oblivious, my mom is cold and unpredictable, and I have to disappear." Brea wiped her eyes and cleared her throat.

"It isn't fair," Hayden repeated back Brea's words. "Hey, could you reach into the backseat and grab the blanket?" he asked, pointing behind him. Brea reached into the backseat for the wool blanket and then resumed her prior position with her legs on Hayden's lap. Unfolding it, she tossed one end to Hayden to cover themselves.

Neither of them minded the clock. As time passed, the conversation slowed and as they listened to the sound of the waves crashing on the shore, they grew drowsy and eventually fell asleep. They slept for hours, occasionally stirring for a moment, only to close their eyes again, enjoying the comfort of one another's presence.

Just before dawn, Brea woke and she would have to go home soon. Watching Hayden as he slept with his lips parted, Brea smiled, appreciating how peaceful and endearing he looked at this moment.

"Look at us, Hayden, we're friends," she whispered and closed her eyes again.

A moment passed, and she heard Hayden reply, "Not sure about that. I still don't know what we are."

Hayden dropped Brea off at home as the sun rose. Handing her a piece of gum, he joked it was only for her breath—not an invitation to make out with him. She laughed when she took it from his hand, said goodbye, then hurried into her house. Relieved to discover her parents were still asleep, Brea crept up the stairs and into her room undetected.

After removing her dress, she put on her pajamas and slipped under her comforter. It had been a dark period for her, lasting many months, but now, as she lay in her bed, a seed of optimism sprouted. Being with Hayden last night, hope for a better future and placidity filled her—she fell asleep within several minutes.

Chapter Forty-One

The Past

Loud knocking on the door startled Brea. "Yeah," she called out, eager to make the obnoxious banging stop.

It was her mother. "Brea, you need to wake up. Your friend Tory is downstairs." Sitting up and pushing off her blanket, Brea scanned her room. Outside it was bright. Checking her alarm clock, she saw it was eleven o'clock.

"Tell her to come up, Mom," Brea replied as she rolled out of bed and crawled to her desk for a hair elastic. Her mouth had a slight cinnamon taste, but not enough to cover up the morning breath and alcohol from the previous night. Looking in the mirror, she attempted to rub away the makeup smudged into half circles under each eye.

Tory entered the room without knocking. "Brea," she said, out of breath.

"Hold on, Tory, let me go brush my teeth and wash my face. I just woke up."

"No, listen. Trevor called me this morning. Callie saw you last night at the supermarket with Hayden. She saw you both kissing, and Aaron's telling everyone he knew something happened with you and Hayden when you were with Jaimie. He's saying you guys lied about it, and—Jaime knows. Is it true, Brea?"

Brea sat down on the bed with her hand covering her mouth as her brain attempted to digest Tory's words. "How could I have been so stupid?" She rubbed her forehead and looked up at Tory. Tory shook her head, confused and at a loss what to tell Brea to comfort her. Shaking her head, Brea closed her eyes. Jaime now knew without a doubt she had lied.

"What is everyone saying? Do you know if Jaime has seen Hayden yet?"

Tory sat beside Brea on the bed. "I don't know. I don't think so."

Brea did not cry—she was stunned.

"Brea, what's been going on with you and Hayden?"

She sighed and met Tory's eyes. There would be no point in hiding anything now. As she shared the entire story, Tory's mouth hung open, dumbstruck. Similar to Allegra, she empathized and did not judge Brea.

"Why didn't you tell me? I would've understood," Tory said with a half-smile as she wrapped her arm around Brea.

"I couldn't, sorry." Brea shut her eyes, filled with dread, knowing she would have to face not only Jaime but Vienna as well on Monday.

"What am I going to do, Tory? I know I deserve the worst. I'm a liar, I cheated, all of it—"

Brea dropped her head in her hands and groaned. Shame washed over her, and she had only herself to blame. Hayden said the rules did not apply to them—but they did. Brea's betrayal of Jaime and Vienna would brand her a slut and untrustworthy under the scrutinizing lens of her high school peers.

"Look, go brush your teeth, take a shower, put on some clothes, and we'll figure it out. I brought you a coffee and a bagel. It's on the kitchen table downstairs—I'll get it for you." Tory stood to leave the room, leaving Brea on the bed. Before going to the bathroom, Brea needed to speak with Hayden. Picking up the phone, she grabbed her notebook and found his number. The phone rang half a dozen times, then went to voicemail.

In the bathroom, she brushed her teeth, then cleaned her face with soap and a washcloth to remove any traces of eye makeup. The aggressive scrubbing left her face pink and raw. She stepped into the steamy shower and the hot water seared her skin. It felt painful but soothing as she contemplated the mess she would need to climb out of.

Reluctant to waste time, Brea turned off the faucet after a shampoo. The cold air chilled her, and a wave of sadness washed over her as tears dropped from her eyes onto her cheeks. Though the humiliation stung, and she had little self-love to soothe herself, she would need to bury her tears and find Hayden before tomorrow. With him, they could figure out a strategy, and she would not have to face Harvey Slate alone. Wrapping herself in a towel and suppressing her distress, Brea headed back to her room. Tory sat at the desk, holding Brea's coffee in her hand.

"Thank you, you're amazing," Brea proclaimed as she took the cup from Tory, then drank a large sip. Although no longer hot, she welcomed the caffeine, and regardless, it tasted delicious. Slipping into a pair of denim shorts and a gray long-sleeved T-shirt, Brea towel-dried her hair and dabbed a touch of concealer under her eyes.

Tory held out the bagel to Brea. "No thanks, I have to go to Hayden's. We need to talk about what we're going to do tomorrow," she said and waved away the bagel.

"I'm not leaving until you eat," Tory replied in an assertive tone of voice.

"Half," Brea bargained and grabbed it out of Tory's hand. She had no appetite, but ate. Satisfied, Tory walked downstairs and out of the house with Brea.

"I can drive you to Hayden's," Tory offered as they stepped onto the porch.

"No thanks. I'm going to ride my bike. Thanks for everything and I'll call you later." Brea embraced Tory, appreciating her loyalty and friendship, then sprinted down the driveway to fetch her bicycle in the garage.

CHAPTER
FORTY-TWO

THE PAST

B rea arrived at Hayden's house twenty minutes later after pushing herself to ride as fast as possible. Hayden lived five miles from her house with only a few short hills to climb, making the route manageable. Upon turning the corner onto his street, Brea was out of breath with beads of sweat dripping down her forehead.

At the end of his driveway, she slowed to a stop—his black Lexus was parked outside the garage. Brea slid off the seat and set the stand on her bike. Her heart raced as she made her way up the walkway. Knowing what she did about Hayden's father and his volatile temper, she hoped he would not answer the door.

Scanning the exterior of the home and landscaping, she felt uneasy. There was an off-putting air of perfection coupled with the evergreen shrubs pruned into urn-like shapes lining the front of the home. Brea's fingers trembled as she raised her right hand to ring the bell. After pressing the button, she took a step back to wait and drew in a deep breath to calm her nerves.

No one answered the door. Waiting another minute, she rang the bell again. Brea detected no sounds or movements from inside the house and wondered if Hayden was asleep, or rather avoiding answering the door, believing it might be Jaime or Vienna. Looking around, she stepped off the pathway onto the lawn to walk around the side of the house. If Hayden was home and sleeping, she could knock on his glass doors and wake him up. Brea made it halfway across the front lawn when a voice stopped her in her tracks.

"Can I help you, miss?" Startled, Brea whipped around with her hand over her heart.

"Oh, I'm sorry I scared you," an older man said, dressed in a light-blue button-down shirt and tan trousers, with a round face, a bushy gray moustache and a US Marines cap on his head.

"Oh, no, I'm fine. I'm looking for Hayden—Hayden Botero. I see his car parked in the driveway, but no one is answering when I ring the doorbell."

"No one is home, miss. They left behind the ambulance a couple of hours ago. Mr. Botero asked me to keep an eye on the house for the next few days."

Brea felt as though something had slammed into her and knocked the air out of her chest. Closing her eyes and shaking her head, she desperately hoped she had misheard what the man had said. "I'm sorry, I don't understand. What happened?"

Her heart thumped, and a sick feeling sprouted in her core, terrified something had happened to Hayden. Knowing what she did about Hayden's father and his having stayed out all night with her, perhaps his father had caught Hayden coming home in the morning and hurt him.

"Miss, the boy found his mother dead this morning coming home. She was already gone, found by the boy on the sofa in the living room. There wasn't anything they could do. It's a tragic thing, still a young woman and all. All morning there was a lot of activity with the ambulance and police here. I'm assuming you're a friend of the boy?"

"Yes," she replied, her voice flat. Brea blinked her eyes and shook her head. "Do you know how she died?" Brea felt compelled to ask, though uncertain she wanted to know the truth.

"No, Miss, I don't. I live across the street and can't say I spoke with the family very much. They kept to themselves, but my wife chatted from time to time with Mrs. Botero. Said she was a lovely woman," he answered, appearing troubled as he turned his head to look at the front door of Hayden's home. "Mr. Botero and the boy will stay with family for some time. It's a genuine tragedy. My wife and I are just shaken up about it. We're the Hammonds, by the way, if you would like to write a note and leave it with us. I'll be holding onto their mail for the time being."

Brea gave Mr. Hammond a brief nod, her body otherwise remained motionless. "Thank you," she replied with a strained voice.

He gave Brea a gentle smile, then turned to walk across the lawn. She watched Mr. Hammond cross the street and disappear after he entered his home, leaving her standing alone in the middle of Hayden's yard. Lightheaded and worried for Hayden, Brea plodded to her bike. She paused and covered her face, picturing Hayden walking into his home and finding his mother dead—it broke her heart, and she could not bear it.

The truth coming out about Brea and Hayden mattered little now. Their indiscretion, trivial and juvenile, meant nothing compared to what happened to his mother. She would face Harvey Slate alone the following day to absorb the responsibility of what they had done. Hayden had been there for her when she needed him—tomorrow she would face the fallout alone and take the brunt of it for him.

Chapter Forty-Three

The Past

Returning home from Hayden's, Brea tried again to reach him on his mobile phone. He did not answer. After leaving him a message, she called Allegra. Tearful and distraught, she informed Allegra of the news about Hayden's mother and Callie witnessing their kiss at the supermarket.

Allegra offered to come over, though Brea declined, needing time alone. She made plans with Allegra to meet the following evening and over a long conversation, Allegra did her best to comfort Brea and provide reassurance that time would pass, and the upset would settle. Upon hanging up the phone, Brea stared out her window for several minutes. Restless and overwhelmed, she needed to leave her house.

Brea packed a blanket, a sandwich, and a soda before cycling off to the park. The afternoon weather was temperate, with a clear blue sky and a soft breeze. Strolling through the park, she followed a winding path until finding an idyllic spot on a hill with shade to set down her things. After spreading out her blanket, she ate her lunch, then lay down to gaze into the endless tapestry of branches and leaves above her.

Meditating on the trees, she wondered why some branches grew long and others short on the same tree. Was it predestined and built into the tree's DNA, or were trees like people, and their environment affected its growth? Were some branches favored by the amount of sunlight and water they received and others influenced by the force of gravity or damage they sustained after a storm?

If Brea had been a tree, she wondered what her branches would look like. She pictured it in her mind—short on love, long on will and determination, and some burned and scarred with no hope of growing leaves again. Would she bend with the wind and grow crooked or adapt and grow tall? It was too soon to tell.

Tomorrow, she would walk onto the Harvey Slate campus and face what came in her path. She had a choice—wither, shrink, or accept responsibility and endure. Deep inside, she knew the latter was the only viable option.

The following morning, Brea met Tory and Anjali in front of the administration building at Harvey Slate. Being excellent friends, they insisted on walking with Brea through the courtyard and escorting her to her first class. With her head held high, flanked on either side by her friends, she walked through the courtyard among the batches of students lingering and catching up on the weekend news. Brea and Hayden were on everyone's lips, and as she walked, heads turned and eyes followed her.

Tara and Callie, both with vile smirks and wicked twinkles in their eyes, fixed their gaze on Brea. She did not shy away from making direct eye contact with them as she walked past.

"Hi, girls." Brea greeted them with a broad smile and a confident tone. Tory and Anjali slipped their arms through Brea's in solidarity. Reaching her building, she nodded to her friends, letting them know she would survive the day, surprised by her own strength.

Although the day was far from over, Brea had a strategy. Most of the students in Brea's classes were honors students and uninvolved with the Harvey Slate elite social set—they would find her drama inconsequential and instead focus on their upcoming rounds of tests. In the afternoon, Brea avoided the dining hall and, during her gym period, joined in a volleyball game. The alternative would have been to walk on the track and endure endless questions about Hayden.

As Brea headed to the locker room to change after gym class, several of her classmates attempted to corner her with rapid-fire questions about Hayden. She was evasive, admitting that she and Hayden *"had a complicated history,"* and *"no, we're not together."* Unsatisfied with her reserved demeanor and clipped answers, they gave up on pressing her further.

After school in the courtyard, Brea waited for Tory on a bench. She had not seen Jaime all day, but her luck had run out as she watched Vienna, dressed in her navy Harvey Slate skirt, white-collared shirt, and black pumps, walking towards her. Brea rose and braced herself, ready to face Vienna.

"Brea, I can't say I'm surprised you went after Hayden. I'm not bothered. I was done with him last year, so don't think that you won anything over me," Vienna laid out with a pompous air.

Shaking her head, Brea let out a chuckle. "Vienna, why do you think everyone is out to get you? I never tried to steal Hayden from you, and we never intended to hurt anyone. What happened between us was—complicated. But I am sorry for the way everything turned out—for lots of things." Brea paused and inhaled, hoping she could reach Vienna. "Look, it doesn't have to be like this with us—we're family. Is there any way we could talk and fix things?"

Tipping her head to the side, Vienna licked her upper lip and crossed her arms. "Always so virtuous and sweet. The thing is, I know it's all bullshit, Brea. You just hide it so damn well, and Hayden is too stupid to see who you really are," she spat back, her face flushed and her eyes filled with contempt.

"Vienna, why can't you believe that I'm not your enemy?"

Vienna rolled her eyes. "My enemy? You are too pathetic to be considered an enemy. And actually, I have to laugh—you did all the work for me this past year by ruining your relationship with Jaime and falling off the ladder of Harvey Slate to the bottom rung. Cylis didn't want you, and Jaime didn't want you. I didn't have to lift a finger, so I'm going to laugh my ass all the way home today." Vienna raised her eyebrows, believing she had won the war against Brea, and with a malicious grin, turned on her heels and walked off.

Brea sighed and sat down.

"Hey, I saw Vienna walking away. Was it brutal?" Tory asked, joining Brea on the bench.

Brea chuckled and raised her eyes. "No, she only wanted the last word, and I let her have it. She isn't worth it. Let's go."

Once settled in Tory's car, Brea released a sigh of relief having made it through the day. The Harvey Slate fallout Brea had expected had not been as hostile as she had feared, or perhaps Brea had matured enough to realize that what people at school thought about her did not matter after all. When they neared Brea's home, they gasped, seeing Jaime's car parked in front of the house and Jaime leaning against the driver's side door.

"Do you want me to stay or come out with you?" Tory asked with wide eyes.

"No thanks, it's fine. I should talk to him alone. I'll call you tonight, and thanks for everything." Brea gave Tory a quick hug, then stepped out of the car.

Bracing herself with a deep breath, she went to Jaime slowly, keeping her eyes fixed on the ground until she neared him, halted, then met his eyes. She had to appreciate the irony of her final thoughts before seeing him—what a clever move, catching her off guard after she thought she had avoided him the entire day.

"Hey B," he said, holding her gaze. He had changed out of his uniform and wore jeans, a black T-shirt, and his favorite vintage Brazil National Football Team hat. His demeanor remained neutral, with no hint of anger. Brea dropped her shoulders and relaxed her stance. Before she spoke, she armored herself with another deep breath to face Jaime once and for all with the truth.

"Hi Jamie," she replied, willing herself to maintain eye contact. They stood in silence for a moment. Jaime frowned with his eyebrows knitted together.

"So, is it true about you and Hayden? Did you lie to me last summer?"

"Not entirely, but yes. We did not have sex, but we did hook up, and Aaron was right. That night at Hayden's party, I was with him in his room. I won't share all the details, but it happened more than once while we were dating."

Jamie winced after she had said, "*more than once*." Sucking in a breath, he looked up and remained silent as he processed her admission. Brea paused a moment and licked her lips.

"Jaime, what I did—it wasn't something that you deserved. I didn't plan on it happening, but it happened, and there were various reasons why I lied to you. The main reason being I was selfish, and I didn't want to lose you. There isn't any excuse for what I did, and I'm sorry."

"B, I feel like an idiot. I thought you liked me. I thought—that you loved me," he said and looked away. It was difficult for Brea to bear witness to Jaime's vulnerability, not because there was shame in it, but because she had caused him pain. Although Jaime was wealthy, good-looking, confident, and the high school equivalent of royalty, he was still a teenage boy who had fallen hard for his girlfriend, and she had betrayed him.

"Jaime, I felt those things, especially in the beginning. Then, the longer we were together, I realized we weren't a good fit. I couldn't be myself with you, and that was not your fault. And instead of being honest with you, I lied because I was too afraid to hurt you and to be alone." Jaime crossed his arms over his chest and inhaled a deep breath as he listened to her speak.

Brea continued. "I have spent the past five years, even longer, wanting to be someone else—the most beautiful, charming, envied, and confident girl—someone like Vienna. Maybe even like your new girlfriend Bianca, but with more facial expressions. The truth is, I'm just not built to be that type of girl."

Jaime chuckled. They stood before one another in silence for a moment until he spoke again. "Look, B, Hayden's a nice guy. I'm not happy that you lied, and I wish you had come to me and told me what was going on with you, but I won't go after him. It's in the past, and I'm not standing in the way."

Brea nodded. "Thank you, but honestly, I'm pretty screwed up right now. I care about Hayden a lot, but I think I need to be alone for a while until I can figure out some things. Looking back, it's what I should have done all year."

Jaime nodded, neither of them having anything further to say on the subject.

"Have you talked to Hayden?" Brea asked.

"No. But Trevor told me before I left school he heard about his mom—that she died."

Brea looked at the ground between them, then turned her head to look down the street. "Does anyone know when he's coming back?"

"I don't know. How come you don't?" he asked, shuffling his feet.

"He isn't picking up his phone." Brea laced her fingers together and exhaled.

Jaime leaned his head to the side. Brea met his eyes and smiled. There was nothing left to say. They looked at one another in recognition of what they had together—the truth had been told, and there was no need to hide behind the lies. Now free, Brea could begin to forgive herself and move forward.

"Bye B." Jaime tapped on his car door with his hand before opening it, then turned to climb in and switched on the engine. Brea watched him drive off from where she stood on the sidewalk.

Tilting her head back to look into the sky, Brea closed her eyes. And what about Hayden? She questioned what might have been if she and Hayden had found the courage to tell Jaime and Vienna the truth after their first night together in her garage. Would she and Hayden be together? Would she have ever met Cylis—found herself trapped in his home and experienced the worst day of her life?

Brea shook her head. It would not be a good idea for her to torture herself with imagined scenarios as she might fall into a hole she could not climb out of. Keep going, write a new chapter, and don't look back. Her survival depended on that.

Chapter Forty-Four

The Past

Five weeks passed, and Hayden had neither reappeared at school, nor had he returned any of Brea's phone calls. Few details had circulated around Harvey Slate regarding his mother's death. Upon returning home to collect his mail and pay bills, Hayden's father told Mr. and Mrs. Hammond that she had died from heart failure, caused by a side effect from one of her prescribed medications. The family desired privacy and did not want flowers or food donations brought to the home.

Many, assuming Brea and Hayden were dating, approached her to ask about him and whether he would return for finals and graduation. She answered with the truth as she knew it, *"I don't know."*

Every day she thought of Hayden and wished she could talk to him. Most afternoons, to cope with her emotions, Brea would ride her bike to the park or take walks around her neighborhood when needing a break from studying. She even put aside her poetry and writing for a few weeks to give herself a break from perseverating on the things that triggered sadness or provoked intense feelings.

Brea doubted Hayden would ever return home, wondering if the school had allowed him to take his finals and graduate without completing the semester in person. He was to begin at MIT in a couple of months, and if he did not reappear, the last time she saw him would have been their night at the beach. Though it would be a tender ending to their messy, undefined relationship, she still desired a proper goodbye.

On Sunday evening before the start of finals week, Brea planned to spend the night studying for her American history exam in the kitchen. After finishing a quick dinner of buttered spaghetti, she settled down at the table with her notes, midterm, and interim quizzes from the year. As she poured herself a large mug of peppermint tea, the phone rang. It was six-thirty, and she assumed Allegra would be on the other end of the line, panicking about her Spanish final. This year, for the first time, she faced an oral exam and had convinced herself she would fail.

Brea picked up the phone. "Allegra, stop freaking out and watch a telenovela. I promise it will help," she teased.

A brief pause followed. "Hi, it's not Allegra, it's Hayden."

Brea's mouth opened, unable to speak for a moment. "Hayden. How are you?" Stunned, Brea had difficulty finding the words to say anything else.

"I'm—I don't know—sorry I haven't called. I came home two days ago, and I needed some time. It's been very difficult." His voice, so different, hoarse and somber, startled her.

"Of course. Hayden, you don't have to explain anything to me or apologize. I'm so sorry about your mom. I tried to find you, but I didn't know how to reach you, and you weren't picking up your phone." She wanted to comfort him, though struggled with what to say. His voice, brimming with grief, made her heart ache for him.

"Thanks. I was staying at my aunt's and my phone died. I didn't bother charging it until a few days ago. I couldn't talk—to anyone—for a long time."

His voice broke Brea's heart, wavering, and when Brea thought he might become emotional, he yanked himself back into control. It was as though he walked on a tightrope, needing to maintain the utmost concentration or he would fall fifty feet.

"Hayden, I—"

"I ran into Trevor at the gas station, and he told me about Callie and everyone finding out about us. I'm sorry you had to deal with that all by yourself—that I wasn't here to help you."

"It's all right. The whole thing has blown over. Jamie even found me, and we talked. I apologized, and it went way better than I thought it would. Oh, and Vienna was pleased I had dug my grave over the year and she didn't have to lift a finger to ruin my reputation."

Hayden cleared his throat. "That's a relief. Listen, I can't talk long. I was thinking maybe after finals on Saturday we could do something together. I can pick you up around seven?"

"Sure. Are you going to be in school this week?"

"Not really. They're allowing me to finish the year at home. I'm only coming in to take finals in the office. I'll go to graduation—not that I want to," he answered with an edge in his tone.

"Can I help Hayden? I can bring you food, books, anything?" she asked, struggling to find something that might bring him back to life even for a moment.

"No, I'm good. I only—want to see you. So, I'll be at your house on Saturday. I have to go."

They said goodbye and hung up. Brea reached for her tea. She blew over the top twice to cool it down and took a sip. Hearing Hayden's voice weighed down with grief had been painful for her to hear. There was no question she would be there for Hayden, but she would need to be clear with him when she saw him—they were friends and, for now, that was all they could be. He would leave for college, continue to grieve the loss of his mother, and after everything Brea had been through the past year, she needed to be alone for a while with no romantic confusion.

Brea's father entered the kitchen, interrupting Brea's thoughts. He paused and glimpsed her notes spread out on the table before walking to the refrigerator to take out another can of beer.

"You like history a lot, huh?" he asked as he popped the tab to open the can and poured its contents into a glass.

"Nope, I can't wait for it to be over. I'm studying for my finals. Remember, I like English and writing, Dad," Brea reminded him.

"Right. Well, I'll leave you to it," he said, tossing the can into the garbage can before leaving the room.

Returning to her notes, Brea sighed. Despite her strange and distant relationship with her parents, she could not imagine life without them, or the grief of either dying young. In preparation to study, she rolled her neck in a circle and turned her attention to her notebook, hoping to spend the rest of the night studying without interruption.

On Thursday, Brea and Allegra met at the public library. To avoid disturbing others with any potential chatter, they secured a private room. Brea needed to study for her pre-calculus final, and Allegra, for chemistry. Laying out their notebooks, old exams, snacks, and water bottles, they settled into their chairs to begin.

Prioritizing her quizzes, Brea opened a blank notebook and set to work methodically, reviewing the most challenging problems. An hour had passed before either of them looked up from their papers to take a break.

"Brea, are you hungry?" Allegra asked as she dumped out the contents of a brown lunch bag, scattering various snacks on the table—muffins, candy bars, and apples. "Ten-minute break," Allegra announced, checking her watch.

Brea sorted through the snacks and chose an apple. Allegra pushed out a second chair from under the table to prop up her legs, and Brea kicked off her shoes and pulled her knees up to her chest.

After eating a sizeable chunk of a Twix bar, Allegra yawned and stretched her arms above her head. She studied Brea, rolling the apple on the table in front of her. "So, Saturday. Do you want to see a movie?"

Brea continued to roll the apple back and forth under her palm. "I don't know, maybe." Not wanting to lie to Allegra, she gave her a noncommittal answer.

Allegra sensed Brea hid something from her. "What's going on, Brea? What's happening?" she asked with suspicion.

Picking up the apple, Brea took a small bite, avoiding eye contact with Allegra. "Hayden is picking me up on Saturday so we can hang out."

Allegra shook her head and raised her eyes to the ceiling. "Big mistake, Brea. Have you lost your mind? I can't imagine what he's been going through, but I don't understand why you keep doing this to yourself. You are not strong enough to only be friends with him. And don't forget that he put you in a shitty situation. Do you realize that? You keep blaming yourself for cheating on Jaime as though it was only your fault—he did that to you, Brea. If he had left you alone, none of the drama would have happened."

Rolling her eyes, Brea shook her head. "You don't understand."

Allegra raised her voice. "If he wanted to be with you, he would have done everything he could have to be with you. He was selfish, and he used you. You're going to get sucked in again, and you're going to get hurt."

Brea glared at Allegra and her body tensed. Matching the volume of Allegra's voice, Brea slammed a fist on the table. "You understand nothing about what happened between me and Hayden! Don't lecture me about what you think you know about us."

Allegra's eyes grew wide in disbelief—Brea and Allegra had never spoken to one another in this way. "You're delusional, Brea. This is exhausting! I can't stand by again and witness you in this cycle of obsessing over a guy and thinking it's the only important thing in life—being someone's girlfriend."

Brea pushed her chair back to put on her shoes. Her anger overtook her as she grabbed her papers and books to shove into her bag. Allegra's mouth gaped open and her face flushed red. "Stop—don't leave. Stop pushing me away. I'm trying to help you, but you don't want to listen!"

Too angry to respond, Brea grabbed her backpack and hurried out of the room. Striding across the lobby with her eyes fixed ahead of her, she burst through the doors, startling the other patrons with the loud crash.

Once outside, she could not walk fast enough to escape the library or the storm of thoughts whipping through her mind—so she ran. She ran to avoid thinking about her mistakes, failed attempts at finding love, her flaws, the inescapable pain and loneliness she lived with, and the possibility that if what Allegra said about Hayden was true, then she was so damaged she could not trust her own mind and instincts—and she truly was alone.

Chapter Forty-Five

The Past

B rea dragged herself out of bed the following morning, exhausted after a restless night of sleep. Dressed in a crumpled school uniform she neglected to press, Brea stood in the kitchen waiting for the coffee to finish brewing. Her eyes were puffy, and she wore her unwashed hair in a loose braid. The only grooming she had accomplished was to brush her teeth and splash cold water on her face.

The harshness of Allegra's perception of Hayden gnawed at Brea, though she was ashamed of her own behavior in the library. Losing control of her emotions had been a frightening feeling for her, and the embarrassment she now felt was difficult to sit with.

Brea's mother entered the kitchen and paused upon seeing her appearance. "You look terrible. Are you sick?" she asked with a look of disgust, as though a foul odor had wafted into the room.

"No, I had a fight with Allegra yesterday. She said some horrible things to me, and I couldn't sleep."

"Friends always fight. You will move past it," she replied with a cool and detached air.

"I'm not sure. I don't think Allegra will want to talk to me after what happened yesterday. I might lose her." Brea swallowed. "Mom, the thing is, it's not only the fight with Allegra. So many things have happened since I changed schools, and I think—I need some help." Brea held back her tears, though her voice wavered as she spoke. She needed a mother right now—this was her moment to recognize that her daughter was suffering and lost, and to offer her comfort and compassion.

Her mother raised her eyes to study Brea for a moment with a vacuous facial expression. "Well, she wouldn't be much of a friend, and you'd be better off alone," she stated with no warmth or recognition of Brea's distress. Brea's father walked into the kitchen to signal he was ready to drive her to school.

"You'll be fine. Brea, no one wants to see a sad face. Have a good day at school."

The words spun out of her mother's mouth like toxic cotton candy. Before her mother had entered the kitchen, Brea thought she could not feel any worse, but now she did. The pain within her would have to be hers and hers alone.

As though Brea had already left the room, her mother returned her attention to her notepad. After drinking a large gulp of burning hot coffee, Brea slammed the mug onto the counter and left behind the coffee splatters as a purposeful reminder of her existence to her mother.

"Brea, please," her mother muttered upon hearing the ceramic mug bang against the counter.

After school, with finals week over, the adrenaline that had pumped throughout Brea's body to push her to the other side of exams petered out. Walking home from the bus stop, exhausted and anxious, Brea's thoughts turned over a piece of news she received earlier that morning.

The administrative aide had summoned Brea to the administration building near the end of English class. Mrs. Joyce, her guidance counselor, knew someone in need of a summer assistant at her shop. Believing Brea to be perfect for the job, she offered to arrange an interview with Trina Rose, the owner of Black Rose Paper Boutique.

The charming store sat in the shopping district of Black Harbor, selling greeting cards, novelty books, small collectibles, and stationery. Besides keeping her occupied over the summer, having a job would help Brea save enough money to buy a used car in the winter, an exciting and welcomed step that would bring her closer to freedom from Black Harbor.

Brea arrived home after school, eager to sit down and rest. Thirsty, she went to the kitchen to pour herself a glass of water when the telephone rang. She hesitated, knowing it was likely Allegra calling, and stood immobile near the phone. On the fifth ring, her desire for reconciliation won over her unease, and she picked up.

"Hey, it's me. Don't hang up," Brea heard Allegra's voice say.

"Hi. I'm surprised you're calling. Or am I delusional and hallucinating right now?" Brea replied, laden with sarcasm.

Allegra sighed. "I know you're upset, and I don't blame you. I said some shitty things to you yesterday. I talked through everything with my mom last night, and I'm sorry. Look, I know you aren't crazy, but I can't lie to you, Brea—I'm worried about you. You have been so lost this past year, and it has been frustrating seeing you spin in circles around these boys. I don't think Hayden is a bad guy, but you're my best friend, and I don't want to see you get hurt again."

Brea softened upon hearing Allegra's sincere apology. "I'm sorry too, for how I reacted. But you need to believe me when I say that with Hayden, we are more friends than anything else. It's a different, complicated type of friendship, and yes—there has been this physical thing with us, but I know what I'm doing. We understand each other, and I want to help him."

"Okay, I hear you, and no matter what happens, I'll be here for you. Can I call you on Sunday to find out how everything went and maybe we can meet up for coffee or see a movie?" Allegra asked.

"Yes, of course, yes. I'll call you on Sunday. I know you're only trying to protect me, and this past year—I did kind of go off the rails. This year will be different, and if it isn't, I promise I'll see the school psychologist in the fall and send you weekly reports."

Allegra laughed. "That sounds like a good deal to me."

Before saying goodbye and hanging up the phone, Brea chuckled. Relieved that her friendship with Allegra remained intact and that finals were behind her, Brea went upstairs to change out of her uniform. She planned to hide out in the garage and spend the rest of the afternoon reading a novel. Thinking about Hayden, she looked forward to seeing him and, with hope, defining their relationship as good friends for the near future without confusion or ambiguity.

Chapter

Forty-Six

The Past

B rea finished her turkey sandwich, wiped the crumbs off her mouth and checked the clock—short on time, she rushed up the stairs to slip into her new pale-pink halter sundress. With the unforgiving humid weather, the thin cotton fabric would allow her skin to breathe, and as she did not know where Hayden planned to take her, the style of the dress made it appropriate for multiple settings.

The temperature, stifling both inside her room and outside, made it unthinkable to leave her hair down loose. Brea brushed and clipped her hair into a loose knot with several pieces left out to frame her face, then blotted the sweat off her forehead with a dry washcloth. Other than applying light eye makeup and sheer pink lip gloss, she did not bother with making up her face. With ten minutes left until Hayden would arrive, she sat at her desk with the fan set to full speed and waited.

At seven, Brea clicked off her fan, then fled down the staircase and out the front door without saying goodbye to her parents. Stepping onto her porch, she groaned. Despite the evening temperature having dropped, the air, hot and heavy, weighed down on her body. Less than a minute passed, and Hayden pulled up in front of her house.

As she walked to the car, she glimpsed Hayden through the windshield and, meeting his eyes, his mouth curved into a smile. Once seated, they looked at one another, uncertain of what to say or who should speak first. Brea leaned over to embrace him.

"Hayden, I'm so sorry." They held each other for a minute before Brea pulled back, took his hand in hers, and squeezed it.

"Thanks," he replied, looking into Brea's eyes, appearing relieved to see her. She pulled back her hand to fasten her seatbelt.

"I love the blasting air conditioning," she commented, unsure what else to say. She closed her eyes, moved her face closer to the vents, and Hayden chuckled. Brea often shared with him how she loathed her home in the summer months because of the intolerable heat boxed in between its walls.

"You look nice," Hayden complimented.

"Thanks, you too," she replied, seeing him dressed in a mint green polo shirt, blue shorts and white tennis shoes. He appeared more relaxed than she expected, considering his tone of voice on the phone earlier in the week. From his demeanor and appearance, if Brea had not known his mother died, she never would have imagined that only six weeks ago he had experienced such a traumatic loss.

"Where are we going?"

Hayden watched the road. "Well, I had an idea. I don't know if it was a good one, but it's a surprise," he announced mysteriously.

Brea smiled and fixed her eyes on Hayden. "Am I dressed for wherever we're going?"

"Yeah, we're not climbing a mountain or anything like that," he answered with a teasing smile.

"Good. I'm not in the mood for anything outdoors unless it involves a swimming pool."

As they drove, Brea shared with Hayden school-related news he had missed and told him about her job interview on Friday at Black Rose Paper Boutique.

"The best part is if I save enough money, then I am going to buy my car in the winter."

"Brea, you on the road—is terrifying. I may need to intervene and take it upon myself to teach you how to drive," Hayden joked.

"Well, you'll be gone soon, so you don't have to be too scared."

"I'm not going to another planet. I'll be back often, and we'll see each other. We don't have to hide anymore."

Brea pressed her lips together. Later, she would need to find a delicate way to tell him they needed to establish some boundaries as friends to avoid any romantic complications for the near future. They drove for several more miles until reaching Hayden's neighborhood—Brea turned to face him with a puzzled facial expression.

"So, the surprise is I am going to make us dessert. To be specific, I mean with my two hands, then put it in the oven to bake."

Brea laughed out loud. "Oh no, Hayden—do you know how to bake or cook anything at all?"

"No. But I figure you'll be there for damage control if needed. My dad is out of town for the weekend, so I thought we could relax, eat a lot of sugar, and watch a movie or something."

"Okay, but only if you have fire safety gear in the house and working smoke detectors."

"Ouch," Hayden replied, feigning offense. "I may have bought some backup desserts in case I destroy the kitchen," he added.

Brea laughed again. "Good idea."

They pulled into the driveway and exited the car. Side by side, they walked to the front door in silence. Entering the foyer, Brea

surveyed the living room. It was as she remembered—impecca-
bly decorated and cozy with the oversized plush ivory sofas she
had once imagined herself stretched out on. A morbid thought
appeared in Brea's mind, wondering on which sofa his mother
had passed away. Shaking her head to exorcise the somber image,
she smiled at Hayden, placed her purse onto a small console
table, and slipped off her sandals.

"So, should we start? I'm going to propose we partner up
like in science lab. That way, we can only blame each other if
something explodes or your house burns down," Brea joked.

Hayden, amused, stretched out his arm and pointed in the
kitchen's direction for Brea to go first. "You know your way
around after snooping last summer."

In jest, Brea let out a dismissive scoff and walked past Hayden
to the kitchen. On the kitchen island, there were several boxes of
cake mixes, frosting, sprinkles, wrappers, bowls, mixing spoons,
and various types of pans. Impressed, she picked up the sprinkles and smiled.

"It's only going to be us, right? I mean, I think I can eat two,
maybe three cupcakes at most, and I'm done for the night," Brea
remarked.

"Well, there isn't much food in the house, so I figure I can live
on the leftovers for the rest of the weekend," he said and picked
up a box to scrutinize it.

"Yikes. Well, I need to borrow one of your mother's aprons.
This is a new dress, and there is no way I want to smear chocolate
all over it. Where does she keep them?"

Hayden did not answer and the blood drained from his face.
He stared at the box in his hand, and his jaw clenched. Brea's
eyes fixed on his right hand, placed on the counter, rubbing his
fingers with his thumb.

"I'm sorry, Hayden. I wasn't thinking. That slipped out."

"Um, sure, my mom kept them here," he said in a controlled,
crisp voice, placing the box on the counter and turning away to

open a drawer by the oven. Brea, frozen in place, stared at the counter, ashamed of how thoughtless she had been. She raised her eyes upon seeing Hayden walking back to her.

Meeting Hayden's eyes, she opened her mouth to apologize again, but he stopped her. "It's fine. Please don't worry about it. I forget she's gone sometimes too." He handed her a folded black kitchen apron. Standing beside Brea, he placed his hands on the counter and lowered his head for a moment before picking up the box again to study what other ingredients they would need.

"Hayden, if you don't want to talk about her tonight, I understand. If you do, I'm here for whatever you need, all right? I wish I only knew what to say. I had no one close to me die before." Brea unfolded the apron and put it on.

"No, I'm good. I don't want to talk about it," Hayden replied and managed a slight smile. "Let's do this one," he added and handed the box of chocolate cake mix to her. Turning the box over, Brea read the instructions out loud as Hayden walked to the refrigerator to take out the eggs and milk, then returned to place them in front of her on the counter. Stepping behind her, he placed his hands on her shoulders to massage them. Hayden's touch, familiar and sensual, filled her with longing.

Allegra was right—if he kissed her, she would not be strong enough to restrain herself from kissing him back. With Hayden, her body could hijack her mind with only a look or a simple touch—she should have known better than to believe she could so easily resist him.

"Do you want a drink? There's some white wine in the refrigerator," Hayden offered.

"Yes, good idea," she answered. Hayden prepared their glasses while Brea arranged the ingredients and tools they would need. He handed Brea her glass of wine and when she took it from his hand, their fingers grazed—she remembered the touch of his hands on her body and blinked her eyes to refocus.

"Wow, this is so good," she proclaimed after taking a large sip.

"Yup, tastes like—wine," Hayden joked, and Brea laughed. Standing side by side, Brea read the instructions aloud as they followed the steps to prepare the batter. Once mixed, Hayden licked the spoon and handed it to Brea to have the rest.

"This is better than the wine." She licked off the remaining chocolate batter while Hayden used a measuring cup to fill one of the cupcake tins with batter, filling it too high and spilling batter over the sides.

"I'll take over with that—this needs a woman's touch," Brea teased. Hayden took a small step back with his hands thrown up in the air in surrender. Brea bumped him with her hip to move him aside. Paying careful attention, she filled up the remaining tins with batter.

"You can eat your monster cupcake," she told Hayden as she stepped back with a grand gesture of her hands to show him her handiwork. Hayden chuckled and carried the pan to place in the oven.

"They need to bake for twenty-two minutes," Brea read off the instructions. Placing her hands on the counter, she hopped up to sit as they waited for the cupcakes to bake and asked Hayden about his plans for the summer. His family had originally planned a vacation in Hawaii at a resort for two weeks in the summer, but his father had cancelled it.

Rather than spending the entire summer at home, his father insisted he begin a college summer program and he would move to Cambridge in mid-July. Brea looked down when Hayden told her the news—he would leave in a month, filling her with sadness though also relief. It would make it easier to be alone and focus on herself for a while.

Hayden, like so many boys who loved cars, changed the topic of the conversation back to Brea's plans for buying a used one. He rattled off various models and specific details she would need to consider. Paying attention, she did her best to absorb as much as she could, as her father would not provide any valuable advice to Brea when the time came for her to select a car. The oven timer sounded, and Brea jumped off the counter, eager to taste a cupcake. Hayden removed the pan from the oven and placed it on the counter to cool.

"Let me have one." Brea reached out her hand to pull one out of the tin. With a playful touch, Hayden pushed her hand away.

"Nope, we have to wait until they cool before we frost them. It says so on the box." Hayden grinned and extended his arm to prevent Brea from reaching the cupcakes. Still, she persisted in her efforts to take one and fixed her grip on his upper arm, firm and muscular. The memory of Hayden shirtless in her garage appeared in her mind, and her heart fluttered.

Through laughter, Hayden warned Brea, "Stop. You're going to burn yourself."

"Fine." Brea let go of his arm and relented. She pretended to pout and crossed her arms over her chest.

"Look, in exchange for your patience, I'll take out what I bought from the bakery this morning."

Brea pressed her lips together, considered his offer and smiled. "Deal."

Hayden went to the refrigerator and removed a white bakery box with a red-and-white striped satin ribbon. After placing it on the counter beside her, he handed her a pair of kitchen scissors to do the honors of cutting the ribbon. Hayden flipped open the top.

"Oh, wow," she exclaimed, surveying the contents of the box as she untied and removed the kitchen apron. Her eyes swept over the pastries—cannoli, fruit tarts, and marzipan rainbow cookies. "I'm going to gain two pounds tonight," she exclaimed with wide eyes.

"Let's pick out a movie to watch," Hayden suggested, then closed the top of the box and led Brea into the family room. He asked Brea to pick out a movie and pointed to a drawer in the built-in entertainment center. Placing the desserts on the coffee table, he left the room to retrieve plates and napkins. Brea took her time, read the movie titles one by one, and settled on a nineteen-eighties cult vampire film.

Brea sat on the large ivory sofa facing the television. The wide cushions, upholstered in a buttery soft chenille and filled with down feathers, felt as though she had sunk into an enormous ball of cotton. Terrified of spilling anything on the sofa, she placed her glass of wine in the middle of the coffee table.

While she waited for Hayden to return, she picked up a large hardcover book with exotic photographs of Greece and flipped through the pages. Halfway through the book, she wondered what was taking Hayden so long with the plates. Five minutes later and on the verge of venturing out to search for him, he returned.

"Please eat at least three desserts or I'll wind up sick by Monday," Hayden joked and placed down the plates and napkins on the coffee table. Brea held up the movie she had chosen and handed it to him.

"Good choice," Hayden commented.

Brea flipped the top of the bakery box and chose a rainbow cookie. It was delicious—chewy, with a subtle sweetness and almond flavor.

"Hayden, you need to taste this. It's so good." She plucked another rainbow cookie out of the box and held it up for him. Hayden leaned down to eat it out of her hand. Brea laughed. "What are you, a dog?" Although humorous, a ripple of desire rushed through her body at the touch of Hayden's lips on her fingers.

Hayden chuckled as he chewed. Brea watched his reaction, pleased when he smiled and nodded in agreement. Settling back into her position with her legs outstretched on the sofa, Hayden sat on the opposite end. Brea's eyes shifted to Hayden. A small breath escaped her lips as she watched him run his hand through his hair. Focusing on the television, she attempted to ignore her internal conflict—her desire to touch Hayden against the logical part of her brain that told her she needed to be alone with no romantic attachments for the near future.

Chapter Forty-Seven

The Past

Brea yawned. The wine had made her drowsy, and one hour into the movie, she was on the verge of falling asleep on the sofa. Hayden paused the film.

"Should we decorate the cupcakes?" he asked. She blinked her eyes and yawned again. Stretching out her arms and legs, she nodded.

"Sure. I don't think I can eat more than one, but we can decorate them and, on the way home, throw them at stop signs."

"Not going to happen. I'm not interested in going to jail tonight," he replied, smiling, as they returned to the kitchen. There were twelve to frost. After some debate, they settled on vanilla frosting for half and chocolate for the other. Brea worked faster and with more skill than Hayden. Finishing her set, she squinted, seeing Hayden struggle with his third one. She watched him with a smile playing on her lips as Hayden frosted his cupcake with an unwieldy hand.

"Hayden, that does not look appetizing. I think you had too much wine, and you lost your motor skills," Brea teased, scrunching her nose as she pulled herself up onto the counter and watched Hayden butcher the cupcake.

"Hey, I'm not a girl," he explained, striving to defend himself.

"You know there are pastry chefs and bakers all over the world who are men," she pointed out with a smirk. Hayden gave her a side-eye. Brea extended a finger to the cupcake in his hand to scoop up a dollop of frosting. He tried to move it away, but she swiped a small amount onto her finger.

Laughing, she attempted to eat it, but Hayden, moving quickly, sacrificed his cupcake and knife to catch her arm by the wrist before she could lick it off. Surprised he could move that quickly, she froze, her eyes wide. Hayden pulled her hand to his mouth, opened it, and licked off the frosting. Brea's lips parted.

"Hayden, what are you doing?" she whispered. Holding her wrist, he stepped in front of her. "You're leaving for school, and after everything that happened this year—I should be alone, no more boys for a while. I want you to kiss me, but this isn't a good idea—it's too complicated."

Hayden looked into Brea's eyes and let go of her wrist. "This is the best idea," he whispered. He leaned in to kiss her, paused an inch from her face and awaited her consent. With one decisive move, her desire triumphed over her logic—Brea kissed him, and he tasted like chocolate.

Placing his hands on her hips, he pulled her close, and Brea wrapped her legs around his waist. Hayden picked her up and carried her through the house to his bedroom. He needed to stop every few feet to make sure he did not hit a piece of furniture or the wall, and they would laugh, amused by the situation—but the thought of breaking their kiss for longer than a second was unthinkable.

Reaching Hayden's room, he sat Brea on his desk to untie the bow holding up her halter top, then let the two pieces of fabric drop and, with it, the top half of her dress. Her chest, now bare, allowed Hayden to run his fingers over her abdomen and breasts. He took a step back, removed his shirt, and pulled Brea close to him again. The touch of his chest against hers, both romantic and erotic, enhanced their desire to hold one another tighter. Hayden moved his lips from her mouth to her neck, just below her ear. She tipped her head back and, with a firm grip, wrapped her fingers around the taught musculature of his upper arms. Picking her up, Hayden carried Brea to lay her on the bed and positioned himself over her.

Kissing her neck, he used his lips to trace along her collarbone, working his way down her chest, and Brea moaned and arched her back. His hand traveled down her leg, circled her knee, then returned along her inner thigh until reaching the strip of fabric between her legs. Brea's mouth opened, and she exhaled a rapid breath as she felt his fingers move rhythmically over the most sensitive spot on her body with a firm pressure.

Hayden slowed his movements, kissed her again, then sat up. Brea opened her eyes, watching Hayden as he rose to remove his shorts, leaving him dressed only in his boxers. Exposed to the cool air blowing from the overhead vent and without the warmth of Hayden on top of her, a shiver rippled throughout her body. As though a switch flipped, Brea's chest tightened, and she could not quite inhale a satisfying breath—a wave of unease washed over her.

Brea's mind raced when Hayden lay back on top of her. She did not understand what was happening to her body as he kissed her neck. "Hayden," Brea whispered, her voice barely audible. He did not hear her. Brea placed her hands on his shoulders with a light touch. "Hayden," she whispered again. Again, he did not hear her. He moved his arms on either side of Brea to prop himself up and to kiss her chest. "Hayden," she said again, louder. He paused and looked up at Brea.

"What is it?" He lowered his head to kiss her on the base of her neck. Brea's hands were shaking. With Hayden's lower body between her legs and her bare chest exposed, an odd and terrifying feeling consumed her, and she felt that her body and surroundings were unreal.

"I'm sorry, Hayden. We can't. We have to stop. I can't breathe. Let's go finish the movie, and when you're ready to drive, take me home." Brea found it difficult to speak, as though she could not control the movements of her mouth. Hayden looked into Brea's eyes, confused by her abrupt shift in demeanor.

"Get off me, Hayden, I can't breathe," Brea shouted.

Hayden moved onto his side, sat up, and adjusted her dress to cover her chest. "Brea, what's wrong?"

Brea sat up and scooted back until reaching the headboard. She closed her eyes and sucked in panicked breaths. A vivid image of Cylis gripping her face flashed through her mind. She did not answer Hayden as she tied the straps of her top.

"Brea. Talk to me. What's going on?" Hayden tugged the skirt of her dress over her thighs and placed one of his hands over hers.

"It's. It's—Cylis," she sputtered out between shallow breaths.

Hayden clenched his jaw. He withdrew his hand from Brea's and sat on the bed's edge with his back to her. Blowing out a forceful breath, he rested his elbows on his knees and buried his face in his hands.

"I'm sorry. I can't. I'm sorry," she whispered.

"You love him? Did you lie to me, Brea? Have you been seeing him this whole time?" Hayden's voice, with a cutting, angry edge, made it difficult for her to think clearly. Brea's eyes darted around the room—she felt as though she were floating outside of her body, and the walls and furniture appeared distorted.

"Are you seeing him? Don't lie to me, Brea. Tell me the truth." Hayden would not look at Brea, expecting a response he did not want to hear.

"No," Brea mouthed. Her voice would not cooperate with her mind's intention to speak. With Hayden's back to her, he missed her denial. She could not speak. Waves of terror coursed through her body, and she feared she staggered on the edge of losing herself in her mind.

Hayden rose and paced the length of the bed, rubbing his neck with one hand. "Everyone knows about us, Brea. It doesn't matter anymore about Jaime or Vienna—we know it was supposed to be us, always. I don't understand what is so damn special about Cylis. Why do you still want him?"

Brea shook her head, though Hayden did not see her, locked inside his state of incredulity and frustration. He continued to pace beside the bed. "After everything that's happened between us, I can't believe you would still choose him."

"No. I don't love him, Hayden. He trapped me in his house, and he hurt me," Brea cried out with tears spilling over her cheeks.

Hayden froze beside his desk. Fixed in place, he only turned his head to look at Brea. His entire body tensed, and something within him shifted. Looking into his eyes, it was as though Hayden had become a different person. He studied Brea with a horrific, knowing look mixed with a tenuously controlled rage in his eyes.

"What did he do to you, Brea?" Hayden asked through gritted teeth. It was clear he struggled to contain himself, teetering on the edge of losing control.

Brea, burying her fingers into her hair, closed her eyes and shook her head, fearing she was on the verge of losing her mind. If she said it, she had to face the horrible truth of what Cylis had done to her. The best she could manage was to say, "I can't say it out loud. I can't. It was my fault what he did to me."

Hayden did not need Brea to say the words. He knew what Cylis had done to her and with his arm, knocked over the stack of books on his desk—they crashed onto the floor with a tremendous bang.

"I'll kill him. I'll fucking kill him!" Hayden screamed as he kicked the chair at his desk. Brea froze and stared ahead. Never had she witnessed such anger in her life. Her mind shut down—she stopped moving and focused only on her breathing.

"No. I don't want anyone to know. It will be fine," Brea managed to articulate in a strained, flat tone of voice.

Hayden gripped his head with his hands in disbelief and shouted, "It's not fine, Brea—nothing is fucking fine!" From his desk, he grabbed a large glass jar and hurled it at the wall several feet over the headboard of his bed. Everything slowed—the jar flew across the room and Brea lowered her head in anticipation of the impact.

Her ears rang from the explosive bang of the glass hitting the wall, crashing and shattering into a hundred pieces with various small objects, pens, and shards of glass raining over her and onto the bed and floor.

Brea gasped, unable to scream or breathe. There were no sounds, and time stalled. Brea was stuck inside her mind and body as though a thick layer of foam had wrapped around her and blanketed her from the world. She felt nothing, nor could she comprehend the words coming out of Hayden's mouth as he crawled towards her on the mattress. All she saw was the blood on the white comforter spreading below his knees, where glass had cut him.

With one hand, Hayden held Brea's arm to keep her still, and with the other, picked out pieces of glass from her hair, shoulders, and dress. Several times he attempted to brush pieces of glass off the bed and winced in pain as he accumulated various cuts on his hands. As he worked, his blood smeared onto her dress and arms.

"Don't move," he repeated, his voice panicked. "Brea, I'm so sorry. I didn't mean to scare you. I would never hurt you. Don't move, or you'll get cut by the glass. Stay here. Don't move." Hayden hurried out of the room.

After he left, Brea's brain switched on and she could inhale a deep breath. As she scanned the room, her instincts kicked in and she scrambled off the bed. Glass cut the backs of her legs as she slid to the bed's edge, and when she stepped onto the floor, her feet landed on shards of glass—she cried out in pain and covered her mouth to muffle any further sounds escaping from her lips.

She needed to hurry, knowing Hayden would soon return. Brea ran to the curtains and pulled them apart. Unlocking the glass doors, she opened them and took off, running into the backyard along the side of the fence. When Hayden returned to his room, she figured he would assume she had run in the direction of the front yard towards the street. Brea felt no pain, only the beating of her heart as she ran.

Once far enough into the yard and concealed by the darkness, she looked over her shoulder to ensure Hayden had not followed her. There were no thoughts, no tears, no hesitation—only the instinct to run. "*Run. Keep running,*" a voice deep inside her willed her to continue moving.

At the end of the property, she saw a wooden fence too tall for her to scale without a boost. Out of breath and panicked like a caged animal, she paced and scanned her surroundings, hoping to find a bucket or something she could stand on. Though surrounded by darkness, when she looked to the right, ten feet away from her, she could make out something silver and shiny.

Brea hurried over to the object, relieved to discover a wheelbarrow sitting beside an assortment of landscaping tools next to a gardening shed. With a firm grip, she used all of her strength and flipped it over. It gave her a two-foot boost to reach the top of the fence. She pulled herself up to straddle it, then slipped, coming over the other side. Brea scraped her left hand and leg as she fell to the ground.

Several bags of yard debris and folded tarps softened the impact of the fall. Brea sat still to ensure she had alerted no one to her presence on the property. Palpating along the bottoms of both her feet, she found a slender shard of glass stuck in the heel of her right foot. She pulled it out, and bit her hand to prevent herself from crying out.

Surveying the yard, it appeared similar in size to Hayden's property, and she would need to cross about seventy feet before reaching the home. Brea rested in place for another minute to catch her breath. The only sounds she heard were the cicadas and a bird chirping in the night.

Ready to run, she took off, once again keeping to the left side of the property rather than running down the middle to conceal herself as best as she could. Reaching the house, she whispered, breathless, "Please, please," hoping to find an easy exit with no need to climb another fence. There were no lights on in the house. The owners were sleeping or away from home.

Garbage cans lined the side of the house against the fence, suggesting a gate would be nearby. Hurrying down the paved path and finding the gate, she exhaled, relieved to see the latch did not have a lock on it. With caution, she opened it, slipped out, and left it open, not wanting to risk making any more noise than necessary by shutting it.

Other than parked cars, the street was empty. If anyone saw her running down the street, barefoot, with streaks of blood on her arms, legs, and dress, they would certainly stop and question her. A worse thought occurred to her—if spotted, a concerned person could even insist on calling the police. On her journey home, she would need to move with stealth.

An hour passed before Brea reached her street. Remaining vigilant the entire way home, she hid behind a fence or a parked car when a vehicle appeared on the road. Upon seeing her house, she felt a wave of relief, albeit short-lived. Placing her hands atop her head, the realization set in—she had left her purse and house keys at Hayden's. Stopping in front of her neighbor's home, she paced. The engine of a car hummed in the distance, and Brea panicked. She ran into her backyard, remembering the garage door would be open.

She slipped inside and collapsed on the loveseat. Frantic, Brea scanned around her for anything useful to help her find a way inside her house. An idea came to her. She could try some windows in the family room. Often her father opened the windows during the evenings and may have left one unlocked. Brea shook her head—she would need to lie to her parents in the morning and tell them she had lost her purse and keys. If she were to sneak into the house tonight, they would ask how she had entered. The only option was to knock on the door.

In the garage corner, she spotted several black plastic garbage bags filled with old clothes piled on a table. In the fall, her mother had planned to donate the clothing to the resale shop. Fortunately, she had forgotten.

Brea grabbed her reading flashlight. Switching it on, she hurried to the bags and ripped one open. The mass of unfolded garments made it difficult for her to find something useful. After pulling out a few pairs of slacks, she found a white dress shirt of her father's that could cover up her arms and dress. In another bag, she spotted her old pair of tennis shoes.

Her fingers worked quickly to button the shirt over her dress, then she slipped into the sneakers. Having removed her hair clip while watching the movie, she ran fingers through her hair and did her best to untangle the large knots when her eyes landed on a thick rubber band on the workbench. She twisted her hair into a loose bun and secured it.

A thought stopped her in her tracks—Hayden could have taken her keys and let himself into her house. What if he was waiting for her in her bedroom? A pounding thump beat in her chest. Walking around the side of her home, she paused upon reaching the edge, then craned her neck to survey the street. Relieved upon seeing no sign of his car, she hurried to her porch and mounted the steps, preparing herself to knock on the door.

Brea shook out her hands to stop them from trembling, raised her arm and knocked three times. After waiting two minutes, she knocked again, louder, then rang the doorbell. Another minute passed, and the foyer light switched on, followed by the porch light. Her father opened the door, rubbed his eyes, and appeared alarmed to find Brea there.

"What's going on, Brea? What happened?"

"Nothing, Dad, sorry I woke you, but my purse disappeared from the party. Someone may have taken it." Waving Brea into the house off the porch, she slipped in and turned off the light in the foyer to minimize the chances her father would notice her appearance.

"Wash up and go to bed. We'll have to call the locksmith in the morning to have all the locks changed." He waited for her to pass by him. "You sure you are all right?" he asked.

Brea spun around and studied her father. She had forgotten how much they resembled each other, sharing the same hair and eye color. The manner in which he looked at her, a look on his face she had not seen before, conveyed that he knew somewhere deep in his body something was wrong.

She shook her head and smiled. "Dad, I'm fine, only tired." Brea witnessed the subtle flash of relief in his eyes. Either he believed her or he was subconsciously relieved she would not tell him the truth—Brea would never know for certain.

"Dad, go back to sleep. I need some water. I'll be up soon." Her father nodded and went upstairs without question.

Brea walked into the kitchen to pour herself a large glass of water from the tap. She drank it down and filled it once more to carry with her to her room. As she climbed the stairs and ambled down the hall, her feet burned and throbbed with every step she took. Once in her bedroom, she paused and drew in a deep breath before placing the glass of water on her dresser and then pulled out the top drawer for a pair of clean pajamas and socks. Limping, she crept down the hall to the bathroom.

After turning on the faucet to the tub, she closed the toilet lid and sat down. Tugging gently, she pulled off the old sneakers and undressed as the bathtub filled with steaming hot water. Under the stream of water, Brea squirted a generous pour of shampoo to disinfect her skin from head-to-toe. A sweet floral fragrance filled the room.

While waiting for the tub to fill, she examined her body for wounds. The bottoms of her feet were black and caked with dirt and dried patches of blood. Her hands were dirty with several scrapes from climbing the fence in Hayden's yard, and the back of her right thigh had a long scratch and a two-inch wound that had stopped bleeding. There were several scratches on her arms, and the cuts on her left leg were minor.

Brea rose and examined her chest and face in the medicine cabinet mirror, relieved to find no cuts or scratches, only a flushed complexion and smeared eye makeup. Staring at her reflection, she felt an odd sense of detachment, as though she were watching herself in a movie. To break her trance, she opened the medicine cabinet door, removed a frosted plastic bottle of rubbing alcohol, gauze, and bandages, and placed them on the toilet seat.

Seeing the tub full, Brea turned off the faucet. She placed one foot at a time into the steaming hot water and excruciating pain seared throughout her body as the water contacted her skin and wounds. She forced herself to endure the discomfort, then with a delicate touch used a washcloth to wipe the dirt and blood off her hands and feet. Once satisfied, Brea sank into the tub and submerged her body under the water—she wished that with the grime and blood, her memory of the past year could also drain down the tub, leaving her mind unsullied.

When she stepped out of the bathtub, several wounds reopened and bled again. With careful attention, she cleaned the cuts with alcohol, then dressed them with gauze and bandages. Until they healed, she would need to wear socks, sneakers, and cover the length of her arms and thighs, despite the hot weather.

Brea dressed in her pajamas, tucked the soiled clothing and old shoes under her arm, and made her way down the hall. Once inside her room, she hid the bundle under her bed—in the morning she would find a garbage bag to throw it all away. She lay in her bed and, disregarding the hot temperature of her room, pulled the bed sheet over her to feel safe.

Stretching out her arm, she clicked on her rotating fan. The warm air blew over her, beginning at her head and moving down the length of her body until reaching her knees and repeating the cycle. She found the faint clicking sound of each pass soothing.

Brea did not bother to wipe the tears that flowed down her cheeks—she was heartbroken. Allegra had warned her seeing Hayden would be a mistake, and now Brea believed with no doubt she could no longer trust her own mind—Hayden was not who she thought he was.

Ashamed and angry with herself, she would tell neither Allegra nor anyone what had happened tonight—she would bury Hayden as she did Cylis. Her eyes fixed on the fan, watching it rotate back and forth as it lulled her into a trance. Brea did not know how much time had passed until she closed her eyes. She listened to the whirling fan blade, and over time, the sound pulled her down into a deep, long sleep.

Chapter Forty-Eight

The Present

Brea shivered. The water in the bathtub, now a murky green from the dissolved bath salts and soap, had cooled. An hour had passed since she had climbed into the tub. Staring at the monochromatic blue abstract painting on the wall, Brea wiped her eyes, now coming back into the present moment.

So much of her past from those years at Harvey Slate, Brea had buried. She had been too afraid to remember, both to avoid the pain and because her mind had not been ready to cope with the trauma of her childhood and what Cylis had done to her.

Brea climbed out of the tub, careful not to slip, and wrapped herself in a plush white bath towel. Tina had taken the children out for the afternoon so Brea could clean up the kitchen and fold laundry. Although preferring to lie in her bed and sleep, she would force herself to accomplish at least a few household chores. Yesterday, Sophie crawled onto Brea's lap while seated on the sofa and asked, "*Why are you always so sad, Mommy? It makes me sad. And our house is dirty.*"

Looking into Sophie's eyes, Brea's heart ached. It served as the wake-up call she needed. Brea had fooled herself, believing she could conceal her sorrow and her failing marriage from her children. Though difficult, she recognized that her denial drew a parallel to her own mother, and the realization dawned on her that burying her pain and trauma might condemn her own children to a similar cycle of suppression.

Brea's skin itched from having sat in the soapy water for too long. She lathered her legs and arms with cream, then wrapped her hair in a towel. Scrutinizing her face in the mirror, she wondered how different she would look to someone from high school seeing her now. Would they see strength or weakness behind her eyes? Brea saw pain, and though frightening, it was honest and the birth of something new. She turned, went into her closet and grabbed a pair of dark blue jeans and a white T-shirt to dress.

In the kitchen, she cleared the dishes off the table and placed them in the dishwasher. As the machine ran, she wiped the table and counters, cleaned out the refrigerator, and took out the garbage. Her stomach ached, and Brea remembered she had not eaten a meal since yesterday. Taking a banana from the counter, she sat on a stool to eat. It was enough to kill the pang of hunger and settle her stomach within moments.

Brea rubbed her shoulders as she looked out the window. The view of the ocean failed to ease her tension. Early this morning, she woke with her heart racing. Restless and unable to fall asleep again, the unthinkable question replayed in her mind, "*What if I went on this trip?*"

Hayden had seen through her mask. To escape the risks of making decisions and mistakes in an uncertain world, she had retreated to the only safety she had known—putting herself back in a cage. Having spent several days reliving every detail she could recall from those two years at Harvey Slate, she had a choice to make—continue to live in denial, hide her sadness, surrender her life to Adam, and live on perpetual autopilot, or allow herself to wake up and take the steps needed to work through her fear and confront her past to reclaim her life.

Brea clasped her hands together to steady them as she walked into her bedroom, knowing she could no longer live as the sanitized version of herself—the charade of contentment, unsustainable, needed to end. Picking up her cell phone, she switched it on, sat on the edge of her bed, and made the call. It rang four times, and he picked up.

"Hi," she heard on the other end.

"Adam, I have some news. It's unexpected, but I received an invitation to take a trip to Mexico next Saturday for a week. Allegra, my old best friend from high school, is eloping to Greece for a small ceremony, but she wanted to have a party first to celebrate with her girlfriends. One woman had to drop out, and Allegra called me out of the blue, seeing if I could take her spot."

Adam did not answer right away and the pause was agonizing for Brea. "Let me think about that for a minute," he replied.

Brea cleared her throat. "I'd really like to go. I haven't taken a girls' trip since we got married, and everything is already paid for. All she is asking is for me to show up."

Adam hummed for a moment. "All right, go ahead. My mother has been begging me to bring the kids up to Santa Barbara. She would love to have Alex and Sophie to herself for a week. I can take them up there and drop them off."

"Great. Well, I'll book the flight then. We'll talk more about the details later. Bye." Brea hung up the phone. Her fingers trembled and she dropped the phone on the floor. She crouched down, lowered her head into her hands, and inhaled a deep breath.

After several minutes, she wiped her eyes and stood to walk through the house and into her backyard. Gazing at the ocean, she turned over a thought that occurred to her, something important she had not allowed herself to recognize about Hayden all those years ago.

Brea grew up in a world of profound emotional neglect and, as a result, she believed herself to be damaged, unworthy, and unloved. She and Hayden had shared a unique connection, and now she understood why—Hayden was wounded and scarred, and it created a bond between them, a recognition unlike any other. It was not logical, but something that lived deep within them, and that is why Hayden knew her down to her bones—because they were the same. And all those years ago, she had missed it—he needed her, too.

A heartbreaking realization washed over her. That last night at Hayden's house, she believed she could neither trust her own mind nor Hayden—but she had been wrong. The truth about Hayden had always been there, locked inside her, but the impact of her childhood and Cylis' assault had made her too fearful and mistrustful to see it. Brea made a mistake about Hayden and shut him out. She thought he was a monster after he fell apart that night, but his own trauma had tormented and overwhelmed him, and learning that Cylis had hurt her pushed him over the edge.

It was neither Brea nor Hayden's fault for what happened to them, but the culminating events of a cruel world that had beaten them up and spit them out. They were only too young to understand and see their way through it.

Brea drew in a deep breath and tilted her head back to gaze into the cloudless sky. To trust herself again and break free, she could not do it alone. She needed the one person who had been the constant in her life during those years, the only person she had felt safe with and who understood her. To change her life, she needed what had been missing the past twenty years—her complicated, undefined relationship with Hayden, and his side of the story.

To Be Continued in Book 2: Unlocked, A Novel by Ella Khort

An Excerpt from Book 2: Unlocked

Chapter 1: Hayden

The ice in the glass had melted, watering down the scotch. Hayden drank it regardless after hanging up the phone. She called. For three days he busied himself with work, wondering, though not allowing himself to hope, whether Brea would accept his proposal. It was five minutes after midnight, and Hayden's flight home to San Francisco would take off at ten in the morning. Falling asleep would be difficult with the sound of Brea's voice echoing in his mind.

He planned to postpone informing Avery about the trip to Mexico until after arriving home. It was not uncommon for him to travel with little notice if one of his subsidiary companies was in crisis, and as a result, it would be unlikely this trip would raise any suspicions. The challenge would be the following week at home, coping with the guilt of lying to Avery.

Switching on his laptop, he pulled on a clean T-shirt and fixed himself another scotch. He emailed his assistant to book his flight and draft a sham itinerary. Ashley would be discreet with no questions why he asked her to do this. Afterward, he wrote an email to his travel agent requesting she book two suites in Puerto Vallarta or Punta Mita in any available luxury resort.

Hayden paused, sipped his scotch, and pictured Brea seated at the counter of Brine several days prior. Her warm smile vanishing upon recognizing him had struck him like a bullet to the chest. He would give anything now to have her look at him as she did twenty years ago.

Though she attempted to mask it throughout the call, her strained voice revealed she was on the verge of tears. He rubbed his eyes, and a wave of guilt washed over him, remembering his last night with her when he lost his control.

To have a week with Brea, hold nothing back, and to prove to her he was not the man she believed him to be, was an unforeseen gift. However insane the idea, he felt certain this trip was the only path to both help her understand the truth of that night and find her way out of her current unhappiness. Hayden stretched his neck and fixed his eyes on the ceiling. He needed to forgive himself as well, but that would only happen if he earned her forgiveness first...

About the Author

Ella Khort is an adult fiction novelist publishing her first two novels, *Locked Away* and *Unlocked*. Her writing draws inspiration from themes of second chances, love, the complexities of the human mind, and resilience. Outside of writing, she enjoys spending time with family, cooking, and painting.

Instagram: @ellakhortauthor
Facebook: Ella Khort Author
Substack: ellakhort.substack.com